The Alchemist's Arms

JONATHAN POSNER

To Steph

I hope you enjoy
it! All the best

Jonathan

CONTENTS

ACKNOWLEDGMENTS

I would like to thank all those who helped make this book happen.

My wife Helena, my friends from the Windsor Writers' Group and especially to Sinead Fitzgibbon for her thorough review and encouragement.

I would also like to thanks the following, who read the book in beta, and were kind enough to give me their honest feedback and support: Sue Armstrong, Chasqui Penguin, Penny Siberry, Ellen Johnson, Luke Moreton, Kathy Johnson, Shirley de Vivo, Mike Cunningham, Marie-Helene Brown and Terry Adlam.

CHAPTER ONE

Southwark, November 1574

The waterman shipped his oars and let the little boat drift slowly up to the dark jetty. As the bow bumped against it, he clambered out and secured the line to a small rusty cleat.

He turned to the two sodden men still hunched in the stern of the boat.

"Southwark, sirs," he muttered. "As bidden."

At first the two men seemed stuck to their seats, as if pressed down by the cold, unrelenting rain that had accompanied them across the Thames from the little wharf at Queenhythe. The waterman stared curiously at their dark shapes silhouetted against the shimmering water, as if unsure how he was going to get them out of his boat. Then he gave a barely perceptible sigh and held out his hand to the nearest man. The man looked at it in disgust, but then grabbed hold and used it to step safely onto the glistening planks of the jetty.

While the first man was shaking the rain out of his hat, the waterman held out his hand to the second.

"I am perfectly capable of disembarking from a wherry!" the second man snapped, and the waterman moved back. With a grunt of annoyance, the man stood up and stepped carefully onto the jetty.

"Wait here," said the first man. "We will be in need of a return to Queenhythe later."

"The bear pit is closed at this time of night," observed the waterman. He gave a small snigger. "If that is why you are here, of course."

There was a heavy silence, punctuated only by the gentle rhythmic thump of the boat against the jetty and the patter of rain on the water. The men stood as still as statues, and the waterman started to wonder if they had even heard him. He cleared his throat and tried again. "Because if it is girls you

5

want…" then suddenly he found himself staggering backwards, propelled by the point of a dagger pushed up into the soft base of his jaw, and ended up pressed hard against a slimy wooden post. "Oh, we are not here for the stews of Southwark, knave," came the voice of the second man, with soft but unmistakable venom. "If that is what you are suggesting."

The waterman said nothing, but pressed his head further back on the wooden post, his eyes fixed on the blade that was just visible in the darkness.

"Nay, knave, we are not here for whores." The blade pressed a little deeper and the waterman winced as he felt it break through the skin. "We are on private business – and if you have any sense you will wait here to carry us back to Queenhythe, then you will most assuredly forget that you ever saw us."

The dagger pressed a little deeper.

The waterman remained silent, unable to speak.

Then the dagger was pulled back, and the man turned away. Immediately the waterman put his hand to his throat to stem the hot blood that started to ooze out.

"Or belike I will seek you out and let my blade here finish the task. Do I make myself clear?"

"Indeed you do, good sir," the waterman answered, his voice coming out as an unnatural, guttural croak. "I will be here to take you back across the river." He rubbed his throat. "No matter how long that might be," he added with an attempt at a thin smile."

"Good. Make sure you are." The man sheathed his dagger then stepped off the jetty and onto the street beyond. "Or I will find you, be assured of that."

---0---

The two companions walked the Southwark streets in silence a few moments, their leather shoes squelching in the mud and filth.

Suddenly the first man stopped. "Why did you threaten that man so, Frances?" he asked sharply.

The other man stopped also. "Nay, Tom, had I not been clear on the consequences, he would be back in his boat and rowing for his life the moment we had stepped away from the jetty. Then we would have been stranded in this hellish mud pit for the night, forced to wait for the bridge to open in the morning. Besides," he added, "a small threat to secure our easier return to civilisation is a fair trade."

"Aye," answered Tom, following close behind, "and raising a hue and cry for the murder of a wherryman would help our cause better?"

"Do not give him the dignity of an honest trade, my friend," snapped Francis. "Did you not take offence, as did I, at his suggestion that we were here for the Southwark stews? Why else, he was suggesting, do gentlemen steal across to Southwark at dead of night?"

"We gave him no better reason." Tom was silent a moment as he trudged through the street; the dark, oppressive houses looming overhead against the night sky. "Perhaps we should have let him think we were here for a couple of whores. 'Tis a better reason than the truth."

"Nonsense. What if his next passenger was someone who knows us? A knave such as he would be sure to boast of the two fine gentlemen he carried across to the brothels of Southwark."

Tom snorted in disbelief. "Now it is you who is talking nonsense." He stopped as his foot sank deep into a puddle, and foul brown water slopped up his ankle. "By the Lord's Wounds, Francis, curse this God-forsaken place! My shoes are ruined! This is my best pair!"

"Stop your whining," snarled Francis. "I will have reason to have a better pair made for you if we succeed in our venture." He marched on through the mud. "And a fine pair for myself as well," he added.

"Aye, but no need of a new hat if it fails," muttered Tom, shaking the muddy water off his shoe and trudging after him through the dark.

---0---

Tom caught up with his companion at the next street corner. Francis had stopped and was scanning each of two possible alleys that forked away in front of them.

"I do not recall which of these I was to follow in the instructions I was given," he muttered.

Tom studied each in turn. "They look much the same to me," he said.

"That does not help."

"Let us try the left first," Tom said reasonably. "Then if that is not correct, we can always re-trace our steps back, and try the right."

Half an hour later they stopped again.

"By the Risen Christ," snarled Francis, peering around in the dark. "I warrant we have been at this corner at least twice before. We are now completely lost."

"At least the rain has stopped," Tom pointed out, trying to sound reasonable.

"Small comfort," Francis snapped back.

"I was sure we were tracing our steps back to the fork in the road."

Francis gave a dismissive snort. "We will walk that way," he muttered, pointing along an alley. It was darkened by oppressive timber houses with their 'jetty' upper stories leaning in towards each other, like giants squaring up for a fight.

It was not long before they came upon a tavern sign swinging in the night air, bearing the name 'The Blue Maid' and a picture of a girl milking a cow. "See here," said Tom, pointing up. "I say we step inside and ask the good men of Southwark if they can help us."

Without waiting for Francis, he walked down a short dark passageway that opened out into a courtyard, brightly lit by several flaming braziers. A half-open door to one side revealed more light and the sound of voices. Tom pushed it open and Francis followed him into the tavern.

As they made their way through the warm fug of candle smoke, Tom spotted a table with two empty seats next to a couple of elderly labourers. He sat down.

Francis sat opposite him and looked round in distaste.

The room held around fifteen wooden tables and benches, each with several men sitting at them nursing tankards of ale. They mostly wore the rough clothes of labourers and peasants, although there were a few better-off yeomen. A couple of peasant girls were travelling round the tables with pitchers of ale, filling tankards as they went.

One of these girls appeared with two tankards and thumped them down on the table. Tom gave her a three-farthing coin, which she bit carefully then pocketed, seeming satisfied with its authenticity. Then she slopped ale into each tankard and moved away. Francis stared down coldly at some solid object floating in the brown liquid, then picked it out and flicked it away.

One of the labourers at their table put down his tankard and stared suspiciously at the two newcomers, then touched his cap in a gesture of servility that seemed to Tom to be only just short of insolence.

"We do not often see fine gentlemen such as yourselves in the Blue Maid," he said, his eyebrow raised.

"Filthy night," answered Tom levelly. "We sought shelter from the downpour."

"Aye, that will be the reason," replied the labourer, with a small knowing smile on his face. "For it is sure not the ale that draws you in." He looked pointedly at Francis.

"Now listen, fellow…" snapped Francis, "mind your ton…" He stopped sharply as Tom kicked him under the table. "By Christ's Wounds, Thomas…?"

The labourer laughed. "Your companion is a sensible fellow, sir, as is his foot," he said.

Francis said nothing, but his mouth closed like a trap and Tom noticed a red flush start to creep out from under his ruff and spread up his cheek.

"You are right, sir," said Tom, with a faint, and he hoped, conciliatory smile. "This is not our usual place to drink." He paused a moment, choosing his words carefully. "But the truth is that while we were indeed seeking shelter, we are in Southwark to find a particular man who lives hereabouts."

"He must be a special fellow," observed the other labourer.

"Or he owes you money," said the first, and gave a great roar of laughter which ended in uncontrolled coughing and gulping of ale.

Tom waited until the paroxysms had died down, then said, "No, we have heard tell of his powers and we sought to meet him."

"He has powers?" asked the first labourer. "Does he practice sorcery?"

"No, no," Tom said quickly. "I do not think his powers come from sorcery. They say he is known as…" he paused, "the Alchemist."

If he was hoping for an awed reaction, he was disappointed.

"Plenty of folk round here known by that name," the labourer said matter-of-factly. "Thriving trade by those who will tell you they have the secret of turning base metal into gold."

"They say," cut in Francis with a tight-lipped smile, "that he can be known by the pictures painted onto his arms." He placed his own arms on the table. "He has two muskets in the form of a cross, on this one," he pointed to his right forearm, "and on the other, a single short-barrelled piece, but which has no lock or other visible sign as to how it could possibly be loaded."

"Ah, that Alchemist." The two labourers exchanged a significant look.

"You know this man?" Tom looked at each in turn, his eyebrows raised.

"Aye."

"And you can direct us to where we might find him?"

"Aye."

"Then please be good enough to do so."

There was a moment's silence. "He is not far from this place," said the first labourer.

"Mighty close," said the second.

"You will soon find him," added the first.

They both drained their tankards, taking their time.

"By thunder!" exploded Francis, rising from the bench with his hand reaching for the dagger at his belt, his face now deep red all over. "Will you tell…?" He sat down abruptly as Tom again kicked him hard under the table.

Tom waited until Francis' face had started to fade back to its more usual colour, then asked quietly, "Where is this Alchemist?"

"That table over there," said the first labourer with a smile. He pointed across the tavern to where a thin man with no hat and dark spiky hair was sitting, talking to two yeomen.

"Over there?" Francis sounded incredulous.

"The very man, sir."

"Christ's Blood, you could have said…"

"Nay, good fellow," Tom held up a restraining hand to Francis, "these worthy men of Southwark have had some sport at our expense – we should leave it at that." He drained his tankard and stood up. "Come, we have business with the Alchemist." He gave a small nod to the two labourers. "Good evening, sirs." Without waiting for Francis, he started threading his way across the tavern to the Alchemist's table.

Francis stood also, gave a hard-eyed stare at each of the labourers in turn, then stepped over the bench and hurried off after Tom. He joined his companion in front of the Alchemist's table.

The three seated men looked up at them, their eyebrows raised in enquiry. "I am told you are the one known as the Alchemist," said Tom, to the spiky-haired man.

The man looked them both up and down in turn, then gave a barely-perceptible nod.

"I am," he said slowly. "Who's asking?"

Tom said, "One who would talk with you in private."

The Alchemist stared at them for what seemed an uncomfortably long time, then he glanced at the two yeomen at his table.

"Leave us."

The yeomen said nothing, but both stood up and made their way to another table.

Tom and Francis sat down in their places, opposite the Alchemist. Tom glanced at the man's arms, which were sleeveless. There were the pictures as had been described; the strange hand-gun on the left and the crossed muskets on the right.

"What do you want from me?" the Alchemist asked.

Tom took a deep breath, glancing around to ensure that in the hubbub of the tavern, their words would not be overheard.

"It is just possible you can help us," he said quietly, "in a matter of the greatest importance to the future of England…"

CHAPTER TWO

Grangedean Manor, February 1575

Lady Mary de Beauvais leaned forward towards her son.

"You will do well to stop looking like you have bitten on a lemon," she whispered, "and start being thankful for these people's kindness."

She stood back. There was a long moment of silence.

"Yes, Lady Mother," the boy muttered.

She leaned forward again. "I mean it, Ambrose," she whispered, this time putting a little more steel in her voice. "The Grenville family are being most kind in taking you into their house and having you educated with their son – it is a real privilege."

"Yes, Lady Mother." The boy's head dropped and he seemed to be studying the hem of her voluminous skirts.

"So would you prefer your father and I sent you to the grammar school instead?" She put her hand under his chin and lifted it up, searching his eyes for some recognition of the sacrifice she was making.

She was sending him away from Grangedean Manor, and it was breaking her heart.

Yes, it was only for one year, but even a few days without her son by her side seemed almost unbearable.

She forced a smile.

"They will teach you better hunting and archery skills, and you will make great friends with Richard Grenville." She stood back again, still holding his chin. "There will be jousting and swordsmanship, too."

"I just want to stay at home, Lady Mother." His big, liquid eyes looked up at her – and that was when the hardness in her heart melted – like butter in a hot pan.

"Oh Bambi," she cried softly, as she pulled his small body into her arms, "I will miss you dreadfully – but I know it is the right thing to do." She kissed him on the forehead and once again stood back. "One day you will be Sir

Ambrose de Beauvais, the head of our family – and you need to know what it is to be a leading member of society. What better way to learn, than to have your schooling with the Grenvilles and see how it is done?"

"You could teach me."

She shook her head slowly. "No, Bambi, I could not. Because..."

She paused a moment. Because the truth was, she simply did not have the background or the knowledge to prepare him fully for his life in 16th century society – but that was something she could never explain to him.

She turned back to her son.

"Do not worry," she smiled reassuringly. "You will soon find the Grenvilles are like a second family. I wager that by the end of the year you will be just as upset to be leaving them, as you are to be leaving your father and me now."

He did not reply.

"Do you know," she continued, her voice becoming strangely flat, "I understand what it is like to leave home, to leave your mother and father, to leave everything that you recognise and hold dear." She shivered, and not just from the cold winter air in the Great Hall. "But you have to learn to accept it. To get on with life – to make the best of it even, and to come to love it." She paused, her eyes looking through him as she stared at visions that only she could ever see; visions of a world she had known that was lost to her forever. Then, with an effort, she pulled herself back to the boy. "I do understand what you are feeling, Bambi, believe me I do." She touched his cheek tenderly. "You will have such a lovely time there."

"But Mother," he whispered urgently, shaking his head. "I will not." He swallowed hard, struggling to get the words out. "They are Catholics, Mother! Kat told me."

Lady Mary resolved to have a word with Kathryn, her middle child. Goodness knows how she had found this prize nugget of information, and yes, the Grenvilles were Catholic. But as her husband Sir William had pointed out, some of the most noble families came from the old faith, and anyway, one doesn't ask too many questions when a family as noble as the Grenvilles agrees to take your son in and start him on the path to a first-class education.

William himself had been quite sanguine about the arrangement.

"I have had a word with Sir Nicholas," he had said when they had first discussed the matter of faith. "He says they follow the law and attend the Protestant church in their village."

"Good," she answered. "I do not want our son getting into any trouble, William. It is dangerous being Catholic right now. Every day they say there are plots to kill the Queen and put Mary of Scotland on the throne." She stared hard at him, her mouth set in a thin line. "Are you sure you are not leading him into danger by putting him in a Catholic household?"

"Of course."

"Well, if you are sure."

"He is an eight-year-old boy, Mary, my love." William patted her arm with a smile. "He is hardly likely to start plotting against the life of the Queen."

So Ambrose already knew. The original plan had been for his father to tell him once they were on the road to the Grenvilles' palatial Hetherington Hall, hundreds of miles away in North Yorkshire.

Mary held up a hand to her son. "Ambrose, please!" she said. "We have to respect other peoples' beliefs."

"No, we do not," he hissed back. "The Queen…"

"The Queen does not want us to fight with the Catholics," his mother cut in quickly. "She wants us to live together in peace."

"That is not what Nicholas Stanmore says," muttered Ambrose. "He says the Queen wants to rid the land of every last Catholic. He says she wants to hang, draw and quarter every one of them for being a damned traitor." He looked up at her with troubled eyes. "And Nicholas said the Pope has told every Catholic it is their duty to kill the Queen."

"Ambrose!" she cried. "Do not say those dreadful things!" She put her hands on her hips. "Nicholas Stanmore is eleven years old and should not be saying such words." She paused. Despite his tender years, Nicholas was factually correct. In the five years since the Pope had issued the *Regnans in Excelsis* bull, excommunicating Elizabeth and exhorting her catholic subjects to commit regicide, she had managed to avoid any assassination, mainly due to the network of spies run by the Secretary of State Lord Burghley and Sir Francis Walsingham. "The Queen is a very great lady," she continued, "who I am confident will rule this land for many years to come, and one day will protect us from our enemies when they try to conquer England."

"You do not know that for certain. You cannot."

"I do…"

Mary stopped herself. The truth was, that she did know that one day Elizabeth would defeat the Spanish Armada, and that her reign would last for forty-four glorious years, but one thing was for sure – she could not tell her son this.

"I do…" she repeated, "*not* know this for certain. But," she continued, "I have every faith in our Queen's best intentions, and I know that she is a very great lady who deserves our respect – and I know she will only execute Catholics, or anyone else, if they are proven to have plotted against her life." She put her hands on his shoulders. "Come now, little Bambi," she said, her tone softening. "It will all be alright, I promise." She squeezed him gently. "Your father and his men-at-arms are waiting to ride with you to Hetherington Hall and it is a very long way."

He stared at her a moment, then gave a weak smile. "Yes, Lady Mother."

He ducked away from her hands and ran to the doors of the Great Hall.

"Oh wait!" she called out suddenly. He skidded to a stop and turned.

"I had forgotten something. I have a small gift for you. I almost let you leave without it." She walked back to the high table, picked up the small jewelled box she had put there earlier and opened it. "Do you want to see it?"

Ambrose was about to answer, when there was the sound of heavy boots along the flagstones and the doors were thrown open.

The man who strode in was tall and athletically-built. He carried himself with an easy grace; and although the trim beard and blonde hair cascading out from under his velvet cap were both peppered with a little grey, his face was remarkably unlined – giving him the look of a man much younger than his thirty-six years.

Sir William de Beauvais was carrying a thick fur cape draped over his arm, similar to the one he wore himself.

"Come, son," he barked, as he draped the cape over the boy's shoulders, "put this on against the cold. We must be away if we are to reach the first stop before nightfall. It is many days' ride to Hetherington."

Ambrose pulled the cape tight. "Yes, Father, but Lady Mother has a gift for me."

"What is that?" There was a twinkle in Sir William's bright eyes. "What does your mother have for you?" He marched across the room and peered at the object that lay on her open palm. "Aha – it is a fine thing this; a golden frame with a perfect painted illumination of your mother's fair face for you to remember her by…" In one quick move he picked it off her hand and tossed it high in the air to his son. "Here, catch it, boy!"

"William, no!" Mary snapped, as the small picture spun lazily across the room, throwing out golden beams of morning sunlight.

Ambrose held out his hands, his eyes fixed on the little object spinning towards him.

He very nearly did catch it – and surely would have done were it not for an unfortunate flash of light from the golden frame that seemed to momentarily distract him.

As it was, the frame caught the edge of his hand, bounced up over his shoulder and dropped onto the top of a large oak chest behind him. William and Mary watched with open mouths as it landed with a thud, then skittered across the top of the chest and dropped quickly out of sight down the back.

There was a moment's silence.

"Oh, William!" Mary gasped. "What on earth did you do that for?"

William gave her a weak smile and a small shrug of his shoulders, for all the world like a guilty schoolboy saying 'sorry', but he said nothing. This was a tactic he had tried many times in their ten-year marriage and usually it melted Mary's heart. Most times she would laugh, punch his shoulder and call him her 'dear, silly man'.

But this time she stood still as his charm bounced off her, much like the golden frame had bounced off Ambrose's hand.

"William!" she barked. "That was a totally, completely and utterly stupid thing to do! It might have caught his eye!"

"But by God's good grace, it did not, my love." He tried another smile, then let it drop.

"No," she answered, "but it was delicate and made of gold – at best it will be bent or scratched!"

"Let us see, my love," said William and strode over to the oak chest. "Come, Ambrose," he said, as he started to pull the chest away from the wall, "help your father."

"Shall I call Simon or another servant?" Ambrose asked uncertainly.

"No son, come and help me now. We must retrieve your gift and set off without waiting for servants."

The boy scampered over to the wall and started to push at the chest, his little muscles bunching and his face quickly reddening. As William pulled and Ambrose pushed, the heavy chest moved slowly away from the wall. Once a sufficient gap had been opened up, Ambrose dived down and retrieved the painting.

"See Lady Mother!" he exclaimed, his eyes sparkling as he held it out to her. "It is wholly undamaged! God has protected it for me to treasure while I am away!"

"There, Mary, my love," said William, with undisguised relief in his voice. "No harm done." He turned to Ambrose. "Come son, we must be away. Say farewell to your mother."

The boy ran into Mary's outstretched arms, still clutching her gift. She kissed the top of his head, savouring the fresh, boyish smell of his hair and wanting so desperately to preserve it in her memory, so she would never, ever forget it...

"Fare thee well, Lady Mother." Ambrose tilted his chin and met her gaze. She could see the tears welling up in his eyes and knew it was a mirror of her own tears. "Fare thee well."

"Take care, my sweet Bambi." She kissed his head again. "Do as you are told and do not get into any trouble."

"No, Ma, I will not."

Sir William came up and put his hand on Ambrose's shoulder. "Come on, son, we must be away."

"Take good care of him on the journey, William," she said.

William looked quickly at her, clearly noticing the catch that she could not hide in her voice. "For sure, Mary."

"And how long will you be gone?"

"A month or two. The snow is fair thick here, and is likely to be thicker in the north – so I warrant we will not make a fast pace."

She nodded. "Well, go safely, keep warm both of you, and William – hurry back."

"Yes." William pulled at the boy. "Come, we must make Reading by nightfall."

Ambrose wriggled out of his mother's arms.

"Fare thee well, Ma," he repeated, then suddenly he was gone, running out with his father to leap on his pony and ride away from her for a year, or maybe more…

---0---

As the doors closed behind William and Ambrose, Lady Mary went over to the high table and flopped down onto one of the benches.

Hot tears started to roll down her cheeks.

You told yourself you wouldn't cry. You promised yourself…

She sniffed loudly and wiped her tears with her handkerchief.

He'll be fine with William and the men-at-arms on the journey, and he'll have the time of his life at Hetherington Hall…

The door from the kitchens opened and an old woman came in, wearing a plain black woollen dress and a white cap. She carried a wooden tray containing a silver goblet and a pitcher, together with some bread and a clean, folded napkin.

"A little draught of wine and some manchet bread to restore your humours, my lady?" she asked softly.

Mary pushed her handkerchief back into her sleeve and looked up with a watery smile. "Oh, thank you Ruth. Perfect timing as always. Just what I needed."

The old woman set the tray down on the table, poured a goblet of wine and handed it over. Then she sat beside her mistress.

"As your housekeeper, I know it is not my place to ask how you are faring, my lady," she said. "But as your friend and confidant, and even the one-time saviour of your life, I feel I have the right to ask and be answered."

Mary took a sip of wine and a deep breath. "Of course." She picked up the napkin and unfolded it carefully, then dabbed her eyes with it, playing for time.

"Dearest Ruth, I know I am doing the right thing by Ambrose, but deep down I keep thinking I have failed him." She dabbed her eyes again. "I am his mother. It should really be me that teaches him how to be a nobleman and a credit to his family, but I cannot." She turned to the housekeeper. "I just do not know enough, even after ten years here…"

Ruth put her hand on Mary's arm.

"As the Lord is my witness, I do understand, my lady. In truth, these ten years you have barely set foot outside Grangedean Manor, and certainly not ventured further than the village. I understand well that you have made a life for yourself here, but it has very narrow boundaries."

Mary shook her head slowly. "Ruth, you know that I once stood accused of witchcraft." She shivered. "When you have every soul shouting at you, calling for your death…"

"I know, my lady, truly I do." Ruth nodded. "And I see how you have built your life here in Grangedean – a life that is comfortable to you and keeps you protected from the unfamiliar outside world that tried to do you harm." She smiled. "If I were in your position, I am sure I would do the same. But you cannot keep Ambrose forever with you, locked inside this house. By sending him to a noble family, you are indeed making sure he steps outside your boundaries and is taught by the very best means possible." She looked directly at Mary, her steady blue eyes clear and certain. "So how can you be failing him? He will come back from the North a better educated child and a future head of the family. Where is the failure in that?"

"I suppose you are right."

Ruth gave a small laugh. "And if you ever want to teach him of the wonders of the world yet to come, you can tell him of the polished stones called 'phones' that talk with the voice of Our Lord, or the covered wagons that travel without a horse to pull them."

"Goodness, no!" Mary exclaimed, her eyes wide. "That would be a disaster – he can never know about those, or the truth about where I am really from!" She paused to gather her thoughts once more. "Ruth, that is our secret – yours, mine and Sarah's. No-one else must ever know how I travelled here across time itself from the distant future."

"No, Lady Mary, it is our secret, my oath upon it. I have not breathed a word to a soul, and nor has my daughter, Sarah."

"Thank you, Ruth; I know you and Sarah would never betray me."

It was a secret the three of them had managed to keep for ten years – and amazingly in all that time no-one else had ever questioned Mary's claim to have been the daughter of a friend of the de Beauvais family.

No-one had subsequently seen through the beautiful gowns, the carefully-applied make-up and the noble bearing of the elegant Lady Mary de Beauvais, to the real, frightened girl that had been kept so painfully hidden for so long.

That girl was called Justine Parker of Hammersmith, West London, who was born in the late 20th century, and who found herself in the wrong place at the wrong time – when an electrical storm opened up a freak wormhole in the fabric of space-time and deposited her, bewildered and alone, in 1565.

Accused of witchcraft by a superstitious serving girl, she had been relentlessly pursued by the witchfinder, one Matthew Hopkirk, determined to try her by ducking her in the Grangedean Manor well. With the help of Ruth and her daughter Sarah – who had been one of the servants – she had managed to thwart Hopkirk.

From there she had married Sir William de Beauvais to become Lady Mary, and ultimately mother to Ambrose, Kathryn and her youngest daughter, little Jane.

Ruth had been given the post of housekeeper and Sarah was made her lady-in-waiting. But it was not just out of loyalty that the secret had been kept – although Mary liked to believe that this was the strongest cause – but practical reasons also. For who would believe such a strange tale? Who in the 1560s or 1570s would even grasp the concept of time travel? To tell the tale would be seen as madness at the very least – just as it had been touch-and-go when Ruth and Sarah had first been told.

And now Justine was Lady Mary de Beauvais, a well-established Elizabethan wife and mother, mistress of Grangedean Manor.

Once she had come to accept that time-travel was a one-way trip and there was no going back, she had found herself embracing Elizabethan life – although without 21st century technology she had to rely instead on 16th century manpower. Fortunately, that was plentiful, and she had soon organised an army of servants to help her run the house.

But it wasn't just the daily tasks that she felt could do with the modern touch; it was the quality of life as well. As Justine in Hammersmith, she had had the radio on at all times, living her life to the sound of chat, banter and music. Now she only had the mobile phone she had brought back with her, carefully hidden in a small locked casket in her bedroom. It was taken out and charged with her solar charger when she was alone – allowing her a few precious minutes for a nostalgic wallow in the few music videos stored inside. The joy of connecting with her previous life through the phone was tempered by the torture of the ever-present 'no signal' message – as well as the fear that despite the charger, one day the precious phone would die completely and sever her last link with the 21st century.

"You look sad, my lady," said Ruth, breaking into her thoughts, and as ever, seeming to read them. "Do you grieve for the life you once led?"

Mary nodded with a rueful smile.

"It must be hard, when you are the only one who knows about the times yet to come, to have no other body to talk to. No one who understands about such things as wagons called cars and polished stones called phones."

"I suppose it is." Mary forced a smile. "But then I think that Kat needs a new kirtle and Ambrose must go to the butts to practice his archery, and maybe the rushes need changing in the bed chamber, and I forget about my old life and I get on with this one."

"Quite right, Mistress."

Mary looked up, and her eye caught the oak chest, still pushed away from the wall.

"Come Ruth, we have to put the oak chest back in its place. Call a servant to help."

Ruth stood and picked up the tray. "As you wish, my lady. Again, I am sorry to have upset you."

Mary stood also. "I am fine, Ruth. My oath upon it."

She even sounded like an Elizabethan!

As Ruth disappeared down the stairs to the kitchens, Mary went over to the chest. There were black marks along wood panelling, showing it had stood close to the wall for many years. She ran her fingers along the back edge and examined the deep dust left on them.

It is filthy! Why did no-one clean behind it? How on earth did I miss this?

A sudden flash of something glinting in the shadows on the floor caught her eye, and she bent down behind the chest to have a look.

She could just make out a small recess in the darkness, caused by the curved edge of a worn floor board not quite touching the panelled wall.

Bending further, she could see there was a metallic object lying deep in the dust. She reached down closer and put her fingers into the hole. She could feel the object – it was cold and very smooth; so smooth that her fingers could not seem to get a purchase.

Bending still further, she pushed her whole hand slowly into the space, and very carefully felt for the edges of the object. Once she had these, she was able to get a grip between her thumb and forefinger. Triumphantly she eased it out.

Standing straight, she went over to the window and examined her trophy. Blowing away the dust, she could see that it was a square brushed steel box. It was not big – it fitted snugly into her palm, and it was made of two parts fitting closely together. She turned it over. On the larger part was a black oval, surrounded by a relief pattern of scrolls and whirls. In the centre of the black oval was a white moulded skull.

Then her heart missed a beat.

It was a 21st century cigarette lighter.

She picked it up with her other hand and flicked the lid open. There was the lighter mechanism. She ran her thumb slowly down the strike wheel a few times, fearing to try lighting it; fearing to be proved that it was what she thought it was.

Then suddenly she found herself pushing hard on the wheel and flicking her thumb down.

A flame shot out of the nozzle.

With a small cry, she snapped it shut again, as she stared, mesmerised, at the little object.

There was only one person she knew who carried such a lighter – she had often seen him use it in the kitchens at Grangedean Manor when it was a modern-day visitor attraction, right up to when she'd got caught in the electrical storm and transported back to 1565.

It belonged to Rick, the spiky-haired catering manager.
Which could only mean one thing…
If the lighter was here, then Rick was here, too.

CHAPTER THREE

Ruth came back up into the Great Hall with a servant in de Beauvais livery.

"Simon will put the chest back, Mistress," she said.

The man went over to the chest and started heaving it back into place.

"Wait!" commanded Mary. He stopped and looked back up at her in surprise at the urgency in her voice.

"Ruth," she asked, "tell me how long this chest has been here against the wall? I do not recall."

Ruth thought a moment. "I believe it was when you were preparing for the birth of little mistress Jane." She nodded to herself. "Yes, I believe the master had some craftsmen make it and install it while you were in your confinement."

Jane was nearly four – which meant that the lighter must have been dropped into the hole at least four years ago, before the oak chest had covered it up. At the time Mary had been preparing for childbirth by being confined to a dark room and resting – as it was believed that the chances of miscarriage were reduced by avoiding any sort of stimulation. It seemed that she had not registered the new chest after emerging from confinement – no doubt with the birth of her third child she had other things on her mind.

So Rick must have been living in Elizabethan England for at least four years.

Four whole years!

What stories could they have shared if she had been able to chat to him? What memories of the future had they in common?

Ruth was wrong – there *was* now another living soul in Elizabethan England who knew what a phone was supposed to do; who understood how cars worked. Another living soul who would truly understand how she felt.

Had it been an electrical storm like hers, that had opened up the wormhole in time and transported him here? Had he been as petrified as she had been when falling into the past – and as surprised to find himself in such a strange time, even if in the same place?

Then suddenly Mary's heart missed a beat.

Rick wouldn't just know about phones. He would also know the answer to her burning question...

He would be able to answer the question that kept her awake at night, the one that had *really* kept her confined to Grangedean and the village, the one that had first forced itself into her head like an unwelcome stranger just after she and William had emerged from the little church as husband and wife all those years ago...

It had started as just a little niggle; a feeling of mild unease, but it had grown stronger and more corrosive with each passing year and with the birth of each child...

Rick was out there somewhere. Somehow, anyhow, she *had* to find him.

Because it was not just their shared experiences she had to discuss. It was also because Rick was the only person alive who could give her one other crucial piece of information...

"Ruth," she asked as casually as she could, nodding to Simon to push the chest back into place, "did you ever see a stranger leaving the Manor at that time? A man with short dark hair that stuck up from his head in spikes, like a hedgehog? A man wearing the strangest of clothes?"

"No, Mistress," Ruth answered slowly, with a sideways look that said she had picked up on the casualness in Mary's voice, and was calculating what it might mean. "What sort of man might that be?"

"No-one. No-one at all."

Ruth looked unconvinced. "Marry, my lady, I do not recall such a man, although I warrant I would have done from your tale of him." She paused. "I can ask the rest of the servants if one of them has seen him?"

"No, it is no matter."

"Indeed, Mistress? 'Tis no matter?"

"None at all, Ruth, believe me." Mary recoiled at the thought of the servants gossiping about the strange spiky-haired man that so interested her. "It is certainly not a matter I wish to have discussed with any other soul in this house."

Ruth nodded, clearly accepting of her mistress's occasional odd behaviour. Then her eyes slid over to the servant Simon. Mary followed her eyes and saw Simon had his back to them, with his hands remaining on the chest. His body was very still; a stillness that plainly said he was straining to hear every word passing between the two women behind him.

"Simon?" They saw him flinch slightly at Ruth's tone, then he slowly stood up and turned to them, a look of studied innocence carefully applied to his face. "You will not talk of this day's dealings with anyone else. Do I make myself understood?"

He gave a sly smile, as if he now had a secret he could not wait to share with all the serving women. "Yes, Mistress Ruth," he answered, although it was plain he did not mean it.

Ruth stared coldly at him. "I am most serious, Simon. If I hear you have talked of this, you will be cast out and will be left to vagrancy."

He swallowed hard and visibly paled. "Yes, Mistress Ruth," he muttered.

"You may go, now."

"Yes, Mistress Ruth." He scurried over the door leading down to the kitchens and was quickly gone.

There was a long, long moment of silence. Then Ruth spoke. "As your sometime saviour and close confidant, I would know the truth." Her voice became steely hard. "I warrant that you asked this question for a reason. This hedgehog man means much to you."

Mary let her breath out slowly. "Ruth, we have known each other many years?" Ruth nodded expectantly. "So I cannot hide from you that I found this." She opened her hand to reveal the lighter. "It belongs to the man with spiky hair – a man I once knew from my own time. And if this is here, then he will be, too."

Ruth picked it up curiously and studied it.

Then suddenly she gave a small cry and the lighter dropped from her hand, falling heavily to the floor.

"Lord a' mercy, my lady!" she gasped, crossing herself several times. "Lord a' mercy! 'Tis the work of the devil!"

Mary picked up the lighter. The white skull shone out starkly against the black enamel. "No, Ruth, this is not the devil's work – it is the work of men, just like all things made in my time."

"Then what of the devil's mark?" Ruth had turned as white as the skull itself.

"It is…" Mary stopped, suddenly unsure. The 21st century iconography of a skull in this context could surely be explained without ironic reference to hell, but in the moment she couldn't think how. "It is the work of men," she said lamely. "Look." She opened the lid and flicked the wheel. A flame shot out. "It has only one purpose – to light fires."

Again, Ruth gasped and crossed herself as she stared at the bright flame dancing in Mary's hand. "A tinder box! 'Tis a miniature tinder box!"

"Yes, and it works the same way, too." Mary flicked the lid shut, putting out the flame, then opened it again and flicked the wheel once more. "Turning the wheel strikes a spark, which lights the oil stored inside."

Ruth looked slowly up at her. "You make polished stones called 'phones' that talk with the voice of the Lord," she said, shaking her head, "and tinder boxes no bigger than a pebble – these are truly wonders." She held out her hand. Mary flicked the lighter shut and put it on Ruth's palm. Ruth studied it carefully a moment, then tried to light it as Mary had done. It took a few goes before she too had the flame dancing off it. "Ha! 'Tis not natural, that would have a fire lit without a normal tinder box."

She closed the lighter and handed it back.

"Your friend that would be a hedgehog – he will be concerned to find this wonderful thing again. He must have lost it when he came here like you did, on a witch's curse."

Mary had forgotten she had concocted the story of a witch sending her back in time – as she believed this would actually be more credible to 16th century women than the space-time wormhole she believed was the true cause.

"Yes, and I would like to give it back to him."

And to ask him the question…

"I warrant you would." Ruth smiled. "And talk together of the times yet to come, but which for you both are but memories."

"Yes, Ruth, I would like to talk with him." Mary said, then paused. "But…"

"What ails, my lady?"

"Oh, Ruth, I know it sounds stupid, but…" She faltered to a stop.

Ruth sat slowly on the bench seat. "Pray tell, my lady. There is something that troubles you." She gestured to Mary to sit beside her. "I can see you are deeply a-feared of something."

Mary was about to sit down, when a heavy yawn overtook her. It started deep in her chest and quickly reached up till it popped in her ears, forcing her mouth open and her eyes to screw tight shut. She put her hand up to try and cover it, but there was no hiding it, it was so all-consuming.

"God's truth, my lady, you must a-bed this instant" said Ruth. "I had not seen it before, but now I see that you are as tired as a stag running from the hunt."

"No, I am fine," answered Mary, once she had regained the power of speech. "I'm fine." She flopped down next to Ruth. "I have been very worried about Ambrose," she said. "And in truth I have not slept much these past nights thinking of his journey."

"Pray sit, my lady." Again Ruth patted the seat beside her. "Tell me what troubles you."

Mary sat, and looked into her housekeeper's eyes. Then she sighed and shook her head. "Ruth, I have been worried about Ambrose, but there is something else that has been troubling me for many years – and finding this lighter means I may get the answer."

Ruth stayed silent, as if she were giving Mary the space to speak when she was ready.

"I know it is stupid, Ruth," Mary said after a moment, "but I need to find this man. I want to ask him a question. I want to ask him if… if…

Mary swallowed hard. This was the question that had been eating her from the inside for these last ten years, and now she was about to say it out loud.

What if it sounded completely stupid?

She looked at Ruth.

"I want to know if I will still exist in the future!" she blurted out.

There was a silence. Then Ruth frowned. "I know not what you mean, my lady," she said slowly.

"I mean, I need to find out if I have changed history so much that I have endangered my own existence." Mary paused. Ruth was still looking confused. "If this man does not know who I am, then maybe it is because I do not exist in the future; the future that he knew before he came back in time himself. And if I do not exist for him, then at some point I must stop existing at all," she paused again, searching the housekeeper's eyes for acknowledgement that this was so very difficult, "because I will have changed history."

Ruth stared at her, wide-eyed, with her mouth pursed. "But you lived in your time, did you not? And you were transported here on a witch's curse – so what is to think on?"

Mary put her hand on Ruth's arm. "Dearest Ruth," she said, "I know. But what have I done since I got here?"

"You have married the master and become established as a fine wife and mother, beloved of all."

"That is lovely to hear, but what I have really done is to change everything." She leaned in towards Ruth. "I saved Sir William when history said he was to die, and I had three children, who will grow up and have lives of their own."

Ruth nodded slowly, as understanding started to show in her eyes. "And you fear that all five of you, who were never here in the original history – the one that led to your birth – will create new consequences…" she said slowly.

"Exactly. Consequences that may mean that events will go this way and that way – until one day, something happens that means that maybe my grandparents are not born at all, or never meet each other…"

"…And so you will not be born either." Ruth shook her head.

"You see?" Mary said. "If the man who owns this lighter knows who I am, then I still exist in his time – the future that runs on from where we are now, with me, William and the children all existing."

"And if he knows you not?"

Mary sighed deeply and grimaced. "Then at some point perhaps I will just… disappear."

Ruth stroked Mary's cheek. "My dear lady," she said softly, "I am sure that cannot be. You are a good person, who goes to church at all times required by God and by the law. God will not let you disappear, my word upon it."

"That is good, I am sure," Mary answered, "but I need to know." She shook her head and stood up again. "So I want to go to the village this evening and start asking if anyone has seen this man."

"You can be away in the morning," said Ruth, her eyes narrowing and her voice becoming firmer. "I will have your horse Juno made ready for you to ride out, after you break your fast."

Mary gave a small inward shudder. To spend the rest of the day and all night trapped in Grangedean Manor, thinking on what she had found and not doing anything but trying to sleep – that would be unbearable!

"I cannot wait until morning, Ruth; truly I will not," Mary said firmly. "I must go to the village now and start asking. I can be back by nightfall."

"But the hedgehog man has been here four winters or more – belike he can wait one more day to be found?"

"No, my mind is firm on this, Ruth." Mary drew herself up and lifted her chin. "I will go to the village this hour and see if I can find out more."

"Alone?" Ruth fixed her with an accusing eye. "That is not seemly. You must take a servant or some men-at-arms with you."

Suddenly Mary was a teenager again, standing in front of her mother being told not to go out 'dressed like that.' She wanted to stamp her foot and shout "I am a 21st century woman – I can go wherever I please!" But instead she took a breath, smiled and said, "No, Ruth, please have Juno saddled now."

Ruth observed her silently a moment, then seemed to try a different approach. "My lady," she said, "you will fall from the very saddle, you are so very tired." The old woman's expression softened as she put a hand to her mistress's sleeve and looked up at her. "Your eyes are like the tiniest flakes of coal deep in the snow," she said softly. "Please, let it rest, let *you* rest but a few hours, and go a-freshed in the morning."

Mary smiled. "Ruth, you have always looked after me like you were my own mother, and I respect you for it, but on this matter, I will not be swayed."

"Then take Simon to look out for you."

Mary glanced across at the door where the servant Simon had so sheepishly departed a few minutes before. "Right now, Ruth, I would rather not. I will go alone."

Ruth bowed her head. "As you wish, my lady." She looked up and nodded briefly. "As you wish."

She turned and walked slowly to the doors.

CHAPTER FOUR

The low winter sun was already turning the sky from grey to red as Lady Mary de Beauvais pushed open the heavy wooden door and stepped into the village tavern.

Although she had been inside once or twice over the years, the sight of the stark room with its blackened wooden tables and spluttering tallow candles never failed to give her a sickening shiver of fear, as she re-lived the events of that fateful night ten years before. It was the night when William had been accused of witchcraft by the snake-like magistrate, Hopkirk, and so nearly drowned in a barrel in a witch-trial. When that had been thwarted, Hopkirk had tried to attack William with his wicked knife.

Mary shuddered again.

Historically, William should have died that night. All the 21st century historical records had told how he was killed in a tavern brawl on the 31st of July 1565.

But this time she had been there too, in disguise. When the moment came – a split-second moment when history would have taken its course and William's life would have been brutally cut short – she had acted instinctively.

She had rushed at Hopkirk and knocked him down, stopping him from stabbing William.

So it was the night when history had been changed forever. Sir William de Beauvais, far from dying as a young man, was now very much alive. And instead of dying childless as history had ordained, he was the father of Ambrose, Kathryn and Jane.

So history had been set on a new path – a path that could lead to Justine Parker, now Lady Mary, no longer existing.

What would happen if she were to disappear? Would it be as if she had never existed at all? And what of William, Ambrose, Kat and Jane – would they too disappear? Would history re-establish itself as if she had never travelled back in time? But then the events that led to her birth would re-establish themselves as well! So then she would suddenly reappear… and maybe end up bouncing between existence and non-existence like a paradoxical tennis ball…

Mary shook her head. This was ridiculous.

Life – real life – must go on. And right now, that was in Elizabethan England.

She looked around the tavern.

It seemed nearly empty, with just a couple of village men at one table. She sat down away from them, and looked round for the innkeeper Luke, or his wife, Agnes.

Luke and Agnes had taken over the ownership and management of the tavern some five years before on the death of Agnes's father, old Jake. He had been quite the village character, padding around the tavern in his dirty smock like a grey ghost; his grizzled beard so long that it would have reached the floor, had it not had to pass first across his enormous belly. But Jake could not go on forever, and one day he had been dispensing his customary pearls of wisdom to a group of villagers, when he had suddenly turned bright red, made a noise like the hiss of steam escaping a boiling kettle, and, as the villagers stared transfixed, had toppled slowly forward face-first like a felled tree. He was apparently dead before he hit the floor, according to the tales that spread like wildfire among the villagers after the unfortunate event.

Mary and William had attended the funeral in the little village church, sitting calmly in the front row of the pews reserved for them, while the rest of the village were crammed noisily in behind them. Mary had wanted to buy Jake a coffin, but as William pointed out, Jake had been a willing associate of Hopkirk on the night he was nearly killed, and it was hard to forgive that, even in death. So Jake had been buried in just a shroud. The village had paid their respects – and Elizabethan country life carried on. Agnes and Luke were established as the new owners of the tavern, and they had done well to maintain the warmth and atmosphere established by Jake.

Only that warmth appeared to be lacking this evening, as the two men sitting across the room suddenly noticed Mary. Immediately they stopped talking and stared at her with dark, hostile looks.

In that moment, she felt very exposed.

These men were clearly finding it unacceptable to come across a single woman in the tavern. Mary shifted uncomfortably on the bench as a cold flush flooded through her like a tidal wave. What on earth had she been thinking, to come to the tavern unaccompanied? She should have listened to Ruth instead of being so headstrong…

She dropped her head and stared down at the table, wondering whether she should get up and go, scurrying back to her little bubble of comfort in Grangedean Manor like a naughty schoolgirl…

No. She could look after herself.

A chill wind blew across the back of her neck as the door opened.

She glanced behind her and saw some more villagers shambling in, clapping and blowing on their hands to get some heat into them after the cold outside. As they started to make themselves comfortable at the next table, one of them looked her up and down, then nudged his companion, muttering something. His companion laughed.

"Art all alone, lady?" the first man asked, his mouth twisted into a sneer. "I think 'tis a bit late for you to be out without your husband."

Mary looked at the man. He was a red-faced labourer with few teeth and little hair, dressed in a moth-eaten woollen jerkin and filthy breeches.

Suddenly Mary knew what she had to do. She was a 21st century woman and she was lady of the manor. She was not going to be told where she could go and when – and certainly not by a man as filthy as this.

Very slowly and carefully she stood up, then lifted her chin defiantly.

"My husband," she said firmly, "is your master, Sir William de Beauvais, and he is away at this moment." The man looked surprised – clearly he had not known who she was. "And I will not be told by you, or by any other man, where I can go." She lifted her chin a little higher. "Do you understand me?"

The man looked down. "Yes, my lady," he muttered.

"I did not hear you."

He looked up. "Yes, my lady," he repeated. "Begging your pardon, my lady."

"What is your name?"

"Simeon, my lady."

"Well, Simeon, I thank you to keep your opinions to yourself in future."

"Yes, my lady." He sat down and there was silence in the tavern.

"Good." Mary sat also, trying to look calmer than she felt.

Gradually conversation resumed.

As if this was her cue, Agnes appeared with a full pitcher of ale in one hand and a fistful of tankards in the other. She was a small, plump woman with a pinched face, eyes that seemed too close together and mousy hair hanging in straggly tendrils round her face. Mary was put in mind of Mrs Tiggywinkle from the Beatrix Potter books of her childhood; a look which was reinforced by the plain brown woollen dress and white ale-stained apron.

"Ale, my lady?" she asked. Mary nodded, and Agnes put a tankard down, filled it with a flourish, then stood back, pushing a tendril of hair behind her ear. "There," she said. "A fine ale just for my lady. The first of a new barrel."

"Thank you, Agnes," said Mary, putting a three-farthing coin on the table. Agnes scooped it into a pocket on the front of her apron.

"I wanted to ask you a question, Agnes," Mary said, quite levelly. "If you have a moment."

Agnes smiled; a thin, shallow smile that didn't quite manage to reach her small eyes. "For sure, my lady. But by your leave, I would first attend to these folk." She gestured over to Simeon and his friends.

"Go to it."

Agnes gave a small nod. "I will return most presently." She moved over to the villagers' table and started serving, laughing quickly at some quip by one of the men and responding with a comment of her own that drew a great roar of laughter in return.

Mary couldn't help wondering if she had been the butt of their joke, and decided she probably had been. She sighed. Elizabethan England was such a strange land – and it was clear that even after living in it for ten years she knew so little of how it worked. But now that Rick was out there somewhere, she was going to have to step out of the safe, comfortable world of Grangedean Manor and explore it…

Agnes sat down opposite Mary and folded her arms under her ample bosom.

"You wanted to ask me a question, my lady?"

"Yes, Agnes, I did." She took a sip of her ale.

"About four years ago, did a stranger come into the tavern? A strange man in strange clothes, with no hat and hair that stuck up in spikes like a hedgehog?"

As she said it, she knew how slim her chances were of Agnes remembering one customer from such a long time ago – however strange he might have been.

But never in a million years, could she have imagined the reaction she would get from the little woman across the table. The colour drained from Agnes's face, and she stared open-mouthed at Mary. After a while, small intermittent mewling sounds started coming from the back of her throat.

"So you knew this man?" Mary hazarded.

Agnes nodded, wide-eyed but still said nothing. Mary pushed her tankard across the table, and Agnes drained it in a single gulp.

"Tell me about him, Agnes." Mary said gently.

Agnes pushed a tendril of hair behind her ear and took a deep breath.

"My lady, how is it that you know of him?

Mary frowned. "Tell me what you know, first."

Agnes leaned forward. "My lady," she said, pleading with her eyes. "This is not a good man. He is godless and Heaven knows he lacks a soul. What e're your business be with him, please, I beg you to think again on it."

"Tell me how you came to know him."

Agnes leaned further forward. "It was not more than ten or twelve months since my father had died, God rest his soul," she began. "I was alone in here one morning, when this man staggered in. He looked frightened, like he had seen an evil spirit, but I was a-frighted also when I saw him."

"Why was that?"

"As you said, he had no hat, and his hair was in spikes like giant thorns.

Or a hedgehog, yes." She nodded to herself as she stared at the images in her head. "He was wearing loose blue breeches with yellow stitching, that I had never seen on a man before." She suddenly fixed her gaze back onto Mary. "They reached right down to his ankles! Would you believe it?"

Mary shook her head. "No," she answered.

"His unshaped jerkin had only the smallest of sleeves," Agnes continued, her eyes glazing over as once again she was lost in her memories, "and on his arms were painted pictures of muskets."

Mary nodded. Rick had had tattoos of guns on both arms – she remembered now. He was always talking about guns, and had once showed her the tattoos as they sat outside the Grangedean Manor visitor café having a coffee. "The ones on my right arm, these are AK47s," he had told her. "Over a million of them around – developed after the war and still going strong. Very reliable. On my left arm, a .44 Magnum. You seen *Dirty Harry* or *Taxi Driver*? .44 Magnum," he had sniggered, holding his two fingers to her temple as if they were a gun. "Go ahead, make my day!"

She had found the whole thing a bit sickening, and had said so.

"Yeah, well, it's good to have a hobby," he had answered. "One day I'll have a .44 Magnum, or an AK47. Or a sniper rifle, like in *Day of the Jackal*. Awesome killing weapon, that."

Mary said to Agnes, "You must have found him frightening."

"Aye." Agnes nodded again. "He begged me for a pint of ale, though he had no coin upon him that I recognised."

"Did he offer coin?"

"He did – smooth silvery tokens bearing the head of a queen, but not a queen I knew. I told him we only accept Queen Elizabeth's coin here."

"What did he say to that?"

"He insisted that it was Queen Elizabeth – but I refused to accept it, saying it was not. But he was so desperate for vittles and ale, that I took pity and gave him some."

"Where did he go after he had eaten and drunk?"

Agnes shook her head slowly. "Oh no, my lady, he never went to any place! No – he stayed here."

"He stayed here? In the tavern?" Mary asked. "For how long?"

"A few months. He told me he had some experience of preparing food, so I gave him work in my small kitchen, and a truckle bed to sleep on at the day's end."

So Rick had been living and working only a couple of miles from Grangedean Manor for a few months – and Mary had had no idea! She might even have come in to the tavern after Jane had been born, and been completely unaware that someone she knew – someone who also came from the 21st century – was there as well.

She could have found out already if he knew her. If she still existed in his time…

31

"So what happened after a few months?" Mary asked. "Why did he go, and where?"

"Oh, my lady!" Agnes stared at her as a tear suddenly appeared and started to roll down her cheek. "He had to go. We had to turn him out."

"Why?"

Agnes swallowed hard, and a second tear appeared. "Because he tried to force himself upon me while I were a-bed," she whispered, "and Luke came in and caught him in the attempt."

"Oh, how awful!"

"Aye." Agnes sniffed loudly and wiped her eyes on her sleeve. "Luke cast him out that very night."

"Luke cast him out? Where did he go?" Mary asked again.

"I cared not, but I heard tell he fetched up at Master Melrose's house, and worked for him a while." Agnes sniffed again. "Had I been asked, I would have warned Master Melrose against the man, but I was not told where he had gone until after he had moved on again."

Mary paused, as Agnes wiped her eyes and sniffed once more. Then she said, "Thank you, Agnes. You have been most helpful."

Agnes looked up at her with pink eyes. "He was a godless man, as I have said, my lady. A godless man. And God willing you will not find him, for if you do, I warrant he will only bring you misery."

CHAPTER FIVE

Reading, February 1575

Ambrose de Beauvais lay back on the thin, hard bed and studied the gold-framed picture clutched tightly in his small hand.

Slowly he traced a finger down his mother's face.

"Good night, Ma," he murmured. "God save thee well this cold night."

He let out a slow breath. "Pa and I – we have ridden far this day, and I am so tired Ma, truly I am. I would sleep this moment like I were dead to the world, only it is all so strange here, and there are such loud noises of the men drinking downstairs that I could not sleep. I would be in my own bed at home, Ma, with you to tell me a story so I could lay my head to my pillow and feel your hand on my brow and hear one of your wondrous tales." He blinked away a small tear and sniffed. "Will you tell me again of gentle Cinderella, Ma, or the tragic Princess Diana?"

His mother's picture smiled up at him, staying resolutely silent. "But I have a story to tell you, Ma," he murmured, "about what happened to me and Pa on the road this day." He shifted his position to get more comfortable, and began his tale.

"We were some hours in the saddle after we took our leave of you this morn, and I said to Pa that I was sore and hungry. Pa said he was hungry too, and we stopped and dismounted our horses in a clearing, where some other travellers were also stopped. I tied my pony, Thelwell, up, and Pa and the men tied up their horses, and we had just sat down with some bread, cheese and wine when a man galloped past us as fast as the wind. He was riding well, Ma, like you have taught me, with his head close to the horse's mane and his bottom in the air..." Ambrose paused and let out a small giggle. "I beg your pardon, Lady Mother, you always tell me I should not say such words." He took a breath. "...Anyway, he was riding well. But as he passed us, one of the other travellers' horses took fright at the sight, making a great neighing and standing on his hind legs, and this caught the eye of the running horse, causing him to shy most suddenly and toss the man from his back. The man fell so badly and his head hit the ground so hard, that it would not be possible that he would survive. Pa and I ran to the man and Pa felt his neck, but then shook his head and closed the man's eyes, so I knew the man was dead even though Pa did not say it."

Ambrose paused a moment, and swallowed to clear the lump in his throat. "It was terrible, Ma, so terrible. One minute the man was riding hard, the next he was dead. I asked God what had this man done so wrong, that he must be struck down so? And God told me in his own way. Because a moment later some more men rode by, pulling up their horses sharply when they saw what had come to pass. Pa told them the rider was dead, and their leader, an old man with long white hair, got down from his horse and checked the body for himself. Then this leader said how it was a shame that the man was dead, as he may not now be brought to justice. He said the man had 'cheated the hangman'. I was expecting Pa to ask what the man had done, but instead Pa gave a great shout and ran over to the leader, calling him Wychwoode and embracing him warmly. It seems you and Pa know this Master Wychwoode well, as he was part of some adventures you had before you were married and I was born."

Ambrose touched the picture softly. "You never told me anything of these adventures, but the way Master Wychwoode talked of them, it seems they were most dangerous. Why have you not told me, Ma? You tell me many exciting stories, but not those ones. I asked Pa but he would not tell. He said they were stories for another time. Then he asked Master Wychwoode what the unfortunate dead man had done, and Master Wychwoode said the man was part of a papist plot on the life of our Queen. He said the man was called Francis Allcyne, and that spies had found out that he was part of the plot, so Master Wychwoode, who works for a man called Walsingham, was chasing this Alleyne to bring him to justice."

Ambrose put the picture carefully under his pillow and tried to get more comfortable on the hard bed. "And now Pa and this Master Wychwoode are drinking in the tavern downstairs and I am commanded to sleep, but I cannot, for the noise and the hard bed, and for not having you to stroke my head and call me your 'little Bambi', and because this talk of papist plots makes me so concerned, Ma..."

The door swung open and Ambrose looked up, to see his father standing in the doorway.

"Art not yet asleep, my boy?" asked William, swaying slightly and grabbing the door frame for support, before coming over to the bed and staring down on Ambrose, his face looking flushed. "What shall I tell thy mother, sirrah?" he demanded. "Shall I tell her you were falling asleep in the saddle on our travels because you would not sleep in your bed?"

Ambrose shook his head solemnly. "This is not my bed, Pa," he said. "My bed is soft and warm but this one is cold and hard." He sniffed quietly. "And I cannot sleep with the shouting from downstairs."

"Nonsense, son…" began William, then stopped as a loud crashing sound came from below, accompanied by a great roar of laughter. "Yes, well, 'tis but occasional, and you must be so tired after our strange adventure this day, that…" Again he was interrupted, this time by the sound of a heavy punch being thrown, followed by an even louder crash. Father and son then listened as Wychwoode's authoritative voice barked out commands, clearly trying to restore order.

Ambrose waited till there was relative quiet again, then said, "and my Lady Mother is not here to stroke my head and tell me her stories."

William took a deep breath and sat down heavily on the side of the bed. "You would have me tell you a story, son?" he asked, then put out a hesitant hand to his son's head. "What would you have me tell?" he asked, stroking Ambrose's hair cautiously, as if it were too hot to touch.

"No, Pa" answered Ambrose, moving his head away slightly. "Perchance another time."

William quickly withdrew his hand with a barely disguised expression of relief. "That is good, my boy. Another time then." He stood up. "Sleep well, son. We have an early start in the morning." He walked over to the door, then turned. "I will be up to bed myself presently. I trust you will be asleep when I return."

He was just about to leave when Ambrose sat up.

"Pa?" he said, his voice catching. "There is something else…"

William paused, his hand on the door knob. "Yes, son?"

"That man who died today. Master Wychwoode said he was a papist, who would have been hung for his part in a plot to kill the Queen?"

"Yes. But what of it?"

"The Grenvilles are papists, and I am to spend a year or more with them." Ambrose looked at his father with an ashen face. "What if they are also plotting against the life of the Queen?"

William returned to the bedside and again sat down.

"Ambrose, my son," he said, looking into the boy's wide eyes. "I know the Grenville family of old, and they are too well established, and too secure in their position, to let old papist beliefs lead them into treason." He gave a small smile. "I would not take you into danger, I promise."

"You swear, Pa? On Ma's life, and on Kat's and Jane's? You swear?"

"Yes, Ambrose. I swear it." He ruffled the boy's hair. "I swear it, truly I do." He took a deep breath.

"I promise – you will be in no danger at the Grenvilles."

CHAPTER SIX

The sun had barely risen over the white, snow-frosted parklands of Grangedean Manor, when Lady Mary de Beauvais swung herself up into the saddle and wheeled her mare, Juno, round to face the gate. The groom who had been holding the mare's head bowed and retreated to the warmth of the stables.

"I will be back well before sundown," Mary said to her lady-in-waiting, Ruth's daughter Sarah, who was standing close beside Juno and was huddled in her cloak, blowing on her hands to keep them warm. "Please make sure Kat and Jane attend to their needlework, and Ruth has the month's accounts ready to review when I am back.

"Yes, my lady," muttered Sarah without raising her head. There was something in her tone that made Mary look at her sharply.

"Come now, Sarah, be of good cheer!" she said. "What ails you?"

"Naught, my lady."

"Nonsense." Mary pulled back on the reins and Juno's hooves clattered with impatience on the cobbles. "You look as though there has been a death in the family."

"Nay, my lady."

"Then what?"

Sarah looked up slowly. "My mother has told me that you have found out that there is another here, a man from your time."

"Yes! It is amazing news!"

"Nay, my lady," Sarah answered. "I am much a-feared."

"Why?"

Sarah hesitated, clearly wrestling between her sense of propriety and voicing her deep concern. Eventually propriety lost. "My mother says you intend to seek him out – alone, if necessary." She paused again. "It is not seemly, my lady, for you to be searching the land alone, looking for a strange man, while the master is away. And it could be most dangerous." She looked up and stared at Mary, her face pinched and red; her breath misting in the cold morning air. "I do not like it."

"I appreciate your concern, Sarah, truly I do." Mary leaned down and touched her friend's shoulder. "But I do not intend to go chasing off after this man today – just to visit Master Melrose to hear what the man did when he worked there, and where he might have gone afterwards. I shall be back later, and we can decide then what is best to be done."

"But you go alone to Master Melrose?"

"I do, Sarah." Mary answered. "In my time, women would go alone wherever they please. I have hidden myself away for ten years in Grangedean. Now I need to get out and experience England."

"But this man could be anywhere in the land by now."

"Then, yes, I will seek him out."

Sarah frowned. "But my lady, in truth, what do you know of this land? In the time since you came here from the far future, you have not once gone further than the village. You are as much a stranger today as you were ten years ago. You have always said it is best for you not to travel away from Grangedean Manor."

"I know, Sarah, but if Master Melrose can point me in the direction that this man has gone, then I will find him. I must, and I will go on my own if necessary, because it is my quest and no-one else's." Mary put a little steel in her voice. "Last evening I faced a villager down who questioned me being out alone, and if I could do it to him, I can do it again." She smiled. "And as I say, I come from a time and place where women can go as they please, without needing a man to guide them."

She dug her heels into Juno's flanks and headed for the gate. Then she added over her shoulder, "So how hard can it be?"

---0---

Thomas Melrose stared at Mary, his mouth hanging open like a piece of loose sacking. He closed it with what seemed an effort, but his thin face stayed as white as the rolling snow-covered hills outside his pebble-thick leaded windows.

"I do not see you outside Grangedean Manor these past ten years, yet now you plan to travel the land in search of that man, Richard?" Mary nodded. "But why? The man is poison."

"I would ask him some questions which only he can answer."

"Well, I am sure you have your reasons, Lady Mary, but I would not be in that man's presence again for all the silk of the Orient."

"Why?" she asked. "What did he do?" Although from other reports of Rick's behaviour, it wasn't hard to guess.

Melrose shook his head. "I trusted the man. I took him in. I gave him shelter and an honest workman's wage. And how did he repay me?

"How?"

"He tried to bed my daughter, my sweet Olivia." Melrose drained the goblet of wine in his hand and refilled it from the pewter flagon in front of him. "I stopped the man in time, but if I had not been so fortunate to be passing her chamber and hear her cries, he would have succeeded."

"Then he would have been arraigned on a charge of rape?"

"Belike." He took another sip of wine. "But how to prove it?"

"By the word of your daughter." Mary said indignantly. "If the crime was against her, she would be the accuser and witness."

Melrose stared at her with a half-smile. "Lord a' mercy, Mary, you have hidden yourself away from us all these last ten years, but even so, you should know that this is not how such things work."

"How so?"

He paused a moment, regarding her over the top of his goblet. "I have no doubt Sir William treats you most kindly, and does not beat you as he is entitled to do, but..."

"He would not dare," she interrupted.

"...quite so – and in truth I cannot imagine him wanting to do so, either. But the law permits it, because the law is always on the side of the man. So the outcome of any arraignment and trial for rape is almost always that the word of the man is believed." He gave a hollow laugh. "Unless, of course, a child ensues and it is conclusive that it is his. But even then he may claim consent, or choose to marry the girl – in which case it becomes a case of fornication before marriage rather than rape."

"So even if Richard had raped Olivia, the chances of him being found guilty..." she began.

"...would be very low," he said. "Yes. And I would certainly not have allowed a marriage."

"But that is awful." Mary bit her lip. So Rick had tried it on with Agnes, then with Olivia Melrose, and who knew who else besides? The man had clearly decided to let his basest nature loose once he had arrived in Elizabethan society; once he was freed from the norms of the 21st century. And this was the man she wanted to have a cosy fireside chat with, reminiscing about the joys of 21st century life? She felt sick at the thought; the man was clearly a monster. And one with a very short fuse as she now remembered – such as the time he'd bawled out a temporary waitress for tripping on the stairs and dropping some plates.

But being a bad-tempered sex maniac didn't alter the fact that she had to see if he knew her in the future.

"As may be, Mary," continued Melrose, "but that is very much the world we live in. A man is generally presumed innocent if the victim of his crime is a woman."

"And that is acceptable to you?" She fixed him with a firm stare. Thomas

Melrose might be an Elizabethan, but surely even he could see that was wrong?

He inclined his head. "I do not say that it is acceptable to me that this man would bed my daughter against her will. Certainly not." He paused. "But I do accept that men have dominance over women, for that is the natural order of things, ever since Eve submitted to the serpent and so tempted Adam to eat the apple and fall from grace."

Mary almost bit her tongue.

Better to stay silent than decry a social order favouring male dominance – based on a fantasy text written by men.

She took a breath, then forced a smile. "But what if a woman refuses to accept male dominance?"

"Then she is both brave and foolish." He narrowed his eyes. "And are you that woman, Mary?"

"If necessary, yes."

"Ever since you took charge of the fight against Hopkirk and his men," he said, "you have been the controlling force in your family." He took another sip of wine. "And when the Lord Jesus himself spoke to all assembled, telling them that you were a virtuous woman not a witch, it gave you an unassailable authority for such behaviour."

"But I have never, ever referenced that, not even to William in private," she observed. And that was true, because she knew it had actually been an app on her phone that produced the voice and nothing to do with Jesus at all. But that didn't mean it wasn't the elephant in the room whenever they were together, making William somewhat wary of her, so she could sometimes play on it to get her way. Poor William – unknowingly married to a headstrong, modern time-traveller, and emasculated because of his own religious beliefs.

"I know," Melrose answered. "William has been clear that you have always behaved with virtue, so nothing needed to be said."

"But you feel I should still play the subservient wife?"

He nodded slightly. "Yes, but not because it is an act. Because it is how things should be. The natural order."

"Well, it is not natural to me."

"That is clear."

"And you do not approve?" she asked.

"No."

"And even if Richard attacked your daughter, you would accept it is the natural order?"

He paused, eyeing her thoughtfully. "As a father, no. But as a man, yes."

"Well, I am sorry, Thomas, but I simply do not agree."

"That is your prerogative. But I would still take a stick to this man Richard and beat him close to death for what he did."

"As would I."

He smiled and drained his goblet. "You would indeed? Although he is strong, and determined?"

"You mean that as a woman, I would not be a match for him?"

He laughed. "As a woman, no. But as Mary de Beauvais, beloved of God and one I saw ten years ago as a brave, strong woman, then maybe."

"Then maybe one day I will," she laughed back. "But I have to find him first."

"And ask him your questions?"

Mary hesitated. "I know that part of it makes no sense," she said eventually, "but I have to. I really have to find him."

"Aye," he said, "if you insist, then I am clearly powerless to stop you."

"So will you help me by saying where he went?"

"It was some time ago – he will doubtless have moved on by now."

"He may well have done, Thomas," Mary was unable to keep the edge of irritation from her voice, "but I would know where he went initially, so I can continue my quest."

Melrose stared at her a moment, his eyes searching across her face as if trying to see inside her and understand her true motives. Eventually, he said, "He said he was going to London."

"A big city."

"He mentioned Southwark – a place he had known as a child." Melrose sat back, clearly unsure if he should give the further information in his possession.

Mary waited.

"He said he wanted to see what it was like today."

Not sure if there was more to come, Mary waited further. Talking of Rick was clearly painful for Melrose, but he looked as if he would probably volunteer more information. Eventually her patience was rewarded.

"I recall asking if Southwark was but a small village in his youth, that would now have grown in size," he said eventually. "It was most strange. He laughed as if I had made the funniest joke, and when he had regained his breath, he said that it was more likely that Southwark had substantially shrunk." Melrose gave a weak smile. "I did not understand the man. I thought at the time that he should perhaps be better held in Bedlam." Melrose shook his head. "Marry, you are like to get just such nonsense yourself when you find him. That is if he is still living this day," he added. "A man such as he would surely have found the sharp edge of another's sword by now. Another father or husband who took great exception to the man's behaviour."

Mary shook her head, although she could not prevent a broad grin appearing. Southwark had *shrunk*? That could only mean that the Rick she sought was from the future like her. It was definitely the right man.

"Thank you, Thomas," she said. "I will see if I can follow the trail you have given me." She looked him in the eye. "I will set off for London tomorrow."

Melrose was about to answer, but stopped as a girl swept into the room and came up to touch his shoulder. She looked around eighteen, had long black hair, the brightest hazel eyes and was dressed in the simplest of pale blue velvet gowns. She had a dark, almost Spanish look about her, in marked contrast to Melrose's thin, drawn features and grey hair.

Melrose put his hand on hers and his face lit up in a beaming smile. "Ahh, my sweet child!" He stood and took the girl's hand across the table. "Lady Mary de Beauvais, allow me to present my daughter, Olivia."

Mary smiled at the girl. "I believe I made Olivia's acquaintance ten years ago," she said. The girl paused in front of her, one eyebrow raised in enquiry.

"We have met before?" she asked. "I do not recall."

"I believe you were a bridesmaid at my wedding." Mary remembered three small, excited, giggling girls holding her train and frequently having to be shushed by Sarah as her maid of honour. "But were you not Olivia Dowland at that time?"

"Ahh, yes." This was Melrose. "When Olivia's father was sadly killed in the defence of your honour and your integrity in the face of that dreadful magistrate, Hopkirk, I took in Olivia and her mother." He smiled warmly. "And I found that in return they both stole my heart. I was married to her mother for four happy years until she was cruelly taken from me by a dreadful chill…" he shook his head, "and I have raised her child as my own."

"I am so sorry for your loss," said Mary.

Olivia was staring at Mary, seeming bound in her own thoughts. "Of course – Lady de Beauvais," she said. "I think I remember your wedding. It was such a beautiful day and I felt like you were a lovely princess marrying your prince. I was very young, though, was I not?"

"It was some ten years since," agreed Mary.

"I am eighteen now," said Olivia. Then she blurted out, "And I am bidden to serve in the household of Lady Burnham! She has a town-house on the Strand in London and a magnificent estate in Essex! Is that not such a wondrous honour?" Olivia giggled, then added, "And so much fun to be had in London, I am sure!"

"Olivia is required to attend on my Lady Burnham at his lordship's house on the Strand on the first day of March," said Melrose proudly.

The girl turned sharply to her father. "Did I not hear as I came in, that Lady Mary is setting off for London tomorrow?"

Mary answered for him, "Yes, that is my plan."

"Why then, Papa, that is perfect! I am to go to London in but three days! I can travel with Lady Mary and her retinue. She can see me safely to the Strand in good time!"

Melrose looked down at the table. "I would not want to impose on Lady de Beauvais, my dear."

"But it would be such fun to travel together!" Olivia turned to Mary and took one hand in both of hers. "Please, Lady Mary, please say you will!" She turned on Mary, challenging her to agree.

Mary could see that Melrose was looking uncomfortable, and, being mindful not to challenge his authority after their earlier conversation, she said, "I would you let your father decide on this, my dear."

Olivia turned to Melrose, dropping her head in a gesture of supplication, then looking back up at him. Mary could not see Olivia's face in full, but she could see Melrose was struggling under the full force of his daughter's eyes.

"We agreed, my dear," he stammered. "I was to take you myself and keep you safe. You cannot ask the same of Lady Mary." Then he hesitated, and muttered, "Although I can think of no other woman who could do the task better."

"You are handy with a sword, Father, I will admit," answered Olivia, then her head lifted as a thought seemed to hit her. "But I have the perfect answer! We can all go together! Lady Mary would be better with another man to look out for her, and you will still be taking me as we agreed!" Olivia clapped her hands. "It is perfect! We shall set off in the morning!"

"Now wait, my child," Melrose countered, with a small, pained smile and a hastily raised palm, "but a moment, please." He looked first at his daughter, beaming with the brilliance of her idea, then at Mary, who found herself unable to meet his eyes. There was a silence which went on a bit longer than was comfortable, then Melrose said, "This is all to presume greatly on Lady de Beauvais's goodwill. I say we must travel separately as we had originally planned, and not impose upon her – nor upon her quest to find this… this man she seeks."

But Olivia was oblivious to the discomfort in the room.

"Nonsense, Father. It makes perfect sense for us to travel together." She turned, and the full impact of her large eyes now landed on Mary. "What say you, Lady Mary? Would it not be such fun?"

"It may be, my dear," answered Mary, forcing herself to look away, "but your father is perhaps not so keen on the idea as you are, and…"

"Father will come round – he always does," interrupted Olivia. "And we will have so much to talk about on the journey, you and I, that I simply cannot let this opportunity pass!"

"But…" Mary tried half-heartedly – although this cause seemed all but lost.

"I must ask you all about fine households!" continued Olivia, as if Mary had not spoken. "You can tell me what is to be done by ladies-in-waiting. What should I wear each day? May I paint my face and wear my finest silver, or must I be as a nun, all chaste and plain?" She put her hands together as if in prayer and her lips moved silently. Then she smiled and said, "I am most observant in my prayers and worship, Lady Mary, truly I am and God knows this well, but I do so love to wear the finest gowns and jewels!" She leaned forward and whispered, "In truth, I would make a perfectly awful nun!" She leaned back, then she drew a sharp breath. "My hair! How must I wear my hair? Can I let it fall to my waist or must I braid it each day?" She turned to her father. "You see?" she said seriously, "I have so much to ask of Lady Mary – so many questions! I could not possibly travel without her." She leaned over and took his hand in hers. "You would be failing in your duty as a kind and loving father if you were not to allow this."

But Mary's blood was running cold as Olivia excitedly set out these topics of conversation. How could she possibly answer a single one of these questions? In truth, Olivia at eighteen would know far more about Elizabethan society than she ever did – and that meant there was no way she could let this girl accompany her.

"Well, perhaps, but…" Melrose began.

"Good, then that is settled." Olivia took Melrose's goblet and drained it in a single gulp. "Hmmm" she said with a knowing smile at Mary, "we will need to take some finer Rhenish than this on the journey, or we will die of thirst!" She refilled the goblet from a pewter tankard and tried it again. "Ahh, but perhaps it improves with each sup. We shall see. Who is the man you are chasing and why, Lady Mary? It sounds so mysterious. You must tell me all."

Momentarily wrong-footed by this sudden change of subject, Mary wasn't able to think of an answer immediately, and Melrose cut in. "Lady Mary seeks Richard, the man who behaved so badly that he must be turned out."

"Oh him." A ghost of a smile flickered quickly across Olivia's face, passing so fast that Mary wasn't sure she had actually seen it, before the girl's expression hardened. "That dreadful man," she said. "Why in Our Lord's name would you want to find him?"

Mary was about to give a bland explanation about just wanting to ask Rick some questions, when Melrose spoke sharply. "We should not be asking Lady Mary such things, my dear," he said. "It is her business, not ours."

"But it was our business when we took him in, and when he … he tried to use me so harshly." Again, the briefest of smiles. "You turned him out, yet Lady Mary seeks him now." She spread her arms wide as if to emphasise her point. "That is most definitely our business, Father. Come Lady Mary," she said, "tell me all."

But Mary didn't answer. Instead she stood up quickly, causing Olivia to step back. She announced, "I do apologise, but it is getting late and I must be back at Grangedean Manor presently. I am so sorry, my dear Olivia, but I feel it is best for you and your father to travel to London in a few days as planned. I, meanwhile, will make my way there tomorrow. Alone." She took both of the girl's hands in her own and gave her warmest smile. "I am sure you will have a splendid time in the household of Lady Burnham, and I wish you all the very best of fortune there." She turned to Melrose. "And I must thank you, Thomas, for your information on Richard's movements, and I will trouble you no more on this matter." She nodded at both of them to signify that she had made her decision and would not be turned, then she walked calmly out.

CHAPTER SEVEN

The early morning snow lay thick on the ground as Sir William and Ambrose de Beauvais, together with their two men-at-arms, stumbled bleary-eyed out of the inn to saddle up their horses. The dark, freezing air numbed their fingers despite thick leather gloves, and made their breath turn to clouds of steam in the light of the burning braziers.

Ambrose's pony, Thelwell, skittered and shied as the boy struggled to get the heavy saddle on its back; its hooves clattering on the cobbles. William finished saddling his horse, checked the men-at-arms were mounted, then tethered his own horse and came over.

"By the Lord's Wounds, son, this beast of yours is making a din," he muttered, a pained expression on his face. "The sound is passing through my head like a red-hot poker."

"He will not stay still so I can saddle him, Pa" said Ambrose.

"Here, let me." William took the saddle from his son and placed it on Thelwell's back, stroking the pony's neck and making 'shh-ing' noises. Thelwell settled after a moment, and William stood back. "There, son. Now, let us be away."

Ambrose looked around for a mounting step, but did not see one. With a sigh William picked the boy up by his waist and lifted him easily into the saddle. "Come, we have no time to tarry. We have many miles to cover this day."

Ambrose was just settling himself in the saddle and gathering his reins when the door of the inn opened and Robert Wychwoode strode out.

"Good morrow, Sir William" he said jovially. "And to you also, young Master Ambrose."

"Good morrow, Master Wychwoode," William answered.

"Which way are you headed?" asked Wychwoode.

"Did I not say last evening?" said William. "We are headed for Stratford-upon-Avon – we hope to make it there tomorrow."

"Stratford?" Wychwoode exclaimed. "I am also on the same road; I am bidden there to question a man."

"Some legal case?" inquired William.

"Nay." Wychwoode seemed to wrestle with his conscience a moment, as if he was making up his mind whether or not to reveal some nugget of information. He cleared his throat. "'Tis concerned with that man who fell from his horse yesterday, and met his untimely end."

Ambrose gripped his reins tightly. "Does this man in Stratford know more of the papist plot to kill the Queen?" he asked. "Will you make him tell you all?"

Wychwoode smiled slowly. "I know not, young Ambrose," he said, "but I will know more when I have questioned him."

One of Wychwoode's men led a horse out of the stable, ready saddled up. Wychwoode swung himself up and settled into the saddle, as his other men emerged and all mounted up around him. He turned to William. "Come de Beauvais, let us ride together, at least until Stratford. It will be good to have your company."

William nodded and mounted his own horse.

"But what of this man?" Ambrose urged. "What of the papist plot?"

"In good time, son," cut in William. "We will ride together, and I am sure Master Wychwoode will tell us what he can, when he is ready."

"But Pa..."

"Nay, shush, son." William turned his horse's head in the direction of the gate at the far end of the inn's courtyard and encouraged it to a brisk walk. "Do not put pressure on Master Wychwoode."

The party filed out of the courtyard, with Ambrose bringing up the rear, his head down and the cold starting to bite into his bones even before he made it out onto the frosty track.

----0----

As the pale wintery sun struggled to show itself above the black skeletal trees, Ambrose allowed himself to contemplate the possibility that maybe, just maybe, he would at some point start to feel a little warmer. Even a bit warmer, just a little bit, would be so good. But until that point, there was nothing for it but to huddle into his coat, grip the reins in his numb fingers, and concentrate on... on what?

On the horse in front.

Left leg forward. Right leg forward. Left leg. Right leg.

Tail swish!

How stiff is a horse's leg? Why does it not bend as a man's leg does as the horse moves? Ambrose clicked his tongue. Of course! Because its knee is facing backwards.

Left leg. Right leg...

What would Ma be doing now?

Would she be rising from her bed, and waking Kat and Jane? Would she be chiding Kat for not seeing to her hair? Or picking up Jane and giving her a big hug because she had had another bad dream?

Left leg. Right leg…

Tail swish.

She would be taking Kat and Jane to the Great Hall to break their fast. There would be bread, and cake and ale, and Kat would eat too much because she was but a small pig who lived for her stomach, while Jane would cross her arms and say 'no' and Ma would have to make a game of the food to make her eat it. Ma would say the piece of bread was a wondrous bird, that would fly into Jane's little mouth, so she must catch it before it would swoop away again…

Left leg. Right leg.

Biting cold.

Tail swish.

----0----

"Francis Alleyne was a very bad man. A very bad man indeed."

Robert Wychwoode leaned back and stared at William and Ambrose in turn, his eyes flickering orange in the firelight as if there were sparks shooting out of them. "He was part of a plot against the life of the Queen, and would have put Mary of Scotland in her place."

"How did you know, Master Wychwoode?" asked Ambrose. "What led you to him?"

"Ahh, young Ambrose – straight to the point." Wychwoode leaned forward and stoked the fire with the black poker so that more sparks flew up from the glowing logs. "You are truly your mother's son." He smiled. "She has the clearest mind I have ever seen in a woman. Calculating and sharp."

"Aye," said William with a small nod, "I do not dispute that. Especially if I am late to bed after a flagon of wine." Both men laughed.

"Do not talk of Ma in such a way," said Ambrose, then realised he was talking to grown men. "Please," he added, somewhat lamely.

There was a moment's silence. "Well spoken, young man," observed Wychwoode. "Well spoken." He looked across at William. "He has her spirit, too, I see. You must watch your son, my dear de Beauvais, lest one day you find he has got the better of you."

William smiled. "I do not fear that day. What father would?"

"So what led you to this man Alleyne, Master Wychwoode?" Ambrose repeated, determined to get an answer and feeling emboldened by his father's approval. "Please tell me, sir."

"Yes, young man, I will." Wychwoode glanced behind them, but it was clear they were alone, sitting by the fire in the parlour.

The evening had come eventually, and they had stopped at a small inn for the night. After some boiled ham and ale, Ambrose had felt much better, and was starting to feel the warmth of the parlour fire work its welcome way into his bones.

"Francis Alleyne was a name that my master, Walsingham, had heard from two or three papists that he was…" Wychwoode hesitated, as if searching for the right word, "…interested in. So I was tasked with locating him, and putting one of my men close to him to see if he was indeed a plotter."

"You had a man spy on him?" asked Ambrose. "Pretend to be his friend, when all the time he was planning to betray him?" Ambrose could not believe grown men could do such a thing, for betrayal of friendship was surely the basest of behaviour?

"Aye, for that is the best way to find out information."

"If my friend Nicholas Stanmore betrayed me, I would never forgive him."

"Indeed you would not, and nor should you." Wychwoode shook his head slowly. "But Alleyne was plotting the life of the Queen, which would have put England in the hands of the papists. This would be worse than a friendship betrayed, much worse. So we must take equally strong measures to stop this happening."

Ambrose tried to imagine what it would be like if Nicholas were to give up a secret they shared – not that any of their secrets were anywhere near as big as this man Alleyne's. But it would still be a dreadful thing. How could you trust someone if they might betray you? Ambrose decided that the world of men was not a pleasant place. He shivered, despite the heat of the fire.

"How goes it, son?" asked William, putting his hand gingerly on Ambrose's shoulder. "Art tired and ready for bed?"

"No Pa," he answered quickly. "I am well, but I do not like to hear of a friend's betrayal."

"For sure, Ambrose," said William, "for I know how much betrayal can hurt." There was a long silence while he stared unblinking into the fire. When he spoke again, his voice was strange – hoarse and guttural. "Aye, and when it is from a man I considered a friend since we were your age, it hurts all the more."

Again there was a long silence. Ambrose was trying to understand who had betrayed Pa, and how anyone could do such a thing, when Wychwoode spoke.

"But all was well in the end," he said. "Your wife's good council prevailed and the friendship was made strong again."

Ambrose looked from his father to Wychwoode and back. Suddenly he had understood. "These are the tales of your adventures with Ma!" he exclaimed. "I would know more of these tales! Pa, please tell me!"

"Another time, son." William patted Ambrose's shoulder before withdrawing his hand. "Another time."

Ambrose crossed his arms and stared angrily into the fire. William put his hand on his leg. "Nay, son, do not frown and cross your arms so. The tales of your mother's and my adventures can surely wait. For now I say we would hear more of this tale from Master Wychwoode." He turned to the older man. "So your fellow let the plot continue till there was enough evidence, then came to you?"

"Yes, indeed. Our man, Tom Cobham, followed the plot until contact was made with a mysterious man in Southwark known as the Alchemist, and a large sum of money was offered to this man, that he would kill the Queen."

"Did you capture the Alchemist, too?" asked Ambrose, reluctantly switching his attention back to Wychwoode. Ma and Pa's story might have to wait, but he would definitely hear it. That was for sure.

"Nay, he has slipped though our hands and we have lost him." Wychwoode shook his head. "In truth, we do not know where he has gone."

"But now you have Alleyne dead, belike the plot is over?" asked William. "It has lost its leader so it is like a headless corpse. The Alchemist is cut loose and has no direction, so we have naught to fear from him."

"Unfortunately not." Wychwoode drained his cup and poured more wine from a pitcher on the table next to them. "We believe there was someone else behind the plot – another, more active leader than Alleyne – someone who we believe Alleyne himself was working for. We do not know for sure who this man is, nor do we know where this Alchemist has gone. And with Alleyne dead, we have lost our best source of information."

"But what of Tom Cobham? asked William. "Can he not make a guess where the Alchemist has gone?"

"No, the meetings with the Alchemist were held in a tavern or, I understand, in the street behind it to avoid overhearing, and Tom was not able to learn any more about him."

"So the plot is still alive, and the Alchemist is still at large, planning to kill the Queen on behalf of an unknown papist plotter?"

"Yes," said Wychwoode drily, "that is a fair summary of the situation."

"And the man in Stratford?" asked Ambrose suddenly. "What of him?"

"Aye," added William, "what of this man?"

Wychwoode looked at them both in turn. "I trust you, de Beauvais, and this is to go no further." He nodded, as if convincing himself to continue. "Cobham told me he had heard brief mention of a John Tyler of Stratford, so I must follow every lead. I have no great expectation of this Tyler of Stratford, but I will seek him out." He leaned back in his chair and again drained his cup. "I will find this man and see if he gives me any clue on the identity of the true leader of the plot."

"But what if he will not tell you?" asked Ambrose.

Wychwoode put his cup down carefully and fixed the boy with a stern, steady gaze.

"Oh, if he knows anything of this plot, anything at all," Wychwoode nodded very slightly, as if he were reassuring himself as much as Ambrose, "then he will tell it to me. As the Lord is my witness, he will tell it to me."

CHAPTER EIGHT

Lady Mary held the piece of bread high above the mouth of her youngest daughter, Jane. "A beautiful, magnificent bird, flying high above you!"

The little girl's eyes followed it closely as it swooped and dived above her. "Ickle bird, ickle bird!" she chuckled, as the bread passed close to her mouth, then climbed high again, out of reach.

"Please Ma, just give it to her," sighed Kathryn. "Must we do this every morn?"

The bread came to roost in Jane's mouth, and the four-year-old started to chew on it happily.

"Yes, Kat, if it gets your sister to eat."

"You do not play such games with me, Ma."

"No, and I do not have to, as you will eat any food put in front of you." Mary eyed the seven-year-old girl with a warm smile. "Which is a good thing, my sweet child."

"Jane eats well enough when Ruth is with her. Last night when you were away, she ate the whole leg of a pheasant."

"Did she? Did she really?" Mary's warmth turned to mild suspicion. "This is not you telling one of your tall tales?"

"No Ma," Kat stared back with the clearest, widest blue eyes. "She ate the whole leg, and Ruth did not need to make a game of it, or pretend it was a bird."

"But it was a b… no matter." Mary smiled again. "Then she will eat well for the next few days, as I have to go to London shortly, and Ruth and Sarah will be looking after you."

There was a silence as Kat stared at her.

"You are going away?" she asked eventually.

"Yes, my sweet."

"Without me, or Jane?"

Mary smiled gently and nodded.

There was another moment's silence. "But… how long will you be gone?"

Kat asked, her lower lip now starting to tremble slightly.

"No more than a week or so, I am sure," answered Mary, smiling inwardly at Kat's swift transition from petulance to dependence. "I will be back soon, I promise."

"Will you take Sarah, too?"

"No, it will just be me – I have said that Sarah will help look after you and Jane while I am gone."

"Take Simon."

"He is needed here – I cannot spare him." Simon was the only serving man left in the Manor now that William had taken his men-at-arms, so it was important he stay to help Ruth and Sarah. Also, Mary could still not forget the man's rather sickening sly smile on hearing of her interest in Rick.

"So you will be on your own?"

"Yes." Mary put her hand on Kat's shoulder. "I will be fine on my own. I can take care of myself." She knew as she said it, that it was as much to reassure herself as Kat.

Then she squared her shoulders.

She had hidden away for too long! Now it was time to get out and prove she could look after herself.

"But a bad man might attack you."

"I can take care of myself, Kat. Really."

"But what if a bad man creeps up?" Kat's lower lip was trembling more. "What if he creeps up when you are not looking?"

"Then I will make sure I am always looking out for him."

Kat changed tack. "Why do you need to go anyway, when Pa and Ambrose are gone too?"

"It is just something I need to do. Someone I need to see."

"Why?"

"It is what I need to do, Kat. I will be back soon, I promise. Really."

"You promise? Really, really, really?" Kat looked at her solemnly. "Cross your heart and hope to die?"

Mary leaned over and gave Kat a hug, pressing her daughter's head into her chest. "I promise," she whispered into the little girl's ear. She sat back and crossed herself. "Cross my heart..."

But very much hoping not to die.

The main doors swung open and a serving girl came in and bowed.

"There is a Mistress Melrose here to see you, my lady."

The girl had barely stepped back when Olivia swept majestically into the hall, her fur travelling cloak sending the rushes on the floor scattering behind her like waves in the wake of a boat.

"Ahh, Lady Mary!" she said, taking off her hat and shaking out her long dark hair. "I am so pleased to find you still here, and not yet set off for London!"

"Mistress Melrose, Olivia, what a surprise," answered Mary, putting an edge of polite coldness into her voice. "No, I will be setting off shortly, but for now I am breaking fast with my children."

Olivia studied each little girl for a moment, seeming quite oblivious to Mary's disapproval.

"Such sweet children" she said. "What are their names?"

"This is Kathryn, and this is Jane."

"So lovely. What a credit they are to you. Are they yet betrothed?"

"At four and seven?" Mary shook her head. "Certainly not."

"'Tis no matter." Olivia said dismissively, reaching for a cup and pouring herself some ale. "Time a' plenty for that." She drained the cup and poured some more.

Mary stared at her, not quite believing that the girl had the gall to help herself to ale without so much as a 'by your leave'. "It is indeed a pleasure to see you again so soon, Olivia," she began, although she could hear the flatness in her tone that said the opposite. "May I ask…?"

"For sure," Olivia cut in. She was clearly expecting the question, and gave Mary the full force of her most dazzling smile. "You want to know why I have called on you this frosty morn?"

Mary nodded slowly and deliberately. "Well yes, I did wonder." Although now she was beginning to have an inkling.

"I have come to beg a small favour."

"A small favour?" Mary prepared herself to say once and for all that she was not going to have Olivia as a travelling companion to London. The thought of having this spoiled girl tagging along – no doubt asking unanswerable questions on the ways of Elizabethan nobility – put a cold shiver up her spine.

Olivia took a breath and put her cup down on the table. "Aye. My dear grandmother, my father's mother, has been taken unwell with a fever. My father is loathe to leave her, and has bade me come hither to ask if I may accompany you to London."

And there it was.

There was a moment's silence.

"Accompany me?" asked Mary, her voice frostier than the cold drifts of snow outside the Great Hall.

"Aye." Olivia paused. "To London."

Another silence. Then Mary leaned forward. "Now, listen, Mistress Melrose, I…"

"Can you make sure a bad man does not attack my Ma?" interrupted Kat suddenly.

"Kat!" snapped Mary in annoyance. "This is grown-up talk."

But Olivia moved over to the wide-eyed little girl and sank gracefully down in front of her until their faces were level. "It is Kathryn, is it not?" she asked sweetly.

"Yes, Livia. But my Ma and Pa call me Kat."

"Kat." Olivia stroked the girl's head. "Such lovely hair you have, my sweet child. So soft and so pretty. Well, Kat, my little puss, do you want me to go with Ma to London?"

"Yes, if you promise to keep her safe."

"Of course I will, my sweet one. Your Ma will be as safe as safe can be, if she is with me."

"You promise?"

Mary frowned at her eldest daughter. "Shh, Kat. I said I can look after myself."

Kat looked up at her. "But Livia says she will make sure you are safe. She promised."

"Well, it is very kind of Mistress Melrose," said Mary, with a forced smile. And yes, it was lovely that Kat was so concerned to stop her going to London alone, even if her concern was misplaced. "But I am not sure it is necessary…"

"But she said!" Kat looked hard at Olivia. "You said!"

Olivia put her hand over Kat's in a sickeningly sweet gesture. "I did, little puss."

"So you go with my Ma, then. You keep her safe."

"I will." Olivia stood up. "For you, Kat." She turned and gave her dazzling smile to Jane, who was clutching a last piece of bread and watching with big eyes. "And you, little Jane, do you want me to keep Ma safe?"

"Please, Olivia," Mary cut in, alarmed that this charade was going on forever. "I am sure Jane will agree with you. She is only four."

"Good." Olivia's smile disappeared immediately and her expression became firm as she put on her hat. "When do we set off?"

Mary had one last try. "It is awfully kind of you, Olivia, but I really would prefer to travel alone…"

"But Ma!" squeaked Kat. "Livia said she would keep you safe!"

"I know she did, Kat, but…"

Kat stared at her, and Mary saw the tears well up and spill over her cheeks, like a tap had been turned on. "I want you to be safe, Ma…"

That was when Mary knew she was beaten.

She gave a deep sigh. "You will need to go home first," she said to Olivia, "to gather your belongings and tell your father."

"Nay, I have all I need with me, now, and my father has already given his blessing." Olivia produced another of her bright smiles. "He holds you in high regard, and has spoken at length of your courage and resource."

"He is most kind."

"My horse is ready," continued Olivia, "and I have a small box-cart tethered to it with all my clothes inside."

Mary looked at her two daughters, their little faces staring up at her. Jane still clutched her last piece of bread, which would need to fly like a bird before it could be eaten. "Then allow me to finish the meal with my children and prepare myself. We will leave within the hour."

---0---

Mary and Olivia urged their horses up a small slope, to be faced with a fast-flowing stream crossing their path just ahead.

"I would we rest a while, Lady Mary," muttered Olivia. "I am tired to my bones and sick with cold."

Mary looked at the stream in the flat afternoon light. Although it looked deep and at least fifteen feet wide, the path ran straight up to the nearest bank, then emerged immediately opposite on the far side. "It looks like we can ford the stream on this path," she said, taking out and studying the map that Luke the innkeeper had drawn for her. "This is most likely the Black Bull Ditch, which means that over there," she pointed to where some dark smoke could just be seen on the horizon against the grey sky, "is the village of Hammersmith. We can be there in half an hour, then we can rest up and get warm in an inn."

The village of Hammersmith. Mary had always known that the suburb where she had once lived as Justine had started life as a small village, but to be on the verge of seeing it – of walking the streets that would be one day become her familiar landmarks – that was a wonder indeed. It was not surprising that Rick had headed for his own home of Southwark – the fascination with seeing how it looked way back in history was utterly compelling. And how great to be able to swap notes with Rick when she actually met him...

"But the box-cart, my lady."

"...Eh? What's that?"

"The box-cart." Olivia turned in her saddle and pointed back. "It will get water inside and my best gowns will be ruined if we ford the stream. We must find a bridge."

Mary looked at the troublesome object. It was a wooden box of about four feet square, with a large wheel either side on a single axle. Two long handles came out of the front and each was tethered to a strap behind Olivia's saddle.

Mary sighed.

They were three hours from Grangedean Manor, and should have been much further on by now. But their progress had been slowed considerably by this box-cart trundling along behind Olivia's horse. It should not have caused any problem if the roads had been well-made, but on the rough snow-covered paths they had travelled, its axle had frequently seized up with ice, caught on large stones or got stuck on hidden roots. If anyone was tired it shouldn't be Olivia, who had remained resolutely in her saddle each time the axle jammed, but Mary, who had to dismount and free it.

"For sure," Mary muttered. "We will find a bridge."

It took half an hour and directions from a couple of labourers, before they came across a small wooden bridge within a tiny hamlet of rough cottages. Mary crossed the bridge then headed in the direction she thought would take them back towards Hammersmith.

"I would still like to rest, Lady Mary," Olivia called after her. "It has been a half hour for sure. Maybe we should have seen if one of those little houses could have taken us in?" Mary did not turn round, or answer. "They all had smoke from their roofs," continued the girl, "so they would have had a fire for us to rest by and warm ourselves."

Mary stopped and turned back with a pained smile. "We have no surety of a warm welcome, though. We need to find a proper inn at Hammersmith." She turned back and was about to walk her horse on, then shifted round again in her saddle and added, "We would have been there by now if we had used the ford to cross the stream."

Olivia did not answer, and their slow progress resumed, the atmosphere between them as cold as the snow draped on the bushes and the surrounding fields.

The journey had started well enough, with Olivia chattering happily as they made slow progress along the path, asking questions about noble living that Mary had deflected as best she could, until the chatter turned to speculation on what life would be like with Lady Burnham.

Mary then found herself tuning out Olivia's voice, and instead started wondering how she would find Rick when she got to Southwark. Could you just go up to someone and say, 'Do you know a man with spikey hair and tattoos of guns on his arms?' She suspected a tavern would be the best place to start; 21st century Rick had always liked his beer, and it was likely that 16th century Rick would be no different. She could imagine him standing on a table with a tankard of ale in his fist, singing drunken songs, to the amusement – or perhaps bemusement – of his 16th century companions. Yes, she'd start in a tavern and see where that took her.

But her wandering thoughts were interrupted by the first tortured screech of the wooden axle of the box-cart as it iced up, followed by her eventual dismount and fumbling with freezing fingers to free it – once it was clear that Olivia was not going to get off her horse and free it herself.

Many similar stops had then occurred, leading to the gradual cooling of relations with Olivia as it became clear that this spoiled little girl could not – or would not – do anything to help.

The light had become very grey as they eventually rode into a village of squat black and white houses, each with smoke coming from their roofs.

As large flakes of snow started to drift down, Mary took a brief glance at

Olivia. The girl had snowflakes caking up her eyelashes, making her look as if she had aged twenty years. Mary assumed she herself looked much the same.

"We are in Hammersmith, I believe," Mary said, trying to sound more confident than she actually felt, "and we are sure to find an inn here." But unfortunately, none of the buildings looked like an inn, and in the flat light and increasingly heavy snow, it would soon be hard to make out any buildings at all.

Mary was debating whether to knock on the nearest door and beg for shelter, when she just made out a long, low building ahead that looked different to the surrounding houses. Moving closer, she could see a painted sign on the wall announcing itself as 'The Cock and Magpie'.

"Here we are," she said, trying to put a cheery note into her voice.

They rode under a low arch and emerged into a courtyard, under the watchful gaze of several horses in stables to one side. They found a couple of empty stalls, and once the horses were comfortable, made their way into the inn.

Inside, Mary could see that the Cock and Magpie was not much different to the village tavern at Grangedean – just bigger. There were plenty of blackened oak tables with brightly lit tallow candles and bench seats. Mary started towards the nearest empty table and was about to sit, when she noticed Olivia had already walked up to two well-dressed gentlemen sitting by the fire.

"Good sirs," she heard Olivia say, "we are two ladies travelling to London and the snow has chilled us to the bone. May we join you at the fire?" She indicated a couple of spare chairs. "We shall be no trouble, and glad of good company." Mary could not see Olivia's eyes, but she knew that these two gentlemen, both of whom were fine-looking men, one in his late twenties and one nearer forty, would be powerless to resist them.

"For sure, mistress," said the younger man, standing and bowing. "We would be glad of the company of such fine gentlewomen as yourself and…" he turned and bowed at Mary, "your delightful companion."

"Good sirs," said Mary, with a stern glare at Olivia, "we should not impose upon you." She forced a smile, despite her annoyance. "Please excuse…"

"Nonsense, my dear," interrupted the older man, also standing and bowing, "we should be most offended if you were to abandon us now. Please," he waved at the two spare chairs, "be seated. The fire has warmth enough for us all."

With another angry glance at Olivia – which was rebuffed with a bright, innocent-looking smile – Mary pulled off her travelling cape and sat down.

The men insisted on ordering large glasses of mulled wine all round. While they waited for the drinks to arrive, Mary stretched her toes out to the fire, starting to let the delicious warmth flow through them like the sunrise advancing across the fields at dawn. She had not intended to interact with anyone other than when absolutely necessary – for clearly it was foolish to risk showing her ignorance of Elizabethan life – but as the warmth enveloped her, she found herself starting to relax.

"Have you come far?" asked the younger man.

"From Grangedean," answered Olivia. "And we are on our way to London, where I am to serve in the household of Lady Burnham."

"Indeed," said the older man. He paused a moment "I am sorry, mistress, we do not know your name?"

"Olivia. Olivia Melrose."

He nodded. "Honoured to make your acquaintance, Mistress Melrose." He turned to Mary. "And are you to serve in the same household?"

"Oh no!" exclaimed Olivia, before Mary could answer. "This is Lady Mary de Beauvais, of Grangedean Manor." She gave a silvery laugh, making Mary wince. "She is not to serve in any household, but to be served in her own! For now she is on her way to London to seek out a man."

The older man raised an eyebrow. "That is most forward, Lady Mary." He shook his head slightly. "What would Sir William have to say?"

"You know my husband?" Mary was surprised.

"Sir William de Beauvais of Grangedean Manor? I know of him, but by name only." He regarded her quizzically a moment. "Allow me to introduce myself. I am Sir Robert Standing of the City of London, and this is my good friend Lionel Shelton. We are on our way from London to Birmingham."

Shelton bowed his head briefly. "Delighted, my lady, delighted."

"How wonderful!" laughed Olivia. She put her hand on Shelton's arm. "We are like ships that pass in the night," she said conspiratorially. "One evening to make merry, then never to see each other again!"

Shelton put his other hand over hers. "Indeed, Mistress Melrose, we must make merry if we can."

"Olivia, please. Call me Olivia!"

Just then the drinks arrived. Mary took a cautious sip of hers, and found it to be rather pleasant; full-bodied and spicy. She settled back in her chair and stared into the flames, letting the heat of the fire and the richness of the wine wash over her. She was vaguely aware that Olivia was chattering away brightly, and that Sir Robert and Shelton were hanging on every word and each musical laugh, but she really wasn't listening. Olivia had the admiring male audience she so clearly relished – Mary was resigned to letting her get on with entertaining them. The warmth enveloped her, and her eyes began to close…

"You must tell me of the man you seek, Lady Mary."

Mary opened her eyes. Sir Robert was smiling at her. Beyond him, she could see Shelton carefully brushing a stray lock of hair back from Olivia's forehead.

"Oh," she murmured, "it is just an old friend. I have not seen him for many years, and have heard tell he is now living in London."

"An old… friend?" He smiled again, but this time there was a more quizzical edge.

Mary shook her head. "I fear you misjudge me, Sir Robert. I am the wife of Sir William de Beauvais, and like to remain so. My interest in seeking this man is purely in renewing a very old friendship, nothing more. And anyway," she fixed him with her steeliest stare, "with respect, sir, it is no business of yours."

"You are right, Lady Mary. It is no business of mine. Please forgive my impertinent curiosity."

"'Tis no matter."

Sir Robert stared into the flames a moment, then drained his glass. "So you are escorting the delightful Mistress Melrose to London, so she can find her place in society?"

Mary nodded. Sir Robert glanced across at Shelton and Olivia, who were now giggling together, oblivious to anything but each other. "Such a charming child, is she not?" asked Sir Robert. "She and my companion Master Shelton, seem to have formed a close bond in such little time."

"I think that is her way. She has a character that men find attractive."

"And she is most fair of face as well…" he murmured.

Now it was Mary's turn to look quizzical. "That is very forward of you. The grey in your beard suggests you are old enough to be her father." She sat back in her chair and eyed him over the rim of her glass. "Is there not a Lady Standing who would object to that remark?"

"There is, aye." He paused a moment. "You are right. And anyway," he glanced across to where Olivia was now stroking Shelton's beard, "I fear I have lost out to a man who is much closer to her age than I."

---0---

The winter sun struggled weakly through the rough sacking covering Lady Mary's bedroom window. She opened her eyes and stared blankly at the chipped plaster ceiling, unsure for a moment where she was. Then it came back to her: yesterday's snow; stopping at the Cock and Magpie in the village of Hammersmith; drinking mulled wine with the two strangers by the fire; Olivia flirting shamelessly with one of them, before Mary had insisted they take their leave and had dragged the unwilling girl away and up to their room…

She sat up and looked across at the other bed – Olivia's.

The covers were flung back and it was empty.

Mary got up, and with muttered curses under her breath, started getting dressed as fast as she could. She was about to head out into the narrow passageway to start searching for Shelton's room – where no doubt she would now find the wayward Olivia – when she heard a thud against the door, followed by a small sob.

She pulled the door open, and had to step back as Olivia fell into the room at her feet, wearing nothing but a dirty and bloodied undershift.

"Oh, my goodness, Olivia!" she exclaimed. "What has happened to you?"

The girl squinted up at her through puffy red eyes, one of which was starting to blacken with a dark purple bruise. She tried to speak – but her mouth was too swollen, and all that Mary could hear was another sob.

"Come, we must get you on the bed this instant." Mary took Olivia by the arm and started to pull the girl up, but this caused an agonised howl, so she quickly let the arm drop back again. "Come, you need to be on the bed in more comfort." With a hard stare through her slit eyes Olivia held up her other arm. Mary grabbed it, and after much struggling, cursing and many yelps of pain from both of them, she finally got Olivia onto the bed.

Once the girl was laid out, Mary stood back and assessed the situation.

The rapidly blackening red marks around Olivia's eyes and mouth suggested she had been punched in the face. The undershift had streaks of dirt down one side, as if she had been pulled along the floor. But it was the blood staining the garment lower down that spoke of the worst part of this attack. Mary gently pulled at the undershift, easing it up to reveal the tops of Olivia's legs, but the girl shrieked and pushed it down again.

"By Christ, Olivia," said Mary quietly, "what has happened to you?"

As Olivia stared again at Mary her eyes started to brim with tears and she gave another great tortured sob. Mary immediately dropped to her knees and put her arms round the girl, hugging Olivia's head to her chest, rocking her back and forward as the sobs grew louder and more pained.

"Oh, my child, my poor, poor child," Mary whispered, stroking Olivia's hair, "my poor sweet child...."

The sobs continued, each one racking the girl's whole body in a convulsion of pain. Mary held her tight throughout, continuing to stroke her head and soothe her with soft shushing sounds, until the sobs started to die down, and eventually stopped altogether.

Mary eased Olivia's head down onto the pillow and slid her arms gently out from underneath. Olivia's head lolled sideways and her breathing became regular as she fell into what seemed like a deep sleep.

Mary stood up slowly. She stretched her arms out wide, feeling her back and shoulders cracking as they protested at the strain of holding the girl for so long.

At least Olivia looked peaceful as she slept – were it not for now blackened bruising on her face and the blood at the base of her belly... Mary again pulled the bottom of the shift up, exposing the girl's groin, but this time there was no howl from Olivia. Instead, just the evidence that Shelton – and it had to have been Shelton – had cruelly robbed Olivia of her innocence...

Mary eased the shift up further, to reveal the grazing down Olivia's side where she must have been dragged along the floor. Mary could imagine her fear as she tried to get away from the man, only to be dragged back and flung down on the bed, before...

Mary stood back.

This man Shelton must be made to answer for this brutal attack – an attack made on an innocent girl by an opportunist stranger with not a care for anyone's feelings but his own. The words of Thomas Melrose came back to her. "A man is generally presumed innocent if the victim of his crime is a woman." Well, this man Shelton *must* be made to answer for this crime.

Leaving Olivia asleep, Mary marched down the stairs to the main tavern. A middle-aged woman was scraping the used candles from the tables and putting out fresh ones.

"Tell me," Mary said, "are Master Shelton and Sir Robert Standing to be found? I would talk with them."

The woman paused and shook her head. "Nay, mistress. They have been gone this half an hour." She started putting out candles again. "They seemed in a fair haste to be away, despite the snowfall." She thought a moment. "The younger man in particular. Could not be away fast enough, though he was laughing and jesting with his older companion as he went."

Mary had to force herself not to kick over a nearby bench seat in her anger.

"Art well, mistress?" asked the woman, with concern in her voice. "Your face is flushed redder than a beetroot."

"I am well, thank you," Mary answered, breathing deeply.

"You look as if you have just seen a spirit," observed the woman.

"I am fine, really I am." Mary repeated. She took a couple more breaths to calm herself. She was about to make her way back upstairs to the room, when she stopped and turned back to the woman. She said, "My companion has been taken unwell. We were expecting to continue our own journey today, but I now think we will need to stay a week or maybe two while she recovers."

The woman froze, then looked at Mary with wide eyes. "She has not a fever?" she asked, her voice rising up to an unnatural-sounding level. "She has the sweating or sneezing?"

"No, she does not," Mary answered. "She has taken a bad fall and will need time to restore herself."

The woman let out her breath and once again resumed putting out fresh candles. "Then if she needs to rest, let her rest," she said over her shoulder. "I have precious few travellers stopping at this time of year, so the room is yours to stay as long as you want."

---0---

"But I must be with Lady Burnham's household on the Strand by the first day of March!" cried Olivia, when Mary told her later of the decision to stay a while in Hammersmith. "She is expecting me and I cannot disappoint her!"

She started to sit up from the bed where she was lying.

"My dear girl, lie back," said Mary, pushing her gently down again. "Do you really think you can attend Lady Burnham while your face looks like that? She will refuse to accept you."

"Like what?" Olivia asked. "What is wrong with my face?" She fingered her eye and mouth, then winced at her own touch.

Mary fetched a polished metal mirror from her bag and offered it over. Olivia took it and held it up gingerly to her face – then gasped and dropped it, as if it had suddenly become white hot. "By the Risen Lord, Lady Mary, look at me!" Olivia picked the mirror up and stared into it again. "I am disfigured! I shall never again be able to turn a man's head with my looks!"

"I should think after this night, that is the very last thing you would want to do," muttered Mary. "And anyway, a couple of weeks and you will be back to your best again, I have no doubt."

"Then yes, we must stay here until my face has healed. Until I am fully healed..." Olivia stopped suddenly, staring at Mary. Once again her eyes filled with tears and she gave another sob. "But I shall never be healed, shall I? Because I can never be wed!" She stared at Mary, her eyes as wide as they could go with the bruising. "I can never be wed for I am no longer a maid..."

"My dear child, that is not going to be a problem unless we let it be a problem." Mary smiled at her. "Not every man who thinks he has married a maid is correct. Many are fooled by a small bag of pig's blood judiciously applied to the bedding in the morning."

Olivia looked cautiously hopeful. "Oh!" she said in a small voice. "You are sure?"

"I am indeed." Mary handed her a lace handkerchief.

Olivia wiped her eyes and gave a watery smile. "Then there may be hope?"

"I am sure that when the time comes, we will find a way."

Olivia paused and put the mirror carefully down beside her on the bed. "I have been something of a nuisance to you, have I not?" she said slowly. She looked up at Mary. "I was content for you to fix the box-cart each time it froze up, and to go out of your way to find the bridge..." There was a moment's silence, "and now I have been a silly girl, and we must stop our journey for one or maybe two weeks because of my stupid, wilful behaviour..."

Mary dropped to her knees by the bed, and clasped Olivia's hand in both of her own. "My dear sweet child," she said fiercely, "you must never, never,

64

ever, blame yourself for the actions of a man – do you hear me?" Olivia gave a small but hesitant nod. "It is never a girl's fault if a man decides to act like a coward and a beast!" She stood up. "If Lionel Shelton forced himself upon you, then it is for his conscience, not yours, to answer for it."

"But as a girl, I must submit to a man's will. It is as God has ordained," said Olivia in a small voice. "My conscience must answer for refusing to submit, so that is why he has need to become angry, and to strike me, and to…"

"No!" snapped Mary, so loud and so sudden that Olivia gasped in fright. "I will not accept that!" She paced away from the bed, then turned back, her hands on her hips. "If society tells you that men may use a girl as they please, then society is wrong – and this subservience has got to stop! Do you know," she continued, "there was a time when I lived in a land where a woman's worth is measured equal to a man's, and I will respect no man unless he earns it, and nor should you!" She paced away again, then turned back and fixed Olivia with a stern look. "No man has the right to attack a girl, or to force himself on her." Then she added in a quieter voice, "And I am sure God will understand that."

"You do have the strangest way of seeing things, Lady Mary." Olivia tried to smile, although it was hard to tell with her bruises. "So you say I must not blame myself for this?"

"No, Olivia, you have been badly used by a cruel, selfish man. You should direct your anger at him, not yourself."

Olivia was silent a while, as she took this in. "Then I do that," she muttered. "I blame Lionel Shelton." She paused again. "And I do apologise to you, Lady Mary, for being a wilful girl, and for using you so thoughtlessly."

Mary smiled. "I thank you for your apology – which I accept." She paused, considering her words carefully. "And I too, apologise, for I wanted to be alone on my journey – such that I did not value your company, and did not stop you going to that man, Shelton…"

"You were asleep." Olivia observed.

"But I should have stayed awake…" Mary answered. "I have failed you my child – failed in my duty of care." Mary wiped away a small tear with her sleeve. "And for that I am truly sorry."

"So we can be friends now? asked Olivia in a small voice.

"Yes," said Mary, "we can. And now," she continued, "we must help you recover from this dreadful attack and get you better as quick as we can. Then we can get you to Lady Burnham, fully restored to your health and beauty."

"And no more talk of Lionel Shelton?"

"None at all." Mary nodded. Then she gave a small chuckle. "No more mention of Master Lionel blasted Shelton."

"Or Lionel cursed Shelton?" suggested Olivia, with as much of a smile as she could manage.

"Nay. Nor Lionel fopdoodle Shelton!" said Mary. This was a word she had heard Ruth using about the servant Simon, when he had apparently done something particularly foolish.

"A filthy yaldson!" laughed Olivia. "For his mother was a whore!" She put her hand to her mouth in sudden shock. "By Heaven, Lady Mary," she gasped, "we are using words that no lady of standing should ever utter!"

Mary took Olivia's hand. "It's good to curse this man, Olivia. For he has used you so badly, that if I ever see him again, I swear to you, he will live to regret it."

CHAPTER NINE

March 1575, North Yorkshire

Ambrose, William and the men-at-arms emerged from the dark forest into the grey afternoon light and found themselves on the edge of a high ridge.

The ridge was sliced through the middle by a deep wooded ravine, as if giant hands had pulled the sides apart and left an ugly, gaping wound. To get across, they would have to descend to the base of the ravine, then climb up the far side.

The wind drove heavy snow into their faces.

William pulled up his horse. Ambrose and the others stopped beside him.

"There, my boy, see that?" William pointed across to the far side of the ravine. Ambrose peered through the misty air, squinting against the wind and snow.

"No, Pa. What is it?"

"There. You can just see the chimneys. That, my boy, is Hetherington Hall."

Ambrose stared hard across the ridge, till he thought he saw what looked like some trees that were straight, and unlike all the others around, had no snow-laden branches.

Chimneys!

"Is it there, Pa?" he asked, "is that really it? Where the Grenvilles live and I am to make my home?"

"Indeed it is." William smiled at him – or at least he might have smiled: it was hard to tell when his beard was so caked with snow.

"Then come, Pa," Ambrose said, as he turned Thelwell onto the narrow path that disappeared down the side of the ravine into the mist. "We must make haste. My feet and hands are as cold as they ever were, and I would get to the house and warm them quickly." He rode on, following the path, and disappeared over the edge.

---0---

William indicated for the men to follow him, then urged his horse on and soon caught up with his son. Ambrose and Thelwell were picking their way carefully down the path, keeping close to the bleak rocks to one side in order to avoid the sheer drop on the other.

"Have a care, son," called William.

"I am, Pa," Ambrose replied over his shoulder, as he steered Thelwell round a hairpin bend and continued on down. "The path is wide enough for two." He let Thelwell speed up, so that William had to increase his own pace.

"I said, have a care, son!" he repeated, torn between a sudden feeling of pride in his son's horsemanship, and concern for his safety.

"Do not fret, Pa," Ambrose chuckled, as he urged his pony on. He looked back over his shoulder again. "Thelwell is as keen as I am to reach a warm stable!"

"Ambrose!" yelled William, suddenly seeing his son heading into real danger. "For Our Saviour's sake, have a care! The path narrows!"

Ambrose turned back and must have seen what William had seen – that the path in front of him curved around a rocky outcrop, and as it did so, narrowed to a single horse's width. He tried to pull his pony up, but the packed snow underfoot had become icy, and Thelwell's hooves could not find grip.

Together the pony and rider slid towards the edge of the path, and William could see that it was only a matter of moments before they must disappear over and be dashed to death on the trees and rocks below.

Urging his horse forward, he grabbed at a thick branch that grew out of a fissure in the rock, then leaned forward as far as he could and at the last possible second, grabbed the back of Ambrose's saddle with his other hand.

The weight of the pony and its forward momentum meant that it was a slim chance he would be able to stop them sliding over, but he had to try. As the muscles in his back and shoulders screamed in protest, he hung on with strength he did not know he possessed, fighting as he felt his arms being torn from their sockets.

Ambrose and Thelwell came to a stop just inches from the edge.

There was a moment as they both gathered themselves, then the pony and rider backed carefully towards William.

Feeling that he had just been split into two on the rack, William slowly released his grip on the branch and then on Ambrose's saddle.

"Oh Heavens, Pa," said Ambrose over his shoulder, "that was close!" He turned slowly in the saddle and William could see that even against the snow on the ground and the flat, colourless skies, his face was a sickly white.

"Come, son," said William quietly, "let us continue carefully to the valley floor. I would not be on this ledge a second more."

Ambrose nodded, and encouraged a reluctant Thelwell to start down the path once more.

William turned to the two men-at-arms. They had stopped just up the path, the shock on their faces no doubt a mirror of his own. He nodded to them to follow on.

A short while later they were riding through the wild sycamore trees that populated the floor of the ravine, picking their way over roots and branches that lay in soft-edged mounds under the thick carpet of snow.

"What is that, Pa?" asked Ambrose, pointing ahead. Now it was William's turn to squint through the trees, seeing nothing but brown and white shapes all the way to the far side of the dark ravine floor. Then he saw it – a small hut with a thatched roof, sitting alone in the middle of the forest.

They approached it with caution; William dismounting and walking up first. He could see no light through the window, nor smoke from the hole in the roof.

"Stay back son," he warned. Then he tried the door. It opened easily, and he peered inside. Then he reappeared.

"Come Ambrose," he ordered with a smile, "there is no one here."

There was nothing inside except a bed, a small table and a wooden chest. There was a small grate to one side, with logs piled beside it.

William sat on the bed and indicated for Ambrose to sit as well. William put his arm around the boy. "Art well?" he whispered. Ambrose nodded and looked up at his father. Suddenly his eyes were full of tears.

"I would have perished in that instant, Pa."

"Nay," said William, brushing his son's tears away. "Not while I was there to look after you. I would never let harm come to you, my boy. Never."

Ambrose snuggled deeper into his father's embrace, and then put his head down onto William's lap. William started gently stroking his soft hair, and after a few minutes he could tell from the regular breathing, that his son was fast asleep.

William laid him gently down on the bed, then went outside to where the two men-at-arms were waiting, their horses pawing the snowy ground and their breath steaming in the cold air.

"My son is exhausted, and has suffered some shock at nearly falling up there," he said. "I would he stays here tonight and tomorrow if needs be, until he has recovered himself." The men nodded. "I will stay here with him, and we will have a fire for warmth and food from our packs. You two head on up to Hetherington and we will meet again tomorrow."

The two men wheeled their horses round and started riding towards the far side of the ravine, and the path that led up towards the house, as William went back into the hut and prepared to light the fire.

---0---

The snow was still falling the next day in the flat afternoon light, as William and Ambrose arrived in the stable yard of Hetherington Hall.

Ambrose slithered off Thelwell's back and his boots crunched as they landed on the snow-covered cobbles.

A liveried servant ran out from the stables and held out his hand to take the reins.

"Welcome, young Master de Beauvais. We have been expecting you this many a day," the man said. "Let me take your pony while you go inside and warm yourself." Ambrose stared at the man, surprised at a total stranger addressing him by name.

"Give him your reins, son," said William.

Ambrose handed them over. "Thank you, young master," said the servant. "Your pony has got himself warm coming up the valley – I will rub him down and give him water and mash before he catches a chill." The man started leading Thelwell away, then turned back. "And the same for you – you run into the house with Edgar here, and warm yourself by fire."

Ambrose looked round, to find another servant had suddenly appeared beside him, like a ghost in the grey light.

"Welcome, Master de Beauvais," the man said and took Ambrose's arm. "This way, please. Let us get you inside, and in front of the fire."

Ambrose looked back at William, who nodded his approval to go with the servant.

Together they went through a side door and into a long, echoing corridor paved with flagstones. It was lit by burning braziers mounted periodically along the walls; the orange light of the fires flickering off the arched ceiling and making the bricks seem to dance brightly. Just being out of the cold wind made Ambrose feel a little warmer, and by the time they reached the Great Hall with its magnificent roaring fire, he was starting to feel the familiar throbbing of the warmth coming back into his fingers and toes.

"Stop here, and I will fetch the Master," said the man Edgar, and left them alone in the hall.

"How do you fare, son?" asked William softly, as he lifted the thick fur coat off Ambrose's shoulders. "Here, let me see your hands." He pulled each of his son's gloves off. "Aye, they are more white than pink right now, but that will soon be mended. Hold them to the fire, and let us get the heat back into them."

Ambrose held them as close as he dared to the dancing flames. The throbbing got worse, as it always did when he warmed his frozen hands, then started to get a little better.

"There, son. You will soon be warmed through." William took off his own gloves and held his hands to the flames as well. "We do not want you to catch a chill, either."

"No, Pa."

"You are strong, though." William said. "This weather is worse than I have ever seen, and we have been over three weeks on the road. Yet you have kept riding on, and never a sneeze or even a cough." He looked his son up and down a moment. "You are a fine boy, Ambrose, and will make a fine young man."

"Thanks to you, Pa," replied Ambrose with a smile.

---0---

As Ambrose knelt to warm himself by the fire, the doors swung open and William saw a large, red-faced man with a full beard stride in, followed by a slim woman with grey hair. She seemed to glide effortlessly across the floor like a serene ghost.

"God save you, good Sir Nicholas," William said, bowing to the man. "And God save you also, Lady Grenville," he added, taking the woman's arm and giving her hand a brief kiss.

Sir Nicholas and Lady Grenville returned the greetings, as a servant entered with a tray of silver wine goblets and a matching jug, then proceeded to pour the wine and hand round the goblets.

"It has been many months since we last met, my dear Sir William," boomed Sir Nicholas, "when we agreed that your fine son could be tutored in Latin, Greek and suchlike with my own Richard." He drained his goblet in one gulp and thrust it out beside him for a refill without taking his eyes off William. "The boys will have a fine time together, believe me, for it is not just classes they must attend, but their archery practice in the butts will be daily once the snow clears, and there will be hunting and other such pastimes for them!"

He beamed jovially at William, then frowned. "But by the Lord's Wounds, my dear fellow, I forget myself as a host! You must be chilled to the bone!"

"Aye, but it is not my bones that matter," said William, gesturing to Ambrose. "It is my son who needs to be made warm again, after so many weeks in the cold and wind."

"Indeed," said Lady Grenville, gesturing at Ambrose, "come hither, child – let me see you."

Ambrose stood up, but stayed close to the fire.

"Oh my, how could I be so thoughtless!" she cried. "You must not leave its warmth until all the chill is gone from you." She wafted over and took his hands in hers. "Your hands are as blocks of ice, are they not?" She took each in turn and rubbed it between her own. "There, child, we will soon have you restored!"

"Thank you, my lady," Ambrose muttered.

"I want you to think of this as your own house, my child," she said. "Is that not so, Nicholas?"

"That is so," he answered.

Ambrose looked carefully up at Lady Grenville. "And what of worship?" he asked. "Are we to attend Catholic mass?"

There was a brief pause, and William thought he saw a look pass between Sir Nicholas and his wife, then she smiled sweetly and said, "Good heavens, no! Queen Elizabeth has forbidden such things. What a forward young man you are, Ambrose de Beauvais!" She patted his head and William saw him flinch slightly. "There is a fine little church in the village and we attend services there, exactly as the law says we must."

Sir Nicholas drained his cup again.

He turned to the servant who was refilling it. "Have Richard brought in," he ordered. "He can meet our young guest who is to be his companion in the schoolroom and the butts."

"And Master Topsham, also," added his wife, "who is to provide their schooling each day."

"Then we will eat," said Sir Nicholas. "My wife tells me that a boar has been well roasted and will certainly warm us all!"

---0---

That night, Ambrose lay in the soft, warm bed and studied the gold-framed miniature of his mother. The frame was looking a little faded and scratched, but the smiling face was as bright and as colourful as ever.

"We have arrived, Ma," he whispered softly to her. "I have been cold, and I have been hungry, but we have finally arrived, Pa and me. We have had some adventures on the way, Ma, like I told you before, with the man Alleyne falling from his horse and being killed, and Master Wychwoode joining us till he turned off at Stratford to question a man called John Tyler about a Catholic plot to kill the Queen – which I know would upset you so much, Ma, because you have said what a great lady the Queen is, and what she will do to make England the best nation in the world one day."

He stroked the side of his mother's face. "And I all but fell off the side of a ravine, Ma, but Pa was there and he hung onto me and stopped me from falling." He took a deep breath to clear the memory of sliding towards the edge of the icy path. "Then Pa and I found a small hut and we slept there the night and through the morning as well as we were tired and it was warm under some blankets we found there and with the fire." He smiled at the little picture. "And now we have arrived, Ma, we have actually arrived. Hetherington Hall is a fine house. So far I have only seen the Great Hall and my bed chamber, for they said I must rest after supper, but I feel sure it will be good here." He stroked his mother's face again, and she smiled back at him.

"I have met Sir Nicholas and Lady Grenville, and they have said I am to imagine this is my own home, although it is not, is it, Ma? My home is Grangedean Manor with you and Pa – but I will do my best to be part of their family while I am here, and be a credit to you and Pa, and to the Grenvilles." He wriggled down the bed to get more comfortable, enjoying the feel of real bedsheets and a soft mattress; so much nicer than the rough blankets and hard pallet beds he had endured in the taverns on the journey.

"And I have met Richard Grenville, who is nine, and I must be assured we will be good friends, although he has a slightly mean look, and Master Topsham, who is to be my tutor in classes with Richard, who seems to be a kindly man." He paused. "Also I have met a man called Lambert Moreton, who is Sir Nicholas's nephew and is staying here for a few weeks. He came in when we were eating our supper of roast boar, but he would not eat with us, and instead he was much pre-occupied with some important matters. He would not discuss these where Pa and I could overhear, so he demanded Sir Nicholas to come out of the hall with him to carry on the conversation, which I thought was not polite, and if I had done that, you would have scolded me for it, Ma, I am sure you would." Ambrose smiled drowsily. "Although I would rather have you here and scolding me, Ma, than hundreds of miles away at home. Are you thinking of me, Ma, like I am thinking of you?" He shook his head. "I am sure you are too busy with Kat and Jane to think of me, aren't you? But maybe you do." He looked up and across to the glowing embers of the fire, then back at his mother. "I have asked Pa to tell you how much I love you and I miss you, when he gets back home, and he says he will, and he ruffled my hair and said I am a fine boy. But Pa has said he will not yet set off on his homeward journey as the snow is already so thick and it falls heavily. But when he does, and he gets home, he will tell you, because I asked him too… because I asked… because…"

The miniature dropped out of Ambrose's fingers and onto the bed, as he slipped gently into a deep sleep.

CHAPTER TEN

The Strand, London, late March 1575

Lady Burnham stared down her nose as Mary and Olivia were ushered into her presence in the Long Gallery.

"Mistress Olivia Melrose?" she demanded with an audible sniff of disapproval. "You are two weeks late. I should refuse now to take you in."

"We do most humbly beg your pardon, my lady," said Mary. "But we were unavoidably detained in the village of Hammersmith. The snow was so thick we could not leave the village, nor find any messenger able to get word to you."

This was mostly true – the snow had fallen heavily ever since they had arrived at The Cock and Magpie and it would have been foolish to try and travel while it lay so thick on the ground. But it had thawed enough to travel a good few days before Olivia's face and outer scars had healed enough to be concealed under make-up. By then Mary thought it too late to send a messenger; as he would only be a day or two ahead of them. So, once Olivia was fully restored to health, they had pressed on into London and were able to present themselves at Lady Burnham's magnificent riverside house, hoping she was there and still disposed to see them.

"Indeed," said Lady Burnham to Olivia, "and who is this who has brought you here, Mistress Melrose, and speaks for you while you look to the floor?" She glared at Mary, then back to Olivia. "Is this Mistress Melrose, your mother?"

"Oh no, Lady Burnham," said Olivia, "my mother has sadly passed away. This is Lady Mary de Beauvais of Grangedean Manor, who has very kindly brought me here."

"Lady Mary de Beauvais?" Lady Burnham appeared to attempt a cold smile, "I have heard of your husband, of course – Sir William. Yes, I have heard of him…" She left it there, seeming to imply that not having heard of Mary as well was somehow Mary's own fault.

Then Lady Burnham rang a small hand bell, and a few moments later a liveried servant appeared.

"Take Mistress Melrose to her rooms and ensure she is settled in. Introduce her to Mistress Tyndall, who is to share rooms with her. They will join me and my other ladies at supper."

The servant bowed and showed Olivia to the door. Olivia followed him with her head still down, and was almost out of the room when she suddenly turned and ran back to Mary, flinging her arms around Mary's neck and hugging her tightly. "Fare thee well, dearest Lady Mary, I shall miss you so, truly I will!" She pulled back and looked at Mary with tearful eyes. "You have been so good to me, and I am sure I did not deserve your patience and love – I have been such a foolish girl!"

"Nay, child," whispered Mary, "you may have been wilful to start, but I warrant you have learned some valuable lessons these few weeks. I would you mark them well."

Olivia nodded.

"So remember what I told you," Mary said quietly, taking a silk handkerchief out of her sleeve. Then she dropped her voice so Lady Burnham could not possibly hear. "What that man did to you was wrong, and unforgiveable, and if you ever have the chance, you should find a way to make him pay for what he did." She wiped Olivia's cheeks where the tears had fallen, then cupped the girl's face in her hands and looked deep into her eyes. "No man has the right to take you against your will," she whispered fiercely, "and you must never, ever, ever blame yourself for a man's weakness. As I told you when we were in Hammersmith, I once lived in a land where a woman's worth is measured equal to a man's, and I will respect no man unless he earns it, and nor should you." She leaned forward and kissed Olivia on the forehead, then let the girl go and stood back. "Now my beautiful child," she said aloud, "hold your head high, and be the brilliant person that I know you can be."

Olivia nodded, then gave Mary one last watery smile, and was gone.

There was a long moment's silence after the door had closed, then Lady Burnham observed drily, "If you were that girl's mother you could not love her more. I warrant she has gained much from having you as a travelling companion."

Mary nodded slowly. "Aye. She is young and I will admit I thought her very foolish and self-centred when we first met, but the time we spent together has made me grow to see her as a young woman with a good heart, and maybe I saw something of myself as a girl in her. She is both willing and able, and I am sure she will serve you well." Then Mary fixed the older woman with a firm eye.

"And I trust, Lady Burnham, that you will do the same for her."

---0---

A few minutes later, Mary stepped out of Lady Burnham's house and paused on the step, looking down into the hustle and bustle of the Strand, trying to pick her moment to join the mass of people that were progressing in both directions in the slush and mud.

Some were on horseback, some on foot, and many were pushing wooden carts laden with produce. These enterprising merchants had either stopped and were selling to the rest of the crowd, or were pushing on, seeming desperate to get somewhere else.

A gap opened briefly in the crowd and Mary grabbed her opportunity. She lifted her skirts clear of the mud and stepped briskly into the flow of people and carts. As she started walking she could see a cart just up ahead loaded with bread in baskets, and a sudden rumble in her stomach reminded her that she hadn't eaten in many hours.

It was not easy to get through the crowd, but finally she caught up and grabbed a rough-looking loaf from one of the baskets.

"One farthing, lady," the man called out, stopping his cart.

She paid and he was about to push on, when she said, "Pray tell me, sir, how may I get to Southwark from here?"

"Southwark, lady?" He paused a moment, considering. "You can walk across the bridge, but that is a long walk, or you can just step down to the riverside right there," he indicated a gap between two houses close by, "and take a wherry across." He looked her up and down. "Hath not a husband to tell you this and to take you?"

Mary forced herself to smile sweetly and said, "My husband is not with me now, but we shall soon be re-united."

The man grunted. "Fare thee well, mistress," he said, and pushed his cart back into the stream of people.

Clutching the loaf, Mary turned down some steps to a small landing stage. A waterman was sitting in a boat tied to the stage, as it bobbed gently up and down on the brown waters of the Thames.

"Would you take me to Southwark?" she asked.

He nodded and she stepped down into the boat, arranging her skirts as she sat on the worn leather-covered seat in the stern. The waterman cast off, settled himself on the thwart and started to row.

As they headed out into the Thames, Mary took a few small bites of the bread. It was dry and tasteless, but at least it was reasonably filling.

The river was teeming with hundreds of boats, large and small. Some were crossing in the same direction as them, but there were also many boats coming up or down river across their path. The waterman seemed oblivious to the danger and steered safely past every possible collision without ever once taking his eyes off her loaf of bread, which made her feel quite uncomfortable.

Twenty minutes later he was helping her up onto a landing stage.

Mary thanked him and handed him the agreed coin, and after a moment's pause, the rest of her loaf.

"Thank you," he muttered, and was about to climb back into his boat, when Mary had a sudden thought. "Excuse me," she said. "But I need to find a particular man. I am told he lives in Southwark, but I do not know his address."

The waterman stared at her blankly and she immediately regretted asking. It had been a spur-of-the-moment thing – almost as a return favour for the remains of the bread – but now she could see how very odd it sounded.

"I am sorry," she said, "it is no matter. I should not have asked…"

"This man you seek – belike it is not your husband?"

"Well, no, but I do not see…"

"Hmm." The man shook his head slowly. There was a long silence. Mary was about to thank him anyway and walk off, when he said, "You have a name?" before breaking off a large piece of bread with brown teeth and chewing on it slowly and noisily. She nodded, mesmerised by the sight and sound of the chewing. It reminded her of a cement mixer she had once seen as a child.

He continued chewing for what seemed like forever, then eventually he swallowed and said, "Start at the Blue Maid." He looked about to break off some more bread, and Mary stole herself for another long bout of chewing, but thankfully he muttered instead, "The men in there know everyone. Tell them what your fellow looks like and happen they will know where to find him." Then he turned without any further word, stepped back into his boat and pushed off for the northern bank.

Mary paused a moment, trying to get the image of the waterman's chewing out of her mind, then cleared it with a shake of her head and set off through the streets. It seemed she'd had the right idea herself to start at a tavern, so she walked with her head high and hope rising that she would soon be able to meet Rick – and ask him her all-important question.

But the Blue Maid wasn't easy to find at first. After several wrong turns, many double-backs and a series of confusing directions from locals, she was starting to believe that maybe the waterman had been playing with her – deliberately sending her on a fool's errand. Had he been put out by her being a woman alone, or by the way she had stared at him when he was chewing the bread? But she had given it to him, after all… Then she spotted the sign of a girl milking a cow swinging lazily on a building up a side road.

With a small sigh of relief and a mental slap on the wrist for being paranoid, she hurried along to the sign and was relieved to see that it bore the name 'The Blue Maid'.

Mary entered the tavern and stood a moment in the doorway, adjusting her eyes to the dim light coming from the candles stuttering on the tables and the warm fire in the chimney breast close by. She started to make out the throng of men laughing and shouting at the blackened wooden tables; men dressed in the sombre colours of yeomen or the dirty smocks of peasant land-workers; also a few in fashionable doublets. Women in ale-stained aprons weaved round the tables with trays of tankards or wooden platters of food, leaning across the tables to serve the men; getting their bottoms slapped or having to push away hands that tried to stroke their hair.

At first no-one seemed to notice her. The noise of laughter and conversation continued unchecked, ebbing and flowing around the room. Then one man in a rough leather jerkin sitting at the table nearest the door happened to look up and stopped talking abruptly. His companion followed his gaze and stopped with his tankard raised part-way to his mouth. This aroused the curiosity in the men at the next table – and from there the next – until within half a minute the whole tavern was staring open-mouthed at her in stony silence that went on for an uncomfortably long time.

Mary shivered, despite the warmth of the fire.

What seemed like a hundred dirty, bearded faces were staring at her; their eyes boring into her with expressions ranging from idle curiosity through to unhealthy interest. Suddenly she was back in the Grangedean tavern on the night ten years before, when she stood accused of witchcraft and knew that behind the eyes of every man, woman and child in the place was a desire to see her burned to death.

Now it was clear why everyone had been so concerned that she should not travel alone.

Mary cursed inwardly. What had she been thinking – to assume that just because she came from the 21st century, she was immune to the basest instincts of 16th century men? Had she learned nothing from Lionel blasted Shelton?

A moment later her worst fears were confirmed.

"Art alone, mistress?" called out the man who first noticed her. "Or is your husband to be found presently?" The men around him sniggered.

Before she could think of a suitable answer, another man spoke up. "The stews are closed down now, mistress, if that is the home you seek." There was laughter from a few of the men. "Although," he continued, "there are plenty of new brothels in their place."

"Art well dressed for a whore," said a small, swarthy man with a scar down his cheek. "But I have a good purse and," he stood up and thrust his hips forward suggestively, "a hearty appetite!" There was much laughter and he came over to where she stood. "I shall take a piece of this in the back room!" he announced to the rest of the tavern. Then he grabbed her sleeve. "Come my lovely, and earn your keep!" She recoiled from the man – from the foul smell of his breath and his body. Desperately she tried to pull away, but he had a firm grip on her sleeve and was not about to let go. He rounded on her, his rough, scarred face close to hers and the stench of his ale-laden breath filling her nose and mouth. "I said to come my lovely, so come," he growled.

"Get away from me!" Mary snapped, then added in the firmest voice she could muster. "I am no whore!"

Unfortunately this revelation did not result in him releasing her sleeve and apologising for his dreadful mistake.

"I care not," he said, pulling at her again. "I want a piece, and it is all the better if I do not need to pay."

Mary was just drawing breath to scream as loud as she could – however futile that might be, when she heard a firm voice say, "Unhand her, Jake!"

Another man had stood up. With hope rising, Mary could only assume that these words meant he was on her side. She recognised him as the first one to have noticed her just now.

She and Jake watched as this man came over.

"I said, unhand her," the man repeated.

"Nay, Ned, she is to be my fun this afternoon," Jake snarled. "You wait your turn."

"Leave her, Jake," said the man called Ned. Then he smiled at Mary. She smiled back, and was about to thank him profusely for rescuing her, when slowly and deliberately, and with his eyes fixed on hers, he licked his lips.

Her blood ran cold.

His next words confirmed her worst fears. He said, "I saw her first, so I have her first. You wait your turn."

But Jake was not going to give up easily. "She is mine, Ned!" he snarled. "So be gone before I make you!"

"Nay, she is mine, I tell you!" answered Ned, and suddenly an evil-looking knife appeared in his free hand. Jake took a step back, staring at the blade, which allowed Ned to grab Mary and start pulling her towards a door at the back of the room.

"Let me be!" she cried, looking around for someone – anyone – to help her. "I am Lady Mary de Beauvais!" But all the faces seemed like stone, all watching impassively as she was dragged past them. Desperately she looked for the higher-ranking men she had seen initially – anyone in a fine doublet who might come to her rescue, but those she saw had their heads down, although one did look up as she passed, and she saw him shake his head sorrowfully.

Ned flung her through the door, then he closed it behind him.

"Get away from me," she yelled as she backed into the room, "or you will regret it!"

"I think not, mistress," he said with another evil grin, advancing on her with the knife raised. "I too have an appetite, and you are just the wench to fill it."

"Did you not hear what I said? I am Lady Mary de Beauvais," she repeated, trying to keep her voice steady, "and my husband is Sir William de Beauvais. Perhaps you have heard of him?"

"Nay. Never."

"If you do this, he will find you and he will kill you."

"I care not if you are cousin to the Queen herself," he answered. She bumped up against the far wall and heard herself whimpering in fear.

He came right up to her and put his knife to her throat.

As she tried to shrink from the blade, he reached down with his free hand and untied his breeches. As they dropped to the floor, she felt his hand grasp her skirts and work its way under them, then she felt him position himself closer to her body.

So, this was how she was to learn the lesson not to go out alone in Elizabethan London. What were all her fine words to Olivia worth, if she ended up walking into a situation where it happened to her?

Mary screwed her eyes shut and held her breath. Nothing happened.

She opened her eyes.

Ned's coarse face was burning bright red in front of hers; his eyes bulging and his tongue sticking out between blue lips.

A pair of hands were around his throat, throttling him.

With a gurgling sigh his face dropped out of her sight – to be replaced by that of the man who had been standing just behind him.

It was the well-dressed man who had shaken his head as she had passed by a minute earlier.

She stared at him, struggling to find any words appropriate to the situation.

The man flexed his fingers, with a grimace of pain. Then he smiled.

"Lady Mary de Beauvais, eh?" he said. "I have heard of your husband Sir William, of course, but have not had the pleasure of making your acquaintance before now."

Mary took a deep breath to steady her nerves, and waited a few moments for her heartbeat to get back to something like normality. "You shook your head as I passed," she said slowly. "Yet now you come in and stop this man?" She paused. For all his fine clothing, this man might be no better than Ned and Jake. "Or are you merely going to replace him yourself?" she asked with an edge of resignation in her voice.

He gave a small barking laugh. "Nay." He shook his head. "You need have no fear on that score. No. I could not countenance such a fine lady being so ill-used." He paused. "I could see that all the men in the tavern back yonder were on the side of Master Ned here, and that to deny those of them who wanted to take a turn at you, as I fear they were planning, would make rescuing you at best difficult – and at worst suicidal."

"So why...?"

"Ahh. Then I remembered that this room has a side entrance from the street, so giving me a way in unseen and us both an effective escape route." He looked down at Ned, who was groaning and coughing at their feet. "And I think we should effect that escape before Master Ned here recovers sufficiently to raise the alarm, or anyone else comes in for their turn."

He took her arm and guided her across to the far corner of the room, where there was a wooden door partly obscured behind some stacked beer barrels. He pushed it open and led her out into the street.

"I found this when I was here a while ago and needed to conduct some private business away from the tavern," he said conversationally. "A useful thing to know."

He took her quickly along the street and through several turns before she found herself stepping down onto the same small jetty where she had originally arrived in Southwark. Another wherry was tied up and bobbing alongside, and her rescuer helped her down into it. They settled themselves side by side on the seat at the back.

"Queenhythe as fast as you can, sirrah," he snapped. The waterman cast them off and started to row.

Mary glanced back at the Southwark jetty, but there was no sign of pursuit, so she turned back and studied the man next to her.

He was clearly a gentleman. He was well dressed, with a fine embroidered doublet, well-fitted hose and soft leather shoes. His beard was trim, and the hair that curled back over his ears was thick and dark.

Mary realised that in all the drama of her rescue, she had not shown this man her deep gratitude. "I must thank you, sir," she said, "for your action today. You have saved me from dishonour by that foul brute of a man."

"Aye." He turned to her and smiled. "But I must ask what in heaven's name you were doing entering a Southwark tavern alone? Did you not know that men such as Jake and Ned would see you as fair game?"

Mary paused, staring across the river and trying to decide what her story should be. The only sound was the waterman's oars splashing rhythmically as she considered her options. Eventually she decided that this man had an honest, open face, bright blue eyes, and should be trusted.

"I was looking for an old friend, and I had heard he was in Southwark. I wanted to ask if anyone could help me find him."

"An old friend?" She sensed an edge of humour in his voice and turned to him. He had an eyebrow raised.

"Yes. Is that so bad?"

"No, but it raises more questions than it answers."

"Well, I am not prepared to answer them right now. And anyway," she said carefully, "I do not even know your name."

He removed his cap and made a small bow from the waist.

"Tom Cobham at your service, Lady de Beauvais."

CHAPTER ELEVEN

Hetherington Hall, late March 1575

Sir William and Ambrose were standing at the edge of the woods, looking out over the misty ravine.

It had become their habit to meet there every morning, despite the cold wind and driving snow. It was good to spend a few minutes alone together; time when they could share stories and observations about their lives at Hetherington Hall without being overheard.

William huddled into his thick fur coat. "Art well, son?" he asked.

"Yes, Pa."

"And becoming friends with young Richard Grenville? You said yesterday that he was spiting you occasionally."

"We are good friends."

Something in Ambrose's voice made William look hard at his son. "You are sure?"

Ambrose was silent a moment, then said, "He called me a name, Pa." He paused while a strong gust of wind howled around them. "So I knocked him down."

"What name?"

"It was nothing."

William put his arm on Ambrose's. "What name, son?" he repeated.

Ambrose was silent and William waited. After a moment Ambrose said, "He called me a heretic."

"A heretic?"

Ambrose nodded.

"I suppose he knows no different with his Catholic upbringing," said William. "So you knocked some sense into him, eh?"

"Yes Pa." Ambrose paused. "And now we are friends, truly."

"Belike he respects you now, for standing up to him."

"Yes, I think he does."

William waited while another gust of wind howled around them. "And what learning have you had this past day?" he asked.

"Latin mostly – we have been learning how verbs should be declined."

"And divinity? Have you been learning the true faith?"

"Aye, Pa. I have my divinity lesson each day at the same hour of the afternoon."

"But no papist heresy?"

"No, I am instructed about the true faith by Master Topsham."

William turned to him. "And Richard? He called you a heretic, but he should not call you that name. Does he not baulk at learning how faith should be practiced according to God's true wishes?"

"He is never there for my divinity lesson. Master Topsham and I are always alone."

There was silence as William considered this. "And this is the same time each day?" he asked slowly. "Is it by chance," he swallowed, "at five in the afternoon?"

"Yes, always at the same hour. Always five in the afternoon."

"And you are sure Richard is never there?"

"Never." Ambrose looked at his father. "Why?"

William shook his head. "No," he said slowly. "'Tis no matter" He looked at his son with a weak smile. "No matter at all – I am mistaken."

But that was just to protect Ambrose, for he was not mistaken. Five in the afternoon was when he too was always left alone. Whatever was happening, whether he was talking to Sir Nicholas or Lady Grenville, or even to Lambert Moreton, just before five they would always make some excuse and leave him alone – not to re-appear for at least an hour.

William stared across the ridge; the harsh edges of the ravine softened by the snow.

What would be the one thing the Grenvilles might do as a Catholic family all together, which they would want to keep secret from him and Ambrose? A Catholic family that were making an outward show of conformity by attending the Protestant church in the village – but in truth, could not let go of their heretical practices?

It would be to hold a secret Catholic mass somewhere in the house, every day at five.

William resolved to find out if he was right. He would try to follow them and see where they went.

Because if they were holding mass, it was treason – and not only were they putting themselves in danger, but he and Ambrose could potentially be implicated too.

His words to Ambrose came suddenly back to him, cutting into his head like the wind howling across the ravine.

Son, I promise you will be safe at the Grenvilles.

William felt sick. Here he was, not a couple of weeks into his son's time at Hetherington Hall – and already these words had become a hollow, empty promise.

He cursed his stupidity for ever taking Grenville at his word. But Grenville had been so convincing; so open and honest when they had met in London, that although the family were Catholics in the past, they had accepted the new laws and moved on. But now he thought on it, Grenville had been at such pains to explain how the family were conforming to the law and attending Protestant church, that perhaps he had been just a little too eager.

But why? What purpose would it serve to have Ambrose in the house if their mass was discovered?

If indeed they were holding mass.

He had to find out, so he could decide what action he must take to protect his son.

And it would have to be this afternoon – he could not wait another day with this uncertainty.

----0----

"Good Sir William, I would you give me leave just now – I have matters I must attend to in the kitchens regarding the evening meal." Lady Grenville gave thin smile. "I am sure you can devise some entertainment of your own?"

"Indeed, my lady," William answered with a smile that was as thin as hers. "I have my bible to study and my prayers to make – I pray God will cause this snow to melt so I can soon be on my way home and no longer be a burden on your kind hospitality."

"It is no burden, my dear Sir William." She floated gracefully over to the door; her skirts gliding across the floor without any rise and fall. "It has been a pleasure to have you as our guest and I know it is a comfort to your charming son." She paused with her hand on the door. "You are welcome as long as God sees fit to keep the snow from thawing."

She wafted through the door and closed it sharply behind her.

William waited around ten minutes, hoping this would give the family enough time to make their way to their secret mass, then he slipped off his shoes and padded silently to the door.

Where would they have gone? There were a number of possibilities he had considered since the morning meeting with Ambrose – and the one he felt most probable was the east wing, where he knew there were some empty guest rooms on the upper floor which were locked for the winter.

He emerged into the narrow corridor and checked left and right to make sure there was no one else in sight. Then he crept softly along until he came to the main stairway. Again he checked he was alone, then stepped as quietly as he could to the top of the cold stone stairs. There he stopped, listening intently, trying to ignore the sound of his heart thumping like a galloping horse. After some minutes, he made his way slowly along the corridor towards the east wing, checking each floorboard before committing his full weight to it, in case of tell-tale creaks.

He arrived at the door to the first of the three closed-up rooms on the corridor. He put his ear to it, but there was no sound from within. The same was true of the second, and also of the last. He was about to walk away, when suddenly he thought he heard a distant male voice.

He stopped, every nerve on edge, straining to hear it.

Nothing. He was about to leave when – there it was again.

Distant. Faint. But definitely a male voice.

Perhaps it was someone talking elsewhere in the house? There was no reason to suppose anything sinister if it was just two servants talking...

Then it came again. Louder. Clearer.

And now he could hear the words.

"Benedictus qui venit in nomine Domini."

William gasped. "Blessed is he who comes in the name of the Lord."

So it was true!

The Grenvilles were indeed committing treason by celebrating the Catholic mass in secret.

He moved closer to the door of the third room, and put his ear gently against it. He could still hear the voice, but if anything, it was slightly less clear. Very slowly he eased the latch up, then pushed the door open by no more than an inch. Still the sound remained faint, forcing him to conclude that wherever the mass was taking place, it was not in this particular room.

But where? Stepping back into the corridor he looked at the wood panelling that closed it off at the end. He tried to recall what was below this corridor – some formal rooms for receiving guests? And the main receiving room at the end of the wing, with windows on all three sides and magnificent views over the snowy gardens and parklands? If it was, and William was pretty sure it was, then why was this corridor above it blocked off short? There had to be a room beyond.

He went up to the wood panelling and gingerly put his ear to it.

"In nomine patris et filii et spiritus sancti, Amen," came the man's voice, much clearer now and sounding like it was only a few feet away on the other side of the panelling. It was followed by an "Amen" from the congregation.

William pulled back as if the panel had suddenly become white hot, then stood still a moment. So there was a room beyond the panelling – which presumably the Grenvilles accessed through a secret door in this corridor or in the third room.

William hesitated, unsure whether to run and risk being heard, or to creep slowly away and risk being spotted.

Then there was a louder sound – one that made his heart miss a beat.

It was the sound of chairs scraping back.

"The mass is ended. Go in peace to love and serve the Lord."

He only had seconds to get away before the family would emerge from their secret mass.

Throwing caution to the wind, he ran back down the corridor as quickly as he could and almost fell down the stairs, then sprinted across to the room where he had left his shoes. He put his head round the door – thankfully there was no one there – and slipped quietly inside.

He ran softly to the place where he had left his shoes.

They were not there. They had gone.

In rising panic, he looked everywhere around the room.

They were nowhere to be seen.

With a stream of muttered curses, he headed back up the stairs and made for his rooms. He would have to get another pair as quickly as possible before he ran into any member of the family and had some explaining to do.

Arriving at his door, he glanced around to check he was still unseen, then slipped inside.

With a sharp intake of breath, he spotted his missing shoes immediately.

There was no mistaking them; they had been placed clearly in the middle of the floor.

So someone had found them in the room downstairs, and brought them up to his rooms.

Which could only mean that someone – presumably a servant – had seen them, knew they were his, and had taken them to his room.

Which, in turn, meant that a servant knew he had been creeping around the house with no shoes, at precisely the time when the Grenvilles were attending their secret mass.

And if a servant knew, then how likely would it be that the Grenvilles would soon know as well?

William sat on his bed and looked blankly at the drapes hanging around it.

If the Grenvilles knew that he was aware of their treasonous masses in Hetherington Hall, then he had suddenly become a significant threat to their security. They could hardly risk him leaving the Hall.

And if they knew, then it was not just discovery by the authorities that put him and Ambrose in mortal danger – now it was the Grenvilles themselves.

CHAPTER TWELVE

Tom Cobham's eyes were fixed unwaveringly on Lady Mary's over the rim of his glass. He stared hard at her as he swilled his wine round.

"My dear lady, let me understand this," he said, as the wine spun lazily in the glass. "You have left your home and your children to come to London to seek this man you call Richard?"

She nodded.

"Yet you have nothing more to go on than you know his name and the possible chance that he lives in Southwark?"

Again, she nodded.

"And this is because you knew him ten years ago, and you would like to see him again?"

"There are questions I would ask him that only he can answer."

"Marry, I trust there are. He had better have answers that the Lord himself could not give, for you to have put yourself in the gravest danger in seeking him out."

"It seemed the right place to start looking."

"Aye, and look how it nearly ended." He continued to swill the wine around his glass. She smiled.

"Again, I owe you my thanks."

"That man Ned was acting as a wild beast, which was according to his nature. I used the only force he would understand."

"And I am deeply grateful."

There was a silence as Tom continued to stare hard at her. She wasn't sure which was the easiest thing to look at – his piercing blue eyes or the mesmeric circular movement of the wine. She chose his eyes.

"How would you have recognised this man – even if you had managed to find him?"

Mary thought a moment. She had decided in the boat across from Southwark to trust Tom. He had saved her honour, and possibly her life. And now he had taken her to the safety of his small house near Blackfriars, made her comfortable, fed her and given her some wine.

Maybe he could help her find Rick. He certainly seemed to be confident, resourceful and knowledgeable. She leaned forward.

"Last time I saw this man, he had spiky hair like a hedgehog."

"As do many men. You would have needed more."

"He had two tattoos – pictures – on his forearms. They were of guns... of weapons that look a bit like small muskets."

Mary was totally unprepared for the effect that this had on Tom.

The glass froze so abruptly in his hand that wine slopped out and splashed across the table. But Tom ignored it, his face suddenly turned ashen white as he stared at Mary with a look of total horror.

"By the Risen Lord," he whispered slowly. "You seek the Alchemist?"

Mary raised an eyebrow. "If that is what you call him. I knew him as Rick, or Richard."

"No, no, this is not possible..." Tom shook his head fiercely. "This cannot be – it is too much of a coincidence."

"Why?"

"Because I, too, seek the Alchemist." He frowned, his blue eyes searching hers. "But I cannot find trace of him." He poured himself more wine and drank it in a single draught. "He has not been seen for many days. Something caused him to disappear – it was around a week ago."

Now it was Mary's turn for a sudden shocked reaction.

"A week? No!" She banged on the table with her hand, making him jump. "No! If only Olivia had not..." She stopped herself.

"By the Lord's Wounds, if only Olivia – who e're she might be – had not... what?"

"No." She shook her head. "It was not her fault..."

"But...?" he asked.

Mary paused, waiting for her ragged breathing and racing heartbeat to subside. Eventually she said, "I agreed to take a young girl with me from Grangedean Manor to London, as she had been offered a position in the household of Lady Burnham in her place on the Strand. We were in Hammersmith when she was... when she was..."

Suddenly Tom's room disappeared and she was once again in the back room of The Blue Maid. She flinched as the foul pockmarked face of Ned appeared in front of her again and she could feel his hands fumbling at her skirts, smell his evil breath in her face; feel the sharp point of his knife pricking at her throat. She gave a small cry and put her hand to her neck as if to protect herself from him.

She heard a voice say, "Lady Mary! Art unwell?"

She stared at Ned, recoiling from the rough touch of his hand on her leg... then she felt a hard shake on her shoulder, and as she looked at Ned, his twisted, evil features slowly faded and were replaced by the open, honest and very worried face of Tom Cobham.

"Lady Mary," he repeated. "What is it?" He put his hand over hers. "Were you back in the Blue Maid just then, with that wretch Ned? You looked as if you were re-living his attack."

She nodded, wide-eyed.

"My dear lady." He pushed a glass wine towards her. "Drink this – it will restore you."

Mary took a small sip, and felt the wine fill her head with a warm glow.

She forced herself to breathe normally. "I am fine," she said, as much to reassure herself as him. She could feel Ned slipping back into the shadows of her mind again.

Tom gave her the time she needed to recover.

"Olivia was…" she began again.

"Nay, tell me not," he said, "if it once more brings back your memories of the Blue Maid."

"No, it is right that I tell you," she said. "And I can control my memories now." She took another sip of wine, then a deep breath. "Olivia was attacked by a man called Shelton, who left her bloodied and bruised so she could not be seen in polite society. We had to wait two weeks in Hammersmith before she was fit to travel to London." She paused. "Two weeks that meant I missed Rick." She shook her head, her eyes closed tight. "I would have found Rick if Olivia had not…"

"If Olivia had not led this man Shelton on?"

Mary opened her eyes. "No, that's not…"

"Not what you would say to Olivia?" He smiled thinly. "But it is what you were thinking."

"If Olivia had not been attacked," she corrected him. "He hit her in the face and dragged her roughly across the floor. It was certainly no fault of hers."

"He was clearly not a true gentleman, this Master Shelton."

"No more than Ned – for all he dressed as befitting a much higher rank."

Tom stood and fetched some rags from a bucket in the corner, then mopped up the spilled wine. Mary waited until he had thrown the rags back in the bucket, then asked, "And why do you seek Rick, or the Alchemist as you call him, Master Cobham?"

Tom sat down and poured himself some more wine, very slowly and deliberately, as though he was giving himself extra time to think.

"Let us just say that he is a person that some very influential men of my acquaintance would like to speak to. They too have questions that only he can answer."

"Oh." She thought a moment, then said, "Is he mixed up in a Catholic plot or some such thing? He is not a Catholic as far as I remember."

Tom stood up again. "Lady Mary de Beauvais," he said, "I must tell you that the man you call Richard, and I know as the Alchemist, is indeed part of a Catholic plot against the life of our sovereign lady Elizabeth. And the fact that he has disappeared is extremely concerning for me and my master, one Robert Wychwoode, as it is highly likely that the one man in this realm who can truly succeed in taking the Queen's life, is this Alchemist."

He looked as if she should be impressed with the gravity of this pronouncement, but instead she squeaked, "Robert Wychwoode?" He nodded. "But I know a Robert Wychwoode! Is he tall with long grey hair, and a lawyer by profession?"

"Yes, that is my master in this matter."

"Oh yes! I know him! Ten years ago he helped me and my husband William defeat a dreadful man called Hopkirk. He saved us both, in a way." She smiled. "How can I help?"

"Lady Mary, it is most fitting that you know my master, but I must ask you to consider this from my view." He leaned forward with his hands on the table. "Through the oddest of coincidence, you and I seek the same man. We came together by chance encounter. In my line of work I view such apparent randomness with the deepest suspicion. I must ask you this – and I demand a straight answer on pain of your eternal soul. Did you engineer this meeting? Are you part of the plot I seek to foil?"

A hundred different responses flashed through Mary's mind, ranging from flippant to sarcastic. She paused a moment. Surely the best was response was to treat the question was with the gravity it deserved?

"No, Master Cobham," she said slowly and deliberately. "Everything I have told you is God's truth. I swear it on the lives of my husband and my three young children."

He continued to stare at her silently for some time, then he whispered. "Even though you have not told me everything? Oh, I can see that what you have told me is true – I believe you on that, but if I am to trust you completely, I must know that you will tell me all." He paused, then said, "Why did you withhold from me the rape of Olivia?"

Now it was Mary's turn to stare in silence. "How did you know?" she asked eventually.

"I guessed, from what you said, and what you did not," he answered. "And now I know. Why?"

Mary took a deep breath. "It was our secret. She has to be seen a maid or she will never be wed. Surely you would have guessed that was the reason?"

"Aye." He stood up, and looked down at her. "But I have to trust you if we are to seek the Alchemist together, and any secret must be between us, not setting us apart."

----0----

It was later that evening and they were settled in front of the fire, both with full glasses of hot mulled wine from a large pitcher warming by the flames.

"I promised to tell you the reason I am seeking the Alchemist," Tom began, "so I will tell you all."

Mary sat back in her chair and took a sip of her drink, letting the warmth flood through her. It was surprisingly good, much like the wine she had had in front of the fire in Hammersmith. At least she was with Tom, so she was safe; not like that piece of vermin, Lionel blasted Shelton.

Shelton was nothing like Tom. She studied him as he talked. The way his mouth turned up at the corner as he spoke showed he was honest... The way his eyes crinkled just a little bit – making him look like he was smiling all the time – that spoke of trustworthiness. The way his Adam's apple bobbed in and out of his beard...

Focus.

"...when I was drinking with some acquaintances in a London tavern and one of my companions had too much to drink. So much so, that he was making disparaging remarks about the Queen."

"Oh!" She took a sip of her wine, then gulped down the rest of the glass. It really was delicious. "What did he say?"

"He cast doubt upon her purity, questioning if she was truly a virgin, or some such. He cited Thomas Seymour and the Earl of Leicester as possible lovers, but as I say, he was much taken with drink."

"What did you do?"

Tom refilled her glass from the pitcher. "I told him that what he uttered was nonsense as best, and in truth would be seen as treason. I said that had he made the same remark when sober, he would have been arrested. After that no more was said on the matter, till I was leaving the tavern and this tall, white-haired old man pulled me to one side."

"Wychwoode?"

"Yes. He had overheard what had passed, and asked if I took pride in defending our Queen's honour. I told him that I did. So then he asked me if I would do so again, for him. After a brief hesitation, I said I would consider it." Tom looked up. "In truth I was finding life somewhat tiring, and I was intrigued by the possibility of some excitement. Wychwoode suggested that I come to his chambers in Lincoln's Inn to discuss this further. When I was there, he asked many questions about my upbringing and religious beliefs. When he had assured himself that I was to be trusted, he told me that there was word of a Catholic plot to take the life of the Queen and to put Mary of Scotland on her throne. He knew from other spies that it was afoot, but he had no knowledge of the master plotter behind it. So he had devised a plan that would reveal who this was."

Tom paused a moment, and refilled his glass.

Mary realised she had been staring at him again. Now she was seeing the way his blue eyes seemed to glow, and the way his hair curled back over his ear. His strong hands with their fine down of dark hair. Hands that had closed around Ned's neck; hands that had saved her honour…

Focus.

Plots. He had been talking about a Catholic plot…

"But are there not many such plots?" Mary asked, brightly. "What made this one different?"

"For sure there are many, and most are not worthy of the name 'plot' – they are simply gatherings of self-righteous Catholics who discuss their fanciful ideas with no real means of carrying them out. But this was different, and it was different because of the Alchemist." He paused. "The Alchemist was rumoured to have spent many months using tools he had constructed himself, to make a special form of musket that only he knew how to make. This musket was as thin as the width of a sword, and could be loaded with a singular metal capsule containing both powder and ball, and could be discharged many hundreds of yards from its target, but yet it would hit such a target with unerring accuracy. This meant that a plotter would not need to get close to the Queen in order to have any chance of striking her with a fatal shot – and thus be pulled away or run through with a guard's sword – but could remain hidden at great distance and strike with impunity."

"A sniper!" Mary blurted out.

"A sniper? What is that?"

"Oh, it is a name I once heard for such an assassin."

"A sniper? A killer who strikes in secret from a distance? I have learned a new word, eh?" Tom smiled. "Well, whatever name you give him, we understood him to be called the Alchemist."

Mary considered this a moment. "So the man I know as Rick is a dangerous assassin?"

"It would seem so."

"And you know him as the Alchemist?"

"Aye."

"But why do you call him that?" Mary paused, trying to remember what she had once heard about alchemy. "Is it not all about finding the Philosopher's Stone or turning base metal to gold or some such? What is that to do with Rick making a weapon?"

"I admit that he is not what you would call a traditional alchemist. But he was heard to say that his special musket was made of base metal, and he would accept only gold in payment for using it. So in a sense he was turning base metal into gold, and the name stuck."

Mary sipped her wine, letting this news sink in. So Rick, the catering manager with a passion for guns, had landed in Tudor England like her, but unlike her, he had decided to use his future knowledge – and his lack of morality – to make himself a rich man. She could imagine him working quietly away in some back room in Southwark on the tools he needed to construct his gun, then maybe when he'd made it, taking it to a forest to practice, like in *The Day of The Jackal*. Then letting it be known that he had such a weapon, to flush out a master plotter with enough gold to make him very rich.

"You said there was a plan to find the person behind the plot?" she asked.

"Aye," he said, refilling her glass again from the pitcher. "We knew that there was a man involved by the name of Francis Alleyne. We also knew he was planning to seek out the Alchemist and pay gold for the man to use his special musket as a – what was it?"

"A sniper."

"A sniper – that was it. But we needed to know who was providing the gold to Alleyne. In order to gain his trust, I pretended to be an ardent Catholic and persuaded him to let me join him on his planned trip to Southwark to seek out the Alchemist. We found him, in The Blue Maid as it happens. We offered him many hundreds of gold sovereigns; the condition being that he would take a shot at the Queen with his special musket, and kill her."

"But how would this give you the name of the master plotter?"

"I needed Alleyne to trust me enough that he would reveal the name – either in casual conversation or by reference that I could interpret." He shook his head sorrowfully. "And I believe Alleyne would have done at some point, had he not been suddenly killed."

"Killed?" Mary asked in surprise. "How did that happen?"

"Wychwoode and some of his men were secretly following him, but somehow Alleyne spotted them and took flight. In the ensuing chase, Alleyne's horse shied at some other travellers. He was thrown to the ground and died on the spot."

"So you do not know who is the mastermind behind the plot?"

Tom refilled her wine, then shook his head. "Unfortunately, we are no nearer to finding him." He paused, staring quietly at her over the rim of his glass. "However, there is still one man who we believe is part of the plot that may hold the key – a man in Stratford-upon-Avon called Tyler. Wychwoode has gone there to find him and see what he knows, and I think we should go there too, and find Wychwoode. You must tell him all you know of this Alchemist."

"We must," Mary said, putting her glass down on the table. "We must go at first light tomorrow."

Tom raised an eyebrow, then smiled. "'Tis short notice indeed, but if you wish, Lady Mary, then we will."

"I do," she answered. "Because Rick is out there with the most powerful sniper musket in existence, and we do not know where he is or when he will strike. The life of Queen Elizabeth is in our hands and we have to do whatever it takes to stop him."

"I admire your fervour," he observed.

"I am concerned for the Queen's safety," she answered.

But it wasn't just the Queen that was her primary concern – it was also preservation of her own life and her family's. For what had just become clear was that Rick now presented a new and horribly credible threat to the life of Elizabeth. Which meant that there was a very real possibility that the Queen would die now – and not in 1603 as history originally decreed.

Mary shuddered inwardly. If Elizabeth died now and Mary, Queen of Scots came to the throne, England would revert to Catholicism. And there was every chance that Mary of Scotland would be just as vindictive against Protestants as her namesake Mary I had been. So Protestant families such as hers would be in very real danger. Indeed, it was only three years since the massacre of the Protestant Huguenots on St. Bartholomew's Day in Paris – and who was to say that the accession of Mary II would not lead to the same outcome in England?

But that was not the only threat. For if Elizabeth were to die now, then the changes to history – the history that had led to the birth of Justine in the 1980s – would be cataclysmic. The possible alterations to the historical timeline caused when she had saved William and given birth to her children would pale in comparison.

So if Elizabeth were to die now, then what would be the chance of her being born at all?

Mary looked up at Tom with wide eyes.

If the Catholics did not kill her, then history most likely would.

CHAPTER THIRTEEN

Hetherington Hall, mid-April 1575

William leaned forward and glanced to his right along the high table. Sir Nicholas Grenville was deep in conversation with his wife. William listened intently, but was unable to catch any part of their conversation over the hubbub of supper in the Great Hall.

Did they suspect him of knowing about their daily mass? There had been no outright accusations in the few weeks since his shoes were found, but that had not stopped him behaving like a guilty schoolboy, nervously examining every word said to him by Sir Nicholas or Lady Grenville for signs that they knew.

Lady Grenville turned suddenly and stared at him, as if he were the subject of their conversation.

William smiled weakly at her, and she smiled back.

Was her smile forced? Was it proof she knew that he had discovered their treasonous and heretical secret? That despite their outward conformity to the law by attending Protestant services in the village, they were also attending clandestine masses in a closed-off room every afternoon? And presumably, therefore, hiding the priest somewhere in the house?

William sat back and stared around the magnificent Great Hall. If there was a priest living here, then he would have to eat. So maybe he was in the hall, brazenly and openly sharing supper with the other friends and hangers-on who always seemed to be present at Grenville's meals? William studied the men at the two side tables running down either side of the hall. Perhaps it was the elderly white-haired man in the high ruff at the side table on the right? Or the middle-aged man on the left, smiling serenely as he broke a small loaf of bread?

William leaned forward again, as a man seated at the far end of the high table caught his eye. He was a young man with thick brown hair in a gaudy doublet that seemed at odds with his sombre face. Despite the doublet, something about him suggested an otherworldly air. Yes, this young man was the most likely the priest.

If so, then they were brazenly hiding him in plain sight, openly treating him as a guest or a member of the family. William bit his lip. Maybe it was not even a secret – maybe everyone else in the room knew it – and only he, William, was the one supposed to be in the dark.

Except that now he did know.

Maybe the servant who had found the shoes had casually mentioned this to one of the family, and conclusions had been drawn? Maybe even now Sir Nicholas and Lady Grenville were deciding what was to be done with him – and with Ambrose.

"Sir William, you look quite pale. Are you well?"

William glanced to his left at Lambert Moreton, who appeared concerned.

"I am quite well, I assure you," William answered. He looked at Moreton, as if seeing him for the first time. The man was very thin – almost to the point of emaciation – looking as if a breath of wind would blow him down. His sandy hair fell across one eye and his beard was so wispy that it needed some shadow across his face to see it was there at all.

"I am glad to hear it." Moreton pulled a plate of roast goose closer, then held a sharp knife up to William's face. "Can I cut you another slice of goose flesh?"

"Thank you, yes, indeed, that would be very kind of you." William cringed at this answer; he sounded like a nervous maid at her first banquet.

Moreton cut a couple of slices, then put them on William's plate. "Are you enjoying your stay at Hetherington Hall, Sir William?" he asked, his voice conversational and quite neutral. "Are you being treated well while the weather continues to force you to stay these many weeks? I have never known the snows to stay so long, although now that we are half-way through April, I am sure the Lord will see fit to start the thaw and bring spring at last."

"Yes, indeed," William answered, trying to match Moreton's conversational tone. "Being here as Sir Nicholas's guest gives me more time with my son, and the unexpected pleasure of being in his company for a while longer."

"Of course." Moreton cut some goose for himself. "And plenty of time to explore Hetherington," he added casually.

William felt as if a bucket of cold water had been emptied over him. He stared at the man, unable to think of a single thing to say.

"Is it as big or as grand as your own Grangedean Manor, I wonder?" Moreton continued, seemingly unaware of the effect his words were having. "My uncle has some magnificent rooms, do you not agree?" William found himself nodding weakly. "Indeed," Moreton continued with a small smile, "there are many interesting rooms just waiting to be discovered, are there not?" Again, William nodded. "It will be such a shame when the thaw does finally come and you wish to leave us. So many more interesting times we could have enjoyed in your company. And your charming son will be disconsolate, if his father is not there to keep him safe."

'Keep him safe?' Was that an open threat to Ambrose?

William took a deep breath and squared his shoulders.

He could not give anything away – he had to be assured, confident and strong. For Ambrose.

He cleared his throat. "Ambrose will be happy with his studies, and his swordsmanship lessons, and his archery," he said. "That is what Sir Nicholas and I have agreed for him."

"Of course, but Sir Nicholas would want to be sure he was quite safe. Swordsmanship and archery can be quite a danger for a young boy such as he."

There it was again! A threat that Ambrose could come to some harm, no doubt if William revealed their secret. He turned round and faced Moreton directly.

The man's thin features were open and his eyes were clear.

Perhaps William was misreading this conversation? Maybe it was all just innocent chatter?

He smiled slowly. "Indeed, Master Moreton, but I have entrusted the care of my son to Sir Nicholas, a man of honour who lives by his word. And Sir Nicholas has given his word that Ambrose will be safe in his care."

"My dear Sir William," Moreton said, "the Grenvilles are an ancient and honourable family. I am sure no harm will befall your son, particularly while you are here to keep watch on him."

Was Sir Nicholas using this feeble-looking young man as a mouthpiece; making it clear what would happen if he were to bring the attention of the authorities to their secret Catholic practices and hidden priest? But surely they realised he would be putting his own son in danger if he brought such an accusation – for all in the house would be implicated.

"Ambrose's safety will always be my prime concern," he said. "I would never do anything that places him in a position of danger."

"I am sure you would not, Sir William. You are a cautious man I am sure – one not wishing to take any unnecessary risks."

"Indeed so," answered William. "Which is why I shall be pleased to stay as long as I am welcome, and avoid the treacherous snow and ice that lies thick on my path to the south."

"Oh, you are welcome to remain here as long as you feel able." Moreton took a drink of wine. "If you are willing to stay beyond the thaw, you would be an honoured guest."

"That would be most pleasant," William replied, "but I am keen to get back to my wife and other children as soon as I can."

"A pity. But I am sure Sir Nicholas will be most understanding." Moreton stood. "Now if you will excuse me, Sir William, but I have some business to attend to." He gave a small bow. "By your leave," he said, and walked out of the Great Hall, pausing only to exchange a few quick words with Sir Nicholas. After Moreton had gone, Sir Nicholas leaned forward and jovially raised his glass. William returned the gesture with a weak grin.

Was the broad smile on Sir Nicholas's face a sign that he thought his secret was still safe?

Or that his suspicions were confirmed?

As William saw it, he had three options – none of which were particularly appealing.

He could escape now with Ambrose, but that would be as good as an admission of knowledge of the mass and the hidden priest – or why would he need to escape? The Grenvilles would realise the danger this put them in; they could not risk that he would reveal their secret. They would no doubt give chase with dogs. He had met their two large mastiffs and did not fancy his and Ambrose's chances of outrunning those fierce creatures in the heavy snow and across that deep, wooded ravine.

But if he stayed at Hetherington Hall once the snow had thawed, then he would again be giving a clear signal that he knew of the secret worship – for why would he stay if not to protect his son from danger?

And finally, if he left as soon as the thaw came, he was abandoning his son in a treasonous house. What if the house was raided and the priest discovered? Ambrose could be implicated, or at least questioned, and that was not something he could willingly contemplate for his son.

William's hand trembled as he took a drink of wine.

CHAPTER FOURTEEN

Stratford-upon-Avon

The Alchemist drew back into the shadows, pressing himself against the wall and hearing the footsteps getting louder.

They stopped at the end of the passageway.

He held his breath and waited for what seemed like eternity, his head turned away from the street so his pale face would not stand out in the darkness. Then he heard the sound of a shoe scraping on the rough cobbles – the sound of someone turning.

If the man walked even a few steps into the passage, then all would be lost.

The footsteps started again – and quickly faded into the distance.

The Alchemist let out a sigh of relief.

He waited a few more minutes just to be sure, then moved out of the shadows and peered slowly round the corner onto the street.

It was empty.

He walked quickly in the opposite direction to the footsteps. A few turns later he came across a small tavern. Without hesitating, he pushed open the door and went in, found a table in the corner near the fire and sank into the seat.

That was close – too close. If he had arrived just five minutes earlier at John Tyler's house in Stratford, he would have been taken. He had just been approaching the house when the door had opened and a tall man in black with long grey hair had emerged.

Wychwoode.

He had recognised the man from Francis Alleyne's description. And Wychwoode worked for Walsingham, the Queen's recently appointed spymaster.

The Alchemist shuddered at what had happened next. Wychwoode had stood back to let three men out of the house. Two were clearly his own men

– rough looking and dressed in black like their master. But it was the sight of the one that they supported between them, wearing only a blood-stained shirt and torn hose, that made the Alchemist's own blood run cold. It was Tyler – clearly wounded and being led away, no doubt for further questioning. And there was no possibility Tyler would stay silent – Wychwoode would make sure of that.

The Alchemist ordered a tankard of ale, and when it arrived, drank most of it down in one go.

Now Wychwoode had Tyler, it would only be a matter of time before the whole plot would be blown wide open. Tyler knew too much – and when they got him to London and that infernal Tower, he would no doubt tell all. In which case the Alchemist, as the lone assassin, would be a hunted man.

Unless he could stay one step ahead… He gave himself a wry grin. Considering his pursuers were nothing but medieval dimwits, with no means of communicating faster than a man can ride a horse, that shouldn't be too hard a task.

The Alchemist beckoned a serving girl over, and she refilled his tankard.

Idly, he slapped her bottom as she turned and she gave a satisfyingly indignant squeak.

So now he would have to change his plans.

He had been due to stay in Stratford with John Tyler, keeping safely out of sight until the arranged time to travel to the agreed place, set up the gun and take the shot at the Queen. But that was no longer an option, so he would need to find somewhere else to stay.

He finished his ale and stared into the fire.

Was he being realistic, planning to keep this plot going? Now they had Tyler and would make him talk, maybe the leader would then want him to abandon it?

The Alchemist hoped not. The opportunity to change history – no, no, to *make* history – was too appealing to abandon. To kill Queen Elizabeth would make him famous throughout the realm; throughout history. And rather than go to the gallows for it, he would be hailed as a hero by the new regime under Mary, Queen of Scots. He would be feted by royalty and probably knighted too.

Oh yes. Sir Richard Hornby – it had a good ring to it.

Hadn't he come a long way from doing the catering at Grangedean Manor in 2015 – working with a bunch of misfit actors and corporate guests, all living in fantasy-land and pretending to be high and mighty Tudors? Well now he would be the real thing – a real Tudor noble. Books would be written about him, films would be made of his exploits and generations of school kids would have to learn his name! Serve the little pests right.

So he would see this thing through; he would kill the Queen and he would change history.

Whatever that meant.

But there was no doubt he would have to do this alone. He would have to stay low; keeping out of sight, living off his wits and trusting no-one until the job was done. Then he would make contact with the leader and claim his rightful due – his riches and his title.

If he was going to have to live in this dreadful medieval time, then he was not going to live as a peasant labourer. He might as well live in as much style as he could.

The Alchemist reached down and patted the long bag made of rough sacking at his feet. This was the gun that was going to make it happen. All the hard work in creating it was finally going to pay off. The months spent making rudimentary tools, perfecting them until they were fit for purpose, then seeking out raw materials and spending further months working them. The rejects thrown away or melted down and used again and again, the long days and nights spent covered in soot and sweat to make something that could be factory-made with ease in the 21st century – all this would be worth it when he got that famous pale red-head in the cross hairs and gently squeezed the trigger…

The Alchemist ordered a third tankard of ale and some bread. When he had finished, he picked up his bag and slipped quietly out of the tavern.

---0---

The little cottage stood alone in a forest clearing around a mile out of Stratford, with smoke drifting lazily out of a hole in the wood-tiled roof. It had no windows and just one blackened oak door with a large key-hole and handle.

The Alchemist circled cautiously round it several times, using trees to shield himself from any possible view. Once he was satisfied that no-one was observing him, he walked up to the door and knocked.

It was opened by an old man with unkempt grey hair and beard, dressed in a rough woollen smock and wearing a filthy woollen cap.

He stared suspiciously at the Alchemist.

"What do you want?" he asked.

"I am traveling north and need a bed for a few days to break my journey. Can you let me stay?"

"You are not a vagrant?"

The Alchemist smiled. "No, I have a house in Southwark, but I have come through Stratford on my way to meet my brother in York." The invented brother was the simplest story he could think of.

"No pox or sneezes?"

"No, and not near anyone with those these last few weeks." The Alchemist had heard the same question enough times, starting with the dumpy little landlady at the Grangedean tavern, to know that fear of strangers in these times was mostly fear of the spread of plague.

"Hmm." The man continued to stare at him suspiciously. "You will not stay in an inn?"

"No."

The man stood silent.

"I have some coin," offered the Alchemist. "If that would help?"

"You can agree the payment with my daughter," the man said eventually, then called over his shoulder, "come here, lass."

A moment later, a dark-haired girl of about twenty appeared in the doorway. She looked the Alchemist up and down. "What is it father?" she asked.

"This man would stay with us a few days," the man said. "Name a fair price."

The girl stood silent a moment, then gave a small nod and stood back from the doorway. "Ha'pence a day and you will sleep on the floor."

"Thank you," the Alchemist replied, then picked up his bag and stepped into the cottage.

It was dark inside, with the only light coming from a small fire in a free-standing grate in the middle of the single room – which itself seemed no bigger than an average 21st century double garage. A small pot was bubbling on the grate.

The Alchemist stood a moment while his eyes adjusted to the darkness. Gradually he made out a few more pots and pans and a couple of wooden plates on a small table in the corner, two truckle beds against the walls, and two wooden stools by the fire.

"That will be your corner," said the girl, pointing to the opposite side of the room from the two beds. The Alchemist went over and put his bag down, pushing it as deep as possible into the shadows.

"My name is Richard," he said. "What is yours?"

"I am Ursula," she answered, "and my pa is Walter."

The Alchemist reached into his purse and took out two coins. "There are two pennies," he said. "I will not be more than four days."

She took the coins with a small smile and quickly pocketed them in her apron. "I have some broth," she said. "Art hungry?"

He nodded. The meagre bread and ale he had in the tavern was a while ago.

Walter pulled the table out and put the two stools by it, as well as another he produced from underneath. The men sat while Ursula served the broth, and Walter poured ale from a pitcher.

"York, you say?" he asked. "That is a long way to go from Southwark to see your brother."

"Yes. I have not seen him for some years."

Walter acknowledged this with a grunt and carried on eating.

Ursula, however, was still curious. "Was that when he moved to York — when you last saw him some years ago," she asked, her eyes twinkling in the firelight, "or were you split at birth?"

"Have a mind, lass," snapped Walter. "You will not be prying into Master Richard's affairs — he is our guest."

"He has paid me tuppence for four days — so he is a paying guest. I got a right to ask."

"It is no problem," said the Alchemist. He smiled at Ursula and was rewarded with a smile in return. "I have not seen my brother in over four years."

"There is the answer, lass," muttered Walter. "Now leave the man be."

Once the meal was over, the Alchemist retired to his corner, pushing the sacking bag deeper into the shadows as he sat down. He had just got comfortable sitting on the floor with his back to the wall, when he looked up to find Ursula standing over him.

"Here," she said, "a blanket to sleep under."

"Thank you." He opened up the rough woollen blanket she offered him, then put it over his knees. She sat next to him. "Tell me of your life in Southwark," she said.

"Have you been there?" he asked.

"Nay," she said quietly. "I have never been further than Stratford. I go there often — for the market." There was a silence for a moment. Then she said, "Is it a big place?"

"Big enough."

"Bigger than Stratford?" Her eyes were wide.

"Yes — and it is just across the river from the City of London."

"London?" She bit her lip. "I have heard tell of London. They say the streets are paved with gold?"

He smiled. "Are the streets of Stratford paved with gold?"

"Nay." She shook her head. "Of course not."

"Well, neither are the streets of London."

She smiled hesitantly, searching his eyes as if checking to see if he was teasing or serious. He laughed and after a moment she laughed back.

"You are a naughty man," she said, punching him softly on the shoulder, "to jest with me so." She smiled again, winding a lock of hair thoughtfully round her finger as she looked at him. "I shall have to watch my words, lest you turn them into something I never meant."

The Alchemist was about to reply, when Walter appeared in front of them.

"I go out to catch a coney or a hare for supper," he muttered.

The Alchemist started to stand up. "I can come and help."

"Nay," Walter answered, "I hunt alone."

The old man went to the door and took a slingshot off a hook, then put some small rocks from a pile into a bag and hefted it over his shoulder. He picked up a large cudgel, which looked a bit like a baseball bat. "I will be back presently," he said, and was gone.

There was a silence in the little cottage, as the two of them sat together. Then Ursula got up and walked over to the table. "You can tell me of London and Southwark," she said over her shoulder, "and tales of the folk that live in such places."

"They are ordinary folk, like you and me."

"Are you ordinary, Master Richard?" She turned. "You seem not like any of the folk I know."

"Why is that?"

She studied him as he sat on the floor of the dark cottage. "You come to our cottage that is away from other dwellings instead of stopping at one of the inns you must have passed to get here... you carry no clothes save a rough bag with shiny iron sticks within, that you hide away with much trouble..."

He raised an eyebrow. "Have you looked in my bag?"

"I would not have done so. But I saw inside just as you came in the cottage, for all I was not meaning to do so."

The Alchemist thought quickly. "It is a gift for my brother."

She smiled. "Yet you hide it away?"

"It took me many weeks to make. I do not want any harm to come to it."

"For sure." She seemed to lose interest in the bag and its contents. "But still you have not answered my question."

"I do not remember you asking a question."

"That I did. Why you did not stop at an inn?"

"I do not like inns." She raised an enquiring eyebrow. "I worked in one for a while, so I know what kind of places they are." He stood up and went over to her. "I prefer honest folk and honest food."

She did not move. "What if my pa and I are not honest folk?"

"Oh, you are." He moved closer. "You are both honest as the day is long." He put a hand up to her cheek and stroked it softly. For a moment she let his hand caress her skin, then she took it gently and moved it away. "Have a care, Master Richard," she said quietly. "You have paid for bed and board – no more."

He stepped back and smiled carefully. "For sure, Mistress Ursula, that is understood."

There was an uncomfortable silence, then suddenly the door opened and light flooded in. They moved quickly apart; the Alchemist returning to his corner and Ursula busying herself with pots and pans at the table.

Walter entered the cottage, closed the door, then threw a rabbit carcass onto the table. "A coney in the first few minutes," he announced. "I saw it at first but a few yards from the door. A good hunt, for all it took every stone I had to hit the thing as it ran. But I had him eventually." He took his bag off and hung it back on the hook. "Plenty there for a rich stew, lass. Do you have vegetables?"

"Yes," Ursula answered. "Enough for today. I will get more in a day or two from the market."

She picked up the rabbit. "A fine beast." She handed the Alchemist a sharp knife. "You can help me skin it."

The Alchemist picked up the rabbit and started skinning and gutting it, working quickly and with precision. Ursula stopped and stared.

"By Heaven, Master Richard, you have some skill with the knife!"

"I told you, I worked in a tavern," he answered, separating the skin from the flesh. "Preparing a rab… I mean a coney, for the stew was everyday work."

"It was a trade well learned," she said. "You are a man of many parts."

Walter came over and watched as the Alchemist finished preparing the meat, cutting it into cubes ready for the pot. "The lass is right, Master Richard," he observed. "You have a talent. Use it well and you will never go hungry."

---0---

The Alchemist woke with a start the next morning. Walter and Ursula were already up, and were moving around the cottage, making plenty of noise with spoons and plates as they prepared breakfast. He lay on his back and stared up at the hole in the roof that served as a chimney. There was no sunlight coming through.

"Art awake?" asked Ursula, coming over to where he lay.

"Yes."

"'Tis nearly first light. We shall eat shortly, then my pa is going into Stratford – he has some business there for the day." She studied him as he lay. "What would you do?"

"I do not know – what needs to be done?"

"Bread to be made," she said. "You can help."

"Aye." He stood up and pushed the blanket into the corner.

Walter was already at the table. The Alchemist sat and stared bleakly at the food. What he wouldn't give for a proper 21st century breakfast of bacon, eggs, sausage and tomato, all washed down with a large orange juice and a steaming mug of black coffee… He sighed. Instead he was marooned in the 16th century, with nothing but blackened bread and watery ale, in the company of two uncouth, unwashed peasants…

At least when he was Sir Richard, he would eat as well as anyone in this appalling era.

"…Amen."

Richard looked up. Ursula and Walter were staring at him expectantly – waiting for him to speak.

"Yes, yes, sorry… Amen."

Walter grunted in approval, then tore off a hunk of bread and poured himself some ale. Ursula did the same, so the Alchemist took a small piece of bread and tried it. It was dry and sooty, with a heavy taste of rye and something bitter, which he decided was very similar to the taste of the ale. Not only was it nothing like 21st century bread, but it was even drier and harder to swallow than the pale bread he bought from the market in Southwark.

"You do not like it?" Ursula was staring at him, and he realised he had been making his dislike obvious.

"It is different from what I have been used to, that is all."

"It stops us from starving, lad," said Walter firmly. "And the lass makes it well. That is all there is to be said on the matter."

They ate on in silence, then Walter drained his mug of ale and stood up. "I will be gone till nightfall, lass," he muttered, and left the cottage.

The Alchemist and Ursula finished their meal.

"Now is the time to make more bread," she said. "As you would have done when you worked in a tavern?"

He shook his head. "That was a task I was never given."

She gave a small smile. "Then mayhap if you see how it is made, you may like it more." Reaching down under the table, she brought up a hessian sack, about the size of a 21st century box of cereal, and a large wooden plate.

She opened the sack and scooped out a handful of dark brown flour, which she poured into a pile on the middle of the plate. Then she added a small amount of ale from the pitcher and worked the mixture with her hands until it was a sticky-looking dough. Then she added some more flour and ale and worked those into the mixture. The Alchemist watched, fascinated, as her long slim fingers moved deftly through the ball of dough, quickly working more flour and ale in until it was roughly the size of a large potato.

"Here," she said, looking up from her work, "you can do as I have done until you have doubled this in size." She pushed the plate towards him. "I shall make ready the bread oven outside." She walked out of the cottage, leaving the Alchemist with the dough.

After a moment, he reached for the flour and poured a small amount onto the board next to the ball of dough. Then he did as Ursula had done, adding a few drops of ale and working the mixture with his fingers. He soon found it to be unpleasantly sticky, so he added a bit more flour to try and dry it out. Unfortunately, this was too successful, and soon the resulting piece of dough was horribly dry and flaky. More ale just made it sticky again, so he decided to try folding it into the main ball. This seemed to work – the new larger ball was not too different in consistency, so he repeated the process.

By the time Ursula came back into the cottage, he was sitting in front of a ball of dough of the right size and, he felt, pretty good consistency.

"There," he said, pushing it towards her. "Done."

She picked it up and studied it, kneading it gently. Then she nodded and put it down. "Good. You have done well. We will prove it by the fire."

She took a piece of grey cloth and wrapped the dough inside it, then put it on the plate next to the fire. "Come, this will need some time. You can help me tend the oven."

He followed her outside, then round to the back of the cottage. There was a small extension off the back wall built of rough bricks, with a wooden door set near the top. Ursula opened the door and a blast of heat hit the Alchemist.

"Pass me some faggots, please," she said. He glanced around and saw some tied bundles of twigs in the corner. He grabbed one and passed it over. She threw it in the oven, then held out her hand again. He gave her another bundle, then a third, and she threw each one in. She closed the door and stepped back.

"Thank you. We have some time to wait until the dough has proved."

She sat against the wall of the cottage and stretched out her long legs. She patted the ground next to her, inviting him to sit as well.

"How long will you stay with your brother?" she asked.

He shook his head. "I have no fixed plans." He stared at the forest, squinting at the bright sun flashing through the trees as it rose.

"Does your brother have a trade?" she asked.

The Alchemist thought about this. What might this mythical brother do for a living in York? Suddenly Shakespeare came to mind. "He is a writer of plays."

"Oh." It was a good answer – she had no knowledge of the theatre.

"Has he a family in York?"

"Yes." Again, this brother's fantasy life needed fleshing out. This was getting a little tiresome. "He has a wife and… er, two sons."

"Is that all? Only two?"

He shrugged. "He may have more by now."

"And you?" she asked. "No wife waiting on you in Southwark?"

He turned sharply to look at her. "No."

She was silent for so long that the Alchemist almost drifted off to sleep. "Why so?" she asked.

"What?"

"Why so – that there is no wife waiting on you?"

"I do not know. I have not yet found a wife."

The truth was, after he had arrived in the strange world of 1571 from 2015 by freak accident, his first thought had been that this was only temporary –

so he might as well have some fun without worrying about the consequences. He had quickly started to eye up the girls. The squinty-eyed pub landlady had been giving him all the signs – hands on hips, winking at him, calling him 'my sweeting' – so it was hardly surprising he thought she was looking for a real man for a change, and had crept into her bed chamber when he thought her husband was away for the day. Only it turned out that not only was she totally frigid, but the man had come home early, and together they had thrown him out.

Then there had been that stunning young gypsy-like girl, Olivia Melrose. At first he'd trod warily around her – she was very young and treated him like dirt, but he'd softened her up eventually with flattery and compliments – until he was sure she was about ready to submit. He'd cornered her alone and was just making real progress when her sallow, humourless father had poked his long nose in and stopped them. It was not surprising that he got thrown out again – the girl had accused him of forcing himself upon her, when in truth she'd been giving him all the signs as well.

So when he had finally come to the conclusion that time-travel was a one-way trip and he was stuck in the 1570s – and had settled in Southwark – the thought of finding a wife had rather lost its appeal. Instead he had thrown himself into making the sniper rifle.

The rifle was his ticket to fame and fortune. And once he was Sir Richard, he'd have his pick of the women. They would be falling over themselves to be his wife.

That was for the future. For now, this peasant girl was warming up nicely…

A few minutes later, they went back inside the cottage. Ursula partially unwrapped the cloth bundle and peered inside. The ball of dough was clearly bigger. "Good," she said, opening it fully. She placed it on the wooden plate and looked up at him. "Work it some more."

He started kneading it again. It was less sticky now and warmed his fingers. He continued a minute or two longer, until his fingers started to ache, making him stop kneading and stretch out his hands with a small wince of pain.

She moved round the table to stand close to him, her hip and shoulder touching his. "But you have still to build strength in your fingers." She pulled the plate towards her and started working the dough herself. "You must work it so," she said, "with slower movements, thus."

The Alchemist found himself staring at Ursula's hands as they caressed the dough, watching as she squeezed it in her fist so it grew longer, then folded it on itself and pushed it out, before pulling it back again and squeezing it once more…

She turned to look at him. Their faces were almost touching. "You see?" she said. "It is but a slow, gentle movement."

His head started to move forward, his lips seeking hers, his hand starting to come up behind her back.

She put the bread down and stood back quickly.

"Nay," she whispered. "Bed and board – I have said that is all."

She picked up the dough and again wrapped it in the cloth. Then she placed it back by the fire.

"Come," she said, "we must keep the blaze burning in the bread oven at the back." While he stood motionless, she went outside once again.

He found her by the oven, poking the glowing embers inside with a stick.

"The dough will soon be ready and the fire is hot," she said, with her back still to him.

"Yes," he said, "the fire is hot."

There was a heavy edge to his voice that caused her to turn quickly.

He was standing close behind her. Again, their faces were almost touching. This time he gave her no chance to pull away, but put his hand behind her head and pulled her towards him.

Their lips met and her mouth opened, her tongue darting out to meet his, and for a brief moment she kissed him with real passion. Then suddenly she drew away, her eyes locked onto his, and she shook her head.

"Bed and board is all," she murmured. "Bed... is all..."

Then their lips came together again and she kissed him hard, kissed him with a hunger, as if she could not get enough of him, with small mewling noises in the back of her throat as she kissed.

His hand moved down from her head, and fastened on her bottom, pushing her onto him, so she could not fail to feel his hardness. Then his other hand started bunching up her skirts, lifting the thick layers of material until it was resting on the bare skin of her upper thigh, before starting to make its way up and inward...

She broke off and stood back, her skirt dropping heavily down again.

"The bread..." she muttered. "We must put it in to bake." Leaving him standing once more, she hurried into the cottage, before reappearing a few minutes later carrying a small metal bucket. She showed him that the dough was inside, then she put it in the oven.

He had not moved a single muscle since they had broken off.

She took his hand. "Come," she said. "There is some soft heather in that clearing over there, and while the bread bakes we have time to know each other better..."

---0---

It was a while later, and the Alchemist and Ursula were lying naked on their backs on the heather. She had her head on his left shoulder, and he was stroking her belly.

She picked up his right arm and studied it. "What are these pictures?" she asked.

"They are called assault rifles," he answered.

"Salt rifles?" She studied the tattoos closely. "I know not what this means. To me they are like muskets…" She twisted his arm round. "What is this curved piece in the middle?"

"It is where the…er… balls are stored."

"Oh." She was silent a while. "Why do you have pictures of such muskets on your arm?"

"Because I am interested in them."

She dropped his arm and twisted to look at him. "Is that what the shiny iron sticks in your bag are? Are they pieces of a musket like this one?"

"No, they are… for decoration in my brother's house."

"Oh." She was silent again. Then suddenly she jumped up. "The bread! It will burn!" She ran round the clearing gathering up her clothes, struggled quickly into them, and ran off towards the cottage.

The Alchemist stayed where he was for a few more minutes, enjoying the peace of the forest, then dressed and walked slowly back to the cottage.

As his eyes became used to the darkness inside, he saw the bread on the table. He picked it up and studied it – but it looked largely unburned. As he put it back on the table, some movement in the corner caught his eye.

It was Ursula, and she was sitting in his corner with his bag open.

She was lifting out the metal tubes that formed the sniper rifle, and was studying each piece.

He hurried over. "What the heck are you doing?"

"This is no decoration," she said slowly. "It is a salt rifle like the ones in the pictures on your arms." She held up the stock. "See, here is the part where your finger fits and pulls on this lever to make it fire." She looked up at him. "Why do you bring such a thing into my home?"

He squatted down. "It is for my brother."

"What does he want with it?"

"So he can hunt coneys better."

"You will show me."

Just then the door opened and Walter came in. "My business in Stratford is done early," he announced. Then he saw Ursula. "What hast there, lass?" he asked. "Sticks that shine like the moon."

"It is a salt rifle that belongs to Richard," she answered. "For hunting coneys."

"Aye?" Walter moved closer and peered at the rifle barrel. "How does it do that?"

"Richard will show us."

The Alchemist sighed deeply. He hated to be forced to show the gun, even to these two peasants, but he couldn't see an alternative right now. He reached into the bag and took out the two steel tubes, the scope and the butt, and took the breech block off Ursula.

As they watched mesmerised, he screwed one tube into the breech block to create the barrel, and the second, shorter tube into the other end of the block, then screwed the wooden butt onto this tube. Then he fitted the scope to the top of the block, and presented the weapon to Walter.

The old man picked it up and held it with one hand on the barrel and the other on the breech, with his finger on the trigger. "A musket, this?" he breathed. "Though not like any musket I saw when I was a lad fighting the French." He studied it in the glow of the fire, then went over to the door and opened it to get the better light. "How do you load and prime it?"

The Alchemist reached into his bag for one of the twenty or so cartridges he had made, then took the gun from Walter, snapped open the breech and slipped the cartridge inside. Then he stepped out of the cottage and said, "Find me a coney."

Walter scanned the undergrowth for a moment, then pointed wordlessly at the base of a tree about twenty yards away. The Alchemist followed the man's finger, and saw a small brown shape just beside the tree. He lifted the gun to his shoulder, took careful aim through the scope and squeezed the trigger. There was a crack like the breaking of a branch, a puff of smoke from the barrel, and the rabbit disappeared from view. As the gun went off, both father and daughter jumped, and Ursula gave out a small cry of alarm.

Walter was the first to recover. "By heaven, you made the coney disappear! What art of Satan is this?"

"None," said the Alchemist. "As you said, it is a musket. I have simply hit the coney with the ball."

"From this far?" Walter shook his head. "To hit from this far in one shot is sorcery indeed."

"You made the creature disappear, I swear to it," Ursula said.

"Wait here," the Alchemist said, and walked over to the tree. He soon found the remains of the rabbit a further ten yards back. The bullet had passed straight through its chest, killing it instantly. He picked it up and carried it back to where the others were standing.

"There," he said, handing it to Ursula, "shot through the chest."

There was a silence, as Walter looked from the gun to the rabbit, then to the Alchemist. He appeared to be trying to make a decision – then he said quietly, "Be gone my house this instant. Whatever piece of musketry you have there, I want it gone. And you. Right now."

Ursula said, "But, Pa…"

"Nay, lass, I want this man gone, and that is the end of the matter." He pushed Ursula into the cottage. At the door she turned and looked back longingly at the Alchemist, before Walter pushed her again and she disappeared inside.

The door slammed, and the Alchemist heard the key turn in the lock. With a sigh he dismantled the gun, put it in the bag and hefted the bag over his shoulder.

Then he set off through the forest.

CHAPTER FIFTEEN

Stratford-upon-Avon

Mary looked around her in wonder in the early spring sunshine, as she and Tom rode into the centre of Stratford-upon-Avon. The snows in the fields had melted fast as they had journeyed up from London, and now the only sign that the winter had finally departed was the occasional mound of slush remaining in the deep shadows.

The streets were full of timber-beamed houses, leaning into each other across the cobbled street, their tall upper storeys periodically blocking out the sunshine. But it was the very normality of the houses that caused Mary to stare about her and catch her breath as she rode. Stratford was the town that embodied Tudor England to the people of the 21st century. As the birthplace of William Shakespeare, Stratford had a magic about it that connected you directly to the Tudors – and now here she was, riding into Stratford behind a real Tudor man, and seeing it in its real Tudor splendour.

Not that it was particularly splendid. The stench of human waste and rotting food was indescribable, and she held her lavender nosegay close to her face to block it out as much as she could. Best not to look down, either. A sewer channel running along the centre of the cobbles was clearly the source of the smell, with things floating in it that did not bear close inspection. Instead she focused on Tom's broad back and the thick dark hair escaping from under his cap.

Maybe sensing her gaze, Tom turned his head slightly and she caught sight of his profile and a half-smile.

Then, just for a moment, it was William's profile she saw; strong, open and honest, and she felt a small stab of guilt.

But no. She shook her head to herself. She had nothing to be guilty about. She and Tom had just got a little tipsy that night in his house – that was all.

There had been a moment after Tom's explanation of the Alchemist's plot when the conversation had faltered, then stalled completely, and then they were left in silence, each searching the other's eyes…

God, he was handsome…

And kind, and gentle, and he'd saved her from Ned, so he could be a man of action when he needed to be…

Then the moment when their heads had moved naturally together, and he had started to lean to one side as he moved in, which was nearly the point of no return, and if she didn't do anything or say anything then she would be helpless and it would be too late, and William would never, ever forgive her, and she would never forgive herself, and it would be too late, too late…

So she had pulled back.

"Nay, Tom," she had muttered. "This is not seemly."

And he had nodded, and smiled, and sat back, and said, "For sure, my dear Lady Mary, for sure," and they had got on with planning the trip to Stratford, as if this had never happened, which of course it hadn't, so she had nothing to be guilty about…

Suddenly a small boy appeared as if from nowhere and ran across the road in front of her. No sooner had she realised he was there, than she saw his foot catch on the edge of the sewer channel and he started to fall. With a shrill squeak of alarm, she realised he was falling directly into the path of Juno's hooves. Just when it seemed certain he would be killed or maimed, he pushed off the ground with both hands and emerged unscathed, seemingly from right under the hooves. With a laugh and a brief wave, he ran off down an alley.

Tom stopped and turned in the saddle. "Art well?" he asked, a concerned frown on his face. "I heard you cry out."

"I am well, Tom," she answered. "A boy nearly ran under my horse, but no harm came."

"Good," he said, and turned back in his saddle. He was about to ride on, when Mary called out "Wait!"

Tom turned back again. "What is it, Lady Mary?" he asked, then paused and added, "You are as pale as a bed sheet. What ails you?"

"That boy," she said. "I might have killed him."

"Aye, but you did not, so as you say, no harm done." Tom walked on.

Mary stopped a moment to catch her breath, then nudged Juno in the flanks and followed.

Sure, that boy might have died. And maybe his death would have had no consequence for the world.

But what if that had not been just any small boy? What if it had been William Shakespeare himself?

He was about the age that Shakespeare would have been, and this was Stratford… She had been day-dreaming and not looking where she was going. It would have been her fault if he had died. Let alone any official punishment, she would have had to live with the knowledge that she had killed Hamlet before he'd even been born. How could she have lived with that loss? Or Macbeth? Or Lear…

For a brief moment, the future of the English language could have been in her hands – and she would have changed it forever.

Mary sniffed on her nosegay. She had to protect the future. It was her future and it needed her to be on her guard – to protect it from threats that only she could see.

Mary shivered, then gave Juno another nudge with her heel and trotted closer to Tom.

"Come Tom," she said, "let us make haste to Master Tyler's house, and see what we can learn that will help us stop this man, the Alchemist."

Tom stopped and turned again in the saddle. "I realise that we do not know where he lives. But I am sure he will be known hereabouts. We must find someone who can tell us."

Just then a man pushing a cart laden with baskets of bread went past them and turned down a side alley. Tom stared at him a moment then laughed and said, "The market – of course! We will ask there – someone is bound to know."

They turned down the lane after the man, and soon found themselves in the noise and the mayhem of the market square.

Mary gazed about her in wonder. There were stalls selling bread, vegetables and ales, as well as stalls with all types of clothing, from hats, shoes and hosiery, to basic doublets, plain breeches, woollen skirts and grey dresses. Several stalls were selling meat such as pig and goat – where the animals were still alive and running around in pens. Mary saw a small goat being pulled from the pen. The stall holder then cut its throat, skinned and butchered it on a wooden slab, before handing over fresh cuts of meat to a woman in a woollen dress.

Where 21st century Justine Parker would have been sick, or fainted; 16th century Mary de Beauvais merely shrugged, and nudged Juno to walk on.

It was then that she realised that while she had been looking around, she had lost sight of Tom.

Desperately she scanned across the square, trying to make out his distinctive hat among the various men on horseback. Then with relief she spotted him making for a long, low fence at the far end of the square. She saw him dismount and tether his horse to it, alongside others already tethered there. 'A car park,' she thought, as she made her way over to the fence and dismounted from Juno, 'or at least the Tudor equivalent.'

Juno neighed and lifted her head. Mary stroked her muzzle. "There, old girl, I will be back soon." She tied the reins to the rail. "Do not worry." Juno gave a small neigh in response, and Mary caught a look in the horse's eye that said, "Don't leave me here among these strange sights and smells…"

"You will be fine, old girl," she answered, "I will not be long, I promise."

Fighting through the crowds, she caught up with Tom. He had made his way to a stall selling vegetables, and was bawling at the man.

"John Tyler! Do you know a John Tyler?" The man nodded and Tom stood back, looking pleased. Then the man said, "Yes, master, we have turnips."

"Not turnips, for Heaven's sake! John Tyler!" The man shook his head. With a muttered curse that Mary didn't hear – but guessed it was about deaf idiots – Tom stamped off to the next stall, and from there to the next and the next again.

After twenty minutes of fruitless search, they stopped at the edge of the square, close to three women who were talking amongst themselves.

"By thunder," admitted Tom, "it was madness to think we could find someone here who knows this man. I would we take a few minutes rest, then be on our way."

Mary nodded, and was about to add a comment, when she overheard what one of the women beside her was saying.

"It was sorcery, I tell you! He pointed the stick at the coney, and it disappeared in a puff of smoke!" The woman mimed lifting a rifle to her shoulder and made a sound like gunfire. "Like sorcery, I tell you! It just disappeared!"

Mary and Tom's eyes met and they shared a knowing look. Maybe coming to the market might help them in their search after all – but for the Alchemist rather than Tyler.

Mary put a hand on the woman's shoulder. "Excuse me," she said, "but I could not but help overhear. What did the man point at the coney?"

The woman looked her up and down, taking in the travel-worn but elegant style of her clothes, clearly deciding that Mary was of the nobility. She made a small curtsey. "Beg pardon, mistress, but it was a thin shiny iron stick. He pointed it at the coney and the stick made a cracking sound and the coney disappeared."

"Was it like a musket?" This was Tom, who had stepped over.

"Aye, a bit like a musket, except it was very small and thin. He called it a 'salt rifle'. And it worked by sorcery."

"And what was this man's name?" asked Mary, her breath catching in her throat.

"Richard was his name, mistress."

Mary gasped. "And did he have pictures painted on his arms of similar looking muskets?"

"Aye, that he did."

"And he had spiky hair, like a hedgehog?"

"Aye, that also, as you mention it." The woman smiled, as if to herself, "Fine hair, I thought it."

"And how did it come about, that he used his thin musket to make the coney disappear?" Mary asked.

"My pa and I live in a cottage in the wood. He knocked on our door and asked for a bed for a few nights." The woman gave a concerned look at her two friends, as if seeking reassurance. They nodded, so she continued. "My pa and I let him in for two pennies, as he said he would not stay in an inn."

Mary nodded. No doubt he wouldn't want to risk staying in an inn, in case he was spotted by one of Wychwoode's men.

"What is your interest in Master Richard, mistress?" the woman asked.

"What is your name?" asked Mary.

"Ursula, mistress."

"Well, Ursula, we believe this man Richard is very dangerous, particularly with his special musket. We want to catch him and stop him before he causes any serious trouble."

Tom asked, "How did he come to show you the musket?"

"I asked him what were the sticks in his bag, and he showed how they were put together to make a small musket – only it was sorcery, the way he disappeared that coney, so we…" she swallowed hard, then continued, "we threw him out."

"And when was that?" asked Tom.

"It was last evening, sir."

"And did you see which way he went?"

"Nay, sir – my pa and I went back in the cottage and he said that was the end of the matter."

Tom paused, tapping rapidly on the hilt of his sword as he thought.

"Can we see your cottage?" he asked.

Ursula nodded slowly. "If it pleases you sir, of course."

"Now?"

"It is about a half hour's walk."

"Good," said Tom. "Then let us start now."

---0---

They approached the cottage with Ursula leading them. There was no sign of movement, other than a small wisp of smoke drifting lazily into the clear sky from the hole in the roof.

"This is where you left him?" asked Tom.

"Aye."

"He has a full day's start on us, but he is on foot." Tom looked around at the trees and undergrowth. "We can see if we can track him on horseback, and catch him up. But we need to take the same path from the start."

Tom crouched down and silently studied the ground around him, but seemed to see nothing that interested him. Then he moved on to another patch of ground, and then another. Then suddenly he let out a low exclamation of triumph and carefully picked up what looked like a small piece of twig. As Mary and Ursula watched, he leaned down and picked up another, similar twig, and studied both carefully.

"See here," he said, showing them to the women, "broken clean in two by a man's foot, and not long ago by the look of how white is the wood inside." He stared at the trees around the spot where he had found the twigs. "And judging by the lie of these on the ground, I would say he was heading that way." He pointed towards a gap in the trees, then moved slowly towards it, studying the ground as he went. Suddenly he stopped again, and pointed at something they couldn't see at his feet. "Another broken twig. We have his direction," he said, with a satisfied smile. "We must ride."

As Tom and Mary mounted up, Mary looked down and said, "Thank you, Ursula. We will track Richard down, and stop him from making trouble."

"God speed, my lady," Ursula replied. She curtseyed again, then went into the cottage.

Mary trotted on. "We must take care," she said when she reached Tom.

"Aye. This Alchemist is…" he looked back at her, "what was the word you used? A sniper?"

"Yes." Mary shivered despite the warmth of the spring sun as she looked around the forest. "He could be watching us even now."

Desperately, she scanned the trees around them, looking for signs of movement or a glimpse of Rick's spiky hair.

"Marry, we are being too alarmed. He does not know we are following him," Tom said. "So he is unlikely to be watching us now. My thought is as I said – he has nigh on a day's start on us, and is already many miles ahead."

But Mary was not reassured as they headed deep into the forest and the trees closed in around them, cutting out much of the sunlight and enclosing them in a cold, dappled world where shapes were difficult to define; a world where every shadow could be Rick standing by a tree, and every brief flash of sunlight could be a home-made telescopic sight trained on them…

She forced herself to try and breathe calmly; to observe each shadow dispassionately as she rode, noting how its shape changed exactly as you would expect if it was indeed a shadow, and not a man with a gun…

Suddenly there was a loud cracking sound. Mary squeaked in alarm.

Tom stopped and smiled. "My horse snapped a branch," he said. "You have naught to fear."

He walked on, and Mary followed. A few minutes later he stopped and dismounted. "Wait," he said, as he crouched down and studied the path. "As I thought." He looked at it some more, "the mark of his foot in the earth. We are still on his trail."

"He could be just ahead," said Mary, as Tom got back on his horse and started forward again. Mary stayed still a moment, listening intently – but all she could hear was the breeze rustling the tops of the trees and birds chirruping softly. There was also a harsh rasping sound that she couldn't initially place, until she realised it was her own laboured breathing. Telling herself not to be so panicky, she squeezed Juno's side and trotted up behind Tom.

A few minutes later they came to a small clearing. Almost immediately Tom stopped, dismounted and went quickly to a small black mound in the middle of the space, crouching down to study it closely and poking at it with a stick. Then he turned with wide eyes, and before Mary could ask what it was, he held his finger to his lips to indicate silence. He looked all round the clearing, before pointing to a nearby tree and indicating that she should dismount and join him there.

With her heart in her mouth, Mary did as he wanted.

"It is a fire," he whispered, "and only recently covered over. He may be close by, even watching us now."

"Oh my Lord," she hissed. "What do we do?"

Tom paused a moment. "If this weapon of his is as good as Ursula says it is, then we are in real danger." Mary said nothing more – her mouth had suddenly become too dry to speak. "So I suggest we mount up slowly," he continued, "and turn back down the path. Then when I give the word, ride as fast as you can back to the cottage. We can seek shelter there while decide our plan."

Mary nodded, and walked slowly over to Juno. Again she listened to the sounds of the forest, but again she could hear nothing untoward. She glanced at the trees around her, but again, no tell-tale flash of sunlight bouncing off metal or glass…

She mounted Juno, and turned to face the way back to the cottage. She heard Tom mount up behind her; heard his horse's hooves start to move, and she walked slowly on herself.

The rasping sound of her own breathing now sounded deafening, as the sounds of the forest died away, until her breathing was the only sound she could hear, then Tom shouted, 'Now!' and suddenly all the sounds of the forest came back as she dug in her heels and Juno leapt forward into a gallop as the path and the trees started to fly by, then a fallen tree trunk appeared in her way so she gathered Juno's reins and muttered, 'Come on old girl,' and Juno took off in a perfect jump and was still in the air when there was a sudden sound like a breaking branch from one side and Juno screamed as a red cloud burst from her neck and she landed on the other side of the trunk and carried on down in a sprawling fall that sent Mary clean over her head and into the undergrowth…

---0---

Mary lay looking up at the sky between the trees for a moment, unsure of where she was and what to do next. She closed her eyes, trying to stop her head from spinning.

When she opened them, there was a man with a gun standing over her.

The gun was pointing right into her face. She could see that the man silhouetted against the sunlight had spiky hair like a hedgehog. She couldn't see his face against the sun, but she could hear his voice.

It was Rick's voice.

"Get up," he ordered. "Get up now."

Then she heard Tom, as if from far away. "You, Alchemist. Leave her."

"Hello, Tom Cobham." The gun did not move an inch. "It has been a while since we last met in the Blue Maid, when you invited me into your little plot. But now it is you chasing me. So which side are you on exactly?"

Tom said nothing, staring at the Alchemist in disgust.

"So am I to take it you are no longer in league with your hot-headed friend, Alleyne?" The Alchemist nodded to himself. "I thought as much. You did not seem to be one of those firebrand Catholics – so perhaps you are actually working for Wychwoode?" Again, Tom was silent. "Fair enough," said the Alchemist, as if answering for Tom, "so even if Tyler talks, the plot is blown open anyway. Thanks, Cobham."

Tom lifted his chin and stared at the barrel of the gun. "Right now, I take only Lady Mary's part, Alchemist. Leave her."

"Lady Mary, eh?" Still the gun didn't move. "I wondered if I would bump into you one day, Justine, after the storm when you disappeared so mysteriously – just like the one which landed me in this fucking fairy-tale country." He paused a moment. "You've done well, haven't you, Justine? Lady Fucking Mary now?" There was that arrogant sneer in his voice that she remembered now, only too well.

Too late.

She got slowly to her feet, testing her weight on each knee and hip to make sure nothing was broken. Everything seemed in order.

She should be scared – but in one heart-stopping moment, she had the answer to her question!

He knew her.

He called her Justine!

So she still existed in his future!

She wanted to sing and dance with joy! Saving William and having her family had not changed anything – she still existed in Rick's future!

Then the reality of the situation hit her.

She still existed for now...

Unless he succeeded in killing the Queen...

She stared at Rick across the barrel of a gun – a gun made to a 21st century design which he was planning to use to kill Queen Elizabeth.

And he seemed to have no qualms about using it. She looked over at Juno.

Her faithful companion of ten years was lying on the ground completely still, except for the tiniest flaring of a nostril and an almost imperceptible rise and fall in the chest.

Suddenly Mary knew that there was nothing more important right now, not even having her own existence confirmed, than to comfort her dearest friend. Ignoring the gun, she ran to Juno's side and lay down beside the horse's head, then stroked the soft, velvety muzzle.

"There old girl, there, it will be alright…"

There was a flicker in the dark liquid eye and it fixed on hers.

"There, there, shh, my sweet," she said, and suddenly all she could see was that first day when Juno had been presented to her by Lady de Beauvais, William's mother, with a stern warning that this feisty young mare would be too much for a girl like Justine to handle… But she and Juno had bonded immediately; a pairing that had lasted ten years, until Juno was her stately 'old girl' and she was the matronly Lady Mary de Beauvais herself… Ten years of friendship and understanding that this monster of a man with his dreadful home-made gun had ended with a single shot…

'There, there, old girl," she whispered. "We will soon get you home and have you tucked up in your stable with a nice warm blanket and some of the oats you love…"

But the eye that looked into hers started to cloud over, until it became completely opaque, and the nostril stopped flaring, and the chest was still…

Then, in a sudden moment, her mood turned to anger.

Mary stood up and faced the Alchemist, ignoring the gun that was still pointing at her.

The elation of a few minutes ago had disappeared like morning mist.

"You filthy little man," she snarled. "You filthy, evil, monster of a man. I will make sure you pay for this…"

"Brave words, Justine, or should I say 'Lady Mary'?" He paused. "You really must tell me your story some day." He briefly waved the barrel of the gun towards the path. "Only it will have to wait, because right now I need your undercover lover-boy here to tie up his horse, then join you."

He turned and pointed the gun unwaveringly at Tom.

There was a moment while Tom tied his horse to a sturdy tree, then he appeared beside Mary. They exchanged a quick glance, and Tom gave her a grim look that seemed to say, 'Play along with this and we'll find a way out.' He took and held her hand, giving it a small squeeze.

"Now," continued the Alchemist, "walk down this path side by side, and I will walk behind you with my gun so I can stop either of you trying to run. And as you have seen from the old nag just now, this gun works." He chuckled. "Touching scene back there, by the way, 'Lady Mary'. Remind me to put you up for an Oscar. You almost had me there." Again, he chuckled. "But the fact is, I have you both, and I have you covered. At this close range,

I could blow your heads off your shoulders – so do not try anything silly. Now walk."

---0---

As they walked back down the path, Mary could see that there wasn't any real opportunity to run. If either of them tried to make a break for it, she had no doubt that the Alchemist would shoot them immediately – and she was not prepared to take the risk for Tom or for herself. So she held on to his hand and walked slowly down the path. She also took extra care stepping over roots and fallen branches, in case she inadvertently tripped. She did not want to give the Alchemist cause to think she was about to try something 'silly'.

It was not long before they were once again outside the cottage door.

"Open it," the Alchemist ordered. Mary pushed it open and they all went in.

As Mary's eyes grew used to the gloom, she could see that Ursula was tending to the fire, while an old man that she assumed must be Ursula's father was at the table skinning a rabbit. They both looked up as Mary and Tom walked in, then Ursula gave a small cry when the Alchemist walked in behind them holding his gun.

"Hello again, Ursula," the Alchemist said cheerfully. "I found these two on the path, and I thought I would bring them here for safe keeping." He waved the barrel of the gun towards the corner where his blanket still lay. "All of you, get in that corner and sit with your backs to the wall."

Reluctantly they complied, except Walter, who stayed by the table. "You," he growled, "leave my dwelling now."

"I said sit!" barked the Alchemist and pointed the gun at the old man! With a scowl, Walter went over to the corner and sat. "Now," said the Alchemist when they were all in a row, looking up at him. "There's a few things I need to do first. But then I will be gone, and will leave you all... resting in peace."

Mary felt her blood turn to ice. "So you're going to shoot us all?" she muttered.

The Alchemist shook his head. "Certainly not. I only made a few cartridges, and I'm hardly going to waste four of them on you lot."

"So what do you want with us?" asked Tom.

"I am heading up north, to finish the job that you asked me to do, Master Cobham," replied the Alchemist. "Even if you are no longer willing to see it through, I find it suits my own plans to finish it. So I will need the horse which you so conveniently left for me on the path, together with some food and some drink for the journey." He took the sacking bag off his shoulder and grabbed the rabbit, some knives, a pot, a costrel for carrying drink and

Walter's slingshot, and threw them in. Still pointing the gun at them, he stood in the middle of the room by the fire.

"I must bid you all farewell," he said. "I doubt we will meet again."

"What you are doing is so wrong!" cried Mary. "Have you no thought for the future?"

"What fucking future, Justine?" he replied with a sneer. "The future that you and I know – the one that has not actually happened yet? Well, now it probably never will. Do you know what? The only fucking place it actually exists is as memories in your head and mine. And the truth is, I do not particularly care about it, and shortly, neither will you."

"You are a monster!"

"Sure, but soon I will be a rich monster, and a hero." The Alchemist kicked the pot away from the fire. "Pity you will not be around to see it."

Then as Mary watched in horror, he took another kick at the grate itself. It flew across the room, scattering burning embers as it went. One ember landed at the foot of the table, and the dry wood caught quickly. Soon flames were licking up the table leg.

The Alchemist waited until the flames reached the table-top, then he grabbed a blanket from Ursula's truckle bed and held it to the flames. When it too was alight, he tossed it back onto the bed, spreading the fire to the other side of the cottage.

Walter stood up, his face red with anger. "What do you think you are doing, you filthy cur?" he yelled. The Alchemist pointed the gun squarely at him. "Be seated again, old man, or I will kill you!"

"I am as like to die anyway!" yelled Walter, and Mary saw him start to run at the Alchemist and his gun.

Immediately there was a cracking sound and a puff of red smoke burst out of Walter's back.

She saw the Alchemist smile as the old man dropped to his knees, then fell forward face-first onto the floor, and was still.

Ursula screamed, and Tom started to get up, but the Alchemist had reloaded the gun and was pointing it at them, snarling, "I do not want to use any more bullets, but I will if I have to."

Tom sank back, his face contorted with rage. Mary leaned across and put her arm round Ursula. The girl buried her face in Mary's shoulder, and Mary felt her whole body shake as she sobbed.

"Right. I am off now," said the Alchemist. He backed to the door, grabbed the key off the hook and let himself out. The last thing Mary saw was the barrel of the gun disappearing through the door as it closed.

Just then the other truckle bed caught fire with a whoosh of sparks. The whole cottage was now burning.

"We have to get out!" yelled Mary.

Tom ran around the burning furniture and over to the door. He pulled and pushed on the handle, but the door remained resolutely closed. He turned back to Mary and Ursula.

"He has locked it!" he yelled over the roar of flames. "We are trapped!"

CHAPTER SIXTEEN

The Strand, London

Olivia Melrose put down her sewing and stood up, smoothing her skirts and patting her hair in place.

"Lady Burnham wants to see us now?" she asked.

The elderly steward nodded. "Yes, Mistress Melrose. She has asked for you and Mistress Tyndall to attend on her presently."

Olivia glanced at Maggie Tyndall. The other girl laughed nervously. "What can she want, do you think?"

"I know not, Maggie," Olivia said. "It is unlike Lady Burnham to call us back so soon after we were dismissed for the afternoon." She walked to the door and nodded her thanks to the steward, who was now holding it open. "But I am sure she has her reasons. Come."

Maggie Tyndall also stood up. Her friend was a small, blonde-haired girl of eighteen with bright blue eyes that seemed too large for her face, but which Olivia knew could have a mischievous twinkle in them that men found irresistible.

The two girls made their way to their mistress's presence chamber and pushed open the door. Lady Burnham was seated in her usual high-backed chair by the fire. A man was standing beside her with his back to them. Olivia thought there was something vaguely familiar about the shape of the hair under his cap, but she dismissed the thought. No doubt all would be explained shortly.

"You asked to see us again, my lady?" she said, after both had given a low curtsey.

"Yes, Olivia, I did." Lady Burnham gave one of her frosty smiles. "I have some news for you both that I think will delight you."

Olivia glanced once more at the man, and wondered why he remained turned away. There was definitely something familiar about him, and now it was starting to make her feel a little uneasy. Lady Burnham continued, "Yes,

I have some wonderful news." Again she gave a smile. "I have been asked to accompany Her Majesty the Queen on her forthcoming progress in the North, and I have decided to take the two of you to attend on me."

Maggie made a small jump. "Oh, my lady! We are to go on progress with the Queen?"

"Yes, dear, you are. I have chosen you both as I believe you have shown me good service." She looked pointedly at Olivia. "Even though you have been with me for only two weeks, Mistress Melrose, I have seen much good in you. You have a wise head on those young shoulders." She paused. "I believe you will be fine ambassadors for my household in the royal presence."

"Ohh, how wonderful, my lady!" squeaked Maggie. "Are we to meet the Queen?"

"Indeed you will, which is why I have asked this gentleman here to school the two of you on royal protocol. He is with the Queen's staff and will accompany us on the progress."

The man turned round slowly and smiled at Olivia.

Suddenly the room seemed to spin and she clutched at Maggie's arm for support.

Lionel Shelton!

She stared in shock as he came up to her. "Hello, Mistress Melrose," he said. "It has been a while since we last met."

Olivia did not answer; she could think of nothing to say.

"Come," barked Shelton, *"and submit!"*

"I wouldst not, Master Shelton! Please no! Do not raise your hand to me again! I beg you!"

"You are a wayward child, that I would teach some manners now!"

"I beg you, no!"

"You already know Master Shelton?" demanded Lady Burnham, glancing suspiciously at each of them.

"Indeed, my lady," Shelton answered easily with a sly grin, removing his cap and bowing to the girls. "Mistress Melrose and I met by chance on a snowy night some weeks ago in the little village of Hammersmith. We passed a most pleasant evening in the bar of a tavern, as I recall."

Olivia continued to stare at the man, still unable to find any words.

"No, Master Shelton, no! By Heaven, do not strike me again!"

"Then do not make me, you wilful girl! Submit now and it will be better for you!"

"Master Shelton has said he has already made your acquaintance, Olivia," said Lady Burnham with a small sniff of displeasure. "Please do him the courtesy of an acknowledgement."

Olivia took a deep breath. She knew what she had to say – '*Indeed, Master Shelton, how nice to see you again…*', but how could she trust herself not to blurt out – '*How dare you come into my presence once again, you filthy monster?*'

She took another deep breath. "Indeed, Master Shelton," she whispered, "how nice to see you again."

"Good." Lady Burnham nodded, seeming oblivious to Olivia's inner distress. "We are to join the Queen's entourage at Greenwich in three days. Until then you will be in Master Shelton's charge; he will school you on how to behave at Court and in the presence of the Queen." She waved her hand in casual dismissal. "Schooling will begin in the morning. Meanwhile, you are free to your own activities until supper."

Olivia and Maggie curtseyed, then walked out of the room.

Lionel Shelton!

As Olivia followed Maggie down the endless corridors back to their rooms, it seemed like the wood-panelled walls were closing in on her, crushing the air out of her body and stopping her from breathing.

Lionel blasted Shelton!

When they eventually reached the sanctuary of their room, Olivia could do nothing except sink down onto the bed and lie immobile, staring up at the ceiling. Maggie, however, was like an excited kitten, unable to keep still for even a moment.

"We are to see the Queen!" she cried. "Oh my, whatever shall I wear at Court?" She threw open her clothes chest and started taking out garments. "I will need new gowns and shoes, of course – these old things will never do…" She stopped a moment. "I shall have to ask Master Shelton what is worn at Court! He will know." Then she jumped onto the bed and leaned over Olivia, her face suddenly filling Olivia's entire field of vision. "I say, Livvy, that Master Shelton is quite a catch, is he not? Quite the handsome man." She frowned. "His eyes, were they blue or grey?" She shook her head. "No matter – I shall observe them most carefully next time we meet." She looked up. "I liked his beard though – well cut and trim. I wonder if he has a wife already? I might make a play for him, Livvy. You do not mind, do you?" She moved closer, so a tendril of her hair hung down by Olivia's nose. "You mind not, do you Livvy dearest, if I make a play for him? You know him already – from some snowy evening – you have no designs on him yourself?" She paused expectantly. "Do you, Livvy? Livvy?

Lionel Shelton! Dear God, no!

It seemed to Olivia at that moment that it was not Maggie Tyndall above her, but now it was Lady Mary, grabbing her shoulders and staring fiercely down at her, saying once again the words spoken so passionately in Hammersmith.

"My dear sweet child, you must never, never, ever, blame yourself for the actions of a man – do you hear me? It is never a girl's fault if a man decides to act like a coward and a beast. If Lionel Shelton forced himself upon you, then it is for his conscience, not yours, to answer for it."

Then it was Maggie once again, looking at her expectantly, waiting for an answer.

"What was that, Maggie?" she muttered.

Maggie squeaked in exasperation. "Oh, Livvy, you have not listened to a word I have said! I am thinking to make a play for Master Shelton. I think his beard is most becoming, and his grey eyes – or perhaps they are blue, I shall have to check – are quite piercing. I asked if you were of a mind to make a play for him yourself."

Olivia stared up at the girl's face.

Such a pretty face.

So how would it look if Shelton punched it as hard as he had punched hers?

Olivia shuddered. Would it change Maggie's bright, innocent personality as much as it had hers, if Shelton also dragged her across the floor, threw her down on the bed, and… and…

That was not going to happen.

"Maggie," she said firmly, "Master Shelton is here to coach us on royal protocol. He is not, I am sure, seeking a wife. I would advise you most strongly to end these silly thoughts of romance, and concentrate on learning how best to behave at Court."

Maggie climbed slowly off the bed and looked down at Olivia.

"And you are not saying this because you want him for yourself? she whispered. "Because you have met him before, drinking in some tavern?"

Olivia stood up and held Maggie's face in her hands. "Maggie Tyndall," she said, "I love you as my best friend in all the world, so please believe me when I say I have no interest in this Lionel Shelton. None whatsoever. And believe me also when I tell you that I know this man, and I know he will not make a good husband – for you, for me, or for any girl." She moved her hands down to Maggie's shoulders. "So let us do no more than learn from Master Shelton how we should behave at Court; let us conduct ourselves properly as befits our station, and let us put aside any thought of romance with him."

There was a long silence as Maggie digested this, then eventually she nodded. "Marry, Livvy, I see you are most sincere in this, so I suppose I must take your advice on the matter."

"Good. Now, let us get dressed for supper, and tomorrow we shall learn how best to attend my lady at Court."

---0---

"When the Queen enters a room, you are to sink to a curtesy – and you must be sure never to raise your head to a level that is higher than hers – although," Lionel Shelton paused and studied both girls, "I doubt either of you is taller than Her Majesty anyway."

"Are we allowed in her presence chamber?" asked Maggie.

"Aye, the Queen likes to have many people around her at all times."

"How exciting!" Maggie breathed. "And what if she speaks to you?"

"You address her as 'Your Grace' and you answer her question succinctly and truthfully."

It was the following morning and the three of them were gathered in the long gallery, bathed in the sunlight that flooded in from the diamond-paned leaded windows overlooking the Thames, making rippling patterns on the opposite wall as the light reflected off the water.

Maggie and Olivia had finished their duties with Lady Burnham after breaking fast, before making their way to meet Shelton in the gallery. Olivia had done all she could to delay the start of the meeting; lingering at breakfast, deciding to change her sleeves, then her shoes, until Maggie could no longer contain her impatience and had dragged Olivia into the room where Shelton was pacing up and down. After pleasantries between Maggie and Shelton, the session had begun, and now it was in full swing.

"And what about the Queen's courtiers?" asked Olivia. "How are we to behave if we meet them?"

"A fine question, Olivia." Shelton gave a slow smile. "I know how like you are to turn a man's head, so…"

"I have learned where such behaviour leads, believe me Master Shelton," Olivia cut in. "And I am not the same girl that I was. Now please, answer my question."

Shelton pursed his lips. "I would say that if you meet one such as The Earl of Leicester or Sir Christopher Hatton, you should be polite and ladylike – and aware of courtly manners."

"What are those?" asked Maggie.

"Such that they may well pay you compliments, or profess love, but such wooing is all part of the game at Court – you are not to act as if it were real."

"Oh." Maggie considered this carefully. "But what if it really were real? What if they really were wooing you? How would you know the difference?"

"It would not be real, believe me," said Shelton. "For the Queen does not approve of her courtiers having romances."

"Then why do they do it, if it is not really real?" asked Maggie, with a frown.

"Because it is how the Court works," he answered. "Compliments and poetry and courtly love are what makes the whole system function. Especially," he added, "in relation to Her Majesty herself."

"But she has now said she is married to England, and will never take a husband," Olivia observed. "So what does it benefit the courtiers to profess love to her?"

"It is the game she likes to play – and she has them play along with her." He gave a small laugh. "And it trickles down to all the ladies at court."

"So how does it work, exactly?" asked Maggie. "Show us."

Shelton looked slowly at each of them in turn. "You would have me show you?"

Olivia shot a furious glance at Maggie, but it rebounded like an arrow off a shield. The girl was staring intently at Shelton, her lips parted and her eyes wide. Olivia heard her say under her breath, "Grey – I knew it."

Shelton walked over to Maggie and bowed. "Mistress Tyndall," he said quietly, taking both her hands in his, "may I say how radiant you look today, as lovely as a soft-petalled rose…" He brushed a stray lock of hair back over her ear. "Nay, for that is to do a disservice to your wondrous beauty for you are a thousand times more fair, my dearest Maggie…"

Maggie smiled sweetly and was about to answer, when Olivia cut in. "Such wooing would not fool a simple child, Master Shelton. Surely they do better than that?"

"Oh, but do go on, Master Shelton," breathed Maggie. Then she shot a stern look at Olivia, before turning back and whispering, "You were saying?"

"Master Shelton was giving you a valuable lesson in the shallow, meaningless tittle-tattle that passes for conversation at Court," snapped Olivia. "And you would do well to heed how shallow it is." She turned and stared out of the window at the boats making their way up, down and across the Thames, trying to control her ragged breathing. When she turned back, Maggie and Shelton were standing just apart, with a studied air of innocence on both their faces.

"You will continue the instruction of us both, Master Shelton," Olivia ordered, "so we may be fully prepared for our life at Court. The instruction will be here each day and," she added, with a furious look at both of them, "I need hardly say that outside of these sessions of instruction, we will not engage you in discourse of any kind. Do I make myself clear?"

---0---

It was two days later that the barge pulled slowly away from the Strand jetty, then made its way up the centre of the river.

Olivia sat quietly in the stern, looking out as the city passed by, watching the hundreds of other barges, wherries and sailing boats criss-cross the Thames. There was the occasional large ship amongst the crowd of smaller vessels, majestically making its way towards the port of London with just one or two sails unfurled; men lining the decks as the vessel slipped through the water. The river was a mass of sounds as well as movement; boatmen shouting for way as others came too close to their wherries, passengers greeting each other as they passed; pilots shouting the depth as they manoeuvred their barges towards the dock – and all accompanied for Olivia by the rhythmic splash of oars from Lady Burnham's rowers.

Olivia glanced back over her shoulder. The house she had called home these last couple of weeks had blended into the mass of buildings along the bank and could no longer be picked out. She turned forward again and looked along the length of the boat. Lady Burnham was close by, seated under the canopy to protect her from the sun and keep her complexion pale – staring down her nose at the rowers, just as one could imagine the Queen might do. Maggie was sitting up at the front of the boat, talking to Shelton and smiling most inappropriately at him.

Olivia frowned. God knew well enough that she had tried her hardest to keep them apart – but it seemed the more she tried to warn Maggie off the man, the more the silly girl seemed to want him. Olivia had therefore switched her tactic to one of total indifference to see if that worked, but it seemed that Maggie was drawn to Shelton like a moth to a flame, and continued to behave in a way that was guaranteed to get the man's interest.

Not that there had been much time when the two of them could have been alone. It had been a frantic few days since Lady Burnham's announcement. There had been Shelton's sessions of instruction – which Olivia got through by concentrating fiercely on the information he was providing and trying to ignore her rising bile every time she looked at the man. Then there were clothes to be selected, trunks to be packed, and Lady Burnham's own travelling wardrobe to be managed. So the time had passed quickly, and now they were on their way to Greenwich to join the Court as it set off to begin the summer progress.

What would Court be like? Shelton had made it sound most strange; a constructed society where false flattery was required in public – especially towards the Queen – but in private the conversation was mainly tittle-tattle and idle gossip. The Olivia of a few weeks ago would have revelled in such artifice – indeed that would have been her natural style – but the Olivia who had suffered at the hand of Shelton was altogether different. Since that dreadful night when she had lost her innocence – no, when he had forced it away from her with unspeakable violence – she had left her childhood pleasures behind, and entered reluctantly into the adult world. But it was not just Shelton's attack that had been responsible – that had only been the start of her transition. In truth, it had been Lady Mary's unexpected kindness that had completed the journey. To have been so caring and understanding, even after Olivia had been as manipulative as she had been on the way to Hammersmith, showed Olivia that other adult behaviour could be kind, selfless and confidence-building. Indeed, Lady Mary had been very clear with her strange notion that a girl had the right not to have to submit automatically to a man.

But then, why should such a view be strange? Was there not a Queen on the throne? Perhaps things were going to change, as Lady Mary had said. Olivia prayed that one day girls would be able to own property in their own right, marry whoever they chose and take part in the government of the land, as Lady Mary had told her with such great confidence.

Lady Burnham leant back and fixed Olivia with a hard stare. "Master Shelton seems remarkably familiar with Mistress Tyndall," she observed. "I would you take the girl aside and tell her not to lead him on in this way."

"I have seen this also, Lady Burnham," answered Olivia, "and I have told her she must be more considered in her behaviour."

"Well, she has either not heard your wise words, or she has rashly chosen to ignore them."

They both viewed the flirting going on at the front of the boat.

"If he decides to act on her inappropriate ways," said Lady Burnham, "then she must accept the consequences. And I do not feel she is suitable marriage material for him, should it get that far."

"He could always restrain himself," muttered Olivia. She did not think she had said it loud enough to be heard, but the breeze must have carried the words to her mistress. "By the Lord's Wounds, Olivia," Lady Burnham exclaimed, her eyebrows almost disappearing under her hood, "what a strange notion!" She stared at the girl a moment. "He is a man – if he decides to act upon her flirtation and take it further, then that is his right – and she must accept that it is her own fault."

Olivia stayed silent, and Lady Burnham turned away.

Again, the image of Lady Mary came unbidden in front of her. "*You must never, never, ever, blame yourself for the actions of a man – do you hear me? It is never a girl's fault if a man decides to act like a coward and a beast.*"

Olivia nodded to herself.

One day, Lionel Shelton, you will pay for your actions that night.

Not long after, they rounded a bend and Olivia caught sight of the royal palace at Greenwich, its magnificent brick towers and chimneys rising above the surrounding trees.

The barge drew up alongside a set of stone steps that descended into the river in the middle of a long waterside wall. A footman in the Queen's livery took hold of the gangplank, then folded it back so that it rested on a step. Shelton jumped down first, then held out his hand to help Lady Burnham off the barge and up the steps. Then he came back for Maggie, and escorted her off as well.

Olivia waited as he turned back and held out his hand to help her down.

"I am perfectly capable of stepping ashore, Master Shelton," she growled.

He shrugged his shoulders without a word, then went over to Lady Burnham and made an exaggerated show of offering her his arm. Together with Maggie they started out towards the palace.

Olivia stepped carefully off the boat and followed them up the path.

CHAPTER SEVENTEEN

The fire was now raging out of control, and there was no way out.

Mary, Tom and Ursula moved ever closer together, until they were huddled in the centre of the cottage, each staring out at the advancing flames.

Tom unsheathed his sword and poked it at the timbers and rushes that blazed around them, pushing them back to try and create a break in the fire. Mary could see that this would only delay the inevitable, as she found herself coughing uncontrollably.

"The smoke!" she gasped. "It is the smoke that kills! We must cover our faces!"

Ursula ripped off a piece of her skirt and tore it into three strips. They each bound the material as masks around their faces, which made breathing a bit easier.

Then Tom turned to Mary. "I would not die from burns or smoke," he said, his eyes narrowed above the mask. "It is not how I choose to go and meet my maker." He put the tip of the sword up to his ribs. "I must end it shortly, then you can do the same."

Mary looked at the shining blade, flashing with orange in the light of the fire.

Was this it?

Justine Parker, the time-travelling adventurer who survived drowning in a well, married a knight, had three kids and – and what?

She pushes a sword into her own heart because there's no hope?

And then what?

She had been so frightened of suddenly disappearing because she had changed history – that she hadn't particularly thought about what would happen if she died anyway.

Rick would have won – that was for sure. He would assassinate the Queen. Then it would be as she had originally feared. The future – her future, the one with cars and phones and planes and TVs that existed only in her memory – might now be very different.

Mary looked up.

Would it disappear, just as that smoke disappeared through the hole in the roof?

If it were not for that hole drawing the smoke and heat upwards to escape into the air, they would surely have been consumed already.

The hole in the roof!

"Tom, quick!" she screamed, pointing up at the hole. "Lift me up!"

Tom looked up and understood immediately. He re-sheathed his sword and yelled to Ursula, "Help me!" Together they grabbed Mary's legs below the knee and lifted her bodily up to the roof in one swift movement. Mary grabbed at the shingles surrounding the hole, then screamed as the heat in the smouldering wood scorched her hands.

Tom and Ursula brought her back down quickly.

"Too hot to hold!" she shouted. Tom and Ursula both took the masks from their faces. Mary wrapped them round her hands and held her arms up ready. Again they lifted her up, and this time she was able to hold on to the shingles. With her arms in agony as she hauled up her full weight, she was able to get her head, then her upper body through the hole. Gasping for breath in the clearer air, she wriggled and squirmed until she was out of the hole and rolling helplessly down the shingles and falling in an ungainly heap by the front door.

The Alchemist had left the key in the lock.

Quickly she turned the key and pushed the door open. A wave of heat and flames blew out, catching her in the face and sending her staggering backwards onto the earth. She struggled to her feet, her breath coming in gasps as she ran back to the door. Inside she could see Tom and Ursula, their faces blackened and their eyes staring. Fierce flames burned between them and the door, making their escape seem impossible.

There was a loud cracking sound over the roar of the flames.

The roof was starting to collapse.

A large burning beam began to fall. Tom leapt out of its way, but Ursula was not so lucky. Mary saw it catch her legs and knock her to the ground, then it fell on top of her and pinned her down across the waist.

Quickly the flames transferred to her clothes and within seconds her skirts were alight.

Tom started trying to lift the beam off her, but it was clear it was too heavy.

Then Ursula yelled something Mary couldn't hear to Tom. He shook his head and tried again to lift the beam. Ursula shouted again and again, but he continued to shake his head and kept trying to free her.

Mary could see that it was a matter of seconds before flames would reach Tom and she screamed "Tom!" at the top of her voice. Then Ursula screamed at him as well. It sounded like, "Please!"

Tom glanced at the flames that were starting to lick at his feet, and made one more attempt to move the beam.

Ursula screamed again, and finally Tom stood up. He stared a moment at Ursula, then at the flames between him and the door. He said something to her, briefly touched her cheek, then ran through the flames towards the door.

He emerged into the open, smoke-blackened and wide-eyed, gasping for air.

As he and Mary watched, another beam started to break away from the roof, and it seemed to Mary it was coming away directly above Ursula. For a moment it hung above the unfortunate girl, but she was trapped like a fly pinned to a board and could not roll away.

Then it started to move again.

As Ursula struggled and Mary screamed, it fell.

At first it seemed to fall in slow motion, then it increased its speed and came down with sickening inevitability.

There was nothing Ursula could do – she did not stand a chance.

It fell with all its weight and a dreadful crash that could clearly be heard over the flames, directly onto her head.

There was a single convulsive spasm, then no further movement in her body.

After that, it seemed that everything happened very fast. The rest of the roof collapsed with a sound like thunder and a whoosh of sparks. The whole cottage was now alight, with heat so intense that Mary and Tom were pushed back, able only to stare helplessly in silence as the fire quickly consumed what was left of the little building. Then it died down almost as quickly, once everything that could burn was finally consumed. Mary was reminded of a modern-day cooker being turned off.

Tom turned to Mary, his face black except for two tear lines down his face. "No more than a few minutes," he muttered, "since that man kicked over the grate." He shook his head. "No more than that to destroy a cottage and kill a good woman."

"And her father."

"Aye." Tom nodded. "And him too." He was silent a moment. "At least it was quick for her. She would have known very little when that second beam took her life."

Mary put her hand on his arm. "What did she say to you?" she asked quietly.

He turned slowly away from the fire and stared at her. Fresh tears rolled down his cheeks.

"She said…" he stopped, his mouth working. "That I must not save her, she wanted to die."

"But why?"

He took a deep breath. "Because she said she was not worthy to live after what she had done." Mary stayed silent, letting him find the words in his own time. Eventually he said, "Because she had lain with that man. She could not suffer herself to live, knowing what sort of a man he was."

"She had lain with him?"

He nodded. "She said that. She begged me not to try and save her, but to save myself." He stared at the cottage, now a blackened and twisted hulk with small fires still burning here and there, then turned back to Mary. "I would have saved her, as God is my witness – I would have done. I would have moved that beam if I had had just a little more time…"

Mary gently brushed away another tear as it ran down his cheek. "I know, Tom. I know."

"She was a good woman." He gave her a watery smile. "She was honest and true. She did not deserve to die."

"She did not."

Tom suddenly grasped her hand. "We must stop that man, the Alchemist," he said. "We must find him and turn him in to Wychwoode. He cannot succeed in this plot." Tom gestured at the smouldering cottage, "and he must be made to pay for what he has done." He nodded, as if to himself. "He is not too far ahead; we must track behind him, unseen and unknown, until we can find a way to capture him." He nodded again. "The sooner we send him to Hell where he belongs, the better."

"I would we wait until the fire is totally out, so we can get to the bodies of Ursula and Walter," said Mary. "They should be taken out of that place and buried with dignity."

"Aye," he answered, "they should. The flames may have died down, but it will take many hours – days even – before it is safe to enter, and we cannot let the Alchemist have such a start on us."

Mary turned sharply to stare at him. "You would leave them there unburied?"

"If it means we have a better chance of catching the man who did this to them, and bringing him to justice, then yes." He looked steadily back at her. "If that is acceptable?"

"Yes, I suppose you are right." Mary stood up. "Then we had better start now, had we not?"

He stood also. "Good. We will go to where I left my horse."

They started walking along the path towards the forest. Mary stopped by the body of Juno, still lying where she had fallen earlier. "Wait," she said, then knelt beside the horse's head and stroked the soft cheek and velvet muzzle, still slightly warm. "Goodbye old girl," she whispered. "Rest in peace, my lovely." Then she put her head onto Juno's neck and lay a moment staring up at the mare's ear, as if she expected it to twitch like it used to. But it stayed resolutely still.

She felt Tom's hand on her shoulder.

"Come, Lady Mary," he said quietly, "we should keep moving."

But with a sudden sob, Mary knew she could not leave Juno, and clung even more tightly to her horse for a few minutes more, feeling the hot tears roll down her face and dissolve into the soft brown coat.

When she finally let go and stood up, Tom was waiting patiently a few feet away.

She nodded, acknowledging that he had left her alone to mourn her friend, and dried her tears on her sleeve. "Thank you," she added, as she walked past him and into the forest, although she could not stop herself continually looking back, until the still brown body had finally disappeared behind the trees.

Tom trotted after her, and together they walked to where he had left his horse. As expected, it had gone.

"Look." He pointed down and she could see the hoof tracks in the soft earth of the path, heading away from them.

Mary was about to march on, when a terrible thought came into her head.

"What if he is waiting for us again with his sniper musket?" she asked, shivering despite the warm air filtering through the trees.

"Surely not," answered Tom. "He will want to be as far away as possible from the fire, now he is on his horse – or rather, on my horse. And besides," he chuckled, "he thinks we are both dead."

They walked further into the forest. Occasionally Tom would stop and study signs on the path or on the trees close by. Mary didn't know what he was seeing that helped him track Rick, but once or twice he darted into the undergrowth to study something Mary couldn't see, then he nodded to himself, and headed on back onto the path.

They were walking on in silence after one such time, when Tom said, "Can I ask you something?"

"For sure," she replied.

He stopped and looked hard at her. "Why did that man the Alchemist call you a different name? What was it; Justine or somesuch?" He narrowed his eyes. "And just before he started the fire, he said something about the future being but a memory for you both. What did he mean by that?" He looked up at the trees around him, as if he was seeking inspiration from their branches and leaves. "What exactly is your connection to the Alchemist, Lady Mary?"

Mary studied her hands, still wrapped in the rough strips of cloth from Ursula's skirts, and realised just how much the burns were hurting. But that was nothing to the painful consequences if she gave the wrong answer to this question. Clearly, the truth was not an option – however much Tom wanted to help her, the risk that he would abandon her or hand her in to a witchfinder if she tried to explain she was a time-traveller, was too great.

"Tom," she said, taking his hands in both of hers and trying not to wince with the pain. "There is indeed some history between me and Rick." He raised a blackened eyebrow and she quickly added, "I always said I was trying to find him to ask him questions." She searched his eyes but he was giving nothing away. "But there is nothing sinister in it, and that is God's honest truth." He stayed silent for so long that she felt compelled to continue, "I swear I will tell you when this is over, but until then I want you to trust me that I am on your side and the Queen's – and I want that man to stop the task you set him, and to pay for what he is done." She gestured back down the path. "I had Juno from when she was not much more than a foal – and more than anything she was my friend. He killed her, and he killed Ursula and Walter." She let go of his hands and stood back. "And for that I want to make him pay."

"There is nothing sinister?" he said eventually. "You swear on your oath?" She nodded. "I swear."

He was silent again for what seemed an uncomfortably long time. "Then I will trust you on this, because I know you are an honest woman, and I respect you greatly." He nodded. "And when this matter is over, I want you to respect me too, and tell me all."

"I will."

"Good." He smiled. "And let us find a stream to wash ourselves quickly and clean your burned hands, for I am tired of being blackened with soot on my skin and my clothes, and I see from the pain in your face that your hands are raw under those rags."

---0---

Eventually they came across a stream. It was about ten feet wide, with clear water running over clean rocks and stones. Mary thought it looked three or four feet deep, which was perfect. She suddenly felt very dirty, and had to fight the urge to throw off her filthy clothes and jump straight in. But first Tom made her kneel on the bank and dangle her bare hands in the cool water, which made the pain in them subside to a dull throb.

He made her keep them there for what seemed like ages, then he took them out of the water and examined them.

"They are still red and raw," he said. He studied them further, then added, "You will need to bind them with a poultice of goose or pig fat, but for now this needs must suffice." Still holding her hands he looked up into her eyes. "So, Mary, how does it?"

"I will live," she answered. "I can manage."

"Good." He let go of her hands and stepped back, still staring into her eyes. "Now I must undress and wash my body and my clothing in the stream." There was a silence, then he added, with a raised eyebrow, "I will be fully unclothed, Lady de Beauvais..."

Mary forced her gaze away from the bright eyes in his blackened face.

"Yes," she muttered. "Unclothed. We cannot be seen together in such a state." She gave a small smile. "I will bathe elsewhere…" She backed away, then followed the stream round a bend to the other side of a thick bramble hedge. There she undressed fully, before taking her torn and tattered gown down to the water and using a rock to scrub the soot out of it.

As she scrubbed, the downstream water ran black, as the dirt and smoke washed out and splashed away across the stones. But just as she thought it was nearly clean, she noticed that the water upstream was black as well, and she wondered for a moment how the dirt could travel the wrong way… Then she realised she must be getting the soot from Tom's washing coming downstream, so after pulling out her gown and laying it on the bank to dry, she peered round the brambles to see if he had finished.

There was no sign of Tom upstream, just his clothes also laid out on the bank to dry, and the winter sun glinting off the surface of the water. She could see both banks and the trees in the distance, but Tom had disappeared.

With a gasp, she started to splash her way towards the spot where his clothes were. Maybe he had drowned? Or someone had taken him while she had been washing her gown…

She was nearly at the spot, when there was a sudden eruption of water that sent her staggering back, and Tom emerged like Neptune from the deep, water flying off him as he stood up and shook his head, his well-shaped body shining in the sunlight as if it had been carved from oiled teak.

Mary stopped transfixed at the sight of his muscled chest and defined abdomen, with its dark streak of hair running down his stomach towards the thick curls of his…

Mary gasped again, and Tom opened his eyes.

At first, they fixed on hers. Then she felt her blood run cold as they moved slowly down, stopping on her breasts, before moving lower to fix on the base of her own belly.

Mary knew she had to move; to turn and wade back round the brambles and out of his sight, but her legs seemed unable to respond, and for what seemed like several minutes they both remained still, like two naked statues facing each other; silent, unmoving.

Then Tom waded forward until he was close enough to touch her. Slowly he reached out and stroked his hand down her cheek.

Mary knew she had to stop this now before it went too far, but instead she found herself leaning in towards his hand as it travelled down to her neck, trapping it briefly onto her shoulder, before it moved softly down over her collar bone and onto the top of her breast.

She heard someone moan gently, then realised it was actually her, as his hand slid down over her breast and cupped it.

Then he came in closer till their bodies were almost touching.

He moved nearer still, and she gasped as they pressed together, his hot skin burning her belly and her breasts as if they were on fire.

His hand moved off her chest and round her back, then down to her bottom, and his mouth closed on hers, his tongue finding hers and caressing it, playing with it, loving it.

She closed her eyes, as again she heard the moan.

As her eyes closed, she saw William.

He was smiling at her as he held out his hand to lead her to the altar in the wedding chapel all those years ago. Then the chapel faded, and now William was in Ruth's cottage, as they lay together in the little bed. Now he was smiling with pride as she handed Ambrose to him, gazing with adoration into the baby's wide blue eyes…

Mary jumped back and out of Tom's grasp.

She realised she was breathing deeply, as if she had just run a marathon.

"Nay Tom," she panted, "this is not seemly. I would not do this."

He said nothing for a long time. Eventually he nodded and stepped back. "Sir William is a fortunate man," he said. "I must respect your will in this, though I like it not."

"Thank you Tom," she answered. "That is the honourable thing."

"Hmm," he agreed, then turned and made his way to the bank, before lifting himself out of the stream and returning to his clothes.

He dressed quickly while she was still wading back to her clothes, then strode off through the forest. Mary struggled quickly into her wet, clingy gown and set off after him as fast as she could, while trying not to trip over roots or turn her ankle in a muddy hole.

Finally she caught up and came level with him, panting hard.

He was striding purposefully along the path, staring straight ahead and no longer searching for hoof prints or other tell-tale signs of Rick's passing. When she asked why not, he just grunted, then muttered something about knowing where the Alchemist was heading anyway. Then he increased his pace so she had to keep running just to stay with him.

Suddenly she had enough.

She stopped abruptly in the path, planted her feet and put her hands on her hips, and waited for him to notice she was no longer there.

Unfortunately, he either did not notice, or chose not to, so she was forced to shout out after him.

"Tom!"

The call echoed around the still forest, bouncing off the tall elms and sycamores; putting up a couple of noisy rooks.

He stopped and turned, then strode back to her with a look of thunder.

"Hush your noise, woman!" he hissed. "What if that murderous friend of yours is near? We would not let him know we still live!"

"Then do not run off and leave me, so I must call your name!" she hissed back. "And anyway, you said he would be miles ahead on his horse…" She thought a moment, "…your horse."

"Aye, but there is a risk he is near, and your calling could be heard in Oxford. Indeed, I have not heard any person shout so loud as you in all my days." He regarded her a moment. "That is some power you have in your chest, Lady Mary."

He turned away and started walking again, so she called out – more softly this time – "Wait!"

He stopped again, this time with his back to her.

"Listen, Thomas Cobham," she ordered, advancing right up behind him and hissing into his ear. "In case you have forgotten, we are following this man so we can stop him trying to kill the Queen, and to make him pay for the killing of Juno, Ursula and Walter." He didn't move. "I am a married woman, Tom," she whispered, "and would not cuckold my husband." She saw him stiffen his shoulders. "So I suggest you stop behaving like a spoiled little boy, and start behaving like a man, because we need to get this Alchemist, and we are not going to do that by behaving like children."

He turned slowly round to face her.

"Hmm," he said slowly. "Then as a man, I suggest we make all haste to the next town, which is Henley-in-Arden. There we can eat, sleep, change our clothing and avail ourselves of a couple of horses so we can make good speed up north…"

---0---

It was only ten miles to Henley-in-Arden; a journey which should have taken them no more than a few hours. However, despite Tom's urgency, Mary found it impossible to make good speed. The forest path was hardly a path at all; more a rough track with frequent obstacles – so she was continually having to lift her heavy, sodden skirts and step over roots, as well as duck under low branches. There were also many thick muddy puddles that were covered in leafy plants and hard to make out, so she was constantly stopping to check the ground before committing herself to the next step.

There were a number of times when Tom, who seemed to have the sure-footedness of a gazelle, was striding so far ahead that she was fearful of losing him altogether. Each time she had to call out to him – not too loudly – so he would stop and wait for her to catch up.

At one point she came to a small fallen tree with a large puddle just in front of it, on a narrow section of the path. The trunk crossed the whole path and disappeared into thick gorse bushes on either side. There was no way round – so she would have to go over. She stopped and studied it carefully, trying to decide if she could get over in one leap, or if she was going to have to risk stepping in the puddle first, before clambering over. As she studied it, she decided that the puddle was just too wide, and the tree trunk too far in front, to be cleared in a single leap. She looked up and saw Tom making his confident way along the path many yards ahead. He must have got over this obstacle with ease.

"Wait!" she called.

She saw him stop and turn, then stand waiting. She picked up a piece of broken-off branch that was lying nearby and used it to test the depth of the puddle. It hit something hard without going too deep, so she decided to risk it.

Lifting her skirts, she put her right foot gingerly into the puddle, letting it down gently till she felt it hit the bottom. The water was cold and glutinous, and she let out a small involuntary yelp as it closed over the top of her shoe.

She looked up. Tom had moved back towards her, and was now watching as she carefully put her left foot in the puddle. This time there was no hard stop, and she felt her foot sink deep into the mud.

"Could'st not have jumped across, like a mountain goat?" he called.

She regarded him with her hardest stare. "Are you calling me a goat?"

"Not if you are stuck in that puddle." Then he laughed. "You look more like a heron, standing on one foot."

"You may have been able to leap about like a goat, but I have heavy skirts on, and smaller legs." She scowled at him. "Are you going to help me?"

"What, and miss the chance to see you fall flat upon your face in the mud?"

"Oh right!" she muttered to herself. "That is how it is going to be, is it?" She looked down at her feet, then up at the tree trunk. "I shall do this myself without your help, Master Thomas bloody Cobham."

She reached forward and put her hands on the trunk, lifting her right leg out of the puddle and positioning her knee up next to her hand. Then she rocked forward in order to get her left leg up.

It was stuck.

She rocked again. There was a gloopy, squelching noise, but it stayed stuck.

"Art now a tree frog, my lady?" he enquired politely.

She chose not to answer, but instead rocked again, pulling at her left foot with all her strength.

It came free with an even louder squelch. With a strangled yell she fell forward, landing in a sprawling, muddy heap on the other side.

She looked up to see Tom above her, laughing uncontrollably.

Without a word she stood up, smoothed down her skirts, tried to pat her hair into place, then walked on past him with her head held high.

Which would have been fine, had she not then tripped over a root and fallen forward, landing flat on her face with a most un-lady-like shriek.

She lay there a moment with her cheek in a puddle.

Damn! That was not supposed to happen.

She felt strong hands grab her under the armpits and lift her easily to her feet. He stood her in front of him.

"There, my lady," he said with a big smile. "Now I have seen you fall flat on your face in the mud. We can continue our journey."

She stared into his eyes. He had splashes of earth all down his cheeks and caking into his beard – although goodness knew what she must look like.

"You are a cruel, heartless man, Thomas Cobham," she said. It was meant as a bit of a light-hearted quip but he seemed to take it seriously. He shook his head, his laughter gone in an instant.

"Nay, Mary. I am not heartless," he said quietly. "Far from it. I have a heart, and it would be yours if it could be." He brushed some mud gently off her nose. "But it cannot be, I know that. I have accepted it." He put his finger to her lips. "Say naught, sweet Mary." Then he touched the same finger to his own lips. "For there is naught to be said."

---0---

By the time dusk fell, it seemed they were still no nearer to habitation.

"We must stop," muttered Mary, as she stumbled over a root. "It gets too dark to walk this path."

"Aye," he answered, "we will have to rest for the night. He looked around. "There is a small clearing there – let us use that."

Mary went into the clearing, swept the undergrowth for sticks and rocks, then sat down. She took out her costrel and shook it. There was hardly any water sloshing around at the bottom, so she finished what was left. "We need to find an inn soon or we will die of thirst," she said. Then there was a loud rumble under her grubby gown. "And hunger," she added.

"My need right now is to keep you warm," he said, busily gathering some twigs and building them up to a conical pyre in the middle of the clearing. Then he picked some dry grasses and pushed them in the base of the pyre, before getting two flinty stones and striking them together to make a spark.

One of the sparks caught on the grasses, and he blew gently on it, until it was firmly alight. Then he piled more grasses and twigs on, until there was a good fire going.

Mary felt in her pocket and caressed the smooth metal and plastic of the 21st century lighter that she carried with her at all times for safekeeping. How easy it would have been to take it out and use it to light the fire – and how many difficult questions would she have had to answer as a result? No, the lighter stayed firmly in her pocket as she stared across at Tom, his face flickering orange in the light of the flames.

"I was thinking how we might get to the Alchemist before he gets to the Queen," he said.

Mary smiled carefully. "You said earlier that you knew where he is going?"

"Aye." Tom took a stick and poked the fire to stir up the flames. "I believe he is planning to shoot at the Queen when she passes through York on her progress."

"This is what you would have asked John Tyler?"

"Aye, although I doubt he would have given this information freely." He poked at the fire again. "I have been giving this much consideration, and I believe York is the place."

She raised an enquiring eyebrow, and he continued, "Her Majesty plans to ride the streets, accompanied by her chief courtiers, such as the Earl of Leicester. There are some streets that are long enough and wide enough for crowds to line them, and there are tall houses in many places that overlook these streets." He regarded her with a half-smile. "We saw how terrible this sniper musket of his can be, with your poor horse…" he shook his head sadly, "so we know he can be many hundreds of yards away from the Queen and still fire upon her with deadly accuracy. I believe that the long streets of York, with the Queen in the open and the Alchemist in a high window at a distance, give him a perfect opportunity."

She nodded. "So we must make haste to York, and search for him."

She pictured the Alchemist, with his high velocity modern-day rifle, taking aim at Elizabeth through his telescopic sight from a safe distance. No Elizabethan security would be effective against him. She shuddered. So they would have to find him and stop him themselves.

"Yes, we must," he answered, "but I warrant he will not be easy to find."

Mary thought a moment. "We know the route Her Majesty will take through York?"

"Aye, well enough."

"And we can see the houses that over-look the route, and the streets that are widest?"

"Aye," he repeated.

"Then, as you say, we must look not to the Queen, but to the top floor windows above her route. We must look for the sight of that musket appearing out of a window, and run up to the room where he has placed himself to stop him."

He observed her levelly. "But if we only see him when the musket appears, we may be too late," he said. "When he slayed old Walter, he had only to raise the weapon and pull on the trigger and the ball did its evil work in no more than a heartbeat. What is to say he could already have slain the Queen thrice over before we burst through the door of his room?"

Mary considered this. Of course, he was right – the Alchemist may only position his gun seconds before the Queen appeared. But somehow she doubted it. "I expect he will prepare well ahead of the Queen's appearance, so I suggest we work together thus." She gazed into the fire a moment while she got the plan clear in her head. "I will walk in advance of the Queen's procession by say five minutes, looking up at the windows. You will walk a couple of minutes behind me, so if the Alchemist does place his musket after I have passed, you may see it." She sat back and smiled. "Then we can be sure of seeing the musket with enough time to work out which house he is in, run in and then stop him."

He shook his head.

"What?" she asked. "I think it is a good plan."

"For sure," he murmured, "except for one thing."

"What?" she repeated.

"If you walk ahead of the procession, you will be walking towards every possible window in full view. I think it is a near certainty that the Alchemist will see you. He will then realise that you escaped the fire in the cottage, and will understand your purpose in an instant. He will slay you as you walk in the street."

Mary give a small sigh. "Indeed, Master Cobham. Then what would you have us do?"

He sat back. "I would walk the other way, so we cannot be seen approaching, and seek out the tell-tale silver musket from below." He paused. "As you say, I would have us walk apart, so that if one misses the sight of the musket, then the other may not."

"But what if we get all the way to the Queen without seeing the Alchemist?" she asked. "Do we then turn round and walk back in full view? It is no different to my plan."

He drummed his fingers on his thigh for a while as he thought. Then he said, "For sure – you shall walk forwards ahead of the procession, but wear a broad hat – and perhaps a boy's clothing – to stop yourself being recognised from above."

"And you?"

"I shall ride with the Queen, so that if you see the Alchemist readying himself to fire, you can make that loud fishwife call of yours, and I shall pull Her Majesty away."

"Good," she said. "Then that is settled. And there is one more matter that must also be addressed."

He raised an expectant eyebrow. "Which is?"

"Hetherington Hall is close to York, is it not?"

He nodded. "I believe so."

"My son Ambrose is there, being tutored with the Grenville boy. I cannot pass so near without seeing him. We will stop there on our way to York."

CHAPTER EIGHTEEN

"We will need some new clothing," Tom observed, as they sat together by the fire in a Henley tavern the following evening. "That gown of yours is no more than a sooty rag, and I do not doubt," he added quickly, before she could comment, "that my attire is not much better."

"We also need to buy horses," Mary added. "The Alchemist has yours, and mine…" She broke off as a lump came to her throat, "and mine," she finished, taking a deep breath to stop the tears that invariably started when she thought of poor Juno, "lies in the forest."

He put his hand on her arm. "I know, dearest Mary," he said. "I know how much she meant to you. If there was any way to bring her back, I would do so in a heartbeat."

She sighed. "No, what is done is done, and I can never have her back. But," she added after a moment, "if I ever get the chance to make that man pay for what he did," she looked hard into his eyes, "then believe me, as God is my witness, I will make him pay." She turned Rick's lighter over and over in her pocket, feeling the smooth steel and shiny plastic skull. Just holding it made her feel as if she held his life in her hand. She opened the lid slightly with her thumbnail, then snapped it shut.

"You say 'what is done is done'," he observed, "yet you have such a look on your face, Mary, that you make me almost frightened." He squeezed her arm. "I would not be in the Alchemist's shoes if you were in a position to do him harm.

---0---

The next morning, they explored Henley's meagre covered market. The only stall they could find that sold women's clothing was one that seemed to have nothing but the plainest dresses – the kind usually worn by serving women. No doubt the quality women of the town had their kirtles, gowns and skirts made by a seamstress, Mary decided, just as she would have done back at Grangedean Manor. Reluctantly she bought the only dress that fitted her; a plain brown one in rough wool.

"I shall be the only gentleman on the road to York this spring accompanied by his own serving maid," observed Tom with a smile, when she tried it on in the tavern.

"Then you had better find clothing as befits a gentleman yourself, Master Thomas Cobham," she responded, squinting into the hand mirror he was holding up and failing to find an angle where the dress looked acceptable, "or I shall be the only such maid on the road to York with her own manservant."

Fortunately for Tom, they found a stall selling more varied men's clothing, and later that day it was a gentleman in a grey doublet, cream nether-stocks slashed with brown, grey hose and black shoes who stepped out with his rather dowdy maid to find a horse trader.

They found one at the back of the market; a small, shifty-looking man with a cast in his eye and ill-fitting wooden teeth. He only had two horses – which, unlike their seller, looked in fairly reasonable condition.

Tom asked the price, and seemed happy to accept it. While he was fishing for coin in his purse, Mary stepped forward.

If Tom was this useless at negotiating, then he needed her help.

As Justine Parker, she had been to Marrakesh on holiday a couple of times – so she knew a thing or two about haggling…

"At that price you are robbing us," she stated firmly. "We will pay half that."

"The deal has been affirmed by your master," sneered the man, "there is an agreement."

"Well, I do not agree," snapped Mary. "No coin has changed hands, so the deal is most definitely not affirmed."

Tom slowly closed his purse and stared at Mary with his mouth slightly open. "I shall be riding one of these horses," she continued, "and I will not ride easy if I know we have been robbed."

"'Tis a fair price," said the man, looking at Tom for confirmation. Tom shrugged and waved his hand in Mary's direction, as if to show he was content to hand over the negotiation to her.

"My master," she said, ignoring the small snort of mirth this brought from Tom, "is a gentleman, and does not regularly buy horses, nor deigns to barter with tradesmen. Whereas I…" she flashed her eyes at the man, who was starting to look uncomfortable, "…I know the price of a horse, and I say again – at the price you ask for these two sorry creatures, you are robbing us."

"I have stated the price…" the man began, but some of his earlier conviction seemed to be ebbing away, and he faltered to a stop.

"And I have said we will pay half that, which as you well know, is fair for these horses."

"And if I say no?"

"Then we will find another trader."

"Ah," said the man, a glint of triumph appearing in his eye, "but there is no other trader within ten miles of Henley. I am the only horse trader here."

"Then we will walk on a further ten miles," answered Mary. "We walked here from Stratford, and we can walk on to the next town."

The man looked again at Tom, as if seeking an ally, but Tom remained silent.

"By the holy cross," the man muttered into his beard, then he looked up. "I'faith," he said, "I accept your offer."

"Good," said Mary. "It is a fair one." She turned to Tom. "Pay the man."

Tom silently opened his purse again, and took out Mary's offered amount.

"Who exactly is the master here?" asked the man, as he took the money, but Tom just smiled, took the reins of both horses and started leading them away.

"I think you know the answer to that," said Mary with a smile. "Fare thee well, good man." She hurried on after Tom.

They rounded a corner and Tom stopped.

"I would never have walked another ten miles."

"I know that," she answered with a small twinkle in her eyes. "You know that. But fortunately…" she patted the muzzle of the smaller horse, then looked over at Tom, "…he did not know that."

---0---

It is around one hundred and fifty miles from Henley-in-Arden to North Yorkshire – a distance that Mary knew would one day take only three or four hours by car on smooth, 21st century motorways. But in 1575 it took them nearly four weeks on horseback across rough tracks, poorly made roads and forest paths.

Not that the journey was without its benefits. As spring took a firm hold, the countryside around them burst gloriously into life. Wild daffodils poked their yellow and orange heads out of the undergrowth and stood to attention as they passed; carpets of bluebells spread out along the forest floors like a colourful welcome mat, and above them the trees started to turn green, softening the spiky canopy of the forest with their soft foliage.

But there was monotony too. Tavern after tavern came and went – all with their rough itchy bedding, homemade pies and ale, and their procession of fellow-travelling humanity. Every evening they found a new one, and every morning they paid and left – and by lunchtime each day, Mary could not remember the name of the tavern, the bedroom she had slept in, or the meals she and Tom had eaten.

And Tom. Tom was always friendly, ever the perfect gentleman, considerate of her needs, playful and irreverent, but never over-stepping the line she had set down for him. Just occasionally she caught him looking at her out of the corner of his eye with a sad, almost hungry expression, which he would quickly replace with a half-smile, then engage her with a new topic of conversation. This was presumably as a form of diversionary tactic, as if to pretend she hadn't seen or understood just how much he was keeping his true feelings in check.

And it was no different for her, either.

The effort it took to keep him at arm's length was eating her up inside. Every time he smiled, cracked a joke for her amusement, or deferred to her wishes when he would clearly have done something different – it was all she could do to stop herself from throwing her arms around his neck and crushing his mouth with hers… But she had made it clear that they were friends not lovers, and that would never change.

So their journey to the north continued in a spirit of companionship, until one fine sunny spring morning they emerged from a dark forest into the bright sunshine and found themselves at the edge of a steep precipice.

As Mary looked, she could see it was actually a wooded ravine, cutting deep through the land as if a giant hand had ripped it in two.

Tom brought his horse up alongside hers and pointed at some chimneys just visible above the trees on the far side.

"Hetherington Hall, I believe."

Mary stared at the distant house, trying to make out the shape of the building against the trees.

Hetherington Hall!

So this was the house where William had brought Ambrose all those weeks ago. Suddenly she felt a warm glow spread throughout her body. Just to see the house where he now lived made Ambrose feel close enough to touch.

To hold her son in her arms once again…

She squinted against the sun as she studied the house. Which one of those tall chimneys was above the room he was in right now? Maybe he was studying with his teacher in a schoolroom under that one on the right wing? Or maybe he was not inside the house at all – instead he was outside at the butts, practicing his archery…

Mary's horse snorted and pawed the ground, as if it was as keen as she was to finish the journey.

"Come," she said to Tom. "We must get there as soon as we can."

Now she switched her focus onto the ravine, looking to see how they could get safely across.

The path ran alongside the ravine for a few more yards, then it seemed to disappear over the edge. Cautiously, she walked her horse forward. As she got closer to the edge, she could see that instead of dropping away completely, the path sloped steeply down the rocky, almost vertical side of the ravine, before making a few hairpin turns lower down on its way to the bottom.

She leaned back towards Tom. "We can follow the path if we take it slowly," she announced.

Tom nodded and they set off in single file with Mary in the lead.

She let her horse pick its way down, trusting that it was sure enough of its way not to falter or slip on the loose stones. At first the horse was extremely careful, placing each leg slowly and testing the surface before committing itself, but after a couple of the turns, the way seemed to become firmer, and soon the horse seemed to gain confidence. Its head came up, its ears went forward, and with a little neigh of pleasure, it began to trot down the path at a good pace.

Soon they were out of the sunshine and Mary shivered as the air grew cold. The rocks beside them were jagged and harsh with only occasional shrubs or branches sprouting from fissures, and here and there some trickling streams of water ran down leaving brown stains in their wake. On her other side was a sheer drop to the floor of the ravine, so Mary stayed as close as possible to the left, leaving plenty of room between her and the edge.

Then they came to a narrow section that curved round a rocky outcrop, and the path reduced to just the width of one horse.

Mary could see that not only was the path frighteningly thin, there were also some patches of loose-looking stones as it curved round the outcrop. The horse's pace, which had been fine when the path was wide and firm, was now dangerously fast. It was clear that the horse thought so too, and it tried to slow down. Unfortunately, just as it passed a sturdy-looking branch growing out of a fissure in the rock, it hit the patch of loose stones and started to scrabble for a foothold.

For one awful moment, Mary was looking into empty space over the horse's head, its ears laid back on its neck in fear. But then the horse managed to regain its footing and carry on down the path, treading with more care and caution. She let it walk slowly on a few more yards, until it was on a wider section of the path and its ears had come back to their more relaxed position. Then she pulled it to a stop, making reassuring 'shh-ing' noises.

"That was close," said Tom from behind her. "That was a narrow and dangerous section of the path – it is most fortunate that your horse is sure-footed."

"Well, I am glad she was." Mary turned in the saddle and looked back into his concerned face.

As she studied him, suddenly her eyes flooded with tears, causing his face to dissolve in an instant into a thousand fragments.

"What ails, Mary?" he asked quietly. "Art quite safe."

"I know." She wiped her eyes with her sleeve. "But I just had a thought.

What if a similar thing happened to Ambrose and William?" She sniffed and blinked a few times. "The winter snows have not been gone long, so it must have been icy when they came down this path. What if one of them lost their grip completely? What if we get to the bottom of this ravine and find they never even made it to Hetherington? What if we find them still there? What if we find them…" she could hardly bear to say the word "…dead?"

"I am sure not, Mary." He gave a weak smile, which looked like he was reassuring himself as much as her. "Sir William is a good horseman, I am sure, and had a care for his son also." He gestured at the far side of the ravine. "I am sure we will find Ambrose safe and well at Hetherington, and Sir William the same back at Grangedean Manor."

"Hmm," she agreed, and gingerly urged her horse to walk on.

As they continued down, the horse seemed to become more cautious, and Mary wondered if it had learned its lesson for itself, or was simply reflecting her own caution. Juno would have instinctively known what Mary was thinking.

They reached the bottom without further incident, and despite Tom's assurances, Mary insisted on them both tracking up and down the foot of the precipice, checking for any signs of William and Ambrose's bodies. Tom picked up a large branch and used it to poke at the mossy mounds and beds of early spring flowers, as well as levering up fallen branches to look beneath. When they had covered all the ground thoroughly – with extra care taken at the spot directly beneath the rocky outcrop – Tom led them back to the path.

"Art sure now, Mary?" he asked.

She wanted to say that they should cover the ground again, and maybe dig in any soft spots – but she could see this would be poorly received. Clearly, as far as Tom was concerned they had checked and found nothing – so she would be pushing her luck to continue. She straightened her back and nodded to Tom. As Tom had said, she should trust to Ambrose and William's horsemanship and expect to find her son where he should be – in Hetherington Hall, and her husband back at Grangedean Manor.

They remounted their horses, and were preparing to ride on, when a sudden pang of guilt made Mary stop.

In all this time, how often had she thought of the family she had left behind at Grangedean? Of Kat and Jane, of Ruth and Sarah? She had promised Kat that she would only be gone a few days – and how long had it been now? More than two months? What must the poor little girl be thinking? An icy chill went up Mary's spine. Would little Kat be wondering if a 'bad man' had got her mother, as she had feared, and had to be comforted by Sarah? And was Jane blithely eating her breakfast, even without her mother there to make it fly like a bird? Or maybe Ruth was working her magic touch and getting the girl to eat.

Mary bit her lip. Was William back home by now? And if so, was he looking after his girls? As a father he could be somewhat distant; so was he now being more attentive to his children's needs? Mary really hoped he was.

Unless, of course, he had left them with Ruth and Sarah, and had decided to go out looking for her. Was he even now scouring the land, anxiously following her trail?

Mary gasped. Had he followed her trail to Southwark? To the Blue Maid? Or to Hammersmith, with tales of his wife's cosy fireside chats with Sir Robert Standing, while Olivia flirted so dangerously with that monster, Shelton?

Mary bit her lip again. What would she say when she got back to Grangedean? How would she look William in the eye and make him understand that nothing had happened?

The stream! With Tom! What of that?

But nothing had happened – she had pulled away. So there was nothing to tell.

She glanced across to where Tom was sitting on his horse, regarding her with one eyebrow raised.

"You appear thoughtful, my dear Lady Mary," he said. "What ails you?"

"Marry, 'tis nothing."

"I doubt that," he answered. "I know that when you bite your own lip it means you are deep in thought about something that bothers you." He cocked his head thoughtfully. "Is it your concern for your son and husband? We have searched most thoroughly and found no trace. Would you have me search again?"

"No," she answered slowly. "It is not just William – it is the girls as well. They know not where I am."

"And you would have them know?"

"Of course, they must be worried sick. For ten years I have hardly set foot outside Grangedean – now I am two months gone with no word."

"For sure." He smiled reassuringly. "We will find a messenger when we can, and see if we can get word to them."

If only we could send a quick text – how easy would that be?

"Then let us continue," he said. "At least you can reassure your son of your safety." He started riding across the floor of the ravine towards the far side.

They had only gone a couple of hundred yards through the sycamores, when suddenly Tom stopped. "What's that?" he said, pointing at something in the distance.

Mary followed his finger, but could not make out anything but trees.

"What?" she asked.

"That," he repeated. She looked harder, and suddenly a shape that looked a bit like a thatched roof seemed to emerge from the jumble of the forest. After that, she could make out walls, a door, a window and the rest of the roof. Once she made it out, she wondered how she could possibly have missed it at first. "It is a hut," she said.

"Aye," he answered. "Let us explore it further."

As they approached it, Mary could see it was very small; no bigger than a 21st century garden shed. Tom tried the door, and it opened easily.

Inside, it was almost empty; the only pieces of furniture being a pallet bed and a small oak chest.

"It is a watchman's hut," said Tom. "That is all." Idly he opened the chest and peered in. "By Heaven!" he exclaimed as he reached inside.

"What is it?" she asked.

With a look of concern, he took out a black metal object that looked like a flattened oval ring with a central bar, with a substantial length of chain hanging off it.

"It is a manacle," he said, examining it and testing the chain. "Someone uses this hut to keep a prisoner." He peered again into the chest, and took out another, identical manacle. "Or two prisoners." Quickly he put them back and closed the lid. "Come," he said, "we must make haste away from this place, lest we suddenly meet the jailer."

---0---

Hetherington Hall was grander up close than Mary had expected, with two broad wings either side of the central house, all brick-built with diamond-paned windows and topped with magnificent twisted chimneys rising into the clear blue sky. The main entrance was up some stone steps, flanked by two balustrades that were themselves each finished off with a fine stone lion, as if guarding the house from intruders.

Mary walked up the steps and pulled on the bell-rope.

The door was opened by a sallow-faced man in what she assumed must be the Grenville livery. "Servants' entrance is at the back," he said, and started to close the door.

Mary stepped forward. "My name is Lady Mary de Beauvais," she announced, emphasising the 'Lady'. He still seemed unimpressed. "My son Ambrose de Beauvais is here under the care of your master, Sir Nicholas Grenville," she added. "I must see him."

"A moment, mistress," the man muttered, then disappeared back into the house, closing the door on her and leaving her standing.

She waited for what seemed like ages, wishing Tom was here to support her. But she had insisted on him staying by the top of the ravine while she went to the house alone – to spare Ambrose from any questions regarding the strange man accompanying her. Tom had pointed out that he was hardly a strange man, and that Ambrose was surely able to understand the idea of a travelling companion, but Mary was insistent, and he had remained behind at the edge of the forest, while Mary had gone on alone to the house.

Eventually the door opened again and the thinnest man Mary had ever seen came out. He had sandy hair that fell across one eye and a beard so fine that she had to strain her eyes to see it. If it were not for his fine doublet, nether-stocks and hose, she would have thought he were a woman.

He looked her up and down, and Mary was conscious that she was still wearing the plain gown that she had bought in Henley-in-Arden – and after nearly four weeks on the road and the occasional wash in a stream, it was not at its best. Not only did she look like a serving-girl-turned-vagabond, but she must have smelled fairly ripe as well. No wonder the liveried man who had first opened the door had thought she was a servant.

"Lady Mary de Beauvais?" the thin man said, in a disbelieving tone.

"Yes," she answered in her best 'Lady of the Manor' voice. "And I must see my son Ambrose, who is in the care of Sir Nicholas."

The man shook his head. "I am afraid that will not be possible."

"Why so?" she asked.

"Because," he said smoothly, "Master Ambrose has gone with Sir Nicholas and Lady Grenville to York to see the progress of the Queen." He looked her up and down again with barely concealed distaste. "And because I cannot believe for one moment that the vagrant serving woman I see before me is the wife of Sir William or the mother of Ambrose de Beauvais."

Mary took a breath and smiled sweetly. "I can see that it may be difficult to tell," she said, "but I can assure you that it is of necessity that I am wearing this garb, and I am indeed Lady Mary, and can verify it as soon as I see my son. I need to see him," she added.

"As you say." The man stepped back. "But I cannot alter the fact that he is staying at the Grenville town-house in York, and will not be back for many days, until the progress of Her Majesty the Queen has passed on."

"I see," Mary said. "But he is well?"

"He is well enough, I warrant, to satisfy a mother's concern."

Mary regarded the man for a moment. Clearly she was not going to get any more information from him.

"Thank you, sir," she said. Then she added with what she hoped was her most disarming smile, "You have me at a disadvantage. I do not know who I have the honour of addressing?"

The man was silent a moment, then he gave a small bow and said, "Lambert Moreton at your service. Sir Nicholas Grenville is my uncle."

"Well, Master Moreton, I am honoured to make your acquaintance."

Moreton gave a thin smile that failed to reach his eyes. "And I yours, Lady Mary, if that is who you are." He bowed again. "Now, by your leave, I have business to attend to in the house, and must repeat that Master Ambrose is not here. I suggest you return once the progress has left York, and he is back." He slammed the door shut in her face.

Mary walked down the steps and made her way to the edge of the ravine.

Tom was sitting with his back to a tree, while the horses grazed quietly nearby. His head was lolled over to one side, and he seemed to be asleep.

She went up to him.

"Tom, Tom!" She shook his shoulder. "Wake up!"

He opened one eye. "Hmm?"

"Ambrose is not here – I am told that he has gone to York to see the Queen."

"Oh." He stood up and put his hands on her shoulders. "I am sorry – I know you were keen to see him."

"Aye. Perhaps we will see him in York. But, Tom…" she paused. "Something was not right…"

"What?" He stood back and searched her eyes. "You have a concern?"

"Yes." She shook her head, as if to clear it of the sinister presence of Lambert Moreton. "It was Sir Nicholas Grenville's nephew who told me, and he was hiding something – I am sure of it." She shook her head again and looked up at him. "Tom, what if something has happened to Ambrose? What if he's not in York and they are covering it up?"

He moved his hands up to cup her cheeks. "My dear Mary, I am sure Ambrose is well and happy, and currently in York, excitedly awaiting the arrival of Queen Elizabeth." He let her go and stood back. "We should go there ourselves as fast as we can. We have our mission – to save the life of the Queen."

CHAPTER NINETEEN

The road to Wyvern Castle, North Yorkshire, early May 1575

Olivia Melrose looked out of the open carriage window at the bleak northern landscape as it rolled past in the warm sunshine. Beside her, Maggie Tyndall was silent, staring out of the opposite window.

Lady Burnham, sitting bolt upright opposite them, looked from one girl to the other. "I have held my peace these last few hours since we left Fambridge Hall," she observed, "but I can hold it no longer. What has happened, that the atmosphere between you two is colder than a December frost?"

Olivia looked at the back of Maggie's head, then at her mistress. "It is nothing, my lady, just a small misunderstanding."

"Well, I would advise you both to clear it up before we reach Wyvern Castle this evening. We are there three days before progressing into York, and I would not want to have all that time with the two of you acting like a couple of angry geese who spit at each other." Lady Burnham folded her hands on her lap. "Do I make myself understood?"

"Yes, my lady." Olivia went back to staring out of the window. Maggie said nothing.

"Mistress Tyndall?" Lady Burnham snapped.

"Yes, my lady," muttered Maggie.

Olivia sighed. The truth was, that Maggie was cross with her because she had been proved right about Shelton…

It had all started when Olivia decided that Maggie's flirtation with Shelton had now gone far enough. They were becoming quite blatant, and knowing Shelton as she did, Olivia was frightened that if it got too heated – and Maggie then tried to resist – his response would be to do to Maggie what he had done to her.

So the previous morning she had found him alone in the long gallery at Fambridge Hall, and it had been the perfect opportunity.

"Master Shelton," she said, "I must speak with you."

"Why, Mistress Melrose," he answered with a raised eyebrow, "this is a surprise. I had thought you were going out of your way to avoid me since we left London."

Olivia ignored this. "I must tell you of Maggie Tyndall."

"I rather think I know more on that topic than you at this moment." He started walking away from her down the gallery. "If we are to go by who is spending the greater time in Mistress Tyndall's company."

She caught up and walked alongside him. "She may spend time in your company, Master Shelton, but she has no real interest in you."

He stopped. "Really, Mistress Melrose? That is not my reading of her behaviour."

"I will not discuss how poor you are at reading a woman's behaviour, Master Shelton," Olivia retorted, then cursed inwardly. She had promised herself to keep this about Maggie and not let him get past her defences. Indeed, she knew that if she did not control the situation correctly, she could find herself once again in trouble from his violent temper.

She took a breath and continued, "I can assure you, she is but a young, inexperienced girl who knows not what effect her beauty has on men. There is no meaning in what she says or her behaviour towards you. She has no real interest in you."

"And she has told you this herself?"

Olivia gritted her teeth. "Of course," she lied. "We talk often."

"And yet she is but a young, inexperienced girl and there is no meaning to what she says?"

"Do not throw my words back at me, Master Shelton," she hissed.

"But I am listening to what you say, Mistress Melrose, and taking most careful note." He gave her a sarcastic smile. "And I do the same with Maggie Tyndall, and do you know what she tells me?" Olivia looked away, as if by not seeing Shelton she could also avoid hearing him. "She tells me that my eyes do please her greatly – both of them in fact – and that she finds my hair and my beard much to her liking, and that my…"

"Enough!" Olivia snapped. "Let me be most clear, Master Shelton. Maggie Tyndall is a sweet, innocent girl who has taken it into her head that you are an honourable man, worthy of her attention. I think we both know you are neither of those things. In fact, as I know to my lifelong cost, you are a thoughtless, heartless monster with no care for the feelings of any person but yourself – indeed I wonder if you deliberately sought the position with my lady Burnham because I told you that was where I was going when we met in Hammersmith, so you could taunt me further..." She thought she saw him flinch very slightly – and decided she had hit the mark. "So I would you leave Maggie alone," she continued, "and do not encourage her any further in her girlish fantasies. I trust I make myself perfectly clear, Master Shelton?"

"A pretty speech, Mistress Melrose. But not, I regret to say, 'perfectly clear'." Shelton assumed a sickly, thoughtful expression. "How is it that on the one hand Mistress Tyndall says to you that she has no interest in me, yet on the other hand, she thinks I am an honourable man, worthy of her attention?" Again he raised an eyebrow. "I merely ask so I can be perfectly clear."

"Do not twist my words, Master Shelton, and you leave Maggie alone," Olivia snarled, "or I will see to it that you suffer harm, just as you made me suffer harm back in Hammersmith."

Suddenly the mask of civility was stripped away, and Shelton once again raised his hand to strike her.

Olivia forced herself not to flinch and stared into his eyes with defiance. After a few seconds, his hand came down.

"Do not threaten me, Olivia Melrose," he hissed, "and know your place as a woman." He brought his face right up to hers, so their noses were almost touching.

Still she did not react, but carried on staring into his eyes.

"Or I will need to instruct you in manners as I instructed you once before."

She forced herself to keep still, and did not blink.

"Do I make myself 'perfectly clear' – *Livvy*?"

With that, he turned on his heel and marched away down the gallery, leaving Olivia standing. As soon as he had slammed the door behind him, she staggered to a bench seat and collapsed onto it, her breathing ragged.

'Livvy?' How dare he take Maggie's pet name for her and twist it into something sick?

She should never have let it get that far – she should never have let him make her angry. She had managed to avoid such a situation ever since London, but now it had happened, and it was her fault for starting it…

Olivia stood up and adjusted her gown. No, it was *not* her fault! Lady Mary had said that she should never blame herself for the actions of a man – and especially not Master Lionel blasted Shelton.

Olivia squared her shoulders and walked steadily to the door at the far end of the Gallery.

Just as she put her hand to the door, it opened.

She stood back, fearing that it was Shelton returning, and prepared herself to confront him once again. But it was not Shelton.

It was the Queen.

She was in conversation with a tall older man dressed in black, with long flowing white hair.

"…Let me assure you, Master Wychwoode," the Queen was saying, "I am placing my trust in your preparations for the progress through York, so the safety of my person is in your hands. But I must stress once again, that I do not want to be seen to be afraid withal. It is not in keeping with the picture I have created, to be as a weakened coward that hides behind her men. So there are to be no extra guards or such-like – do you understand?

"I do, madam," the tall man answered.

"I care not how you make sure I am protected, but I will not have it seen by the people…"

Suddenly the Queen stopped short. Olivia, who had dropped into the lowest curtesy she could manage, could only assume that despite being behind the door, she had just been spotted.

Olivia felt a hand come under her chin, and pull her up.

"Who are you, girl, that would listen to my private counsel with Master Wychwoode?"

Olivia stood as tall as she could. Fortunately her head was still lower than the Queen's.

"Olivia Melrose, Your Grace," she said, then curtseyed again.

"Stand up, girl," snapped the Queen. "Who exactly are you, Mistress Melrose?"

"I attend on Lady Burnham, Your Majesty."

"I see." The Queen considered her a moment with thoughtful eyes. "And how can I be sure you are not a Catholic spy, sent to learn my secrets and so use them against me?"

Then the man Wychwoode suddenly exclaimed, "Olivia Melrose?" Olivia nodded slowly, unsure as to how this tall elderly man could possibly know her.

He studied her face. "Then your father is Thomas Melrose, known to Sir William de Beauvais?" She nodded again.

He looked puzzled. "But I do not see your father in your face…?"

Olivia shook her head. "Nay, good sir," she said. "My true father was killed when I was but a small child. He fought most bravely in the defence of Sir William and Lady de Beauvais. His name was Dowland."

Wychwoode turned to the Queen with a look of triumph. "Your Majesty, I can vouchsafe that this girl is honest and true. I was acquainted not only with both her real and adopted fathers, but with the desperate battle that took Master Dowland's life, and with the honour and courage her new father showed in his own fight. He was a brave man who in a moment of madness made a grave error of judgment, but then he did all he could to right the wrong." He turned to Olivia. "So he took you in and raised you as his own?" She nodded. "Then he has remained a good and honest man. I trust he still lives?"

"He does, indeed."

The Queen smiled, a warm smile that illuminated her pale beauty. "Then child, you are most welcome to us, and we trust you will become better acquainted with us in the coming weeks."

Olivia bowed her head once more, then felt the Queen's hand brush her cheek. She looked up.

"Go, my child, and serve your mistress well. You have found favour in our eyes."

Wychwoode stood back, and Olivia walked out of the door, feeling as if she was floating six inches in the air.

When she arrived back at their rooms, Maggie was not there, so it was not until they met at the table for dinner, that Olivia could speak to her friend.

She decided to keep her meeting with the Queen a secret for the moment, and to concentrate on the other matter.

"I was able to converse with Lionel Shelton this morning," she said casually.

Maybe it was too casual, and Maggie was immediately on her guard. "Why, what passed between you?" She grabbed at Olivia's sleeve. "Is he happy that we are being discreet?" She glanced around the Great Hall to ensure they were not being overheard against the noise of dinner. "Has Lady Burnham said aught about us? Oh!" she put her hand to her mouth and looked across the hall to where Her Majesty was seated. "It is the Queen, is it not?" she whispered. "I knew it, Livvy!" Olivia winced at the name – now tainted by Shelton. "I saw her observe us only yesterday and noted that she did frown so!" Maggie's eyes widened. "Her Majesty has become aware that Master Shelton pays me such attention and she is concerned! We are being too obvious! And Her Majesty has noted this to my lady, has she not, Livvy?"

Olivia held up her hand to stem this flow. "No, sweet Maggie, she has not." Maggie's shoulders sagged in relief. "Nor has my lady said aught, either. But," she continued, "I have spoken with Master Shelton and asked that he pays you less attention, before my lady, or even Her Majesty, *does* say something."

There was a long silence as servants placed large plates of swan, pig and vegetables in front of them. Once they had gone, Olivia saw that Maggie's pretty face had clouded over, like a storm blocking out the sun. The girl spoke slowly and deliberately, as if she was testing a difficult theory.

"You have spoken with Lionel, and you have told him to pay me less attention?"

Olivia nodded.

Maggie's voice became even quieter, so Olivia had to strain to hear her over the noise of the banquet. "And you feel this is your business, Mistress Melrose?"

"I do, for I know Shelton, and I do not think him an honourable man." Then Olivia added, "And I have your best interests at heart, Maggie Tyndall."

Maggie stared at Olivia, then slowly, she shook her head. "I had thought better of you, Mistress Melrose, truly I did." Olivia said nothing. "I knew you disapproved of Lionel and me; oh, yes I did. But I thought you had accepted that we have feelings for each other, and in truth, I thought you were happy for us." Maggie shook her head again. "And now you tell me that not only are you not happy for us, but that you have interfered by asking Lionel to pay me less attention?"

Olivia nodded again.

Maggie stood up. "Then I must take my leave of you, because I cannot remain in your company a moment longer." With that, she flounced out of the hall.

Olivia remained seated, but she saw that Shelton himself had been watching this exchange, for he got up, shot her a look of pure loathing, then followed Maggie out.

Olivia found she had lost her appetite, and a few minutes later she nodded to Lady Burnham to excuse herself, and left the hall also.

She heard the raised voices as she approached their rooms – and it was clear they were the voices of Shelton and Maggie.

Quickly she threw open the door – to find Shelton standing over Maggie, who was lying on her back on the bed. His balled fist was raised, ready to strike her. Maggie had her arms held above her head in self-protection.

Immediately Olivia ran towards Shelton, shouting, "No!"

Shelton looked round, and lowered his hand.

"Be gone, Shelton!" Olivia snapped. "This instant!"

Shelton looked from Maggie on the bed, who was now sobbing, to Olivia, who was pointing imperiously at the door. After a moment, he walked out, without another word.

Olivia immediately ran to Maggie and put her arms around the crying girl. But if she had expected Maggie to cling to her and profess eternal gratitude, she was gravely mistaken.

In fact, Maggie started trying to beat her fists on Olivia's chest as she sobbed, causing Olivia to jump back and stand away from the bed in surprise.

"What did you do that for?" she asked. "When all I had done was stop that man from attacking you?"

"All you had done?" Maggie sat up, wiping her eyes and looking indignant. "All you had done, Mistress Melrose, was to give a sweet, gentle man cause to doubt me – such that he became confused about my feelings for him, and in his confusion, he knew not what he was doing!"

Olivia thought perhaps she must have misheard this – for if she had heard correctly, then surely the words made no sense. "Are you serious? He is a violent, controlling man, who was about to strike you! How was that 'confused'?"

"It is the natural order for a man to be controlling," answered Maggie. "And for a woman to be controlled. So what you told him this morning went against the natural order, and he was confused."

"But he was about to strike you!" exclaimed Olivia.

"And that was because of you!"

"I do not believe I am hearing this!" Olivia yelled, stamping her foot.

"Then do not hear it!" Maggie responded. "Be gone and do not ever talk to me again!"

---0---

Olivia continued to stare out of the open carriage window at the landscape rumbling past, conscious that beside her, Maggie was looking out of the opposite window. They had not exchanged a single word since Maggie had sent Olivia away that morning.

If only Maggie would not be so mutton-headed! Surely she could see that it was Shelton who was the villain here, not Olivia? Why could she not understand that a woman did not need to feel guilty for being attacked by a man – that it was his responsibility, not hers?

Suddenly Olivia shook her head.

No! That was to miss the point! The point was, that girls like Maggie thought it was the natural order of things for the man to be always right, whatever his actions, because the laws and rules of society said this was so. Had she, Olivia, not felt the same, before Lady Mary had opened her eyes to the truth?

If only Lady Mary were here, she would explain it to Maggie with the same passion and conviction that had caused Olivia to change her own mind. If Lady Mary were here, then Maggie would understand why it was no longer acceptable for a woman to be seen as the possession of a man.

Olivia sighed and focused once again on the landscape. Trees, cottages, forests and fields all appeared and disappeared, with the occasional yeoman, farmer or peasant standing with his family like statues and watching as the procession went by.

"We must be close to Wyvern Castle," observed Lady Burnham to no-one in particular. "The local townspeople are gathering to bid good cheer to Her Majesty. Were it not so warm, Olivia, I would have you close the window, for the common folk are apt to smell quite noisome." She reached down and pulled her travelling bag onto her lap. "Instead I will use my lavender nosegay." She started rummaging in the bag.

Olivia nodded politely, then resumed her vigil at the carriage window.

The carriage slowed and rolled to a stop. "The Queen must now be at the gates of Wyvern Castle," said Lady Burnham, looking up from her bag. Then she resumed her search. "I know my nosegay was in here before. Now, where is it?"

Olivia continued to look out of the carriage at the faces of the townspeople as they went by.

Suddenly she stopped and stared hard at one face in particular. She could swear it was a serving woman on a brown horse who looked exactly like Lady

Mary!

Surely not? In truth, she had just been thinking of Lady Mary, so perhaps it was not surprising to imagine that some woman in the crowd was actually her.

She leaned out of the window, looking back and desperately trying to see the woman again, but there was no sign of her. Olivia sat back and shook her head. It had surely been a mistake – for Lady Mary was no doubt long since back at Grangedean Manor, and the possibility that she was even now dressed as a serving woman watching the Queen's progress towards York was arrant madness…

Just then they came to a halt.

Suddenly a face appeared at the open window. It was only there for the briefest instant, but now there was no doubt – it really was Lady Mary! She had her finger to her lips to caution for silence.

Despite the shock of seeing Mary again, Olivia knew she had to stay calm. She glanced quickly back at the others inside the carriage. Neither seemed to be aware of what had just happened. Lady Burnham was still rummaging in her bag and Maggie was staring out of the other window.

By the strangest good fortune, neither had seen what she had seen.

Olivia looked back at the window.

It was empty.

Pretending she was interested in the crowds now lining the road, she leaned out and looked back along the carriage.

Lady Mary was standing just behind, talking to a tall handsome-looking man who held the reins of two horses. Seeing Olivia, she moved forward and stopped by the back wheel of the coach.

"Meet me by the main gate this evening at seven," she hissed.

Olivia nodded, then sat back again, trying to control her breathing and appear normal.

Soon the carriage started to move forward again, and shortly after, passed under a magnificent brick archway and into the grounds of Wyvern Castle.

---0---

Mary waved her hand to ward off the evening midges as they swarmed around her.

She stared at the brick arch above the ornate iron gates to Wyvern Castle. It rose to around six feet above the top of the gates themselves, with a series of bricks standing proud of the wall to create a diamond pattern. At the top was a large stone shield with some form of spacer behind it, as it appeared to float clear of the wall by several inches. The image of what looked like a dragon was carved onto it; it had a dragon's head, body and wings, then a long tail curling round its body that ended in a diamond-shaped tip, but curiously, it had no front legs. She assumed this must be the coat of arms of the Wyvern family.

Strange that there was no guard on the gate, given the importance of the royal visitor and her retinue; Mary supposed that there would be guards by the door to the house itself. Olivia would no doubt have the ingenuity to slip out unseen for their meeting.

Mary looked at the house, just visible through the trees beyond the gates, then up at the tall elms surrounding the wall. If the Alchemist wanted to take his shot from up in one of those, he would have a good view of the house, and presumably a clear line of sight into the grounds. But would he want to risk Elizabeth not coming out, or coming out all too briefly to get the shot? And would he be prepared to wait in a tree for three days on the chance of getting sight of her in the open? No, most likely his plan was as they first thought – to assassinate her when she was more easily visible, passing through the streets of York. So, she would be safe in Wyvern Castle until then, and Mary could decide what she was going to have to do to stop the Alchemist.

There was a rustling of leaves the other side of the gate, and suddenly Olivia was there.

"Lady Mary, by God's good grace!" she exclaimed, peering through the ornate ironwork. "What is your purpose here?" She paused, then added with a smile, "For all that I am most glad to see you!"

"My dear, sweet child," Mary answered, putting her hand through the gate and clasping Olivia's. "Your face is well mended, I see. You are back to your full beauty, as I was sure you would be."

"Aye, and no thanks to that snake Shelton, who is here even now!"

"He is here?" Mary's eyes widened. "How is this so?"

"He is at Court, in the Queen's retinue."

"And do you manage to keep apart from him?"

"Not as much as I would like." Olivia swallowed and looked at her feet. "I have had furious words with him, over his behaviour."

"Why, has he again attacked you?" Mary frowned.

"No, he has not attacked me, but he has made to strike my friend Maggie."

"Is your friend Maggie hurt?"

"Nay," Olivia looked up. "I was able to stop him before harm was caused."

"Well done," Mary said. "And does she also avoid him now?"

"I wish so, but she is too enamoured of him," Olivia answered. "She thinks it is my fault for pouring poison in his ear."

"Then we must make Maggie see him for the man he is." Mary said.

"Yes, we must," answered Olivia. "And I would you talk to her the way you talked to me – you make it seem so clear, how a man should not hold dominion over a woman."

"Indeed," Mary said, nodding. "And we must also think how to make Master Shelton realise the error of his ways," she added. She paused, then said, "All in good time, but now, dear Olivia, I need your help."

"For sure. What can I do?"

"For a start, pray tell me why you are here with the Queen? Are you so soon elevated to a position at Court? I may say," Mary added, "that I was most shocked to see you in the window of that coach. When I left you in the house on the Strand all these weeks ago, I scarcely thought I would see you again in Yorkshire. I had to look twice to be sure it was really you."

"And I could not believe I was seeing Lady Mary dressed as a servant, either," said Olivia with an interested little smile.

"A long story – for another time." Mary answered, a little too quickly.

"Does it involve the fine-looking man you were talking to by my coach?" asked Olivia, her eyebrow raised.

Mary smiled, then shook her head. Trust Olivia to home in on the question she would prefer to avoid. "You have not told me why you are here," she repeated, trying to change the subject.

Olivia paused, her lips pursed. Clearly her interest was piqued, but it looked as though she was prepared to let the subject of Tom drop for now. She said, "My lady Burnham is in the Queen's party for this progress, and she has asked both Maggie and myself to attend her."

"Then that is great good fortune," Mary answered, "as I need the help of someone I can trust who is in the Queen's entourage." She put her other hand through the gate and grasped both of Olivia's firmly. "I have good reason to believe that the life of the Queen is in grave danger, and I need to prevent this attack from happening."

Olivia gasped. "How so?"

"I have been following a man who has both the will, and the means, to kill her. I believe he will make his attack in York, so I need to secure a position within the entourage myself, so I can get close to Her Majesty and stop this happening."

"Yes, you must!" Olivia thought a moment. "There is a man here that the Queen says she trusts to safeguard her person. You must tell your story to him, so he can help you." She paused again, as if deciding how much information to share. Then she said, "He told the Queen that he knew you and Sir William. He said he was part of the desperate fight many years ago that cost my true father his life. A tall old man with long, grey hair."

"Oh!" Now it was Mary's turn to gasp in surprise. "Wychwoode! Wychwoode is here?"

Olivia nodded. "Yes – that was his name."

"Then that is even better! He will be able to help us. Tom and I must see him."

There was a moment's silence. "Tom?" Olivia asked quietly. "Is Tom the man you were talking to?"

Mary smiled. "Tom is one of Wychwoode's men," she said. "We have journeyed together from London with common purpose – to save the Queen. He is even now waiting in the forest, and will join us in the Queen's party. If you and Wychwoode can get us both into the house, and allow us to clean and dress ourselves as befits a courtier, we can finish the task and stop the killer from making his strike."

"And this Tom," Olivia observed, "...he seemed a fine-looking man..."

The statement hung in the air for a moment – sounding more like a question. Then Mary smiled again. "Indeed, but I do not see what...?"

"There it is!" Olivia looked triumphantly at Mary. "Each time you talk of him, you smile. And when I questioned you a few moments ago, you changed the subject most quickly." She pulled her hands away from Mary's. "What is this man to you?" she asked.

Mary sighed. "The truth is, Tom and I have shared many adventures together and have become... close." Then she added, "But nothing has happened, and I have told him most firmly that it never will."

Olivia was silent a while. Then she asked, "And he feels the same?"

Mary was once again in the forest on the way to Henley-in-Arden; standing in front of Tom with his hair and beard full of mud. "He said to me these words... 'I have a heart,' he said, 'and it would be yours if it could be' – but then he accepted it was not to be."

Olivia reached for Mary's hands and took them in her own. "He is a man of honour, then."

"Yes." There was a silence. Mary wondered if she was going to get a lecture on propriety – which, in her heart she knew she deserved – or sympathy instead. Then Olivia burst out, "By Heaven, Mary, you bear this well! This is not easy for you! He seems a good man who cares for you, and you for him, and yet you must push him away! How can you cope with this? Were it me, I am sure I would not have pushed him away! You have such strength, Mary!"

Mary sighed. "Aye, well, I do have strength, because it is the right thing to do. But it is done, and now the most important thing is to get in and meet with Wychwoode."

Maybe a lecture would have been easier.

CHAPTER TWENTY

Hetherington Hall

William de Beauvais looked round as Lambert Moreton approached from the house. He was walking quickly, staring intently at William.

"A moment, son," William said to Ambrose, who was in the act of fitting an arrow to his bow, as Richard Grenville looked on. "Master Moreton comes, and I think he needs must talk with me. You keep practicing your archery." Then he whispered in Ambrose's ear, so Richard would not hear. "You are shooting true, and making your father very proud."

He stepped aside as Ambrose fired the arrow, and turned to face Moreton. "How can I help you?" he asked.

"Sir Nicholas is requesting you ride out to meet him, on a most important matter."

"Sir Nicholas?" William raised an eyebrow. "We spoke only a couple of hours ago in the Great Hall. What has emerged since then?"

"He has had to ride out on a matter of the utmost importance, and is asking that you meet him presently." Moreton paused and looked over at Ambrose. William followed the man's gaze, to see that his son's arrow had hit the bullseye."

"Good shot, Ambrose!" he exclaimed.

Moreton did not offer any comment on the shot. Instead he said, "And your son, too. Sir Nicholas has asked that you both meet him."

"I will call for my men-at-arms – they are close by at the stables."

"Nay," Moreton seemed slightly flustered by this. "There is no time."

William looked at the thin man. "I would prefer to have my men with me and my son," he said firmly.

"There is no call for that," Moreton snapped. "This is but a short ride, and we shall be back most presently." He paused. "Do you not trust, me, Sir William?"

William did not, but felt he could not say as much. "And where is it that we are to meet?" he asked instead.

"I am to lead you to Sir Nicholas," Moreton replied. "I have had both your horse and Master Ambrose's pony saddled up and made ready." He gestured to the side of the house, where a groom was standing with Thelwell, William's horse and another horse as well. "If you will please accompany me?"

William shrugged casually. "I see no reason why not." He went over to Ambrose. "Come son, gather your arrows. We are bidden to ride out and meet Sir Nicholas on some important matter."

"As you say, Pa." Ambrose shot William a quick glance that plainly said, 'Where are we going and why?' William shook his head with a silent reply of 'I know not, but we must take care,' before turning and following Moreton.

Ambrose walked over to the straw target and pulled out all his arrows. Replacing them in his quiver, he trotted after the two men. Richard Grenville started walking back to the house.

William made sure to walk confidently as if he had not a care in the world, although nothing could be further from the truth. Since that fateful day when Moreton had threatened Ambrose's safety, William had been on his guard at all times. Unwilling to leave Ambrose in a traitorous household, he had stuck doggedly by his son's side, continually making excuses as to why he should remain at Hetherington Hall, rather than setting off back to Grangedean and Lady Mary. He had not even found a way to get a messenger to send her news that he was safe. Indeed, it now seemed to be accepted that he was almost a permanent guest; one who would stay as long as his son was being educated in the household.

Many times he had rehearsed the story he would tell Mary when he returned to Grangedean with Ambrose, no doubt to a barrage of questions and cries of "I have been sick with worry, here at Grangedean all these months!" and "I had believed you had perished!" Indeed, it was the thought of Mary, alone and concerned back at Grangedean, that caused him deep anxiety in his day-to-day life, catching him suddenly at times when he was least expecting it – such as when he rode out hunting with Sir Nicholas, or made small talk with Lady Grenville.

The anxiety he felt for Lady Mary was second only to the anxiety caused by the knowledge that he and his precious son were guests of a Catholic family – not a loyal, compliant Catholic family as he had naively assumed all those months ago when he had taken up Sir Nicholas's casual offer to educate Ambrose, but a militant, treacherous Catholic family. For the day before he had overheard a conversation between Sir Nicholas and Moreton that gave him grave concern.

He and Ambrose had just returned from an early ride in the park. His son had put Thelwell in his stable, then headed off to change for his lessons. William had been concerned over a slight heat in his own horse's foreleg, and was crouched down in the stable soothing it with cold water. So when he heard the voices of Lambert Moreton and Sir Nicholas in the yard just outside, he remained low and listened intently.

"I would travel to York to see the procession," Sir Nicholas was saying. "Lady Grenville is set on seeing the Queen. She wishes to confirm to herself how a bastard looks when dressed in finery – like a servant assuming the garb and airs of her mistress."

"And you would go with her?" This was Moreton.

"For sure," answered Sir Nicholas. "I would not have her travel to York alone."

"But is it wise for you both to go?" Moreton asked. "What if some accident or misfortune was to befall Elizabeth the usurper? As a Catholic you would automatically be under suspicion." There was a pause. William could imagine Sir Nicholas's florid face creased in thought. It sounded like Moreton was pressing his point. "Would you not prefer to remain here in Hetherington, and avoid any possible risk?"

"But Lambert, my boy, do you think some such misfortune may occur?"

"Naturally not. But it is a risk, and risks are best avoided. After all," Moreton added, "the sight of that woman encouraging cheering crowds of heretics to adore her will make you sick to your stomach."

Sir Nicholas grunted in agreement. "You are right, Lambert, as usual," he said. "I shall indeed remain here throughout the progress and any man of Walsingham's that cares to visit will find us living a blameless Protestant life."

"That is a wise decision, Uncle," said Moreton, "a wise decision indeed."

There was a long pause – so long that William thought that the men must have gone. With his thighs starting to burn with the pain of crouching, he decided he had to stand up. Just as he was preparing to raise himself, he heard a voice again. Quickly he dropped back down.

"Who was that at the door, that you must attend her?" It was the voice of Sir Nicholas.

"Naught but an itinerant woman," answered Moreton. "She was seeking a position of service."

"Ahh. Did you turn her away?"

"I did. She was most unsavoury."

"Good."

There was the sound of boots scraping across the cobbles as the two men finally walked off. William remained crouched down by his horse's leg a few minutes more, then cautiously he stood up.

The stable yard was empty.

So the Queen was coming on progress to nearby York? William recalled earlier talk of the summer progress, but it had slipped his mind.

Then an idea began to form.

York! It was the perfect opportunity for him and Ambrose to slip away!

To make their escape from this dangerous household, with its threatening young upstarts like Moreton and the ever-present fear of being accused of Catholic practices. William gave a hollow laugh as massaged feeling back into his legs. He had led his son into this viper's nest of heresy, and now here at last was a way he could get the boy back to the warmth and safety of Grangedean Manor.

The more he thought about it, the better it looked.

It would be only natural for Ambrose to want to see the Queen, and only natural for his father to offer to take him. The Grenvilles would be hard-pressed to refuse. And even if they sent an escort of men-at-arms, there were bound to be heavy crowds in York. So it would be no trouble to manufacture a means to become separated, then ride out of the city and set off down south. It would be a while before their absence was noticed, giving them plenty of time to get well ahead of any potential pursuit.

William frowned. Ideally he would want the protection of his own trusted men-at-arms on the journey. But it would raise suspicion if he tried to take them to York. So they would have to be left behind, and he and Ambrose would have to travel alone through hundreds of miles of rough country.

He bit his lip. Could he travel all the way to Grangedean without them? The two of them alone?

He nodded to himself. Of course. The boy was strong. Had he not proved that on the way up to Hetherington? And the snows had gone, so it would be an easier journey.

Then it was settled. He and Ambrose would set off for York, slip away, and leave this hellish house behind them.

With a renewed purpose, William strode out of the stable and marched back up to Hetherington Hall.

---0---

And now he and Ambrose were following Moreton to where the three horses were standing saddled and ready. They mounted up and Moreton led the way out back along the path, with William behind and Ambrose bringing up the rear.

William remained silent as they rode through the parklands towards a side gate in the perimeter wall, waiting to see if Moreton offered any further explanation. As they passed through the gate in silence, there was a fork in the path beyond. One fork led to the village and open fields, while the other led directly to the ravine and on down the side.

Moreton took the path to the ravine.

William glanced back at Ambrose and could see his son's concerned face – which was no doubt a mirror of his own. Why would Moreton be leading them towards the ravine? William made a split-second decision. The York plan was perfect in every way, but it was too late.

This whole situation was now too risky and they had to make their escape right now.

He turned to look at Ambrose again, preparing to wheel his horse around, grab Thelwell's bridle and ride back to the fork in the path. Then they would turn for the village and make all speed away. With the element of surprise, they could get a start on Moreton and open up a good distance from any pursuit.

But as he turned, he saw a sight that made his blood run cold.

Four burly horsemen in Grenville livery were riding out from the gate and coming up fast behind Ambrose. Even as William watched, they reached the boy and surrounded him.

Moreton turned. "My dear Sir William de Beauvais," he called, "I thought you might consider leaving us, so I prepared a little escort. By all means ride off and preserve yourself, but please be aware that you must leave your son in my care." He gave a thin smile. "And I cannot guarantee that my care will be as..." he seemed to be searching for the right word, "...as loving as yours."

"Damn you, Moreton," returned William, all hope of escape now disappearing. "What is the meaning of this?" He decided to try innocent bluster. "Are we not to meet Sir Nicholas as bidden? Why do you threaten my son so?"

Moreton stopped and wheeled his horse round so he was facing William and Ambrose. The horsemen brought Ambrose up close, then stopped also. The small boy and pony seemed dwarfed by them.

"Oh come now, de Beauvais, Sir Nicholas knows nothing of this." Moreton growled, a deep frown appearing on his thin face. "But I am no fool. Did you seriously think I did not know about you creeping about the house back in the winter, spying on us?"

William gripped his reins hard as he tried to maintain a neutral face. "I have no idea what you mean," he said.

"Truly?" Moreton shook his head. "I doubt that very much. Indeed, I will have one of my men ask your son. I am sure he can tell me what you know." He nodded to the man beside Ambrose. The man drew his sword, then grabbed Ambrose's arm and put the point up towards the boy's chest.

"Damn you, Moreton!" snapped William. "He knows naught! You threaten a child?"

"If necessary. Now tell me."

William glanced at his son, whose eyes were wide with fear as he stared down at the point of the sword. William turned back to Moreton. "Devil take you, Moreton," he muttered. "Yes, I did do some quiet exploration. How did you know?"

Moreton smirked at his own cleverness. "An honest man does not leave his shoes behind when abroad in the house, nor does he look guilty later when the talk is of exploring the rooms." He gestured to the man next to Ambrose to sheath his sword.

William breathed a small sigh of relief as the blade slid into its scabbard.

"An honest man does not hold Catholic mass in clear contravention of the law," he answered. "Nor, no doubt, does he hide a priest in the house to conduct such services."

Moreton looked at him as if he were the basest worm. "A man must worship almighty God in the way of truth, or he is neither honest to himself nor to God. But I do not suppose that means anything to you, de Beauvais, who is content to blow with wind and worship as ordered by a heretic bastard."

"You talk treason, Moreton," William said quietly. "Have a care."

"And who is to hear?" Moreton shrugged. "These men are good Catholics, who are loyal to me and to the Grenvilles." He smiled his thin, sickly smile. "And where you are going, neither you nor the boy will be able to tell."

"What are you planning to do with us?" William demanded, trying to put some authority into his voice.

Moreton stared hard at the bushes beside the path a moment, then he laughed, making his thin body shake like a branch in a storm. "My dear Sir William de Beauvais," he said after a moment, "please give no further thought to escape. For you are instrumental to my plans." He laughed again, then suddenly the laughter disappeared from his face as if it had never existed. "I have two plans. One is to keep you both safe – so do not fear. For now. You are my failsafe if aught goes wrong with my other plan."

"Your other plan?" William asked.

But Moreton said nothing more. Instead, he glanced again at the bushes, then he gestured to the men, wheeled his horse round, and set off along the path to the side of the ravine.

William and Ambrose were herded along behind him like a couple of unwilling sheep, as the group headed over the edge of the ravine and started picking their way down the narrow rocky path.

CHAPTER TWENTY-ONE

"How do I look?" asked Mary, as she and Tom prepared to leave their rooms and go down to the Great Hall.

"Magnificent," he answered with a smile. "You are no longer the dirty serving woman or ragged traveller I have known, but are now restored to your full glory." He swept off his cap and bowed low. "After all these weeks, I am honoured finally to meet the noble Lady Mary de Beauvais."

"Oh come now," she said, feeling her cheeks starting to burn, "you have known me in good times and bad. A bath and some proper clothes do not make a difference." Although there was no denying that it had been glorious to finally get out of the threadbare servant's dress and put on the fine pale yellow gown with grey underskirt and sleeves that Olivia had found for her.

"Well, madam," he said, straightening up again, "I beg to disagree." He put on his cap. "Shall we not go down and show the court your nobility and bearing, and see if they are of the same mind as me?"

"Let us go down, for sure, but you mind your tongue, Thomas Cobham, or it could get you into some serious trouble."

"Not just my tongue," he muttered, but just loud enough for her to hear. He opened the door and stood back. "You must lead, good lady, as I am worthy only to follow in your shadow." He gave her a cheeky smile, "and I want better to see the faces of those women you pass – for I am sure they will turn green with envy!"

"Nonsense!" she replied, although she couldn't hide a smile of her own. "And anyway, remember we are only here a couple of days, till everyone goes to York and we can stop the Alchemist."

The thought of that man out there with his awful gun, no doubt hiding in some inn or cottage until the Queen's progress came to York, caused a sudden icy finger of fear to run down her back. She stopped a moment. So much rested on her and Tom's shoulders – not just the safety of the Queen, but the future she remembered, and her own future too.

She shook her head to try and give herself the reassurance and strength she needed to face the challenge ahead.

We have a plan – and it has to work!

At least the first part had been easy – getting into Wyvern Castle and establishing herself and Tom as members of the Queen's entourage. Olivia had been as good as her word, and had gone straight to Wychwoode, who had pulled whatever strings he needed to pull to get them in. They had been sitting chatting idly by the gate for only an hour when Olivia had come back with a sombre-looking elderly man dressed all in black, who turned out to be the Wyvern steward.

"Come, my lady," said Olivia, with a poorly concealed sideways glance that was clearly intended to size up Tom. "You and Master Cobham are bidden to join the progress at the invitation of Master Wychwoode, who says he wishes to avail himself of your good council on the matter of the preparation of the Queen's route through the streets of York. He has made rooms available to you, and has servants ready to bathe and dress you both as befits a courtier."

The sombre man produced an enormous bunch of keys from a leather bag slung round his shoulder, then spent what seemed like an agonising eternity carefully surveying each key before selecting one and opening the gate. Finally, Tom and Mary were able to walk through, as the man locked up again behind them.

Mary looked back at the wall above other side of the gate while the steward was locking up, and saw it had the identical shield above, with the same legless dragon.

"What is that strange beast?" she asked the man.

He regarded her dolefully as he put the keys back in his bag, as if debating whether or not he could trust himself to impart such information. Then he cleared his throat and said slowly, "Madam, 'tis the Wyvern itself – an ancient beast that has been on the arms of the family for over two hundred years." Then he was silent again. Mary was just about to ask if it was chosen for the family name or the other way round, when the man suddenly carried on. "This is known as the hanging gate," he announced, "as it was the old Lord Wyvern's practice to use it to dispose of anyone who challenged or stole from him. He would order a rope to be thrown up behind the shield," he pointed upwards, "and hang the unfortunate by the neck. Indeed," he continued, "so many times has this occurred that the supporting stone behind the shield is worn quite smooth. Which," he added "makes it all the easier to haul a man up to his death."

---0---

Mary took Tom's arm, and they descended the ornate stone stairway with its magnificent wood panelling, together with pictures of the Wyvern family and their illustrious ancestors.

The stairs and the hallway below were crowded with nobility of all sorts; elegant women in gowns of every hue, dripping with emeralds, diamonds, rubies and opals, their hair loose and flowing or contained in different types of hoods. They were accompanied by men in embroidered doublets with slashed nether-stocks, rich coloured hose, and all topped off with a variety of decorative caps and hats. Everyone was talking, which meant they all had to raise their voices nearly to a shout, making a wall of sound that was almost painful to Mary's ears. She also noticed that there was none of the usual smell of sweat she had now grown used to with Elizabethan crowds; instead there were a variety of intriguing and quite pleasant scents. She identified lavender, rose, jasmine and cedar, as well as hints of pine and nutmeg, before she had even reached the foot of the stairs.

She could see the occasional man in the black garb of a lawyer or secretary standing out against the sea of colour, and searched across the crowd for the distinctive white hair of Robert Wychwoode. However, she reached the foot of the stairs without spotting him.

As they passed through a pair of tall oak doors into the Great Hall, she saw Olivia immediately, waiting just inside as agreed. Beside her was a small girl of about eighteen, whose striking beauty was marred by a fearsome scowl as she glared down at the floor.

"My dear Lady de Beauvais," said Olivia, when they had greeted each other with a kiss. "Allow me to present Margaret Tyndall, also in waiting to my lady Burnham."

The girl slowly raised her head and stared defiantly at Mary, who stared back with a slight smile.

"You must be Maggie, of whom I have heard so much," Mary said. Then she stood slightly to one side to let Tom through. "Allow me to present Master Thomas Cobham, who has been most kind and most accommodating on our journey here. We have been through many adventures."

Tom stepped forward, swept off his cap and bowed low to both girls in turn. "Mistress Melrose, Mistress Tyndall, you are both well met."

Olivia nodded her head in acknowledgement. "Indeed, Master Cobham, I am most indebted to you for keeping my friend safe on the journey."

"For sure, Mistress Melrose," Tom answered as he put his cap back on, "I would be well minded not to take the credit for keeping Lady Mary safe, but to say that on just as many occasions, it was she who did such service for me!"

"And the better man for admitting it," said Olivia, with a small sideways glance at Maggie.

"Mistress Melrose, you are too kind," Tom replied.

"Olivia, please! Call me Olivia. And she has done so much for me, too"

"Very well – Olivia – we shall share our tales of Lady Mary's courage and resourcefulness anon, over a glass or two of claret." He smiled, then put a hand on her sleeve. "And I have no doubt that the more claret we drink, the better will be our tales of Lady Mary's bravery and daring!"

Then Tom turned to the girl beside her. "And now, Mistress Tyndall, pray tell me what ails you, that you have such a look of pain on your pretty face?"

"Maggie is upset," explained Olivia, "as she accuses me of trying to end her relationship with one Lionel Shelton, who I do not believe is worthy of her."

"It is not for you to decide," Maggie muttered.

"As one who has experience of this man," Olivia continued, as if Maggie had not spoken, "I know that he does not share your amorous feelings."

Maggie rounded on Olivia, "And pray tell how you know this?"

"Olivia speaks the truth, Mistress Tyndall," Mary cut in quickly, before any argument could start. "I can vouchsafe that this Shelton is a base creature, and best left alone."

"Oh heavens!" cried Maggie, stamping her foot, "Does no one support me in my liaison with Lionel Shelton?"

"No," answered Mary, "and for good reason." She took Maggie's hand in both of her own, and said, "Come with me, child, I have something to tell you." Then she led Maggie away to a window seat where they could sit as far as possible from the crowds.

She indicated to the girl to sit down, which Maggie did by dropping inelegantly onto the seat with a deep sigh and her arms folded.

Mary ignored this. "I could tell you all the dreadful things this man has done to other girls just like you," she said. "Painful things. Selfish things. Wicked things. But I will not. Instead I will ask you to answer just two questions."

Maggie looked up. Mary pressed on while she had the girl's attention. "One, what is the best thing Shelton has ever said or done, and two, what is the worst?"

Maggie hesitated. "Go on," Mary encouraged her.

"The best – he has said my eyes are as the prettiest cornflowers and my hair is as the sunlight itself."

"And the worst?"

Again Maggie was silent, her eyes staring deep into Mary's.

"He made to hit me, because he believed I might have doubted him," she said eventually in a small voice.

Mary said nothing for a while, to see if Maggie would draw her own conclusions. After a moment, the girl nodded. "This is not the behaviour of an honourable man – a man who is in love – is it?"

Mary shook her head. "No, I do not think it is."

"Is it the behaviour of a seasoned courtier who professes love without meaning?" Maggie asked.

Mary nodded.

"But what of the cornflowers?"

"Pretty words do not make a lover," Mary whispered. "But it is the actions that make the man."

"But he was upset. I upset him. It is perfectly right and proper for a man to become angry if a girl upsets him."

"No!" Mary grabbed her shoulders suddenly, causing a couple of nearby courtiers to jump. "No man has the right to strike a girl," she hissed quietly, but with real force in her voice, "however angry he may be!" She let go and sat back. "I know that men have all the rights, but that has to change – and one day it will, I swear. One day women will be as equal to men, and the better for it."

"But…" Maggie looked at her with wide eyes, "no woman can be equal to a man – it is not natural, or as God would wish."

"Why?" Mary responded, leaning forward again and keeping her voice low in order to avoid drawing in any of the surrounding courtiers. "Why must God favour men over women?"

Maggie answered immediately, "Because Eve betrayed Adam."

Mary sat back. There was no point in trying to offer an explanation based on Darwinian evolution to this girl – she would have to take a more sideways approach. "And why did Eve do as she did?"

"Because of the serpent?"

"Indeed," Mary said in triumph. "And was the serpent male or female?"

"Male, of course." Maggie shook her head at Mary's apparent stupidity, then suddenly she stopped, as a light of understanding came into her eyes. "So…" she said slowly, "it was not the woman's fault, but a man's…" She stared at Mary, as she worked it out further. "It is men who tell us we must obey them – yet it is they who make the rules…" She looked in awe at Mary. "So we should recognise that it is not God's law, but…"

"Man's law, yes." Mary finished for her. "And as I say, one day this will change, and women will take their rightful place as men's equals."

"You are sure of this?"

"I am." Mary smiled. "Maybe not in our lifetimes, but one day." She stood up and held out her hand for Maggie to stand as well.

Maggie was silent for a long moment, as she thought it all through. Then she took Mary's hand and stood.

"You are saying that one day my daughters or theirs will benefit?"

"I am."

"Very well, Lady Mary," Maggie gave a small curtsey and smile, "That is a change I would desire."

"So if that is your desire, then you will change yourself now? You will have no more flirtation with Shelton?"

"No, none. He is as the serpent. I see that now, and…" She nodded, as if confirming it to herself, "…and I am quite cured of him." She paused, then added, "I think."

"What you must think, Maggie Tyndall," said Mary, "is that this is a vain, shallow man who is not worthy to kiss the hem of your gown, and you would do well never to forget it."

"I will," Maggie said again, only this time with a bit more conviction. "Yes," she said firmly, "I will."

"Good." Mary stood back to let Maggie go first. "Then let us re-join the others and tell them our news."

They weaved their way back to Olivia and Tom.

Olivia raised an eyebrow in enquiry. Mary said, "Maggie has something to tell us."

Maggie looked down a moment, as if seeking inspiration from the toes of her shoes, then looked back up. "I am no longer enamoured of Lionel," she said slowly. "Indeed, I have seen that he is not an honourable man."

Olivia looked hard at Maggie, as if to say, 'I told you so!' But instead she asked, "And this is how you truly feel?"

Maggie nodded and smiled weakly at Olivia. "I have been quite the little madam, have I not? I am so sorry. Will you ever forgive me?"

Olivia drew the girl into a tight embrace. "Of course I will, you silly goose!"

"I rather think Maggie is now fully cured of Master Shelton," observed Mary to Tom. "Shall we now seek Master Robert Wychwoode? You and I do have some pressing business with him." She looked around the room, and with relief, she finally spotted the tall white-haired lawyer on the other side of the Great Hall.

Together she and Tom pushed their way across the room until the crowds parted and she found herself once again in Wychwoode's presence. He was facing away from her as he was talking to a couple of men, but as Mary approached something made him stop and turn round enquiringly.

He had definitely aged in the last ten years; his face was more lined, and there was a droop to the corners of each eye, but the white flowing hair was as thick as before, and there was still no mistaking the power and authority that emanated from him like an aura. A large beaming smile spread across his face like the rise of the summer sun, then he bowed deeply.

"Lady Mary de Beauvais!" he exclaimed as he stood up. "You are indeed well met!. It must be all of ten years since we thwarted that appalling little witchfinder!" He kissed her in greeting. "Olivia Melrose told me you were here, and we should find space for you and Tom at Court. I trust the rooms we have secured suit you well?" She nodded. "Good." He looked her up and down. "And the clothes we have found do become you most excellently."

Tom pushed forward. "And here is Thomas Cobham, too!" Wychwoode exclaimed. "Art come to report on the matter we started all those months ago?"

Tom nodded, and Wychwoode became serious in a heartbeat. "Then come, we must take a walk in the gardens where we can converse in peace."

Together they made their way out of the Great Hall and through the main doors into the gardens. Soon they were able to talk freely without fear of being overheard.

"I questioned a man called Tyler in Stratford but was not able to get any information from him on the whereabouts of the Alchemist," Wychwoode said. "So I had him transferred to the Tower in London for further questioning." He shook his head. "Which means we have now lost track of this Alchemist. I take it that the reason you are here is that you have knowledge of the Alchemist after Stratford?"

Tom nodded. "Aye, we do. We went to Stratford ourselves to seek out this man Tyler, but we picked up the trail of the Alchemist himself – so we followed him instead." Tom answered. "We found him – or more to the point he found us. He then caused the death of Mary's horse, as well as an honest woodsman and his fair daughter by burning their cottage to the ground. We were also trapped, but escaped only by the greatest good fortune and the resourcefulness of the good Lady Mary."

Wychwoode turned to Mary and nodded. "I have remarked on your courage and resource in the past, Lady Mary," he said with a smile. "I am pleased to see this has not left you." He turned back to Tom, as Mary felt herself blushing for the second time that evening. Tom continued, "We believe the Alchemist is hiding out near here even now."

"Indeed?" Wychwoode raised an enquiring eyebrow.

"We believe he intends to take his shot when Her Majesty is on progress through the streets of York," said Tom.

"With this special musket of his," Wychwoode asked, "the one we heard he had fashioned himself, to find its target even from five hundred yards or more?"

"He has this, and some of his singular cartridges that contain both powder and ball," said Tom.

Wychwoode was silent a moment, deep in thought. "I have sworn to Her Majesty to keep her safe." He looked at each in turn. "We have to get to this man and stop him before he has his chance."

"We do have some thoughts on a plan to stop him," said Mary.

"Pray tell." Wychwoode said.

Mary explained their plan for her to seek out the Alchemist and for Tom to ride close by the Queen.

Wychwoode nodded. "It has the makings of a plan," he said slowly.

"Can you have some of your men available to help us?" asked Tom.

"Aye, Tom, I will," Wychwoode paused, "but all must be done in secret – in the shadows. Her Majesty has made it most clear that she will not be seen to be cowering in fear behind men – rather, she must be clearly visible to all."

"But that is what the Alchemist wants!" exclaimed Tom. "If the Queen is in clear view he can get his shot."

"She does not account for the accuracy of his special musket," added Mary. "This makes it different from every other attempt; the Alchemist can be many hundreds of yards away and still be sure to kill her."

"Aye." Wychwoode agreed. "But the Queen has been most explicit on this, and we cannot go against her wishes on the basis of a possible weapon about which we cannot be certain."

"I have seen it in action," Mary said firmly. "The Alchemist used it to kill my horse, and before he burned the cottage down, he shot the old woodsman dead right in front of us. It is real, believe me."

"I do believe you, my dear Lady Mary, indeed I do," answered Wychwoode. "But I cannot go against the Queen's wishes. This whole operation must be conducted in total secrecy." He looked from Mary to Tom. "I will support you both with a few men, but that is all I can vouchsafe. We will sit together tomorrow and plan this in more detail." He looked at Mary. "Does that meet with your approval, my lady?"

She nodded slowly. "Indeed, Master Wychwoode, it does – as long as we can be sure we can find the Alchemist before he can use his musket." Then she looked down. "But there is one other thing…"

He raised an eyebrow. "Which is, my lady?"

Mary took a breath. For all her concern to protect the Queen, there was something else that had been eating at her, ever since she had been turned away by that strange Lambert Moreton at Hetherington Hall. It was a mother's concern for her son, and knowing that he was here in York while there was a killer on the loose, was a worry that she could not ignore. It seemed only fair that Wychwoode, with all his influence and connections, should offer help in return for all she had done – and was prepared to do – to protect the Queen.

"I have been told that my son, Ambrose de Beauvais, is in York to see the progress," she said. "I am told that he is staying at the town-house of his hosts, the Grenvilles. I am concerned for his safety."

Wychwoode stared at her, chewing on his lip. "My dear lady," he said after a moment, "I am sure your son will be in no danger with the Grenville family. None at all." He gave a reassuring smile. "But I will send a couple of my men to the Grenville town-house to keep watch on him." He touched her on the arm. "Does that reassure you?"

Mary breathed a sigh of relief. "Yes," she said. "Thank you."

She looked at Tom. "Come on," she said brightly, "let us re-join the revelries, then tomorrow we can plan our campaign against this Alchemist."

But Wychwoode held up his hand. "By your leave, Lady Mary," he said,

"I would speak alone with Master Cobham first. He has been working on my orders these past few months, and I would like to have his report in person."

Mary nodded. "Of course," she answered. "Tom. I will see you in the Great Hall shortly." Then she turned and walked alone back to the castle.

---0---

Tom waited until Mary was out of earshot, then turned to Wychwoode.

"I have a feeling this is not about me reporting to you, but perhaps the other way around?" he asked. "You have something you wish to tell me?"

"Aye, I do. What Lady Mary has said raises the gravest of concerns. I would not have this said to her face, but I have information which means that young master Ambrose is indeed in great danger."

Tom checked the retreating figure of Mary to make sure she was definitely out of earshot. "Go on," he replied.

"You may recall I said this man Tyler did not talk in Stratford and we sent him to the Tower for further questions?"

Tom nodded.

"Well, now he has talked."

"Willingly?"

Wychwoode shook his head with a grimace. "Nay, unfortunately not. Let us say that we had to… persuade him… to co-operate."

"Then the information is tainted, surely?" Tom said. "It is well known that a man will say anything he can to stop pain being applied."

"I agree, and I do not use such methods lightly," Wychwoode muttered, "but Walsingham was insistent. This Tyler was a strong man, and held out for nigh on two weeks, it seems, before he died. I have had a messenger only this morning. It seems that before he died, he revealed one piece of information which Walsingham believes is genuine. It may lead us to the man who controls the plot."

Tom thought a moment. If Wychwoode believed that Ambrose de Beauvais was in danger, it could only mean that the household who had taken him in were themselves implicated in the plot. Mary was right to be concerned. "Is it Grenville?" he asked.

Wychwoode nodded. "We think it is. Tyler said only one word that we could clearly define, in response to the question 'where is the plot centred?' He said 'Hetherington'."

"And York is less than an hour's ride from Hetherington Hall, home of the Catholic Sir Nicholas Grenville…" said Tom, finishing the thought. "Then why have you not arrested Grenville and taken him in for questioning?"

"We have no evidence linking him to the Alchemist or Alleyne, other than the word of Tyler."

"Procured under torture." Tom could see the problem. "Are you watching the house?"

Wychwoode nodded. "Indeed, I have now sent men to conduct clandestine observation round the clock from key vantage points. I have my first report due to me tomorrow morning on the current movements in and out of the house." He gave a hollow laugh. "As we get closer to the progress through York, it may be that something incriminating is seen."

"But it may be that the Alchemist is operating alone – under instructions not to make contact with the Grenvilles?"

"Indeed. But let us see when we get the report tomorrow."

"And will you send men to the Grenville town house in the meantime?" Tom asked.

"I will," answered Wychwoode. "I promised the same to Lady Mary, and I will do all I can to deliver on my promise."

Tom was silent a moment, deep in thought. If Mary still thought that Ambrose was in danger, she would not be focused on preventing the assassination of Elizabeth. So as long as she knew Ambrose was safe under observation at the Grenville town house, then that danger was lifted. "But we should not share any of these suspicions with Mary," he said slowly, "unless we have more solid proof."

"I agree," said Wychwoode. "For now she is determined to stop this Alchemist, and her courage and resource will be a key part of our success in doing so. We must keep her mind on that goal – and that goal alone."

CHAPTER TWENTY-TWO

As Mary made her way back into the Great Hall through the crowds of Elizabethan courtiers and hangers-on, the first person she recognised was Lionel Shelton.

He was standing just inside the door, scanning the crowds as if he was looking for someone. As Mary approached and their eyes met, she saw his expression darken as if a thunder cloud had rolled across his face. Then he deliberately turned away as if to carry on searching.

Ignoring the insult, Mary marched up to him. "Master Shelton," she demanded, raising her voice to be heard above the cacophony of noise in the room. She put her hand on his elegantly slit velvet sleeve. "I would speak with you."

He turned back slowly and looked her up and down, paying unnecessarily lengthy attention to her chest. "Yes, my lady?" he drawled, raising his eyes to hers with a sickly smile.

"What you did to Olivia Melrose was a sick, monstrous crime and should not go unpunished," Mary said. She knew it sounded weak when said out loud, and certainly not as good as it had in her head as she was walking over. She stared defiantly at him.

"Indeed, Lady de Beauvais," Shelton answered, seeming impervious to her glare. "And by what spurious authority do you intend to have me charged?" He shook his head. "I would deny any accusation, naturally."

"Yes, I am sure you would," Mary snapped back. "I doubt your conduct as a gentleman extends to honesty and repentance. Anyway," she continued, "an accusation and a trial would undoubtedly affect your reputation. Some would believe you capable of it, even if you were not found guilty."

"I very much doubt that," he said. "It would be the word of a young girl against a gentleman at Court – and a wanton, lascivious young girl at that. Few would give her story credence – even if she were prepared to admit she had carnal relations outside of wedlock." He smiled again, showing yellowing teeth. "For that would reflect poorly on her, such that she could never marry." He paused, "As well you know, my lady."

All Mary knew at that moment was that she was not prepared to let this arrogant, depraved man get away with his crime against Olivia. "I know a time and place where evil creatures like you get the punishment they deserve for raping an innocent girl," she muttered.

"Well, I suggest you go hence to that place, because here and now, I know I can act with impunity."

The look of smug triumph on his face caused a sudden thought to occur. "You would have no hesitation to do it again!" she exclaimed, and he grinned at her, confirming her worst fear. "With Maggie Tyndall!"

He stared over her shoulder into the distance. "She is indeed very comely, and I feel she may be more willing than Mistress Melrose…"

"Oh no, no, no…" Mary shook her head. "That boat has sailed, Shelton. Maggie Tyndall no longer has any regard for you."

He continued to stare into the distance. "So I must either win her back…" he paused, then snapped his head round suddenly and stared at Mary, "or I must disregard her affection entirely. I must have her. She has become an itch that I must scratch."

Then he removed his cap, bowed and said, "But that shall be for later, by your leave my lady, as I have some more," he paused, "important matters to attend to." Leaving Mary feeling sickened to her stomach, he threaded his way to the door, pausing only to bow briefly to Olivia and Maggie as they passed him on their way into the room.

The two girls came straight over to Mary.

"Were you talking to Shelton?" asked Olivia, her eyes wide. "What did you say to him?"

"He smiled at me in a way that I did not like!" complained Maggie. "As if I was but a foolish child who could not be trusted."

Olivia turned to her. "There," she said. "Now you have the measure of him – you see the kind of man he is. As I have told you, he has no real regard for you and he never has."

Mary put her hand on Maggie's sleeve. "We are only looking out for your best interests."

Maggie gave them a watery smile. "I know," she said slowly, "but I did think he had the nicest eyes," she paused, "and I liked his hands as well."

"Which he would have used to strike you," added Olivia. "Had I not come in."

"There is that, I suppose," Maggie admitted.

"Which no man should think he has the right to do," said Mary.

Maggie nodded. Then she said, "I think I will go to my rooms a while." She gave Mary a small curtsey. "By your leave, my lady."

"So," Olivia said, when Maggie had gone, "what did Shelton say just now?"

"That he would take her whether she wants it or not."

"The man is a monster – the very devil!"

"He said she is an itch that he must scratch."

"Then we must stop him, for sure. What are we to do?"

"We have to punish him – we have to teach him a lesson he will never forget." Mary took Olivia's hands in her own. "And I think I have just the plan we need." She paused. "But it will also need Maggie to play her part…"

---0---

A night owl hooted softly as two hooded figures, barely visible in the deep shadows, crept along the back of Wyvern Castle and slipped quietly in through a side entrance.

They passed silently along the dark passageway until they came to a heavy wooden door set into a semi-circular stone wall. The first figure eased the latch up as slowly as possible, then opened the door inch by inch. Suddenly there was a sharp screeching sound from the hinge; unnaturally loud in the still night. Immediately the figure paused, listening for any sounds of footsteps or a shout from someone alerted by the noise. After a minute or more there was no such response, so they resumed opening the door, but slower still. As soon as it was sufficiently open, both figures slipped silently through, then padded quickly up a set of circular stone stairs.

At the top, they paused in front of another door. One of the figures put their hands to their mouth and made a soft owl hoot of their own.

After a moment, the door was opened and candle-light spilled out, illuminating the two hooded figures, as well as the one who had opened the door.

"Is it safe?" hissed one of the visitors.

"Yes," came the answer, and the two entered the room.

Once inside, Mary and Olivia pushed back their hoods. Mary smiled at Maggie, standing back from the door and holding her candle. Her face looked unnatural in the flickering light and shadows. "Then it is done?" Olivia asked.

"Aye." Maggie gestured towards the bed, "He sleeps like an infant."

They looked across to where Lionel Shelton lay spread out on the bed, stark naked. A goblet lay on the floor, leaving red wine stains on the rushes.

"How much sleeping draught did you give him?" asked Olivia.

"As much as you said, and a few drops more for good measure."

"Good," Olivia answered. "That is more than it takes to put my lady Burnham to sleep when she asks for it – but 'tis well done, I see."

"And he had not tried anything untoward first?" asked Mary.

"Nay, I was fortunate that the potion did its work before he was able to," answered Maggie, "though he was most in haste to get unclothed when I said I would lay with him willingly. I had only to unlace my sleeves and he was throwing off his own attire like a man burning with a fever."

"Good." Mary became more business-like. "We need to carry him out to the place I have in mind quickly, in case the potion wears off. Blow out your candle, Maggie – between the three of us we can carry him in the dark."

---0---

The early morning sun beat down on the long column of horses and riders that snaked its way along the path from Wyvern Castle to the front gate.

At the front of the column was Her Majesty Queen Elizabeth, resplendent in white and gold, her red hair rising from her forehead and decorated with pearls and emeralds; her sharp dark eyes looking straight ahead as she rode. Beside her was the Earl of Leicester, more soberly dressed in a grey doublet, and beside him was a hawksman with the Queen's hawk on a leather gauntlet. The bird flapped its wings idly and the hawksman made soothing noises, before slipping a small leather hood over its head to calm it.

As the procession approached the imposing arched gateway, the Earl looked up and sniggered.

The Queen also glanced up briefly, then held up her hand and brought her horse to a stop, causing the column behind her to halt also.

The Queen turned to the Earl and said calmly, "Why is there is a naked man hauled to the top of the archway?" She glanced briefly up at the man. He had been tied with a rope under his arms and then been hoisted up above the gate, almost up to the shield with the legless dragon. The rope then passed over the supporting stone behind the shield, before being tied off securely at the base of one of the brick pillars.

The Earl sniggered again. As if on cue the column of riders behind him all started to laugh, until after a few minutes there was barely a single man who was not roaring with laughter.

The Queen herself did not crack a smile, but held up her hand again, and the laughter died down quickly. "Who is this man?" she demanded. "I can not see his face from this angle, as there are other parts of him which are more – prominent – in my view."

The Earl wheeled his horse round and rode back a few yards to get a better view, then returned to the Queen's side. "I would say it is Master Lionel Shelton, madam," he said.

"And why," the Queen asked quietly, "do you suppose Master Shelton has been pulled up to the top of the brick archway above these gates?"

"I have not a clue, madam," answered the Earl. "Although I warrant this is some form of punishment for bad behaviour – for I understand this is called the hanging gate."

"It is well named," observed the Queen drily. "Although I note he supports his weight with his feet on the brick lintel – so the organiser of this punishment does not wish him to perish by this act."

"Belike he has angered someone and they have simply sought to make him the laughing stock he now is?" suggested the Earl.

"I agree," answered the Queen.

"Shall I have this investigated, madam?" Leicester asked. "To have the perpetrator brought to justice?"

The Queen shook her head. "Nay," she answered. "No doubt this was deserved, and I would commend whoever devised this punishment for their ingenuity." She trotted through the gates without looking up, then stopped and turned back to the Earl. "Enough of this fool – we are set to hunt this morning. Have him taken down and banished from Court for life. I never wish to see him again." She thought a moment, then added, "I fear I have seen quite enough of him as it is."

The hunting party then followed her though the gates, each member looking up and laughing at Shelton, suspended naked in front of the arch above them, his eyes tightly closed – as if somehow by not seeing his tormentors, they could not see him.

CHAPTER TWENTY-THREE

"Master Ambrose *and* Sir William?" asked Tom, staring at the small, anonymous-looking man dressed in a jerkin and breeches that were a patchwork of green and brown. "Are you certain? Sir William was supposed to have journeyed back to Grangedean Manor these many weeks since."

It was later that morning, and Wychwoode and Tom were gathered in the far corner of the Wyvern gardens, behind a maze made of high green hedges. It was the perfect spot for a meeting with Wychwoode's spy.

"Indeed Master Cobham," the man answered. "I have seen with my own eyes the boy and a man of noble bearing addressed as Sir William de Beauvais by Moreton."

Wychwoode asked, "Where was Moreton taking them?"

"I know not, Master Wychwoode, but..."

"Go on," Tom prompted.

"But it was against their will, Master, that much was clear. Moreton had some men-at-arms who threatened the boy, so the father must go along with their orders."

"Did Moreton say anything?"

"He said, and I have this committed to my memory, 'you are my failsafe if aught goes wrong with my plan.' Then he led them away from the house, I know not where."

Wychwoode took out his purse and pressed a coin into the man's hand. "I thank you. Now go and resume your watch on Hetherington."

The man nodded and slipped away. He quickly disappeared into the hedges beyond the maze; his green and brown clothing blending him into the foliage.

Wychwoode watched him go. "He is one of my best men," he observed, "able to hide unseen in any hedgerow." He turned to Tom with a smile. "He could be a couple of feet from you, and you would never know."

"I shall watch my step, then, Master Wychwoode," answered Tom with a laugh, "in case he might be listening and reporting my words back to you."

Wychwoode laughed also. "Then say naught to give me cause for concern – and you have naught to fear."

There was a silence as each man became serious once more, considering the importance of the message they had heard.

"So, the master plotter is this Lambert Moreton," said Wychwoode. "Belike even Sir Nicholas is unaware of this."

"It would seem so."

"Then I am minded to arrest Moreton now…" the older man mused.

"And have Sir William and Ambrose de Beauvais killed?" Tom replied. "Is that not what Moreton meant by a 'failsafe'? And besides, if you arrest Moreton, the Alchemist is not prevented from carrying out his part of the plan."

"True."

"Perhaps…" Tom stopped.

"What?"

"Perhaps Moreton *did* see your man in the hedgerow…"

"Not possible."

"But if he did – maybe he spotted movement – particularly if he was expecting clandestine observers…" Tom shook his head, "then I think he was sending us a message."

There was a pause as Wychwoode considered this. "If so," he said, "if we *do* accept that my man may have been seen, then what Moreton was telling us… is that Sir William and Master Ambrose are his hostages."

"I think so." Tom kicked at a pebble on the path.

"Then we are in the hands of you and Lady Mary tomorrow in York, to find this Alchemist and stop him killing the Queen."

"And if we do, and Moreton hears that the Queen progresses unharmed through the streets of York – then I would not give a fig for the life of the hostages…"

Wychwoode put his hand on the younger man's shoulder. "I need hardly remind you, sir, where your duty lies," he said softly.

Tom kicked the pebble again.

For sure, his duty lay with the life of the Queen – that much was obvious. He must do all in his power to preserve her. But it could not be denied that if he did, then he would most surely be condemning the husband and son of Lady Mary de Beauvais to an untimely end – which did not bear thinking about. But if they were successful in stopping the Alchemist – and as a consequence Sir William met with an unfortunate end, then Lady Mary would become a widow and free to marry once more… To become Mistress Cobham. There was no denying it was an attractive proposition, though he felt sick to the pit of his stomach for even thinking it… No, no. The honourable thing to do as a gentleman would be to find a way to save Sir

William… His feelings for Mary must be put aside. Mary would remain a happily married woman and mother. She would return to Sir William and his brief adventure with her would be over, so they would part… But then, how could he forget the vision of that magnificent body coming up the stream towards him? And the feel of her breasts against his chest, the soft touch of her cheek, and the eyes… the eyes that said they loved him, as sure as day follows night… How would it be to have those lovely eyes look adoringly into his every morning, every evening, every night? As adoringly as he would gaze into hers? And the truth was, it was the best option all round – not only to save the Queen but also win Mary as a prize…

Tom kicked the pebble hard, and it went skittering away into the bushes.

But that would not be the honourable thing to do…

Wychwoode again put his hand on Tom's shoulder. "Your duty lies with the Queen, my friend," he said softly, "for all your heart may lie elsewhere. I have seen the looks you share with my lady."

Tom gave a half-smile. Wychwoode was only seeing half the picture. "I will do all in my power to save the Queen," he said. "You have my word on it – my word as a gentleman."

"And we do not share this with Lady Mary…"

"That will not be an easy thing to countenance," Tom answered. "This is her family…"

"If we stop this Alchemist, I will send men to Hetherington immediately. They can seek out Sir William and Ambrose before word reaches Moreton of the Queen's deliverance from danger." Wychwoode paused a moment. "We also know now that Moreton deliberately deceived Lady Mary. Her son remains at Hetherington Hall, and is not at the Grenville house in York."

"Aye," answered Tom, "he would not have wanted her meeting her son and husband, or she would have upset his plans. He had to get rid of her, and quickly."

"Indeed."

"So you will send men to Hetherington?"

Wychwoode nodded.

"Your word upon it?"

"My word also." Wychwoode agreed. "So 'tis sealed. We have both given our word to do the honourable thing."

---O---

When the banquet ended, the revelries began.

Under the watchful eye of the Queen, a stream of entertainers were brought on to do their turn, then shepherded away again to applause from the gathered throng which matched exactly the Queen's own level of approval. So the jugglers who received a polite handclap and a bored yawn from Her Majesty got no more from the rest of the room, while the dancing girls who did intricate dances with fans and flowers and who got a more sustained clapping and a smiling nod from Elizabeth, received a more raucous reception from the rest of the audience.

As each act was presented, Robert Dudley, Earl of Leicester, made concerned side-glances at the Queen to see how she was taking them, showing visible relief whenever she smiled. On her other side, Sir Thomas Wyvern was looking increasingly horrified as each act came into the Great Hall. As the host, he was bearing much of the cost of the Queen's stay – and perhaps after putting up a couple of hundred voracious courtiers for three days, these performances were the last straw. By the time the last act was completed – a re-creation of the defeat of the French by the British fleet at the Battle of Saint-Mathieu in 1512 using actors wearing model ship costumes – Sir Thomas looked positively unwell. And when the French ship *Cordelière* caught fire and sank using a mixture of fireworks and red silk 'flames', he seemed on the verge of a faint. The only time he was seen to smile, albeit very slightly, was when two ships inadvertently collided, and that section of the dance had to be restarted.

Lady Mary turned her attention back from their unfortunate host, to Wychwoode beside her.

"Now the entertainments are concluded, Lady Mary," he said, "I would we once again talk through our plans for the morrow – for we will have no opportunity for a second chance like those unfortunate actors just now."

"For sure," Mary nodded.

"Now, I have attempted with as much force and vigour as I can to have her Majesty change her route, but Leicester, who is an infernal meddler in these things, has insisted we stick to the plan. He says that no other streets are as wide or as easy to pass along, and he has also had the entire route swept and cleaned, with fresh straw laid along every yard, in order to preserve Her Majesty from the common sights – and smells – of an English town."

Wychwoode paused, and pushed a small piece of bread around on his plate with his knife. "I have advised him that there might be an attack on Her Majesty's person, but have desisted from explaining about the Alchemist and his – what was it Lady Mary called it, Tom – ah yes, his 'sniper' musket. I think that our noble Earl will not believe me were I to try and explain about this fellow, so I have left it only that I have good reason for concern."

"And Her Majesty on her horse?" prompted Tom.

"Aye. I have made it clear that I would prefer Her Majesty to walk, as we can surround her with men and shield her from this dreadful Alchemist. However, Leicester has again insisted that she ride – as he says it not only makes her more visible to the crowds, but makes her also rise majestically above them. He believes it helps create the illusion of her being 'elevated' above her people – which is all of a part in her perception as their glorious monarch."

"Good PR," muttered Mary to herself. There were a few 21st century celebrities who could learn a thing or two from how Elizabeth created her mystique and the cult of 'Gloriana'.

"What was that you said, Lady Mary?" asked Wychwoode.

"Nothing. Please continue."

"So we have no option but to stop this Alchemist before he can strike." He turned to Tom. "Your original plan was workable, so you, Cobham, will ride alongside the Queen as agreed. Look always forwards and upwards to see if you can spot the would-be assassin – as we believe he will most likely be stationed at an open window at the highest point in a building, or possibly on a roof. If you see him, what is your immediate action?"

"I will take hold of Her Majesty's bridle and quickly pull her round out of the line of the man's sight."

"Indeed. But we hope it will not come to this, as Lady Mary will be walking a few minutes ahead of the procession and will be looking to see if the weapon can be spotted further in advance."

"And if I see him?" Mary asked. "I will be a single woman against a man with the most powerful musket ever made."

Wychwoode looked at her closely, as if he was studying her suitability for something. Then he nodded, and said, "I would have you dressed as a boy, with a cap to cover your hair, in case the Alchemist sees you first. As I recall, you disguised yourself as such when we conquered the witchfinder all those years past, and you still have the smoothness in your cheek to fool even the closest observer." He paused. "And two of my men armed with swords and pistols will stay close to you – but not too close, so they are spotted. When you see the Alchemist – and I trust to God you will – you can call on them to help you to disarm him."

"That is good," said Mary. "I need to meet them tomorrow when we get to York and confirm actions."

"That is agreed." Wychwoode stood up. "Now, I have other plans to prepare for tomorrow, so I will take my leave." He looked down at them. "I would you both retire early; we must all be refreshed and ready for the morning."

After Wychwoode had made his way out of the Great Hall, Tom turned to Mary and put his hand over hers. "Whatever the morrow brings," he said, "we have stories to tell, do we not?"

"Aye, Tom," she answered, putting her other hand over his, "but I feel that tomorrow's story will be the one to top them all."

CHAPTER TWENTY-FOUR

York

The streets of York were more crowded than the small local woman in her late thirties had ever known.

She found herself having to push her way through hundreds of men, women and children as they flowed past her like waves around a solitary rock, all rushing to secure the best place to see the Queen. She smiled to herself; they did not have what she had – a top-floor window that overlooked the Queen's procession route. The ramshackle timber-framed house she shared with her husband was only a couple of hundred yards further along the street, although with these crowds, it could have been ten times more for all the progress she was making. Clutching her recent purchases under each arm – a loaf of bread and a keg of ale – she battled her way up the cobbles, breathing a sigh of relief when she finally made it to her small wooden front door. The keg was becoming heavier with every step.

As she lifted the latch, she felt a hand on her arm, and turned.

A thin man in a leather jerkin was standing beside her. He lifted his cap to reveal hair that stood up in spikes, then smiled.

"Good day, mistress," he said, replacing his cap. "Do you live in this house?"

"Aye," she said cautiously.

"I am sure you are most keen to see Her Majesty," he continued, "when she makes her triumphant progress through York."

"Indeed," she replied. "It is a rare honour to see the Queen, but pray tell, what is your purpose?"

The man smiled again. "I have a request which maybe you can help me with."

She shifted the keg under her arm to try and get a little more comfortable. "Well, be quick with it – afore I drop this thing."

"Here," he said, taking it from her, "allow me."

She flexed her arm and shook it to try and clear the stiffness. "Most kind, sir, but I know not what you want."

"I want very much to see the Queen," the man replied, "but I have an uncommon fear of crowds. And as you see…" he waved cautiously at the stream of people still rushing past and starting to line up under the houses on either side, "there are too many people for my comfort down here on the street. So…" he finished with a hopeful raise of the eyebrow.

"So you would come up to the top of our house and watch from there?" the woman finished for him.

He nodded.

"Then yes," she said after a pause while she studied him carefully. "You can come and observe from our window, and you can stay until Her Majesty has passed."

He bowed slightly. "I am in your debt, mistress..?"

"Carter. Beth Carter. Wife of Amos, who waits above for his bread and ale."

"Richard Hornby, at your service."

"Well, Master Hornby," she replied, "Amos and I had planned to watch quietly, without a crowd at our window." She took a small breath, almost as if to reassure herself, and added, "And I have no doubt Amos will protest, but you have shown me kindness and one man is not a crowd, so I will let you up to see the Queen's progress from our window."

Picking up his sacking bag with his free hand, the Alchemist followed Beth up the narrow stairs to the top floor of her house.

---0---

It was half an hour later and the noise of the crowd below the Carters' open window was becoming deafening. The Alchemist shifted his position slightly. The slim gun was beside him on the table, which he had pushed under the window. His last three cartridges, not counting the one already in the breech, were standing in a row alongside the gun.

He took a sip of his ale and glanced round. Beth and Amos Carter were sitting with their backs to the wall. They had their arms tied behind them and linen rags were stuffed in their mouths, then secured round their heads with more rope. As he looked back, Beth struggled against her bonds and glared fiercely at him. Beside her Amos sat quietly, and the Alchemist saw him glance frequently over to a heavy metal poker leaning by the fire.

"I have tied you well, old man," he observed. "So give up all thought of reaching that poker."

Amos glared round at Beth, with eyes that said plainly that it was all her fault for letting this man in. Beth looked down and shook her head, as if to say how sorry she was. The Alchemist gave a small chuckle.

"You will live, fear not," he said. He took a bite out of the loaf of bread. Beth struggled again, her impotent rage clear in her burning stare. "Sit still," he ordered. "If I meant you harm, you would be dead by now, both of you." He turned back to look down the street at the crowds below, before adding over his shoulder, "You are more use to me alive, as I need you to bear witness to what I will do today. So calm down and this will soon be over."

He moved the gun further back on the table, before peering out to scan the crowds. "Best to keep this thing out of sight till the last minute," he said conversationally. "I would not want anyone spotting it before Her Majesty appears, now would I?" He took another gulp of ale and lovingly caressed the stock of the gun. "Everything I have worked for – everything – is for this moment."

---0---

Mary glanced behind as she pushed her way through the excited crowds that lined the street, checking that Wychwoode's two men were still with her. They were a few yards behind as planned, keeping close in case she spotted the Alchemist, but not too close that he would become suspicious. Mary glanced up from under her cap and scanned the windows of the houses above. As expected, they were all open, each with as many people crammed into them as possible, all waving and cheering at the distant royal procession as it made its way up the street behind her.

Mary's breathing was in short, ragged gasps – not only because she was feeling almost sick with fear, but also because the stench of the people she was pushing through was indescribable. At least the street itself had been swept clean of its usual human waste and laid with fresh straw for the Queen.

She came to a place where the pavement narrowed to a few feet, and the space was occupied by a couple of burly yeomen. One was the largest men she had ever seen; he must have been close to six and a half feet tall and had the build to match. She tried to push past but the two men refused to get out of her way.

"Please excuse me," she muttered.

"Hold your peace, boy," answered the giant man. "Wait here and you will see the Queen pass."

Mary took a breath to steady herself, and immediately wished she hadn't. Fighting the urge to retch at the man's smell, she said, "Forgive me sir, but I must get to my master's house up yonder before Her Majesty passes."

"Well wait, boy, and see Her Majesty first." The man chuckled. "What in the name of the Lord is the rush?"

"Belike he wants to find a better spot?" suggested the other man.

"Aye, in truth," said the first, and just as Mary tried to dodge into the open street to get past them, she found herself being grabbed around the waist by two massive arms, and hoisted up onto the man's shoulders as if she weighed no more than a fly.

"Let me down!" she yelled, and kicked at his chest.

The man laughed. "The lad has spirit, I say that!" He grabbed at Mary's legs so she could no longer kick. "Peace boy, you now have the best spot to see the Queen. See – she comes presently."

Mary looked back down the street. From this height she could see the procession clearly. Elizabeth was on her horse at the front, with Tom in a magnificent white doublet riding beside her and the Earl of Leicester on her other side. The Queen was waving at the cheering crowds and smiling, seeming to delight in the adoration of her subjects.

The procession was not more than three hundred yards away.

"Let me down, I say!" she yelled again, but the noise of the crowd meant her words were all but lost.

The procession was getting closer.

She glanced to her right, along the route.

There was a fork in the street ahead, with a small lane branching away up a hill. The lane was empty and had no straw laid down, so it was clearly not part of the royal route. A row of houses ran along the main part of the street backing onto the lane, with a ramshackle house sitting directly in the fork at the junction. She glanced briefly up at the top floor.

The window was wide open, and it was empty.

Every other window was crammed full of people. This window, with a prime view directly along the route below, had no one.

She glanced quickly up again, just in time to see a dark spiky head appear briefly then withdraw into the room.

She looked back at the Queen, sitting high on her horse, now only a couple of hundred yards away, a clear target with full line of sight from the window.

"Let me go!" she shrieked at the man, trying to kick against his arms and chest.

But it was too late.

In sick horror she saw the barrel of the gun glinting in the sunlight as it slid out of the window, and hold steady as it pointed directly at the Queen.

Drawing in her deepest breath she turned towards Tom and yelled as loud as she possibly could, "Tom!"

The yell, coming as it did from above the heads of the crowd, carried across to Tom, just as her yell had done once before in the forest. She saw him look across at her, and she pointed up at the window. She must have been a distant figure but she was high above the crowd so he could not miss her. She saw him lift his head and follow her finger up towards the window. Immediately she saw him grab the Queen's bridle, then he turned Her Majesty away.

At the same moment Mary heard a sound like a breaking branch and saw a puff of smoke come from the window.

She looked back at Tom and the Queen.

The scene appeared frozen still; Tom with his back to her and the Queen out of sight behind him.

Then a small red mark appeared between Tom's broad white shoulders.

It started to get bigger, just as a rosebud opens and grows, until his whole back was bright red.

Then he slowly slid off his horse and disappeared from view.

"Tom!" Mary screamed again, and this time the Queen looked up. Even across the distance between them, Mary could see the fear in the woman's eyes. She was hemmed in by all the courtiers around her, unable to turn and ride away, again exposed to the unseen assassin. If she were hit, then not only would history change forever, but Tom, presumably mortally wounded, would have died in vain.

Mary looked back at the window. The gun barrel had disappeared – presumably the Alchemist was reloading.

Just then one of Wychwoode's men appeared below her, his sword unsheathed. He pushed it up at the yeoman's chest.

"Let her down," he commanded, taking a stance which showed he was prepared to back up his words by thrusting the sword.

The yeoman reached up and lifted Mary off his shoulders. "Her? I thought it was a boy?"

Immediately Mary was back on the ground she called to Wychwoode's man, "That window there!" She pointed up. "Come!"

Together they ran to the door of the end house. The man kicked it in easily, and Mary followed him up the dark stairs. At the top there was another door. The man kicked this one in as well and ran into the room.

Mary saw the Alchemist at the window, leaning along the table, his sleeves rolled up and the tattoos of guns clearly visible on both arms.

The sniper rifle was pointed towards the Queen, and the Alchemist was looking as if he was preparing to take the second shot. At the sound of the door bursting open he swung round and fired at Wychwoode's man. The sound of the gun was unnaturally loud in the small space.

Blood exploded from the man's back and he went down like a felled tree.

Mary froze.

Despite all the preparation for this moment – both mental and physical – she froze.

Now that she was in front of Rick, with the gun in his hand, all her planned responses went out of her head. The only thing in her mind as she watched him pick up one of the two cartridges from the table was the phrase 'rabbit in the headlights'. He opened the breech of the gun, then quickly shook it to release the spent cartridge. It fell out with a puff of smoke. He smoothly slotted the new cartridge in and closed the gun. Then he raised it so it pointed directly at Mary's chest.

"I had thought you had both died in the fire," he said, "till I saw lover boy there leap out in front of the Queen and get his back blown open."

She shook her head. Tom was dead. The thought of it was like a block of ice in place of her heart.

"Yeah," the Alchemist continued, "so it is no surprise that you've showed up like a fucking bad penny."

In the distance, the Queen could be seen starting to wheel her horse round and shouting for the courtiers to let her through. "It looks like I have to make a choice," the Alchemist said. "Do I kill the Queen before she gets away, or you?" He turned back to the window and lined up the shot. "The Queen first, then we'll see about you."

In that moment, Mary's head suddenly cleared and she knew exactly what she had to do.

Leaping swiftly over the body of Wychwoode's man, she grabbed the heavy poker propped up by the fireplace. As the Alchemist started to glance back over his shoulder, she brought it down with all her might on his right arm, directly on the tattoo of the crossed rifles.

It landed with a sickening thud that she felt sure had broken the bone.

The Alchemist gave a thin, agonised shriek and stood up, keeping hold of the stock of the gun in his left hand; his right arm now hanging uselessly at his side.

"You bitch!" he yelled. "You fucking bitch!" He started hefting the gun to get his left hand down towards the trigger, while at the same time raising the barrel towards her chest. Mary lifted the poker again and this time brought it down as hard as she could on his left arm, directly on the tattoo of the single pistol.

The Alchemist let out a bellow of pain and rage and dropped the gun. As it fell, the trigger must have hit the leg of the table, and it fired. Mary saw the shot slam into a wooden chest and the gun recoil across the room into a far corner.

"Damn you Justine, you meddling little bitch!" yelled the Alchemist, standing with both arms hanging by his side. "What the fuck do you think you're trying to achieve?"

"I'm saving history. The history we know." Over his shoulder, she could see the Queen riding away, and men carrying Tom's body back down the street.

"Saving history? What fucking history? It hasn't happened yet," the Alchemist sneered at her. "And now you're here, it probably never will, anyway." He looked her up and down, his mouth twisted in pain. "You had kids?" She nodded. "Then it's never going to be the same, is it? Who knows what changes they'll make? So me killing Gloriana there, that might not be as big a change as you've made already."

"What about you changing things so I'm never born at all?"

"Is that what this is really all about?"

Mary saw the Alchemist's eyes flicker across to where the gun lay, seeming to measure the distance. She wasn't sure what he could achieve with two broken arms, but she gripped the poker and raised it higher just in case. She glanced at his arms; the tattoos of the guns and the pistol had almost disappeared under the rapidly blackening wheals.

"Listen," he said through gritted teeth, "you and me, we were born in the 1980s. At the time we were born, history had not changed. So whatever difference you make now, nothing can alter the fact you were born when you were – and any changes you or I make, it's to a parallel future, not the one we came from." He stopped and his face twisted once again with the pain. "And you're still fucking here aren't you? You haven't suddenly disappeared because of some change to the future, have you?" He shook his head. "More's the fucking pity. So you know what, Justine, you little bitch," he winced in pain, "nothing you or I have done has stopped us being here, but whatever the future will be now, it's never going to be what we knew. That's gone." He nodded across to the open window. "A bit like Gloriana there. Looks like she got away today – but who knows what might happen the next time?" He glanced for a fraction of a second across to the gun. "At least lover boy there took one for the team."

If that was meant to distract Mary so he could get to the gun, it failed.

Keeping hold of the poker tightly in both hands, she flexed her wrists, lifting the tip higher.

Then she waited for her moment.

He stared at the poker, then back at her, with ill-concealed loathing.

She watched his eyes, as intently as a hawk watches a mouse.

No doubt he knew that to look away was a disastrous move, but eventually he stole the briefest glance across at the gun.

It was all she needed.

As his eyes slid off the poker, she hefted it back and in one clean move, swung it down and round as hard as she could on his left shin.

It connected with the noise of an axe hitting a tree trunk, and this time she was sure there was an additional crack as the bone snapped.

Rick went down with a thin scream, hitting his head with a sickening thump on the side of the table as he went. He collapsed on the floor and was immediately still.

She waited what seemed like an age, but he remained motionless.

Was he bluffing?

She crouched down, the poker raised in case he made any move. Slowly, carefully, she touched his eyelid. There was no response. She eased it open, to reveal that his eye had rolled up into his head.

He was out cold.

She looked at his impassive face. Rick, the catering manager at Grangedean Manor who had been nothing more than an annoying colleague in the 21st century, had become a time-traveller like her – and so had become the only person in this strange Elizabethan world who could really understand her. But he had turned out to be a monster, attacking women and trying to assassinate the Queen.

Yet it was he who had worked out the time-travel conundrum – that the time-traveller can never actually endanger their own existence, because their birth took place in a parallel version of the future, one that could never be altered. No changes made to the future by her and her family could possibly prevent her birth in the 1980s.

But was he right? If so, then maybe one good thing would have come from this encounter; she could finally put her concerns about her existence to rest.

She was never going to just 'disappear'…

Mary sighed. All those years of hiding at Grangedean Manor! All those years of fearing to set foot outside in case she changed something pivotal – had that all been a mistake?

What excitement and adventures could she have enjoyed in Elizabethan England, if she had just been a bit braver and a bit bolder?

She glanced down at Rick.

Maybe this adventure had more than made up for it – except that too many good people had got hurt, or worse, along the way. She leaned down over the still body of the Alchemist.

"Rick Hornby," whispered, "I once promised Thomas Melrose I would beat you for what you did to Olivia." She looked at the poker in her hand. "That was for her – and for Agnes and for Ursula," she paused a moment, "and for my dear friend, Juno." She prodded him with the tip of the poker and he groaned slightly. "And, more than anything, that was for Tom."

There was the sound of a different, higher-pitched groan behind her.

She turned and noticed a man and a woman sitting up against the wall, bound and gagged.

Their pleading eyes met hers.

Quickly she untied them, and while they were carefully standing and easing the blood back into their arms and legs, she checked the Alchemist's pulse. It was faint, but still there, so she used the ropes that had so recently bound the two of them to bind his blackened arms tightly behind his back.

"By Heaven, mistress," the man said slowly, "I have ne'er seen such skill with a weapon – and ne'er by a woman – as you showed with that poker." He shook his head and turned to the woman as if for affirmation. "Such targeted strikes to stop the man in his treasonous endeavour! One on each arm and one on the legs, eh Beth?"

"Aye, t'was well done, Amos," replied Beth. "The man got his just rewards."

Just then there was the sound of feet pounding up the stairs, and Wychwoode burst in. He took in the Alchemist lying bloody and bound at Mary's feet and the open window with its view down the street.

"By Heaven, my lady, you have succeeded! The man is stopped while the Queen is safe and unharmed!" A deep frown crossed his face. "But Mary, I have to tell you that Thomas Cobham is hit."

"I know. I saw him killed."

"But no! He lives still. He asks for you."

A sudden hope rose, like a flame coming back to life in a dying fire. "He still lives?" Mary asked, her voice rising unnaturally high. "Where is he? I must see him!"

"There was a barber-surgeon living close to the place where he was hit – it is the house with a green door. He was taken there and the man is doing all he can for Cobham's comfort. Go now, go! I will see to this filthy monster who you have bound so well for me." He crouched down and put a finger to the Alchemist's neck. "By Heaven, he has been beaten most soundly. It is a wonder that he still lives!"

---0---

Mary ran up to the green door. A soldier with a halberd and silver breastplate was standing guard.

"Let me in!" Mary shouted. "I must see Tom Cobham!"

"Art Lady Mary de Beauvais?" asked the man, staring curiously at her clothing.

"Yes!"

He stood aside. "I have been ordered to let you in if you arrived, disguised in the garb of a boy," he said.

Mary ran past him and into the front room, taking off her cap and shaking out her hair as she ran.

It was dark, with only a couple of candles casting a meagre glow in the room. As Mary's eyes became accustomed to the dim light, she could see a man lying on a table, with a woman leaning over him, sponging his forehead gently with a damp cloth. A man in a red velvet cap stood at the end of the table mixing some powders with a pestle and mortar, and a dark-haired nobleman stood beside him. Mary realised that the man on the table who was breathing quick, shallow, ragged breaths was Tom.

Then she gave a small gasp. The woman gently tending to him was Queen Elizabeth.

She went up to the table. She could see that Tom was conscious, as his eyes followed her as she approached.

Mary bowed to Elizabeth. "How is he, Your Majesty?"

Elizabeth looked up. "As well as can be expected, given that he shielded me with his body and took the shot aimed at me." She stared at Mary. "A woman dressed in boy's garb? Then you must be the Lady Mary he has been asking for." Mary nodded. "Then do you wish to tend to Sir Thomas yourself?"

The Queen stood back and handed over the cloth. Mary knelt by the table and stroked Tom's cheek. "Sir Thomas, eh?" she said softly. "That was nice." She wiped his forehead. "What did you have to get yourself shot for?"

"I heard your call," he whispered. "Your loud fishwife shriek was just what we needed."

"But you were supposed to pull Her Majesty out of the way. Not shield her and take the shot yourself."

"Aye." He coughed, his eyes never leaving hers. "But it seemed the right thing to do."

"And it got you wounded."

"It got me killed."

"No!" she whispered.

"Aye. It has to be said. And anyway," he said softly, "it saved the life of the Queen, did it not? See how she lives now, and has seen fit to make me Sir Tom."

"Yes, but…"

He frowned. "Was that not what we intended?"

"Well, yes, but…."

"So, that is settled." He coughed again and some blood appeared at the side of his mouth. Mary wiped it away. "It is a story to tell, is it not? We had some good times together." He coughed another time, and his breathing became more ragged.

The man in the red velvet cap came over with a glass. "Some tonic, Sir Thomas, to restore your health?" The man held the glass below Tom's mouth. Tom took a sip, then the man stepped back. "This fellow is a surgeon, who thinks a tonic will mend the hole in my back," Tom whispered to Mary. "He is either a fool, or he thinks I am one."

"For sure, we will have you restored to health again, Tom," blurted Mary. "For I will die as well if you are not with me."

"Please, my love, do not say such a thing," breathed Tom. "You have a husband who loves you well, and who needs you more than I." He reached out a hand and gently stroked her cheek. "Ask Wychwoode," he breathed. "He will tell you all about Sir William."

"Ask him what?"

"Do but ask him."

"I will."

"Good." He took a couple of laboured breaths. "But I do have one question for you."

"What is that, my love?"

"Back in the forest," he whispered, so faintly that she now had to put her ear right up to his mouth, "the Alchemist called you by some other name, and talked of the future." He coughed again quietly. "At the time I thought it strange, and I must confess I wondered if you were somehow in league with him."

"Nay, my love. I wanted to stop him. I had to stop him," she answered.

"So you were never in league with him." She felt his breath on her cheek as he sighed. "That is good. I needed to be sure of that."

"I swore so at the time," she whispered.

"I know, and I needed to confess to you how I did not fully believe you. I am so sorry, dearest Mary. Will you forgive me? I must know."

She turned and looked into his eyes. "Of course I forgive you, my love."

"Good," he breathed. "Then I go in peace." He paused again as he tried to draw in a ragged breath. Then he said in a louder voice, "Farewell Mary. Fare thee well, my dearest love."

He took two more rasping breaths, then was still.

Mary threw herself onto his neck, as great sobs racked her body. Tom had gone… Tom, who had saved her from that foul man in the Blue Maid; who had been her constant companion and friend; who had always been the perfect gentleman; who had made the ultimate sacrifice to save the Queen's life. Tom, who had said his heart was hers…

She felt a hand on her shoulder. After a moment she looked up. It was the dark-haired nobleman – whom she now recognised as the Earl of Leicester. "Come, Lady Mary," he said gently, "he is gone. We will have him removed for burial."

Mary stood, and Leicester steered her gently out of the room, along the corridor and out into a small courtyard. The Queen followed.

As Mary blinked to re-accustom her eyes to the bright sunlight, there was the sound of boots coming through the house, and once again Wychwoode appeared. He bowed to the Queen, and Mary saw he was carrying the gun.

"This is the weapon, Your Majesty," he said, holding it up. "The man had fashioned it himself." He held up the one remaining cartridge. "He combined both powder and ball into one capsule, so he was able to prime and load the weapon in but a few seconds."

Leicester reached for the gun and turned it over in his hands, then peered through the telescopic sight. "This is a most remarkable piece," he said slowly. "We must study and learn from it, so we can use its superior fire power and accuracy ourselves. It will give us great advantage over our enemies – we will win many more battles with this."

"I agree, but let us address this in good time, Robin," said the Queen. She turned back to Wychwoode. "For now, what of the murderer himself?"

"He is bound and secured, madam," Wychwoode answered, taking the gun back from Leicester.

"He must be dealt with appropriately," the Queen said.

"Of course, madam," answered Wychwoode, then he added, "though he has already taken grievous wounds to both arms and to one of his legs."

The Queen raised an eyebrow. "Why? How did he come by such injuries?"

Wychwoode looked at Mary. "It seems Lady de Beauvais set about him most grievously with a sturdy poker."

"Did she indeed?" Elizabeth turned to Mary. "I must respect your strength."

"I used the poker on the first arm to stop him firing on you after he had shot Tom… Sir Thomas, Your Majesty," Mary answered. "Then he tried to fire the weapon at me, so I hit the other arm. Then…" she stopped, and shook her head. "I wanted to stop him for good, so I hit his leg to bring him down."

"With the force to give it a clean break, madam," added Wychwoode. "The man will surely not walk to the gallows."

"Well, it sounds as if you were successful, my dear Lady Mary." The Queen turned to Leicester. "You see, Robin, a woman can be as strong as a man, if she is driven to it." She thought for a moment, her piercing dark eyes fixed on Mary. "And I saw you in the crowd, did I not? It was your cry that Sir Thomas heard… so, Lady Mary, it was your actions that saved my life – not once, it seems, but twice." Without taking her eyes off Mary, she said, "You know, Robin, I have long been saying that we should look at how much we subjugate women by law. Lady Mary here is perhaps real proof that those laws are in serious need of review."

Leicester nodded. "As you wish, madam."

The Queen turned to Wychwoode. "And what of the man's motive? Is he backed by a Catholic plot or was this a lone action?"

"We believe he has Catholic backers, madam," replied Wychwoode, "and we are in the process of arresting them shortly." He paused. "But we also have some insight into the man's own motives, as he confided in the owner of the house and his wife, who were his unwilling captives. It seems he was not himself a Catholic, nor was he motivated by religious zeal – for all it seems…" he paused, seeming to struggle to contain his emotion, "…it seems, that he worshipped Satan instead." He fished for something in his pocket, then opened his hand to reveal Rick's lighter. The skull looked up at them, glinting wickedly in the sunlight. The Queen drew back with a gasp. "This is a miniature tinder box," explained Wychwoode, "and it is clearly a talisman to Satanic worship. It was found in his bag."

The Queen appeared to go whiter than Mary thought possible. "We shall not have such devilry in our presence," she commanded in a strangled whisper. "Take it away now." She paused a moment, then added, "It shows us how this man is beyond any form of understanding."

Leicester took it and examined it dispassionately, as Wychwoode continued, "It appears his motivation was also self-advancement – he expected ennoblement from the Queen of Scots, were she to have usurped your throne."

"Thanks to the quick actions of Lady Mary and Sir Thomas Cobham, we are spared that disaster, are we not?" said Leicester, handing the lighter back to Wychwoode. "And what of his Catholic backers?"

"We believe we know their ringleader, my lord," answered Wychwoode, wrapping the lighter gingerly in a cloth and putting it back in his pocket.

"I want him found and caught," said the Queen firmly, seeming to have recovered her composure now the lighter was out of sight. "I do not want him to escape justice, nor be free to start another plot."

Wychwoode nodded. "We will be making every effort to apprehend him."

The Queen stared at him a moment. "Well, see that you do. Or I will ask Lady Mary here to do it for you. She seems to have a way of stopping my enemies in their tracks."

Wychwoode bowed but said nothing.

The Queen drew Mary to one side. "I have never seen such devilry as that tinder box," she said, shaking her head. "This man must pay dearly for all he is, and all he has done."

Mary nodded, and said nothing.

"In faith, we are forever in your debt, my dear Lady Mary," the Queen continued quietly. "Your husband is Sir William?" Mary nodded again. "I have heard of him, of course, but never had him presented. You are both most welcome at Court. We would see more of you and greatly enjoy your council in future."

Mary curtseyed. "As you wish, Your Majesty."

Elizabeth studied Mary again with her dark eyes. "You know…" she began, then paused and took a breath, "…when Sir Thomas took the shot in his back, his face was before mine. As close as you are now… I saw the moment he was hit." Mary said nothing; Elizabeth was clearly finding this difficult, but wanted to get out what was on her mind. "When the ball struck… I saw the shock and pain in his eyes – and… he knew it was mortal, but…" she shook her head, "he seemed almost *pleased*… as if he knew he *deserved* it…" Elizabeth nodded. "I wanted you to know, my dear. In case that meant something to you."

"Thank you, madam. Yes, it does."

There was a moment of pure understanding that passed between the two women. It was only brief, but just for a second, Mary felt closer to Elizabeth than she had ever felt to any other adult.

Then the moment passed, and once more the Queen became the decisive monarch. She turned to Leicester. "Come Robin," she said, "we must return to Wyvern Castle. Tomorrow we prepare for our journey back down south. Good-bye, my dear Lady Mary. We shall see you back at Wyvern, no doubt." With that, she swept out, followed by Leicester.

Mary turned to Wychwoode. "Tom said a strange thing before he died. He said there was something I was to ask you about William. What did he mean?"

Wychwoode drew a long, careful breath. "There is indeed some news I have to give you, Lady Mary, concerning your husband Sir William, and your son Ambrose, and the dangerous situation they now find themselves in…"

CHAPTER TWENTY-FIVE

Mary gripped her knees tighter on the saddle and lowered her head, coming down so close to the horse's mane that it whipped across her face with every galloping stride.

Beside her, Olivia Melrose was also crouched low over her own horse's mane, as the two of them thundered along the path from York to Hetherington Hall, their hair flying loose behind them.

It was not more than half an hour since Wychwoode had given her the news that not only had William remained at Hetherington Hall for all this time, but that now he and Ambrose were being held hostage by the lead plotter – and that was Lambert Moreton.

But worst of all, Wychwoode had reason to believe that the lives of her son and husband were dependent on Moreton hearing of the death of Elizabeth. And since she had just prevented that from happening, their lives were now hanging by the slimmest of threads. Which was why it was imperative that she get to Hetherington Hall as fast as possible, before any message reached Moreton from York.

Wychwoode had also muttered something about a promise to Tom to send men to Hetherington, but Mary had neither the time nor inclination to wait while he arranged this – no, this was her mission, her responsibility. With a parting yell to send them as soon as possible if he cared to do so, she had raced out of the surgeon's house and found a mounted soldier. Shouting that she was on the Queen's business, she demanded that he take her to Wyvern Castle with all speed. Fortunately the man had not asked questions, but helped her mount up behind him and had ridden like the wind.

It had been but a few minutes' work to secure a horse from the Wyvern stables, just as Olivia had arrived back in her carriage from York. Seeing Mary so desperate to ride out, Olivia had insisted on coming as well. Despite Mary's protests, the girl had leapt onto the next available horse and galloped out after her.

As she rode, Mary tried to think what she would do to rescue her husband

and son when she arrived at the Hall. What she really needed was a plan.

Although what she did have, was the gun.

She had grabbed it and the last remaining cartridge from Wychwoode as she ran out – with something about her need being greater than his – and it was now strapped to her back as she rode.

As if reading her mind, Olivia shouted across, "What is your plan, my lady?"

"My only thought is to take up position to watch from a distance. Then we can decide what is best to do."

A few minutes later a high stone wall appeared through the woods, and the path turned to follow it. Mary slowed her horse and trotted alongside it for a few minutes. "I think this is the wall of the Hetherington Hall grounds," she said. "We need to get over."

She pulled her horse up and it skittered to a stop, breathing hard and steam rising from its flanks. Mary stood in her stirrups and slowly raised her head over the top of the wall. There was Hetherington Hall. Even from the side it was easy to identify the magnificent wings and the main steps beyond with their guardian stone lions. "Aye, it is," she said.

She sat back in her saddle. "We should tie the horses here, and drop over the wall."

Olivia nodded, and tied her horse to a nearby tree. Mary did the same, then together they stood in their stirrups, stepped up onto their saddles and lifted themselves onto the wall.

Dropping lightly down onto soft earth on the other side, Mary crouched and started studying the land ahead of them. There was a soft thud behind her, then Olivia appeared alongside.

The woodland trees extended a few yards in front of them, before opening out into separate cultivated gardens, each bordered by box hedges at around five or six feet high. Beyond these was an incline up to the side of the house, which rose majestically into the blue sky; its red brick walls set with diamond-paned windows and topped with twisted brick chimneys.

Mary reached behind her and took the gun from its strap, then dropped to her belly, sinking down into the soft leafy earth. She settled herself with the gun pointing up at the house and squinted through the sight. Immediately the building leapt into sharp focus. The Alchemist had certainly known what he was doing – the magnification and clarity were excellent. He had even added cross-hairs for better aiming. Mary shivered as she imagined him centring these on Elizabeth and squeezing the trigger, at precisely the moment that Tom's back had appeared instead.

"Pray tell, my lady, what exactly is that silver stick in your hands?" asked Olivia, lying down beside her.

Mary swept the scope across the side of the house, but saw no movement. "You recall I told you when all this started, that I was going to London seeking out a man? A man that I would ask questions that only he could answer?"

"I do," said Olivia.

"And I also told you when we met at the gates, that there was a plot on the life of the Queen?"

"Of course."

"Well, I found the man. And it turns out I was wrong to seek him. It was he who would kill the Queen – and he made this weapon to carry out the killing."

"By Heaven, my lady!" Olivia squeaked. She paused a moment. "So that was why we at the rear of the progress were sent back to Wyvern early. This man made his attempt on the Queen's life!"

Mary caught some movement out of the corner of her eye and trained the scope on the place she thought she had seen it, but there was nothing more than the branches of a willow tree swaying in the gentle breeze. She moved on to study the side of the house but there was no sign of life. She let her breath out gently; she had not even been aware that she had been holding it. "Yes," she said. "The Queen was saved by Tom, throwing himself in the path of the shot."

"Master Cobham did that?" asked Olivia. "Does he survive?"

Mary looked up and shook her head. After a moment, Olivia put her hand on Mary's and said, "I am so sorry, my lady. I know you were close to Master Cobham."

"Sir Thomas." Mary squinted back down the scope again. "Her Majesty saw fit to knight him before he died."

"Oh. That was kind of her."

There was another flash of movement and Mary swung the gun round.

Then her heart skipped a beat.

Moreton and three men were walking down the main steps and out of the house.

"She is most…" Olivia began, in the same loud conversational tone.

"Shh!" Mary hissed.

Olivia was immediately silent, but perhaps it was already too late. As Mary watched through the scope, Moreton stopped abruptly, signalling to the men behind him to stop also. He stared slowly around, as if searching for the source of the distant sound he had just heard. Mary tried to sink further into the soft earth, but she knew that if she could see Moreton above the box hedges, then he could potentially see her.

She lay as still as she could, scarcely breathing, as Moreton stared across the park. Had he heard Olivia? Something had made him stop – did he know it was a voice, or would he perhaps think it was something else? Beside her, Olivia lay still as well. Both were wearing dull-coloured clothing – with luck they would merge into the leafy floor of the woodland. The stock of the gun felt clammy in her hands. It was still raised, but she dared not move it down, for fear that the movement itself would catch the sunlight and be spotted.

As Mary watched through the scope, Moreton continued to sweep his gaze across the grounds. Her finger hovered over the trigger, as she eased the cross-hairs into position, placing his head dead centre. How easy would it be to squeeze the trigger and rid herself – and Elizabeth – of this vile plotter?

But right now, the gun was not loaded.

Moreton gestured to one of his men, but the man was beyond Mary's view. She remained still, not daring to move the gun a millimetre. The man came into view. She saw Moreton gesture to him again, pointing towards the trees where Mary and Olivia lay. The man nodded, and started walking directly towards them.

Almost as if in slow motion, the man made his way down from the path onto their level. Now Mary could only see the top of his head above the box hedges, heading in their direction. Soon he would emerge onto flat ground and have a clear view of them.

Mary felt in the pocket of her jerkin for the last remaining cartridge. There it was, solid and reassuring. Slowly she grasped it between thumb and forefinger, and eased it out. It may be her only shot, but she couldn't think of any other option than to use the weapon on this man and prevent him finding her and Olivia. Shooting him would give them time to escape back over the wall to their horses, then ride for help in finding William and Ambrose.

She shifted the cartridge into the palm of her hand, so she could release the catch and open the breech with her fingers, just wide enough to insert the cartridge.

The man was now only one hedge away from the open.

Mary winkled the cartridge back towards her thumb and forefinger, ready to slide it into the breech, snap it shut, and shoot.

But her hand was too sweaty.

As she felt the metal case on her fingertip, it slipped out and dropped onto the rough earth at her side.

Desperately she patted the earth around where it fell, trying to find it.

She saw the man turn his head to one side – he was looking for a way round the last hedge. He started walking along it.

As he did so, Mary knew she only had seconds while his attention was diverted, to find the cartridge, load and fire. She looked down at her side, but there were leaves all around, and she could not see it.

But she did see Olivia's arm make a sudden sharp movement and something dark fly out of her hand.

The man came to the break in the hedge and started to turn.

Then there was a sudden loud cawing from a tree further along, as a number of birds shot up into the air. The man looked startled, then craned his head up to watch the birds as they circled noisily overhead.

By the time he looked down again and stepped round the hedge, Mary and Olivia had run back and were now hiding behind nearby trees.

Mary held her breath and waited.

She heard the man shout, "T'was naught but rooks!"

She waited another few minutes, then peered cautiously round the tree. All four men were now walking along the path away from the house, and were nearly out of sight.

Signalling to Olivia to stay where she was, Mary dropped into a crouch and ran back to where they had lain. There was the cartridge, poking out from under a leaf. Picking it up, she ran back to Olivia.

"That was close," she said. "You threw a stone at the tree?"

Olivia nodded. "I saw the rooks up there and took the chance while he looked away."

"Good. Well done. It diverted them all." Mary looked back at where Moreton and his men had gone. "We must follow them. Come."

---0---

Mary squinted through the scope and swung the gun back and forward, but could see nothing but trees, sky and grass. She lowered it slightly, then tried again.

This time Moreton and his men flashed past. She swung it gently back a fraction, and the four men came into view, walking together along the path. She followed them for a moment, then swung the gun past them, looking to see where they were heading. After a moment the magnificent main gates came into view, looking solid and impenetrable in the early afternoon sun. She panned slowly back, once more picking up the four men, but at this distance and with the foreshortening effect of the scope, it was impossible to tell how far they were from the gates. She followed them further, her cross-hairs trained on Moreton's thin, sandy head.

The men reached the heavy wooden gates and stopped.

Then they seemed to wait, standing silently in a small group.

Why did they not go through? What were they waiting for?

"What passes, my lady?" whispered Olivia, her voice no more than a breath in the still air.

"They wait, standing about as if with naught to do." Mary's voice was equally quiet.

"By the gates?" asked Olivia.

"Aye." Mary shifted her position slightly; her arm holding the stock was starting to protest at being kept so long in the same position. "I know not why."

"Belike they await news from York?"

Mary cursed under her breath. Of course! They were waiting for a messenger to tell them news of the Queen. News that would be catastrophic for her husband and son.

Once again, she trained the sight on Moreton.

Should she kill him now, to stop him hearing the news?

She lined up the cross-hairs so that Moreton's head was dead centre. Her finger found the trigger, and started to curl round it. She slowed her breath… and started to pull.

"Oh by the Lord!" Olivia breathed suddenly.

Mary's finger came off the trigger and she looked up at Olivia. "What passes?" she asked, her voice shaking and her breath now rasping in her throat. "I would have killed him in that instant."

"See!" Olivia pointed. "The gate is opening. It must be a messenger who comes!"

Mary looked back through the scope. Sure enough, two of Moreton's men were pulling the heavy wooden gate open, and Moreton was walking towards it with a look of anticipation.

Mary shifted the gun slightly, moving the cross-hairs to head height at the side of the gate, waiting to see a man's head appear.

If this man was a messenger, maybe the better option would be to silence him instead, before he could announce the news that the Queen was not dead.

She brought her finger back to the trigger, and slowed her breath.

The gate continued to swing, until it was fully ninety degrees open. But whoever the man was, he remained hidden, apparently talking to Moreton from behind its solid cover.

"Blast!" muttered Mary, "Why does he not show himself so I can get a shot?"

But suddenly it was too late.

Moreton staggered and clutched at the side of the gate for support. His mouth made a small 'O' shape and he shook his head vigorously. He looked back at the hidden man and asked a question. The man must have answered, most likely confirming the unwelcome news, for Moreton then turned away and let out an anguished howl that could clearly be heard by the watching women. Then he snapped back, and suddenly an evil looking rapier was in his hand, glinting in the sunlight. With another howl, Moreton thrust the rapier out of sight behind the gate, then withdrew it almost as fast.

As Mary watched in horror, a man in a black cape and hat toppled like a felled tree from behind the gate and lay prostrate on the path.

Without a backward glance, Moreton shouted an order to his men, then stepped over the body and walked out of the gate. The other three followed behind. The last man tried to pull the gate shut behind him, but the messenger was in the way. After a brief and half-hearted attempt to kick the man's body aside, he left the gate open and scurried through.

Mary pushed the gun into the makeshift sling on her back and jumped up.

"Come on," she said to Olivia. "We must follow!"

Together they ran across the lawn and soon arrived at the gate.

Mary took in the sight of the man lying on the path, the stones all around him running bright red with his blood. As she reached him, she dropped to her knees and put a finger to his neck. As she suspected, there was no pulse. "We can do nothing for this unfortunate fellow," she muttered, "though I would have killed him sooner myself if I could." Then she ran around him and out of the gate.

They quickly reached a fork in the path.

Mary gave barely a glance to the left fork, and immediately turned right. "This way!" she hissed. "I think I know exactly where they have gone!"

Without waiting for Olivia, Mary ran along the stony path until it reached the edge of the ravine. She skittered to a stop on the loose pebbles and turned to find Olivia right behind her.

"Wait a moment," she whispered.

Together they peered cautiously over the edge of the path. It dropped away from them down the side of the ravine, then zigzagged its way to the floor below. Some way down, they could see the heads of the four men walking along.

Mary pulled back.

"Art well, my lady?" asked Olivia. "You are as white as the snow."

Mary shook her head. "Nay," she muttered. "They go to a watchman's hut at the bottom, I am sure of it. That is where they hold my husband and my son." She looked up at Olivia. "And unless we can stop them, they go to kill both my men."

"We must do something to stop them, my lady!"

"Yes," said Mary, then turned to Olivia. "And I think I have a plan for that – in which you must play a major part."

Olivia smiled. "Whatever I can do, Lady Mary, that I will."

---0---

Mary took aim through the scope, lining up Moreton's thin head once again in the cross-hairs.

"Moreton!" she called out as loud as she could. Her voice echoed around the still air, crashing off the stone walls and whipping around the trees that lined the base of the ravine where he stood.

Moreton turned around and around, spinning on his heel as he tried to locate the source of the call.

"Who's there?" he shouted back. "Reveal yourself!"

"Up here!" called Mary.

He looked up, continuing to spin round. Then he must have spotted her as a distant figure standing on the path high above him and he stopped, staring directly at her; his face in the centre of the scope. Mary moved the cross-hairs up from his sharp, thin nose to the wispy hair falling over his forehead.

"Who's there?" he repeated.

"I am Lady Mary de Beauvais, who you would have dismissed as a vagrant serving woman."

There was a silence, as Moreton continued to stare directly at Mary.

"Then you know I hold your husband and your son," he shouted back. "Do you give me cause that I should not kill them now?"

"I do." Mary called. "For I hold the very weapon that the Alchemist would have used to kill Queen Elizabeth on your orders." She paused. "And I am pointing it directly at your head."

"The very weapon?" He gave a sly smile. "Then I must assume you took it from the Alchemist by force, for I do not think he would have given it up willingly."

"I took it after I stopped him from using it on Queen Elizabeth."

He nodded slowly. "I am impressed. You have shown yourself a match for a man." He whispered something out of the side of his mouth that Mary could not catch – presumably an order to one of his men. "Too bad that your companion, Tom Cobham, was not so fortunate. I never met him, but I was told he cleaved to our cause, and even helped us secure the Alchemist. Now I see he was working against me. Or you turned him – I know not which." He looked away again and nodded to one of his men. "I understand he performed a sterling service for the heretic bastard that styles herself 'queen' – by choosing to die in her place."

Mary's finger tightened on the trigger.

"Aye!" she called back. "A noble gesture, Moreton, if that means anything to you."

"Oh indeed, it means something to me. It means that you and Cobham together have stopped my plan to rid us of this bastard heretic and place the true Queen Mary of Scotland on her throne. Cobham is dealt with, but you are not."

"You forget I am pointing a weapon at your head. I can split it open like a sack of flour."

Moreton did not reply. Instead he smiled broadly at her, then he nodded again to one of the men standing beside him.

Taking her finger off the trigger, Mary looked around the scope to get a full picture of the scene below.

Although the figures were distant, she could see that Moreton was standing a few yards in front of the watchman's hut. Two of his men were standing close to him, and the third was holding a small boy that struggled and wriggled in his arms.

Ambrose!

As Mary watched, Moreton crossed over and took Ambrose from the man. Then he crossed back to where he had been standing.

Mary put her eye back to the scope.

With surprising strength in his thin frame, Moreton was holding the boy up so that Ambrose's body acted as a perfect shield.

"Go ahead, Lady Mary!" Moreton called out from behind Ambrose. "Please discharge the weapon. Marry, you just might cause me a fatal wound, but I fear it is much more likely you will hit this fine boy here."

"Damn you, Moreton! Let my son go!"

"Ma!" called out Ambrose. "Ma! Is that you, Ma? Make him put me down!" He started kicking at Moreton's thighs.

"The boy has spirit, does he not?" called Moreton. "Truly his mother's son! But I warrant that if he does not cease to kick me, I will have his throat cut."

"Stay still, Bambi!" Mary shouted. She studied her son's face in the scope, his little features set into a scowl as he stopped kicking at Moreton.

Then suddenly a knife appeared by his throat.

She swung the gun round, and saw one of Moreton's men was now standing next to Ambrose, holding the knife. The man gave a broad grin in her direction, revealing a mouth containing only a few blackened teeth, then settled his stance.

Mary swung the gun the other way, until she could see the other two men, each standing watching Moreton, her son and their knife-wielding comrade.

She also noted what was happening behind these two men.

It was time to end this.

She shot the man with the knife.

A dark, angry red spot suddenly appeared in the centre of his forehead, and he fell back like an axed tree.

As Moreton turned to see what had happened, his grip on Ambrose loosened and the boy slipped down, until his head was close to Moreton's hand.

"Ambrose!" Mary shouted. "What would Kat do?"

Ambrose bit down hard on Moreton's hand; so hard that Mary saw blood appear.

Moreton screamed and let the boy drop to the ground.

Ambrose immediately scurried off towards the hut, as Olivia appeared behind one of the other men and in one swift movement, pulled the man's own knife from its scabbard and thrust it up to the hilt into his chest. The man gave a grunt, and went down.

His other comrade saw what happened and started to run over, just as William appeared behind him.

William put his foot out and the man stumbled, then went flying forward and landed in a sprawling heap at Olivia's feet.

Olivia wrenched the knife out of the first man's chest, leant forward and thrust it into the second one's back. With a gurgling, rattling yell, the man arched upwards, then flopped forward and was still.

The whole thing had taken no more than twenty seconds.

Moreton looked from one body to the next, then up at Mary. It was clear that he was considering his options – perhaps working out if Mary was able to fire the gun again and he should run, or whether he should stay and keep talking. Then it seemed that he had made his decision – and that was to get away as fast as possible. He turned and started running towards the far side of the ravine. Almost immediately he was out of sight among the trees.

Mary quickly put the gun back in its strap, then set off down the path as fast as she could.

She arrived to find William sitting on a log nursing his foot, while Olivia was cutting away the hose at his ankle. As Mary came up to them, Olivia pulled it up to reveal a blackening bruise darkening the side of his shin.

"I stopped that ruffian, Mary," he said with a wince of pain, "but I think the fellow has broken my leg as he came down. I cannot put weight on it nor walk a step."

There was a moment's silence, as he looked up at her. Then they both spoke at once.

"I thought you were at Grangedean!" Mary said, while he asked, "How are you here and not with the girls at home?"

There was a pause, then Mary said, "Why are you still here, William? You should have set off weeks ago!"

"I was concerned for Ambrose's safety, my love," he answered. "Which I was right to be."

Ambrose! In the heat of the moment, Mary had forgotten how desperate she had been to see her son again. She turned to the small boy who was standing quietly a couple of feet away. She knelt down, then pulled him into her arms and hugged him tight, savouring the smell of him again after all these months. After a moment, she broke off the embrace and looked deep into his eyes. "I am so sorry, Bambi," she said. "I failed you." She stroked his hair. "You said the Grenvilles were Catholic and I made light of it. Will you ever forgive me?"

"Of course, Ma," he answered. "And anyhow, Pa looked after me well."

She walked over to William.

Then suddenly they were in each other's arms, and their mouths came together and Mary kissed her husband with an intensity she never knew she could ever have had.

She pulled back and looked into his blue eyes, as if seeing them for the first time. "Oh William, I have missed you so!"

"And I you, Mary, my love." He smiled. "I thought of you each day, back at Grangedean, worried for my safety."

"And I thought you would be out searching for me!"

"That I would have done, had I arrived home and found you not." He became serious. "But what of Kat and Jane?"

"Oh, William, I know! They will be worried sick, I am sure." She paused. "Or at least Kat will be. She was fearful of a bad man attacking me."

He searched her eyes. "And did any?"

Mary nodded. "One or two did, yes. But I came to no harm. How about you?" she asked quickly, to head off any further discussion about how she had managed to stay safe.

Tom was dead – that was an end to it.

William said, "I thought Ambrose and I were to be slaughtered like a pair of sheep when we were led to that hut and manacled up these two days past. So when that ruffian came in just now and took Ambrose, I thought the worst." He turned to Olivia. "Never did I think that an unknown young girl would then come in and break open my manacles with a bar so I could help slaughter our captors instead. I must thank you for your plan, and your companion – Olivia, is it…?" The girl nodded. "…Olivia here, for carrying it though."

"And it worked," Olivia observed, looking as if she was trying to stay calm despite having just killed a man.

"But I fear I have broken my leg," continued William, "and Moreton has escaped." He winced with pain. "I would follow the rogue and beat him to death for all he has tried to do."

"You are not going anywhere on that leg, William de Beauvais," said Mary. "But I will follow him. It is a steep path up the other side of the ravine, and with luck he will not have got far," she smiled grimly.

She put the gun in its sling.

"All of you, wait for me here."

---0---

Once again, Mary found the scope of the gun invaluable as a telescope.

She aimed it at the path leading up and out of the ravine on the other side, sweeping it across each straight section and around the hairpin turns.

It wasn't long before she picked up the figure of Moreton, walking slowly upwards, some distance above. As she watched, he turned at a hairpin, making the rapier at his waist flash in the sunlight, then he set off up the next section of path, his pace slowing further.

He stopped completely, leaning back against the rock wall, his thin chest heaving for breath.

She put the gun back in its sling and set off in pursuit.

The path was steep and very stony, with loose rocks of many shapes and sizes. Even though she took it slowly in the still, hot sunshine, it was not long before her legs were burning and the air was rasping in her throat.

She rested for a few seconds, then took a deep breath, squared her shoulders and continued after Moreton.

She was making good progress, when suddenly a hail of large stones crashed onto the path in front of her, creating a dust cloud and sending a few smaller stones flying up. She stopped and looked up, but saw nothing.

A minute or so later she had just rounded a hairpin bend and was starting up the next straight, when a single rock the size of a large melon hurtled down with a whooshing sound, followed by an almighty *whump!* as it landed a couple of feet behind her.

Mary gave out a strangled yelp; it was large enough and falling fast enough to have killed her outright.

She looked up again, just in time to see the toe of a man's shoe withdraw from the edge of the path above her.

Mary leapt for the rocky wall beside her, flattening herself against it.

As she did so, another large rock crashed down – this time landing exactly where she had just been standing.

She looked up. Above her the wall sloped forward, giving her natural protection from the overhanging ledge above. She looked down the slope behind her. A few yards back, the wall changed angle and sloped away from the path – so if she went back, she would be exposed.

Ahead, the overhang got steeper – so if she went forward, she would have protection nearly all the way to the next hairpin.

Mary took the gun out of its sling and went forward, gripping the stock tightly.

Staying as close as she could to the wall, she eased her way along inch by inch, trying hard to be silent so that Moreton would not be able to pinpoint her.

Soon she reached the next turn and stopped just before it, while still protected by the overhang.

Leaving its safety to step out onto path and around the hairpin would mean being completely exposed.

She pressed close to the rocky wall, listening hard for any sound, but there was nothing.

Was he standing just above her, holding another rock, waiting to throw it down?

Or was he hidden in a shadow with his rapier drawn, ready to leap out and run her through?

She looked down, and spotted a stone the size of her fist just by her foot. Cautiously she bent and picked it up, then threw it gently down the path she had just climbed.

It made a loud clattering noise in the still air as it landed, and almost immediately there was the sound of footsteps moving away on the path above her.

Quickly she dashed out onto the hairpin, then skidded round the corner.

Moreton was just ahead, standing on a part of the path where it narrowed to just a couple of feet wide. He was hanging on to a branch growing from a fissure in the rocks, and was leaning over the ledge and staring down.

She slithered to a stop. At the noise he pulled himself upright, then turned and drew his rapier.

In response, Mary raised the gun to her shoulder. She pointed it directly at his head.

"See, Moreton," she said, advancing up the slope towards him, "this is the Alchemist's weapon. It is the weapon that killed Tom Cobham, and you saw how it killed the man that held a knife to my son's throat." She steadied herself. "And now it is aimed at your head."

Moreton gave a sneering smile and walked down until he was only a few yards from her, his thin face filling the scope. "So what would you have me do, Lady Mary?" he asked.

"Lay down your rapier."

"And if I do?"

"Then I will take you to Master Wychwoode, who will arrest you."

"And if I do not?"

"Then I will kill you."

Moreton smiled again. "Then you had better kill me," he said. He stepped back a few paces and Mary followed.

"You want me to?"

"Oh yes, Lady Mary." Moreton answered. "For you will be doing me the greatest service. Your killing will perhaps be swift and free of pain – whereas that heretic bastard will have me hung, drawn and quartered."

Mary said nothing, continuing to point the gun at his head.

"I could wound you only."

But I'm bluffing. The gun is not loaded – the last cartridge was used on the man with the knife.

Moreton stared back at her, then sneered again.

"But you do not kill me, nor do you aim elsewhere on my body to wound." He stepped back and again she followed. "Which means that either you have not the will to kill or wound me, or you do not have the means." He raised his rapier. "And since you had no hesitation in killing Charlie down there to free your son, before he wounded me so grievously, I do not think you lack the will." He studied the bite mark on his hand dispassionately, then made another step back. Again, Mary stepped towards him.

"So," Moreton continued, "I surmise you do not have the means. That although the weapon is in your hand, perhaps it is not primed and loaded with shot. In which case," he added, "I would prefer to kill you instead, and make good my escape."

Mary braced herself.

Almost as if in slow motion, she saw the tip of the rapier start to drive towards her. She shifted the grip of her left hand on the barrel of her gun, and in one smooth movement swung the whole gun round, while at the same time turning sideways. The rapier blade sliced harmlessly through the air a couple of inches away, as she brought the stock of the gun swinging round in her left hand with as much force as she could. It made contact with Moreton's arm, sending the rapier clattering down against the rock beside them as he yelled with pain.

Or was it triumph?

Mary suddenly realised why Moreton had been stepping back and she had been so blindly coming up after him – he had been deliberately leading her onto the narrowest section of path.

And now her momentum was taking her over the edge.

She scrabbled to get a grip on the loose stones, but it was too late. She felt her feet slipping.

As she went down, she let go of the gun and reached for the only thing she could.

Moreton's ankles.

The force of her falling pulled both his legs over the edge and he started to fall with her – until he stopped with a sudden arm-wrenching jerk that nearly sent her sliding off.

She looked up.

The only thing stopping them both from plunging down the long drop to the next path below, and possibly on down to the rocks at the bottom of the ravine, was the branch that Moreton was now gripping with both hands.

"Let go of me, you infernal bitch!" he yelled. "For the sake of Sweet Jesus Christ, let go!"

Mary did not answer. Instead she looked across to her right. There was a small outcrop of rock less than a yard away.

It could give her a foothold – if only she could get to it.

She looked up at the rock face above it. There was a small fissure above and to the left.

A hand-hold.

An idea began to form.

She started to swing her legs – first to the left, then to the right.

"Christ's holy cross, what are you doing?" came the cry from above.

Again, Mary did not answer – she was concentrating on reaching the outcrop.

Two more swings, accompanied by increasingly belligerent shouts from above, and she managed to get a toe onto the rock – but it did not hold, and she swung back once more.

"By Heaven, stop this now or I will let go and we both will perish!" shouted Moreton.

The next swing had more momentum and she got her toe on the rock. It held, leaving her suspended at an angle – one foot on the rocky outcrop and both hands hanging onto Moreton's legs.

Mary gripped even more tightly to his left ankle with her left hand, then slowly released her right hand.

"God's wounds!" shrieked Moreton as all her weight went through his left leg. "You vile harridan! You will kill us both!"

"I thought that was what you wanted," Mary muttered.

She eased her right arm towards the fissure, stretching as far over as she could. She nearly got her fingers inside, when suddenly he pulled his leg back and instead of gripping the fissure, her fingers scraped back across the rock and leaving a bright red trail behind them.

Wincing, she looked up.

"I see what you do, you vile jezebel!" Moreton snarled down at her. "But it will not succeed." He pulled again on his leg, scraping her fingers even further away from the fissure, until she felt them hit a small outcrop.

With a gasp of pain as her shoulder nearly dislocated, she clutched at it.

For a moment they were both still; Mary with Moreton's left ankle in the vice-like grip of her left hand, and her right at full stretch with her bloody fingers locked around the small outcrop.

Then she started to pull back.

With her heart thumping and the blood pounding in her ears, she slowly brought Moreton's leg back towards her hand.

"By Christ!" he yelped. "You have Satan's strength!"

Ignoring his shouts, she gathered herself and gave one last pull, then lunged across to grab the edge of the fissure, screaming in pain as her fingers curled into the little gap.

They held firm.

She looked up at him.

"Fare thee well, Lambert Moreton," she said, and gave a sharp pull on his ankle.

Possibly his arms had lost all strength, but it was enough.

Moreton's hands slipped off the branch and he fell past her with a blood-curdling shriek.

The sound cut off abruptly as he hit the path below a sickening thud.

Mary looked down. He was lying on his back with his arms spread out.

She looked back up.

Trying to ignore the pain in her fingers, and the bright red trail of blood dripping down the rock, she searched for a ledge to take her left leg.

There was an outcrop in roughly the right place, but it looked very small.

With little mewling noises coming from the back of her throat, she eased her foot over, pushed the side of her shoe hard into the rock, then let it come down to rest on the tiny ledge.

She clenched her jaw, then raised her right leg and found a small ledge.

Reaching up with her left hand, she scrabbled for a little outcrop, but it was half a hand higher than her full stretch.

Damn!

She took a breath, then reached again.

Again she could not get her fingers onto it.

With a scream of rage and frustration, Mary threw herself upward, using her right hand to pull herself higher, and feeling her left leg come clean off its little outcrop.

It was an all-or-nothing move.

Her hand rose up just beyond the top of the piece of rock, and she crooked her fingers onto it.

Her grip held.

With a further yell to herself, she got her left leg up to another small ledge, then her left hand up to another fissure, and was soon able to get both hands to some rocks at the edge of the path above her.

She pulled herself up over the edge, wriggling like a wet fish on the edge of a boat to get her weight up and over – but she was soon lying safe on the path itself, her breath rasping in her throat as she shook with relief.

Slowly she stood up, then retrieved both the rapier and the gun. As soon as she picked up the gun, she could see that the barrel was badly bent. The Alchemist's work was destroyed – the gun would surely never fire again. She tucked it into the sling on her back and pushed the rapier through her belt, then set off down the path.

Moreton was lying on the path where he had fallen, laid out on his back with his arms outstretched and his legs rocked over to one side.

She approached him carefully, holding out the rapier in case he was bluffing. But when she got to him, she could see his eyes were fluttering and the top half of his body was shaking. She crouched down beside him.

"Moreton?"

His eyes opened and his head turned towards her.

"You servant of Satan," he muttered. "I cannot feel my legs."

Mary looked down at them, then at his lower back, which she could now see was slightly arched. She put her hand under and felt something cold and smooth. She pushed him slightly to his side, and revealed the object.

Moreton had fallen directly onto one of the large rocks that he himself had thrown down at her – and it had severed his spine.

---0---

It was half an hour later and Moreton was laid out on some soft earth at the base of the ravine. He had been roughly carried down the rock face by a couple of Wychwoode's men, screaming and cursing as they went, after the lawyer and his soldiers had arrived at the bottom of the ravine and had been urgently sent up the other side by Olivia and William.

Mary was standing a few yards away from the hut with Wychwoode, William, Ambrose and Olivia.

She turned to Wychwoode. "What will happen to Moreton?" she asked.

"He will be interrogated about possible co-conspirators, then he will be hung, drawn and quartered," the old man answered. "That is the punishment for a treasonous plot on the life of the Queen."

William nodded. "I cannot say in truth that I am sorry. He thought to play me as a cat plays with a mouse. I am well pleased that his plot is ended."

"Please, Master Wychwoode, what of Sir Nicholas and Lady Grenville?" Ambrose asked. He had been standing to one side, holding Olivia's hand.

"I understand they have observed mass in secret and hid a priest," Wychwoode looked at William, "which is an offence in itself." He gestured back to Moreton's prostrate body. "But I also understand they were under the influence of this firebrand here, and have sworn to uphold the law in future and embrace the true religion. They will lose their lands and their position, but not, on this occasion, their lives." He looked at Mary. "Doth please my lady – this outcome?"

"I suppose so," Mary answered. "I have no anger for them." She glanced over at William. He was shaking his head slightly. "What of you, my love?" she asked.

"I have concerns about Sir Nicholas," he answered. "I heard him call Her Majesty a bastard." He paused. "Although I will warrant he knew naught of the plot."

"Then what will be done is for the best," said Wychwoode. "Now," he said, becoming very business-like, "I must take this Moreton into custody. And you, madam," he pointed a bony finger at Mary, "must make haste to Wyvern Castle and once more dress yourself as befits a lady, and one much beloved of our Queen. She has now decided to hold a banquet in your honour this night, and I would not have you be late, or not look as good as I know you can, for this great occasion."

"Me?" squeaked Mary. "Why?"

"If you have to ask, then you are more deserving of the honour than even I thought," said Wychwoode, and he marched off towards the hut.

"Ma!" said Ambrose, his eyes as wide as saucers. "You are to be honoured by the Queen!"

Mary crouched down and scooped Ambrose up in one arm, stood up and pulled William close to her with the other, then nodded at Olivia to come over as well. "Do you know," she said, "that when I was up on that rock face, with nothing more than the tiniest of ledges to stop me falling, the only thing that kept me moving upwards was the thought of seeing you all again." She looked from one to the other. "The only honour I seek," she said, "is to have you men both close to me, and to be home in my beloved Grangedean Manor, with nothing more pressing to concern me than the state of the rushes in the Great Hall, and to have my dearest friend Olivia come and visit me as often as she wishes."

CHAPTER TWENTY-SIX

Mary turned to William and muttered, "Hanging above a hundred foot drop, I was not so fearful as I am now."

"Courage, my love," he muttered back, squeezing her hand, then apologising when she winced with pain. "All will be well, I promise."

They were standing in the dimly-lit antechamber outside the doors to the Great Hall at Wyvern Castle, with William leaning on a stick to support his leg. Beyond the doors, they could hear the noise of more than two hundred people laughing and shouting together, waiting for the banquet to begin.

But that could not happen without the guest of honour.

"What a pair we are," she observed, "you with your leg nearly broken..."

"But thankfully, it turns out, only bruised most sorely," he said.

"...and me with my hands torn to shreds on those rocks." She smiled at him. "We have both had our adventures, have we not?"

"Aye, my love," he agreed, "we have." He paused. "But you have not told me why you set off from Grangedean in the first instance?" He peered at her in the gloom. "And what of this man I am told of – Sir Tom Cobham, was it? What of him?"

The question hung in the air.

Mary took a breath and was about to answer, when there was a heavy knocking from inside the hall, sounding like someone was banging a wooden staff on a table. Then some indistinct voice made an announcement, and slowly the doors swung open. Mary and William were almost blinded by the light that flooded over them, as they stepped forward.

"...And I present to you the Queen's Guest of Honour, and beloved friend, Lady Mary de Beauvais and her husband Sir William de Beauvais!"

It was Leicester who was the Master of Ceremonies, and as William hobbled slowly into the room with Mary beside him, Leicester raised his hands to encourage the cheers from the assembled crowd. Mary smiled nervously at a few people close to her, then looked up to see Queen Elizabeth sitting at the centre of the top table, resplendent in a white and gold gown with an enormous winged headpiece of pale cream silk rising from her shoulders and framing her red hair.

Mary approached the table, then stopped and sank into a low curtsey, while William bowed his head.

The Queen rose slowly to her feet. As if this was the cue everyone had been waiting for, they all stood as well, and the cheering and clapping that was already louder than could be thought possible, increased in volume even further.

Elizabeth gave a small, almost imperceptible nod as a sign of her approval, then indicated the two empty seats, one on either side of her. Mary and William then went round each side of the table to their places.

As Mary sat, the Queen turned to her and said, "You are well met, my dear Lady Mary."

"Thank you, Your Majesty. This is most kind, but…" she almost said 'unnecessary'… "but I was only doing my duty."

"Your duty? Aye," the Queen observed with a half-smile. "But I think you went a little further than that. Let me count the ways." Elizabeth held up her hand and counted off on her slim fingers. "The first, you pursued this Alchemist across many counties and made plans to thwart him. The second, you warned Sir Thomas so that he performed the ultimate sacrifice and saved my life. The third, you stopped the Alchemist from making a further attempt to kill me by the judicious use of a poker on his painted arms. The fourth, you used the said poker to give the Alchemist a beating on his leg that prevented him either escaping or causing any further harm. And the fifth," she made a deliberate show of counting off her little finger, "the fifth, you pursued my Catholic enemy, this Lambert Moreton, to bring him to justice, at considerable risk to your own life." She raised a quizzical eyebrow, "Or have I missed anything?"

Mary shook her head. "Nay, madam, I think you have summed up excellently."

"There, then no more shall be said on the matter." She turned to William and observed, "Your wife is quite the woman of action, Sir William. You must be immensely proud of her."

"Oh, I am, your Majesty…" he answered, and the two of them fell into conversation that Mary could not catch.

She glanced to her left, and caught sight of Wychwoode, seated between Olivia and Ambrose. Wychwoode was clearly regaling them with some story of daring-do – and to judge by the way he was waving his arms about, and the rapt expressions on their faces, he had their complete attention.

Ambrose looked up and caught her eye, giving her a look that said plainly that the stories he was hearing were about her – and that her exploits were causing him to see his mother in a whole new light.

The voice of Jesus, Ma? he mouthed in amazement. No doubt he was referring to the moment ten years before, when a crowd, who had been whipped into a frenzy by the witchfinder Hopkirk and wanted her drowned in a well for sorcery, had heard a divine message telling them that she was not a witch, and should be saved.

She smiled and shrugged. *I am still your Ma, whatever Jesus might say...*

The Queen turned back to her. "I have just set out a course of action to your husband that I wish to be followed," she said.

"Indeed, madam?" answered Mary. She saw William lean slightly forward and smile reassuringly at her.

"Yes. But before I share it, I understand that you, Sir William and your charming son will shortly be setting off to journey back to your home of Grangedean Manor?"

"Yes, madam," Mary answered. "I have two other children, two daughters, and I would see them again as soon as I can."

"I wish you God speed and a safe journey." The queen regarded her thoughtfully. "But I would ensure that this is done as far as possible without troubling the Lord God too greatly, so I shall make available a detachment of my finest guards, as well as a warm and secure carriage, so that your journey is swift, comfortable and untroubled by any brigands."

"Thank you, madam," Mary answered cautiously, "that is most kind."

"Although perhaps I should simply arm you with a poker and let any brigands take their chances?"

Mary smiled. "I am content to travel quietly, and leave my days of action behind me."

Elizabeth smiled back. "I respect that, and would have you attend me at Court, so I may benefit instead from your wisdom and calm council."

"I will be honoured, Your Majesty," answered Mary, still wondering what course of action the Queen had put to William.

"Which brings me to my main point," said the Queen. "This whole episode has been most unfortunate, and I do not want any other would-be armourers thinking to create such a weapon, nor to copy this Alchemist and plot against my life or my crown. I wish for the events of these last few days to be struck from the historical record, as if they never happened. So I shall make my progress down to the Earl of Leicester's castle of Kenilworth in Warwickshire, and we shall record in all documents that there was no progress beyond Kenilworth this summer. York simply did not happen."

Mary must have looked surprised, for the Queen said quickly, "That is not to take anything from your bravery here and your actions, my dear – which you and I will always know and cherish – but the records will only talk of Kenilworth." The Queen regarded her a moment, then added, "Your husband knows that you do not seek any glory for yourself, and he is concerned that if your deeds here became too well known, then you would forever be the subject of conversation – from great halls down to lowly ale-houses. He is anxious for your well-being, and agrees that this as the perfect way to safeguard it."

She leaned forward and again saw her husband smiling at her from the other side of the Queen.

"It is an excellent plan, Your Majesty."

"Indeed." Then the Queen leaned in close and dropped her voice. Once again, they were in the surgeon's house in York; once again two women with a shared bond. "Mary, I understand so well that you have loved and lost." Elizabeth paused. "And that in death the man you loved has given us both the chance to renew our lives. I will use well the opportunity he gave me…" the Queen's dark eyes held Mary's, "and I would you do the same. You have a man right here who loves you most deeply. You have a wonderful future with him, and with your charming son, and your daughters back at Grangedean Manor." The Queen put her hand on Mary's arm. "They are your future, Lady de Beauvais. I would you mark it well."

"I will, madam. Yes – yes I will."

"Good." The Queen leaned back and took her hand off Mary's arm.

Mary also sat back.

Then it seemed that the noise of the room receded into the distance, and for the first time in many months, a warm glow of contentment spread over her.

The Queen was right! Finally, Mary had been given back her future. As the Alchemist had made clear, nothing she had done by saving William or having her children would endanger that. The Alchemist, Moreton and their awful plot were gone, and now she could relax, enjoy her life at Grangedean with her family and, it seemed, her new life at Court as well.

How fortunate she was to be a valued part of Tudor history.

There was a life outside Grangedean, and now she was going to enjoy it!

Mary felt a touch on her other arm and suddenly the sounds of the room came rushing back. She looked round. It was Leicester. She realised with a start that such was the dominant presence of the Queen, and her new-found contentment, she had not even registered that the Earl was next to her as well.

"I must ask you, Lady Mary, what of the Alchemist's incredible musket?"

"Oh." Mary cast her mind back to the path above the ravine. "I dropped it when I fell from the ledge, my lord. It was damaged beyond repair."

His mouth fell. "That is indeed a shame. I would see how it was made so it can be copied." He narrowed his eyes. "Belike its function can still be understood, for all it is damaged?"

Elizabeth leaned across. "Nay, Robin, it is an evil thing; the work of the devil and of a man who worshiped the darkness. We will have naught to do with it." She turned to Mary. "I command you take it to a blacksmith's forge and have it committed to the fire. I want no trace of it to remain."

"But madam…" Leicester started to rise out of his seat. Elizabeth held up her thin, white hand.

"I am resolute, Robin."

He subsided back again. "As you wish, madam."

"I do wish, Robin." She gave a small conspiratorial smile at Mary, then looked at Leicester with wide, innocent eyes. "So Robin, how are you going to impress me at Kenilworth?"

CHAPTER TWENTY-SEVEN

The Tower of London, early June 1575

The thick stone walls glistened in the flickering candlelight, as Wychwoode walked slowly up to the near-naked figure spread-eagled on the platform in the middle of the room; his groin covered with just a dirty cloth.

The platform was made of rough, dark wood, its open grain scuffed from the repeated impact of writhing limbs, and stained almost black by years of being soaked in blood, sweat and urine.

The figure lying on it was tied by ropes around each ankle and wrist. His feet were secured to strong metal rings, while the ropes to his outstretched hands passed round a large wooden drum beyond his head. A muscular man in a leather jerkin stood next to the drum, ready to turn it by means of a cross-bar on the side.

Wychwoode came up to the spread-eagled man's head, and looked down at the short, spikes of hair plastered to the man's sweating skull.

"You will know what this contraption is, I am sure," he said in a dry, flat voice. "We need to know all the details of this plot and your part – and you can either tell me now, or tell me after my associate here has pulled your arms and legs out of their sockets. That is," he added, "if they do not first come apart where Lady Mary has hit them. The choice is yours."

The Alchemist stared at him with hate-filled eyes. "There's nothing to tell," he muttered. "I worked alone."

"But you were in league with Alleyne and Tyler, and were led by Moreton," said Wychwoode. "I do not call that working alone."

"As Cobham must surely have told you, since he was your agent all along," the Alchemist growled, "once Alleyne died and you had Tyler, I contacted no-one. Not even Moreton. There was no others involved."

"What of Grenville?"

"Who?" The Alchemist turned his head away. "I never heard of him."

Wychwoode nodded. "I though as much." He paused, considering the Alchemist's prone figure, with his blackened and bruised arms and leg. "So then tell me, what of this?"

He held up a small metal object with a white skull motif. The Alchemist turned his head back and stared at it in the flickering candlelight. "Is this a sign of devil worship?" Wychwoode asked. "Are you a disciple of Satan? For if so, then you will be burned alive to cast out the devil."

"Where the fuck did you get that?" asked the Alchemist, his eyes wide. "I haven't seen that since…" he stopped himself.

"Since when?"

"Since… fuck. I can't say."

Wychwoode nodded to the man in the leather jerkin, and the man put his weight against the cross-bar to turn the drum.

A few minutes later, once the Alchemist's screams had died down to a soft whimper, Wychwoode asked again.

"Since what?"

"Since… since… oh, fuck it. Since I arrived in this shit-hole time."

"I do not understand. Tell me what you mean." He turned towards the torturer and nodded again. The man started to push on the cross-bar.

"No!" screamed the Alchemist. "Wait! You have to let me explain!"

Wychwoode held his hand up and the man paused.

"Listen," panted the Alchemist, "in life, one day follows the next, right?"

"Yes," said Wychwoode slowly, "but I do not see…"

"So you travel forward through time, always you go forward, right?"

"Yes…"

"But I went the other way. I went backwards."

There was a long silence, then Wychwoode said, "You speak nonsense."

"No, you have got to listen." The Alchemist paused, as if gathering his thoughts. "This year, it is 1575, right?"

"Yes it is."

"What if I said to you, you could wake up tomorrow, and still be the same person, but instead of it being 1575, it was now 1135?"

"Then I would say it was impossible, and against the God's laws."

"Well, it is not impossible, because I have done it."

Wychwoode stared at the Alchemist a while, trying to process what he had just heard. "You mean," he said slowly, "you have travelled *backwards* in time – through four hundred and forty years?"

The Alchemist nodded. "Exactly."

"From the year of our Lord…" Wychwoode paused while he did the calculation, "…2015?"

"Exactly."

"This is arrant nonsense," Wychwoode began, and turned again to the torturer.

"No!" the Alchemist shouted. "You have to believe me! How do you think I made the gun? With future knowledge! How do you think I made the shells – the powder and ball in one capsule? How do you think I made the scope to see the target close up?" He looked down at his arms. "These tatts, pictures, on my arms – they are of weapons from my time! If that fucking bitch hadn't hit them, you'd see more clearly – they're like nothing you would ever find today." He glanced at the object in Wychwoode's hand. "And that lighter you're holding; it's nothing to do with devil worship – total nonsense! It's just a fucking lighter that I must have dropped when I first arrived, that's all."

Wychwoode observed the Alchemist dispassionately. "So you say you travelled here from the year 2015?"

"Yes. Yes, I did."

Wychwoode pursed his lips, then said, "How, exactly? By sorcery?"

"No!" The Alchemist shook his head violently from side to side. "I got caught in a storm. There was lightning – lots of lightning. Then I found myself here."

"I see."

"You believe me?"

Wychwoode was silent a moment, then said, "At this time, no. I am a lawyer by profession. I need to see clear evidence." He paced away from the rack a moment, then turned back. "I assume when this lightning storm sent you to our time, you would have appeared as if by sorcery from thin air. Did any person witness this?"

The Alchemist stared at him with desperate eyes. "No," he said. "But I went to the Grangedean tavern and sought food from Agnes. She will vouch that I was dressed in my future clothes and offered her coin with the head of our Queen on it – the Queen from my time. Ask her. She will confirm it!"

Again, Wychwoode paced away. Was this nonsense? An attempt by a condemned man to create a diversion? He looked at the bruised and battered body on the rack. If it was a diversion, it was remarkable in its invention. What a notion – to come from the distant future... Yet this Alchemist had fashioned a weapon that no man had ever seen before... Such knowledge could be explained by rational means – but equally, it *could* be true... And those pictures on his arms – now more visible since the bruising had started to fade – they also depicted strange types of musket, ones that had no known equivalent... What if this *were* real? But even if so, the talk of lightning was nonsense. What other explanation could there be than this was the devil's sorcery?

Wychwoode again observed the bruised man on the platform. "I am minded to accept that you may be a traveller through time, for there is some proof in the weapon you fashioned and the images on your arms." He paused, considering his words carefully. "But I cannot accept there is any other explanation than sorcery – and the devilry on this object you call a 'lighter' convinces me. So unless you recant this claim, I will have no choice but to have you burned at the stake."

The Alchemist let out a low groan. "And if I do recant?"

"Then you will suffer the fate of a traitor – the same fate as Moreton did these two days past – you will be hung but not killed, then cut down and disembowelled, before your head and limbs are removed."

The Alchemist stared at him for what seemed an age, his eyes glowering in the flickering light. Eventually he said, "So if I recant, I will die as Moreton died. If I do not recant, I will burn as a sorcerer?"

Wychwoode nodded.

"But you know what? You know fucking what?" the Alchemist said slowly. "If I am to burn, then another must burn as well. I am not the only one from the future."

"You would have me believe there are others from the year 2015?" Wychwoode asked sharply.

"Yes, there is – one other. And do you know what? I can prove it!" The Alchemist's voice suddenly rose to a triumphant shout. "Fuck, yes, I can actually prove it!"

"How?"

Despite the pain he must have been in, the Alchemist smiled. "Because I had a conversation with this other time-traveller, and it was in front of witnesses. Honest townspeople of York who will vouch that we spoke of future times and everything the other person said showed that they were as familiar with the future as me."

Wychwoode stared at the man. "If I find your witnesses do support your claim, then I must question this other person also."

"Yes, you must!"

"And if I am satisfied that he is also a sorcerer, then he will burn as well."

"Yes," the Alchemist said, "only it is not a 'he'. It's a 'she'..."

Then he smiled; a broad smile of triumph.

A smile of revenge.

"It's Lady Mary," he said. "It's Lady fucking Mary de Beauvais."

He laughed.

"That bitch is from the future like me, and you're going to burn her to death..."

THE END

BY THE SAME AUTHOR

The Witchfinder's Well

The first book in the series tells the story of Justine Parker, and how she time-travels from 2015 to 1565, and outwits the witchfinder Matthew Hopkirk to become Lady Mary de Beauvais.

Readers have said:
"A must for everyone who loves history and a must for everyone who wants to be whisked away to another time."

"An enchanting and un-put-downable read!"

"A good tale, entertaining, funny, informative, recommended, a good holiday book, one to go back to again and again"

Once Upon and Ending

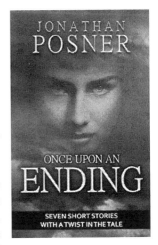

Seven short stories, each with a twist in the tale – and all full of life, love and adventure.

Find out what happens when hard-bitten 1930's New York detective Roscoe Kemp takes on the mysterious Hershenheimsbecker case in 'Private Eyes', and how Granny Vera and Lloyd-George the cat celebrate the new Millennium together.

When Nurse Natalia Davies meets the handsome new doctor in 'One Summer', the course of true love does not go smoothly, and when Mr Alfred meets the gorgeous Zusia in 'A Windsor Tail', he soon finds his comfortable world turned upside down.

Readers have said:
"A varied collection of characters and accomplished storytelling makes Jonathan's well-written book a very enjoyable read."

Both books are available on Amazon.